GEMSTONES,
ELVES,
and other
INSIDIOUS MAGIC

GEMSTONES, ELVES, AND OTHER
INSIDIOUS MAGIC (Dowser 9)
Copyright © 2018 Meghan Ciana Doidge
Published by Old Man in the CrossWalk Productions 2018
Salt Spring Island, BC, Canada
www.oldmaninthecrosswalk.com

Library and Archives Canada
Doidge, Meghan Ciana, 1973 —
Gemstones, Elves, and Other Insidious Magic/
Meghan Ciana Doidge — PAPERBACK

Cover design by: Elizabeth Mackey

ISBN 978-1-927850-89-3

— *Dowser 9* —

GEMSTONES, ELVES, and other INSIDIOUS MAGIC

Meghan Ciana Doidge

Published by Old Man in the CrossWalk Productions
Salt Spring Island, BC, Canada

www.madebymeghan.ca

Author's Note:

Gemstones, Elves, and Other Insidious Magic is the ninth book in the Dowser series, which is set in the same universe as the Oracle and the Reconstructionist series.

While it is not necessary to read all three series, **in order to avoid spoilers** the ideal reading order of the Adept Universe is as follows:

Cupcakes, Trinkets, and Other Deadly Magic (Dowser 1)
Trinkets, Treasures, and Other Bloody Magic (Dowser 2)
Treasures, Demons, and Other Black Magic (Dowser 3)
I See Me (Oracle 1)
Shadows, Maps, and Other Ancient Magic (Dowser 4)
Maps, Artifacts, and Other Arcane Magic (Dowser 5)
I See You (Oracle 2)
Artifacts, Dragons, and Other Lethal Magic (Dowser 6)
I See Us (Oracle 3)
Catching Echoes (Reconstructionist 1)
Tangled Echoes (Reconstructionist 2)
Unleashing Echoes (Reconstructionist 3)
Champagne, Misfits, and Other Shady Magic (Dowser 7)
Misfits, Gemstones, and Other Shattered Magic (Dowser 8)
Graveyards, Visions, and Other Things that Byte (Dowser 8.5)
Gemstones, Elves, and Other Insidious Magic (Dowser 9)

Other books in the Dowser series to follow.

More information can be found at
www.madebymeghan.ca/novels

For Michael
My happily ever after with a cupcake on top.

I'd been compromised, then turned against those I loved. But no one controlled me. No one took anything I didn't willingly offer. Not for long, anyway.

If the elves wanted a war, I'd bring it. The instruments of assassination would come out to play. The dragon slayer would wreak bloody, sticky vengeance. And then I was getting freaking married—no elves invited.

Even a baker of cupcakes and a maker of trinkets occasionally had to set aside the chocolate, the spice, and everything nice to save her friends. And her city.

Chapter One

A man hung suspended in a whirlwind of magic above me.

No...not just a man.

A dragon.

I crouched on the back edge of a six-foot-wide, three-foot-high white platform set above the elven tech I had been tasked to repair, fiddling with a gemstone I'd previously removed. Pretending to work while peering through the maelstrom of golden-tinted magic that fueled the gateway.

The gold of the dragon's magic.

Of his life force.

Energy...magic...life...that was slowly being siphoned away through the elven tech.

Something was wrong with that...scenario. That situation. Terribly, terribly wrong. But whenever I tried to grasp that thought, to fully articulate it in my mind, it hovered just beyond my understanding.

I glanced to my right, then my left. The center section of the stadium grew smaller and smaller each day as the elves erected sections of walls, closing in on the gateway. If I tilted my head, I could still see the upper rows of seating that climbed almost all the way to the domed ceiling. There were fewer rows than there had been the last time I'd counted. Not that I could remember the exact number. Or why that even mattered.

We—the dragon and I—were surrounded by elves, including my liege.

But … we weren't a 'we.'

Were we?

And why would us being surrounded by elves matter?

I'd repaired the tech.

I'd created a pathway at my liege's command, opening a rift between dimensions so that the elves could cross into the earth's dimension from their own.

That much, I knew for certain.

That much, I remembered doing.

Except just the previous day—if my sense of time could be trusted—something else had occurred. Something that had upset my liege, disrupting our connection for a moment that lasted long enough for me to remember … other things. Other ideas.

Ideas that fluttered just out of my reach, even as I gazed up at the dragon fueling the gateway with his life force.

Though my liege's hold on my mind kept slipping, I had come to understand through her that the witches who claimed this territory, this city, had somehow reined the elves in, curtailing my liege's plans.

For the moment.

The stadium was slowly filling with restless warriors as one elf at a time stepped through the gateway. Then waited.

Everyone was on the edge of violence, caught up in that waiting.

Me especially.

The dragon suspended above me appeared to be sleeping. I couldn't shake the feeling that if he would only open his eyes, I would know him. I had thought more than once that I should have been tearing the magic of the gateway down, rather than propping it open and refining it. Gemstone by gemstone, I was harvesting the dragon's magic, his life.

But wasn't he mine to protect?

And wasn't I his?

My liege laid her hand on my shoulder. I returned my attention to the elven device I was still working on, not wanting to invite the pain that came with an admonishment. But her touch was...shaky. Both on my shoulder and in my mind.

She was tired.

She'd have been upset if she knew that I knew. If she understood that I could feel her emotions, even sometimes catching snippets of her thoughts through the connection we shared.

I smoothed my magic, my alchemy, across the milky-white gem I was coaxing into place on the gateway device. The two sections of that device had been reunited. The metal components slotted together in an intricate pattern to form a circle about a foot and a half in diameter. I had slowly been replacing and repairing the gateway's cracked and shattered gemstones, but one large divot on the right remained empty. The elf tech had remained inert until I'd reawakened it with my power—as bidden by my liege. But that wasn't enough. I couldn't fix and fuel the dimensional gateway at the same time.

So the others had been brought in. The others who I'd taken, incapacitated, and stripped of their weapons. The dragon, the vampire, the werewolf, and the guardian.

I was the technician.

They were the power source.

I thought the gateway tech might have been killing them. Slowly draining their lives away. But my liege made certain they were left with a spark within them after each session, allowing them to recuperate so that faint sliver of magic could grow and bloom.

Only to be drained again.

And again.

Unbidden anger coursed through me, through my chest and down my limbs.

Something snapped between my clenched fingers.

The hand on my shoulder tightened.

A hurricane appeared at the edge of my mind.

I had cracked the gemstone I'd been placing in the gateway device. Not enough that I couldn't repair it. But my liege didn't notice. And what she didn't know, didn't ask, I wouldn't tell her.

She wondered why the gateway would still allow only one passenger at a time, why it could recharge only intermittently, about once an hour. She cursed my inability to open it wider, to allow six or a dozen warriors through at once. She fought, argued with Traveler, almost constantly.

But she never asked if I was deliberately limiting the gate, trimming its magic, keeping it only half-functional.

So I didn't tell her I was doing just that.

Though why I would have wanted to sabotage the gateway at all, I had no idea.

"Again?" a large warrior elf snarled from behind me.

Traveler. The teleporter.

He'd noticed the cracked gemstone.

Traveler always noticed, which was why my liege often sent him away, tasked with other duties. Training, organizing, readying the warriors. But what they were being readied for was unknown to me.

I kept my head bowed, even though I desperately wanted to look up again, to check on the dark-blond dragon suspended in the stream of energy emanating from the gateway. Energy that was still tinted with the gold of his magic.

If only he would open his eyes.

If only he would recognize me.

Then maybe I'd know who I was ...

"She's drained." My liege sounded weary. Her tone was labored, heavily accented. Not English, though. Elvish. The translation came through the gemstone embedded into my forehead, anchored in my brain. Though, again, why I would have needed anything to be translated, I didn't know. "I shall set her to sleep. More components will be delivered, and the gateway will be fully functional in a few more hours."

"You've been saying as much for days," the seven-foot-tall warrior elf sneered.

My liege's long cloak brushed against me as she swiveled to face her second-in-command. "What care you for human time, Traveler?"

"I care about being caged in here by the witches. We hold a guardian. How long do you think it will be until the warrior with the golden sword comes?"

"We will be ready."

"I request ... again ... to be allowed to summon an engineer from my realm. She will have the gate fixed moments after she steps through it."

"The alchemist has it in hand."

"A human," Traveler snarled. "Your trust is misplaced. Our most-powerful monarchs grow restless. We have a chance to gain a hold over this dimension and cement our place in—"

Then Traveler grunted, pained.

The boney hand on my shoulder tightened, as if drawing from my strength. I glanced sideways, watching Traveler fight a torment that I knew the feeling of all too well. The hulking elf fell to his knees, panting in unvoiced agony.

He placed a hand across his forehead, as though trying to shield the gemstone embedded there from my liege's power, her assault.

He couldn't.

As I well knew.

"I grow tired of your constant questioning, Traveler." My liege sounded remote, unaffected. But she was holding herself upright with the strength of my back. The strength of my body, my magic.

And I would gladly give it to her.

Wouldn't I?

Traveler met my gaze, his green eyes glistening with rage, with pent-up hatred.

A smile spread across my face, mocking him. Sneering at his pain.

He snarled.

I could shake off my lady's hold. I could lunge, snapping his neck before anyone would have a chance to even see me move.

He lifted his chin in a challenge.

I flipped the cracked gemstone in my hand, threading my alchemy around it and through my fingers. "Try me," I murmured.

He sneered. "Why would I bother? Your head will soon be mine. As will those of your friends."

Friends.

Friends?

I glanced up at the man suspended in the gateway. Was he the one who Traveler threatened? Was he my... friend? The term didn't seem correct somehow... didn't fit the feeling that hovered just out of my reach every time I laid eyes on him—

The magic of the gateway shifted between the suspended dragon and the elven device. A tall, slim elf with sleek hair falling to the back of her knees stepped through the gate, pausing to cast her gaze around the stadium. And for a moment, it felt as though all the elves within viewing distance of the gateway held their collective breath. The newcomer wore a high-collared vest that fell to her ankles, and slim pants tucked into laced-up boots. The long vest was edged with multicolored gems that twinkled with magic.

Traveler scrambled to his feet.

Fear coursed through me. But it wasn't my own.

It was my liege's.

The elves working on the walls returned their attention to the task.

"Problems?" the newcomer asked mockingly. "Already?"

My lady spoke a few words I didn't understand, that didn't automatically translate—a name and a formal greeting, perhaps—dropping her hand from my shoulder and stepping away from me. Silently, Traveler joined her.

I remained kneeling, keeping the newcomer and the dragon in sight without outright staring at either of them.

"We weren't expecting you," my lady said stiffly.

"I heard you had gained a hold in this dimension. A tenuous one, it seems."

Anger filtered through my connection to my liege, even though we were no longer in physical contact. Her anger, not mine.

"I am making great headway, ward builder." Out of the corner of my eye, I caught the sweeping gesture my liege made, encompassing the gateway and the maze of twelve-foot-high walls that had been constructed throughout the lower level of the stadium. She folded her hands before her, appearing tranquil even as I could feel her ire. "I've established a foothold on Earth as none have been able to do before me."

The newcomer's gaze fell on me. I was blocked from continuing work on the elven tech by her booted feet. "A fool's quest, some would say. A flawed attempt to expand a territory that has only been further weakened by your absence. Your imprisonment."

"My daughter has been ruling—"

The female elf waved her hand dismissively. "I'm not here to question you. I understand you seek a prime gem. I have brought you one." A large snow-white gemstone appeared in the palm of her hand. Even without handling it myself, I knew it would fit perfectly into the final empty slot in the device.

Eagerness flashed through me. Not my own. My liege's. I felt only dread. A stone like that could fix all the little things I'd done to hinder the gate's true potential.

"You offer to join us?" my liege asked—a little too keenly.

The newcomer laughed, but the sound was flat and joyless. "I seek only news of my kin."

My liege didn't respond.

The new elf stepped down from the platform, slipping the white gemstone into the outer pocket of her vest. Magic glistened from every inch of the gem-crusted fabric. I curled my fingers in so that I didn't inadvertently reach for the power as she brushed by me.

My liege had called the newcomer 'ward builder.' But judging by the look of her magic, my lady's smothered anger, and Traveler's silent deference, she was much, much more than that.

"My niece?" the ward builder asked, pausing a couple of steps to my left. Even the ends of her bootlaces were beaded with gems. "My nephew?"

"Dead," Traveler said. "Both."

"By whose hand?"

"She kneels beside you," my liege said. "Cowed and entrapped by my might."

"This ... witch?"

"Alchemist."

"She slaughtered my kin, whose safety was entrusted to you by the controller of all the territories. And you allow her to live?"

"She is the reason we were able to open the gateway."

"And after she did so? You continue to allow her to breathe?"

Traveler snorted.

"The alchemist continues to be useful," my liege said bitingly. "Beyond the operation and widening of the gateway. But it is not for you to question me, ward builder. Even though your kin have fallen to the enemy, our realms are allies in this endeavor."

"For now."

Ignoring the snide interruption, my liege continued. "Those who followed me here did so willingly. Their sacrifices were worthy of their position and heritage."

The ward builder abruptly lunged sideways, grabbing me by the neck. I allowed her to pull me to my feet.

Even as drained as I was magically, she wouldn't have been strong enough to move me otherwise.

And though I could have held it easily, I allowed the magic that tied me to the elven tech to snap.

The gateway flickered.

The dragon held within the gate's energy dropped, still hanging at the edge of my peripheral vision.

I met the fierce gaze of the elf as she attempted to choke me. She was a couple of inches taller than I was. Not otherwise touching her, I pressed my neck into her hand.

She gnashed her sharply pointed teeth at me. Then her footing slipped backward a few inches. As I'd assumed, she wasn't strong enough to hold me. Not on her own, anyway.

Her magic rose, writhing along her arm, then around my neck, across my shoulders, and down my own arms, attempting to hold me at bay.

I laughed, but the sound came out as a gurgle. Then I slammed my open palm against her chest. Bone snapped.

Losing her hold on me, the elf flew back, crashing into one of the many walls that had been creeping closer and closer to the gateway for days. Walls erected in an elaborate spiral, forming some sort of maze to protect the passageway to the gate.

Beside me, the magic of that gate collapsed. The dragon tumbled to the floor, rolling off the platform and into the back of my legs. He was heavy, knocking me forward.

Many hands grabbed for me, trying to contain me, to hold me.

I broke a few arms without even trying. The elves who had stepped forward scurried back, nursing their wounds.

The ever-present, simmering hurricane—my liege's power—stormed through my mind.

I ignored it.

I ignored my lady's command to heel.

Ignoring her was becoming easier each time.

To my right, the ward builder had regained her feet, crossing to join the others loosely encircling me. Me and the unconscious dragon. Traveler had manifested a crystalline knife. But I didn't care.

I cared about the dragon. The dragon whose skin was almost the same color as mine. Neither he nor I were finely scaled. Neither he nor I had hair so pale it was almost white...or slightly pointed ears...or sharp teeth.

I found myself wondering suddenly—if the dragon bled, would he bleed red? Red like me? Not the pale green of the elves?

Because I wasn't an elf.

That much I remembered.

That much I knew.

A warrior elf got in my face while I was trying to look at the dragon. Trying to understand what I was feeling, to retrieve knowledge that felt just out of my reach. I took the elf's knife, embedding it deeply within his blood armor before he'd even noticed its theft.

Just for bothering me.

He fell.

Another elf darted forward, dragging the wounded elf away.

The others waited, tightening the circle around me.

The hurricane increased. A tornado slipped through the wound in my forehead, gaining entry through the gemstone embedded into my brain. It threatened the thoughts I was trying to collect. The clues I was trying to connect.

Friend. Traveler had used that word.

Friend.

I knelt by the dragon, placing my hand on his chest. It rose steadily underneath my touch. His magic was dim when it should have been bright. Bright ... and golden ... and tasting like ...

"Not just my friend," I whispered. "Mine ... mine."

Two swords scissored around my neck, then forced me to my feet and away from the dragon. Traveler had appeared behind me without warning, closing the space between us before I could react. Teleporting. I should have followed up on my earlier promise and killed him.

"I'm taking her head!"

"No," my liege shouted. "I have her under control."

"And each time that control slips, she kills one of us!"

"When we conquer this world, those sacrifices will bring glory to us all."

Sacrifices ... I remembered a yellow jacket abandoned in the rain ...

Sacrifices.

I glanced at the newcomer. The ward builder, who had tried to strangle me. She was watching my liege, rubbing her chest. Then she glanced at me, dropping her hand to her side.

"You look like ... Mira," I said, speaking to her. "And her brother. Same ... nose ..." I trailed off, losing track of the thought, of the connection.

"Mira?" The ward builder furrowed her brow.

My liege lunged forward, pressing her fingers to the gemstone in my forehead. A searing agony slammed through my brain.

"Who is Mira?" the ward builder asked.

I lost control of my limbs, collapsing forward against Traveler's twin blades. They sliced into my neck, but my lady snarled a command—backed by a push of her power—and Traveler withdrew his twin crystal swords, allowing me to fall forward across the dragon.

"Mira and her brother," I murmured, trying to speak through the hurricane still rampaging through my mind. Trying to formulate the thought out loud. "My elf...friend...Mira. Illusionist...who wanted to die on her favorite black-sand beach ..."

"Sleep, alchemist," my liege said. "You will retire to your room and sleep."

Blackness encroached on my vision, first taking my sight, then dampening all my other senses.

I slept.

As commanded.

I woke while being dragged by either arm down a short hallway leading to one of the exits of the inner maze. Mentally clawing my way through the magic dampening my thoughts and restricting my movement, I managed to look up. The stairs to the second level were just ahead.

Then I took serious exception to being dragged.

I tucked my knees to my chest. And before my guards could do anything more than tighten their grip on my arms, I kicked out to the sides with both legs, taking their feet out from under them.

They kept hold of me as they stumbled toward me, but I slammed my feet to the ground, straightening and twisting my arms until I could grab both their heads. Then I smashed their skulls together.

Both of them fell before me in a tangle of limbs. Alive. But with cracked gemstones in their foreheads. I stepped over them, continuing toward the stairs with the understanding that I was to return to my room on the level above.

Understanding that I was being compelled to return to my room? To sleep?

I spotted a turtle.

Yep. A turtle. In the hall.

It was a mottled dark green, about six inches across, with red slashes on both sides of its head. It shimmied around the corner at the base of the stairs, as if it had been waiting just beyond the open doorway there. But that doorway led only to restroom facilities, as I had discovered when I first needed to use them. If there was an exterior exit in that direction, it had been walled off.

Was the turtle waiting for me?

I glanced back at my guards. They were still unconscious, sprawled in the center of the white-walled hall.

Pushing away the compulsion that was urging me to continue up the stairs, I hunkered down in front of the turtle. It looked up at me with dead eyes.

I flinched.

A dead turtle?

The creature shuffled closer to the stairs, pausing at the base, then looking back at me.

A tiny black box was attached to its back.

A camera?

Some emotion twisted through me ... fear? No. Anticipation. A smile spread across my face. Unaccustomed to that feeling, I touched my cheeks, touched my lips.

The turtle shuffled slightly to the right, then to the left. As if it wanted to climb the stairs, but couldn't.

A bone-splintering pain—the pain of denying my liege's compulsion—started edging the gemstone in my forehead. Before the ache could grow, could cloud my thoughts, I scooped the turtle up and jogged up the stairs.

On the second level of the stadium, the smooth concrete floors of the lower level gave way to tightly woven beige carpet running down a long hallway. Empty offices branched off on either side.

Hearing my guards begin to stir behind and below me, I tucked the turtle behind the door in the first office. As I placed it on the ground, I felt a tingle of familiar magic. The turtle was wearing a charm made out of a dime around its neck.

The magic felt like...like I should have been able to taste it ...

"It's dangerous," I whispered to the turtle, "for you to be wandering around here ..."

Wait ...

I could do something about that, even drained after working on the gateway device for hours.

I brushed my forefinger across the charmed dime, stirring the magic already stored within it. That magic felt dim, as if it too was drained. As if the spell was running out. That wasn't good either.

I snagged the tiniest trickle of power in the charm—carefully, so as to not accidentally steal it for myself. Then I cemented it with my own magic, informing it that it was to hide the tiny turtle from the sight of its enemies. Not an invisibility spell, exactly. That was beyond my abilities. But an obscuring...a whisper to look away, to look elsewhere.

That would allow the turtle to continue its quest.

But why I felt the need to do anything for the little dead creature, I didn't know.

I heard the elves clambering up the stairs. I quickly exited into the hall and headed to an office halfway along on the left. Crossing through the open door into the room that was mine quieted the compulsion that had forced me to continue moving.

Though I'd also been commanded to sleep, I ignored the neatly made cot against the far wall, walking instead to the room's tiny barred window. The light over the city had changed since I'd last looked out. It was darker now. My liege preferred to work through the daylight hours. Vehicles of all shapes and sizes sped steadily by the stadium, snaking out through the downtown streets and carrying busy people through their busy lives.

I wasn't certain what I was looking for, peering out through the crystalline bars and the magic that coated the window. But I always looked for it just the same.

There was something about the turtle … some connection I was missing …

Magic shifted behind me. In the doorway. I glanced back to see one of my guards snarling at me as he grabbed and slammed the door shut. Locks clicked into place, followed by the magic that sealed the room from … from what?

From me.

I was a prisoner.

There were moments when I thought I might belong. Like I was meant to be with the elves, repairing the gateway. But then …

I wrapped my hands around the window's crystal bars. The magic embedded in them—magic meant to cage me—seared my palms and fingers. But not as badly as each successive time before.

I was becoming immune. Slowly and steadily, I was claiming the elven magic for myself.

Again I scanned the busy streets crisscrossing the city. I saw cars, trucks, buses … stores, apartments, restaurants. Some sort of temporary orange plastic fencing had been erected around the stadium a few days earlier.

But I wasn't looking for any of that.

I was looking for the girl. The young woman.

The turtle belonged to the woman in the red poncho.

That knowledge filled me with an absolute certainty.

I didn't know what the woman in the poncho was doing. Or why the turtle had shown itself to me, asking for help up the stairs.

But I knew one thing.

I knew I wasn't an elf.

A fierceness flooded through me. I tightened my grip on the bars.

They had captured me.

Imprisoned me.

Compelled me.

I didn't know who I was.

But I wasn't a pet.

I wasn't a tool.

I wasn't a pawn.

I placed one foot, then the other, on the wall under the window. Using the strength in my legs, I pulled and pulled and pulled at the bars. They creaked, slowly bending. My feet broke through the drywall, then cracked the concrete underneath.

"No one holds me …" I whispered.

The bars ripped free from the window frame. I flew backward into the opposite wall, then tumbled to the ground. The magic embedded into the bars lashed around my hands, biting into my flesh.

I gained my feet, turning toward the door as the locks shifted, then opened.

Laughing, I took out both my guards as they dashed into the room, swords drawn. Twisting and turning, I dodged their clumsy strikes, beating each of them around the head and neck with the crystal bars. A third elf had apparently joined them, but he remained in the hall.

The first two fell.

I paused, shifting my stance to face the doorway. I raised my newly acquired weapons before me. The crystal bars were slick with the thick, pale-green blood of the two elves unconscious at my feet. I smiled as I absorbed the power, the magic teeming through that blood into the bars. Fortifying them. Claiming them as my own.

I flipped the purloined and remade bars in my hands. Their magic no longer seared my skin. "Come and get me."

The warrior elf hovering in the hall bared his teeth at me, taking two steps forward.

I lunged.

He slammed the door closed.

Unable to stop in time, I stabbed the steel door, impaling it with one of the crystal bars. Locks, then magic, snapped into place.

I shrieked in frustration.

My liege would be called. Woken from her nap. I'd be backed into the corner, and my mind would be ravaged.

Again.

And again.

And I would kneel in the end.

I would kneel!

The second bar crumbled in my hand. I'd been gripping it too tightly. Or perhaps I hadn't fully claimed the elf magic for my own.

And now I had no weapons.

One of the elves at my feet groaned. I kicked him in the gut, childishly.

I was missing something.

I was always missing something.

My gaze fell on the now unbarred window.

What had the woman in the red poncho been doing when I saw her? At the time, I thought she might have been looking for me ...

What if she was looking for a way into the stadium?

I crossed to the window. It was too small for me to fit my shoulders through, let alone my hips. Magic coated every inch of the exterior of the building.

I might not be able to get out of the room. But I could destroy what the elves had erected.

I thrust my hand through the glass of the window, cutting myself. The cuts healed instantly. I grabbed a fistful of the magic there.

"The wards," I whispered.

I gathered the energy to me, thrusting my other hand through the broken window to grip more of it. Then even more. And when I had everything I could hold, I smothered it with my own power. I choked it with my very will, with my need to be free.

Then I tore it asunder.

Magic lashed through the room. The cell. My prison.

I laughed.

I held the torrent of power. I took it for my own.

And I laughed.

The ward magic ebbed, then dissipated. It no longer covered the window. Standing on my tiptoes, I stuck my head outside, craning left, then right, then down. A large swath of the wards had been ripped away from the exterior of the stadium.

I lifted my face to the darkening sky, spotting a few stars peeking through the clouds. But it was raining. Misting. My skin gobbled up the moisture, soothing the ever-present wound in my forehead.

I breathed. I breathed in the cool air. I filled myself with it.

Magic shifted behind me. I stumbled away from the window, pressing my back to the wall, expecting to be attacked.

Nothing moved. The door was still closed and sealed. Two elves were still unconscious on the floor.

And a folded piece of paper was resting on the center of the cot.

That was new.

I slowly crossed the room, feeling a vague sense of the energy shifting within the building. Hearing far-away shouts. The elves were reacting to the breach in the wards.

I leaned over the cot. Then, touching it only at the very edges, I unfolded the thick white paper.

It was a drawing.

A sketch in charcoal.

I peered at its strong, thick lines.

It was a picture of a...a knife. Almost a rapier, really. Simple hilt, blade about the thickness of my thumb.

It looked achingly familiar.

The letter R was scrawled in the bottom right corner of the sketch. I hovered my fingers over that initial. I could feel the magic dancing within the charcoal.

Magic that should have tasted like...apple.

I...I should have been able to taste magic.

I looked back at the rendering of the knife, taking in every inch of it, every shadow, every line...

It was a clue.

A hint.

There was something I had to do...something about the knife.

In the sketch, the knife appeared to be sitting on a bed. Just as the sketch itself was sitting on my cot.

I glanced at the drawing, then at the cot. Then back to the drawing, comparing the top fold of the sheet. The folds were identical. On my cot and in the drawing.

Then...I remembered...

Charcoal drawings tasting of apple...knives...Rochelle...the oracle...the turtle...piloted by Mory...and Warner...

Warner...

Warner.

My Warner trapped in the magic of the dimensional gateway.

"That's my goddamn knife ..."

Called forth by my claim, a blade appeared on the bed. It was carved of green stone and pulsed with magic. Magic I couldn't taste. Because it was mine. My magic.

I grabbed the hilt of the knife. I raised it before me.

My blade.

The dowser's blade.

"Jade ..." I whispered. That was the stone from which I'd carved the knife. A knife with which I could collect magic. A knife with which I could cut through magic. The elves had made me give it up. She...my liege ... Reggie, I had called her. She had forced me to set down the weapon, to abandon my creation.

"Jade."

My name. My knife and my name.

Reggie would never control me again.

Even if I had to die to ensure that promise to myself, I would. Gladly. But first, I would set to rights what had gone wrong, the damage I had wrought under Reggie's command.

I just had to make sure she couldn't get hold of me again. I needed to make it so that when the elves sorted out the breach in the wards, when Reggie came through the door—when she came for me—she wouldn't be able to force me into the corner. She wouldn't press me down with her power. Not anymore.

The movement of the elves through the stadium around me increased. There was more shouted conversation. I could hear them, could feel them through the tear in the wards and the magic I'd claimed as my own. A breach they were already attempting to seal.

But none of that mattered now that I knew who I was. And what I could do. I had to fix the fissure within my own defenses. I had to carve out the weakness, seal the pathway that Reggie had used to tunnel into my mind over and over again.

I ran my fingers along the edge of the jade blade—my blade—savoring the magic that stirred underneath my touch.

The wielder of this weapon kneeled to no one.

I turned the blade toward myself. Tracing the edges of the gemstone with the fingers of my left hand, I wielded the weapon with my right.

Then I sliced through skin and magic.

Ignoring the pain and the blood streaming down my face, I cut into bone. Digging into my skull, I freed the edges of the gemstone. I wedged the knife underneath it, prying at it. Carefully. I didn't want to haphazardly slice through magic that had rooted itself in my brain.

I would have to tease each thread loose, one at a time. Gently. Meticulously. I couldn't miss a single strand …

Pain took my eyesight away. I pressed my knees to the edge of the cot, holding myself upright. My legs were trembling, but they held me.

The gemstone came loose in my shaking hand, but it was still attached to my brain by Reggie's power.

I was going to have to dig deeper.

I was going to have to carve into my brain.

So I did.

No one controlled me.

No one made me hurt my friends.

I was the dowser.

I was the wielder of the instruments of assassination.

I was Jade Godfrey.

Chapter Two

I wasn't completely certain how long I'd been floating in and out of consciousness, lying with my legs curled on the floor and my upper body slumped across the cot. I could still feel the damage I'd inflicted on the wards—the frayed ends of elven magic fluttering through the broken window. The two elves I'd beaten with the purloined crystal bars were thankfully still unconscious, sprawled across the beige carpet. The door was still locked and magically sealed.

But the bedsheets and the charcoal sketch were completely drenched in my blood. A lot of blood. Like, liters of blood. Or maybe cotton and paper were just particularly good at showing it.

I was clutching the gemstone in the palm of my left hand. Tendrils of magic tasting of salt water were tangled within my fingers. Reggie's magic. But for some reason, the gem hadn't crumbled into a fine crystal yet. Perhaps because it had been embedded in my brain? Had it somehow been altered by my magic, claimed by my alchemy even without my knowing it?

Keeping a firm grip on my jade knife—I wasn't misplacing it a second time—I pushed up onto my feet, tucking the gemstone into the front pocket of my jeans. My head felt…wrong. As if it weren't properly

It exploded outward into the hall, crashing through the far wall into an empty office and taking at least one elf with it.

I dispatched two other elves while they were still staring at me in surprise—and with a dawning sense of terror. My blood magic had made my blade sharp. Or maybe, even as wounded as I was, I moved too quickly for them to track.

They should have screamed.

They should have run.

Elves beware.

The dowser was on the loose.

I giggled, amusing myself. Then I lost my footing among the splayed limbs of my downed enemies, stumbling against the wall.

I really wasn't feeling great.

And now that I had a moment to think about it, I wasn't exactly certain what I was doing.

I had my knife.

I'd broken out of my room.

Was I fleeing?

The elves at my feet started to crumble from the inside. I had killed them? I glanced back through the open doorway into my room...no, my prison cell. The two elves in there weren't dead. They could wake and come after me. But I didn't want to kill them for no reason or without provocation.

There was a red exit sign at the far end of the hall, right at the top of the stairs. That seemed like a pretty clear indication of where I was supposed to go. I pushed away from the wall.

A tall, slim elf in a long vest jogged up the stairs—then came to a startled stop when she saw me. Or maybe it was the crumbling bodies of the two warrior elves at my feet that confused her. Her green eyes narrowed, watching me. Waiting for something …

I recognized her. She had come through the gateway, and her arrival had upset Reggie for some reason.

"You tried to kill me earlier…to choke me." I giggled again. That was inappropriate—especially since my forehead began gushing blood in response. But I couldn't seem to stop myself.

"Ineffectually," she said, sneering. Except maybe the scorn was directed at herself, not at me? Her words were accented…but why that struck me as odd or out of place, I wasn't sure.

I wiped away the blood trying to flow into my eyes and obscure my vision. That wouldn't do. Being able to see was important during a knife fight. And while escaping an enemy lair.

I snickered, but managed to get myself under control before I started giggling and gushing blood again.

The elf held her empty hands out to her sides, taking a measured step toward me. She wasn't wearing armor. I glanced down at the decomposing elves at my feet. Each of them had a cracked gemstone embedded in their forehead. The newcomer wore her hair pulled back from her temples in intricate braids, all beaded with jewels of some sort. But her forehead was smooth. Pale and finely scaled, but unblemished.

She took another step toward me.

Without looking away from her, I pushed the leg of the elf corpse nearest to me out of my path with the side of my foot. I raised my knife.

The new elf paused. Again. Her gaze flicked to my blade, then to the two elves slowly decomposing on the carpet. Again. She cleared her throat, raising her hands slightly. It was a gesture of goodwill. It was also a perfect setup for lunging forward and grabbing someone's weapon.

I grinned. She'd have a difficult time disarming me. But unfortunately, I couldn't stand around and play. I could feel more elves heading in our direction. I might not have known what I was meant to be doing, but hanging around in the hall waiting to be besieged seemed like a bad idea.

I took another step back.

"Wait." The elf lifted her hands higher, almost pleadingly. Ward builder. That was what Reggie had called her, wasn't it? "What did you mean by black-sand beach?" she asked. "And the name Mira? An elf you knew? An elf you ... named? An illusionist?"

I frowned, digging for a memory buried beneath the pounding headache that had begun in the center of my forehead but was now stretching over my entire skull and down the back of my neck. "Yes."

"You killed my nephew."

It wasn't a question, but I answered her anyway. "I did ... I think." Another memory surfaced. Of a park at night. "I'm not big on murdering people, but he'd just tried to gut my best friend and had snapped my fiancé's neck."

The ward builder frowned. "I don't understand those words. Those ... designations."

"Well, that explains a lot," I muttered. "My family. Kin. That's what you called your niece and nephew. The warrior elf in the park tried to murder my people. Before I killed him."

She nodded. "And the one you call Mira?"

"Why are you asking?"

"Because it is one thing to die at the end of an enemy's blade in the course of one's duty. And it is completely another to be ... deliberately sacrificed at the altar of an upstart megalomaniac."

"Then you already know the answer."

The elf looked grim. "Yes. But I'd like you to confirm that the rumors are more than simply the disgruntled imaginings of underlings."

I stuck my hand in my front pocket, pulling out the intact gemstone I'd cut from my forehead. Mira's gemstone, covered in my blood. It had tied her to Reggie. Then the telepath had killed the pretty elf in the yellow coat and taken the gemstone from her. To subvert me.

I held the stone aloft between my forefinger and thumb. It glistened with magic—Mira's and Reggie's, and possibly mine. But I couldn't taste my own power.

"A tether stone. One you've apparently somehow cut from your forehead."

"You don't wear one."

She curled her lip in a sneer. "It is beneath my birth and my standing to be commanded in such a ... barbaric fashion. I'm surprised at the number here who have agreed to the subversion. One in particular. Was that stone attached to the elf you called Mira?"

"It was."

"And was she alive when it was harvested? And transferred to you? Was she ... willing?"

"She'd just been murdered for it. By Reggie."

"Reggie?"

"The telepath. Your liege."

The elf laughed harshly. "She is no liege of mine." She spun on her heel, heading back toward the exit sign and the stairs. "They need me to fix the damage you inflicted on the wards. A rather impressive display of wanton destruction. I have deferred action as long as I can. You'll have less than twenty minutes to get out of the building."

"I need to find my people …"

Yes. There it was. That was what I needed to be doing. I needed to find Warner … and Kandy and Kett. And Haoxin. They were all imprisoned in the stadium. Assuming they were still alive.

The elf paused at the top of the stairs, glancing back at me. Her expression was grim. But oddly satisfied. "My name is … Alivia."

"Jade Godfrey."

"You are heading the wrong way, Jade Godfrey." Alivia smiled tightly. "And if you are to fulfill the promise you made to my niece, I suggest you stop bleeding everywhere."

She headed down the stairs before I could question her further. I had no idea what she meant by my 'promise.' But she was certainly right about the blood.

In the wrong hands, it was dangerous.

As I turned to head in the opposite direction, I allowed my alchemy magic to spread out around me, absorbing the residual magic in the blood I'd inadvertently splattered all over the hall. Then I fed that collected energy into my knife. My change in course also took me farther away from the gathering of elves I could feel a level below.

I tugged my T-shirt off and clumsily wrapped it around my head, hoping to staunch my wound. Wandering around in only a bra and blood-splattered jeans wasn't ideal. But at least the bra was a pretty dark green with black lace.

Two more elves came barreling down the corridor toward me, swords drawn.

I dispatched them. Though not before getting a blade to the gut and a wicked slash across my thigh. Both wounds healed quickly enough, but I was sloppy.

Slow.

Badly wounded.

Losing more blood didn't seem like a good idea, even if it was soaking into my jeans instead of decorating the walls.

I made it to another set of carpeted stairs leading to the lower level. But then I felt, more than heard, something whisper to me from farther to the right, along a parallel hall.

Magic.

There was magic down that hall—and that magic belonged to me.

I followed the beguiling whisper, passing more offices. All of them were empty, though none had been converted into holding cells. At the far end, adjacent to another set of stairs, was a boardroom. How large was this freaking building anyway?

Right. Stadium. So...large.

I crossed into the boardroom, moving past the huge table at its center but seeing no elves. A magically sealed door similar to the one that had warded my room stood at the far side.

I easily disabled the magic barring my way with a few flicks of my knife. Opening the door, I stepped into a tiny windowless room beyond. A long, thin desk, a computer, and a bunch of empty cash drawers were stacked to one side, along with one of those machines that counted paper money.

A large magically warded safe took up the remainder of the room. It was taller than me and slightly narrower than the span of my outstretched arms, so about six foot by five foot. Black metal, gold lettering.

I was starting to get an itchy, anxious feeling about how much time I was wasting—what with the stumbling around and the bleeding. I could actually feel the exterior wards beginning to knit back together. The ward builder, Alivia, was working her magic, as she'd said she would. But I felt unable to turn away without investigating the contents of the safe. Compelled, even.

And, yeah, something that could compel me, especially given the state of my damaged brain, was probably a bad thing.

I ignored the wards and didn't bother with the combination lock. Bracing my feet against the bottom corners of the safe, I grabbed the levered handle with two hands, then tried to simply rip through the weak magic that sealed it—by wrenching the door from the safe. The handle snapped off in my hands. I flew back, crushing the narrow desk that cushioned my fall.

Well, that outcome would probably have been predictable to anyone but me.

I scrambled to my feet, noting that I had managed to bend the steel door outward before the handle had given out. It was still sealed at all four corners, but I managed to wiggle my fingers into the gap as high up on the right side as I could, then peeled the top corner free about a quarter of the way down. Placing my palms flat on the top of the safe, I hoisted myself up into a seated position. Then I kicked down, over and over until I'd widened the opening.

I jumped off, peering inside the safe.

A thick-linked gold necklace laden with magic, two sheathed katanas, and a satchel were all arrayed on three of the shelves within the safe. There were other things as well—money and papers shoved to the sides—but I only had eyes for the magic.

"Mine," I whispered.

With my claim, the necklace settled around my neck. I brushed my fingers along the gold chain, the wedding rings, and all three instruments of assassination. Magic writhed underneath my touch as if pleased to see me—pleased to have been let out of the steel box.

There was something dangerous in that sensation...in a magical object feeling as though it were something other than just magic, but I couldn't remember what it was.

I felt more together with the heavy chain around my neck. Calmer. More focused. I twined it around twice more, getting it a little bloody while tugging it over my T-shirt-swaddled head. But I definitely felt more whole than I had in...hours? Days?

I slung the satchel across my chest, keeping my sheathed katana—aka the dragon slayer—in hand. I left the second sword. Though it teemed with potent magic, it wasn't mine to collect. And I couldn't carry more without compromising my ability to fight.

I exited, feeling the need to hurry.

Though actually...where was the sheath for my jade knife?

I glanced back at the open safe, remembering now how Reggie had forced me to deposit my weapons within it. I dug my hand into my satchel, feeling Kandy's cuffs and Warner's knife within its spelled depths and exhaling in relief. My knife should have been in its sheath before I called it to me, after seeing it in Rochelle's sketch.

And at that thought, the sheath in question—spelled invisible by my grandmother years before—cinched around my hips and my right thigh. If I had to loosen my hold on my jade blade, most likely because I needed to wield the katana instead, the knife would return to the sheath automatically.

I smiled—and felt a jolt of pain run through my forehead and back into my brain in response. But with the reclaiming of all my weapons and artifacts, I really was Jade Godfrey again.

I just needed to collect three even more important items—Warner, Kandy, and Kett. And to release a sure-to-be-extremely-pissed-off guardian.

I shuddered at that thought. No matter that Reggie had been in my head, using me as her weapon at the time, Haoxin was going to be seriously aggravated over how I'd used an instrument of assassination on her. I knew Warner would forgive me. Even though I'd tried to strangle him. And Kandy and Kett as well—though it might take a few years for the vampire to actually speak to me again. But that was what love was, right? Being there for each other in our darkest hours?

The guardian of North America, though? I had serious doubts about her ability to view the mind-control/gemstone situation with any compassion.

I stepped into the hall, crossing toward the stairs. The undead turtle was waiting for me at the top. I scooped it up without thinking too much about it, though I had to sheath my knife to do so. The turtle blinked up at me, tasting of toasted marshmallows and strawberry. Mory's magic, animating the undead creature. My mother's magic, likely embedded in the dime charm around its neck.

"Hey Mory," I whispered, peering into the tiny camera on the turtle's back. "Need a lift down the stairs?"

The turtle didn't answer. But then, I wasn't brain-damaged enough to really expect that it would. Well, not after checking first, at least.

Tucking the turtle under my left arm, I started down the stairs. And then realized somewhat belatedly that wandering around a huge stadium on a count-down wasn't going to get me anywhere quickly. Add in a seething head wound and a twisted maze that I vaguely remembered watching the elves building, and I was going to get lost in a hurry. Lost, then sealed back in with a dozen elves looking for me after the distraction of repairing the wards had passed. After they realized that I hadn't torn through their defenses in an attempt to escape, but to rescue my friends.

Not good.

But...I was a freaking dowser, wasn't I?

And I was attempting to rescue people who radiated potent magic just by breathing. How hard could that magic be to find?

Now...if only I could remember the tenor...or taste...of Warner's magic—

An intense panic seized me without warning, constricting my chest. I lost hold of my katana. The weapon tumbled down the stairs as I hunched over, clutching the turtle and struggling to breathe.

I should have been able to remember.

I should have been able to...taste.

But my head...my head hurt.

The turtle shifted in my grasp. I was holding it too tightly. I didn't want to hurt Mory's pet. I didn't want to hurt anyone. Anyone I loved...ever again.

I pressed a steadying hand against the wall to my right, instantly feeling the magic of the elves' wards...shifting...seeking ...

Right.

I inhaled deeply.

I could also feel magic. Even if I couldn't taste it, even if I couldn't remember a specific tenor.

I just had to keep moving. I half walked, half stumbled down the rest of the stairs, pausing to set down the turtle and pick up my katana on the lower level.

I'd bled all over the dead turtle.

"Sorry, Ed," I muttered, wiping my blood across the turtle's hard shell and fortifying the charm around its neck with the residual magic in that blood by instinct. "Keep out of sight. But … you need to get back through the wards soon. Say hi to Mory for me. Tell her … tell her I'm coming. I just have to find Warner, Kandy, and Kett."

The turtle shuffled away, keeping tight to the edge of the white-walled hall. This area looked a lot like the beginning of the elves' interior maze—or at least one of the entrances to that maze.

Warner … Kandy … Kett …

I transferred my katana to my right hand, then dipped my left hand into my satchel, immediately finding the hilt of Warner's knife. The blade reacted pissily to my touch. It didn't like me. Before I'd given it to Warner and tied it to his magic, I had tried to destroy the blood magic I'd used to create the knife. But denying all the death and destruction tied up in that blade was futile. The circumstances that had created it had already occurred. All I could deal with was the aftermath.

"Well, that was awfully insightful," I muttered to myself. "Maybe I should cut into my own brain more often. Trim out the fat." I laughed. And even though the idea wasn't particularly funny and the act of laughing pained me, it also settled me.

I raised Warner's knife before me. Then, in all seriousness, I said, "Take me to your master." Another fit of inappropriate giggles followed that insane command.

Then the knife tugged me left, in the opposite direction the turtle was taking.

"Jesus Christ." I hadn't thought that would work. I mean, I was a dowser, and the knife was tied to Warner, but …

Never mind. Questioning magic was a foolish thing to do.

And even though I was definitely a fool, I was on a serious time limit.

Warner's knife led me deeper into the white-walled maze that radiated out from the gateway situated at the very center of the stadium. I happened upon two more elves, patrolling separately. But even if they'd attempted to quell me together, I wouldn't have had any trouble knocking them out and continuing on. As I traversed the twisted hallways, spiraling closer and closer to the center of the maze, I could feel the energy of the dimensional rift I'd opened under Reggie's command.

It was up and running. Without me operating it.

So had the gemstone that Alivia brought fixed it completely? Or had I inadvertently fixed it enough that it could now be ignited by someone else? It didn't feel as though legions of elves were flooding through into the stadium … yet. But my dowser senses were compromised.

More importantly, though, the gateway being in operation meant that at least one of the people I was looking for was fueling it.

With their life force.

I shoved away that unhelpful thought. I'd find whoever I could, arming them with the extra weapons I carried. Then together, we would take out the gate, freeing whoever was fueling it.

That was a plan. And with my head aching more and more, having a primary focus was less panic inducing than worrying about Reggie managing to pull off her invasion plan while I was stumbling around in a freaking maze.

I paused at a three-way fork in the hall. Magic glistened from the twelve-foot-high, eighteen-inch-thick walls surrounding me, but the three-foot-wide section I stood in was still open to the soaring, domed roof of the stadium. I considered climbing up to see where I was and where the knife was leading me, but dismissed the idea as too risky. Any elves on the upper tier would have no problem spotting a human scrambling around in a bra and bloody jeans with a green T-shirt tied around her head.

The elves had moved quickly, implementing a plan that they—that Reggie—had been concocting ever since they'd broken out of Pulou's prison.

A sudden wave of terror rolled over me so intensely that I gasped, stumbling over my own feet. I'd been so focused on breaking out and rescuing Warner, Kandy, and Kett that I didn't know ... I had no idea who else the elves had harmed. Gran ... my mother ...

No ...

No.

Traveler had said something about the witches trapping the elves in the stadium. And I'd seen Ed. And the appearance of the sketch had to mean that Rochelle was okay.

I got myself under control. Now that I was surrounded by the magic embedded in the maze, I couldn't feel the exterior wards. For all I knew, my twenty minutes had been up twenty minutes before. When the distraction of fixing the boundary magic I'd torn asunder passed, then the elves' focus would turn to corralling me.

But I wasn't going to be contained again.

And faced with as many elves as I'd allowed to pass through the gateway in the previous days—faced with dozens of them—I would die.

Then the people I loved would eventually perish fueling the gateway. I didn't think even Kett could survive having his life force siphoned from him day after day.

"Warner ... Kandy ... Kett ... Haoxin ..." I whispered, turning the names of those loved ones into a mantra. Well, plus one guardian, who might well try to kill me after I freed her. "Warner ... Kandy ... Kett ... Ha oxin."

Warner's knife tugged me to the left again. Away from the center of the stadium and the gateway. I followed the ornery weapon's instructions dutifully, taking two more turns before finding myself in another recently constructed corridor with four evenly spaced steel doors leading from it. Three of the doors were closed. The nearest was standing open.

The hall appeared to dead-end. And, unfortunately, each of the steel-fortified, magically sealed, and most likely triple-locked doors appeared to be guarded by two elves.

So, yeah.

Six elves.

In a fairly narrow hallway. Which meant my katana was near useless.

Spotting me, the two nearest elves shouted, alerting the others to my rather abrupt and ill-conceived arrival. They lunged toward me, manifesting short, broad knives on the fly.

Keeping Warner's knife in my left hand, I dropped my still-sheathed katana, calling my knife into my right hand. Ducking under the first elf's attempt to decapitate me, I spun right and slit the throat of the second elf. Then I smoothly sidestepped as he stumbled forward and went down, hindering the first elf even as he attempted to spin back and reengage me.

I took off the top of the first elf's head with Warner's knife, staring in stunned horror as he crumbled, top down, into a fine crystal. Jesus. The knife was freaking sharp. And utterly wicked. And it was suddenly feeling exceedingly gleeful to be wielded by me.

Also, the elf I'd just murdered should have ducked.

Strong arms wrapped around me from behind, pinning my arms to my sides and lifting me off my feet. I slammed my head back, catching my unseen captor in the chin.

Something snapped, likely his jaw. He grunted.

Black dots swam before my eyes. Pain streaked through my skull, coalescing around the wound in my forehead. Slamming my head into his face had been a bad move on my part. For a moment, it was all I could do to ride out the pain and disorientation while hanging limply in the warrior elf's arms.

Another elf pushed past us, leaping over the disintegrating corpse sprawled across the hall and darting around the second elf—most likely going for reinforcements. The second elf was still breathing, but he was focused on clutching his slowly healing throat.

The agony ravaging my brain settled into a deep throb in the middle of my forehead. I kicked backward, attempting to take out my captor's knee but managing only to wiggle my foot.

Okay, apparently I was more incapacitated than I thought. The pain was draining. Or maybe it was the continual blood loss.

The elf holding me was shouting something. I didn't catch the words. He placed me on my knees, still facing away from him while holding a blade across my neck. Then he tried to disarm me.

Bad idea.

The elf hissed as the magic of Warner's knife seared his skin. Only the sentinel or the maker of the blade, namely me, could touch it without retribution.

Speaking of blades, I'd lost hold of my jade knife, but I could feel it back in its sheath. I must have actually blacked out for a few seconds.

Another elf joined the one who'd originally grabbed me. Together, they yanked my arms back, slamming my face into the ground. I lost my vision for another beat, only regaining my sight when I felt something cool, hard, and teeming with magic snapping around my wrists.

They'd cuffed me.

Jesus. There was blood all over the concrete floor that my cheek was currently harshly pressed against.

Seriously. What the hell good was magical healing if I couldn't dig into my own freaking brain with my own freaking knife?

Something hit the reinforced steel door to my right. The entire wall shook with the blow.

Another hit.

And another.

Someone was trying to break out, to break free from the prison cells.

"Jade!"

His bellow was muted but unmistakable.

Warner.

Warner was just beyond that door. Inches away.

And he knew I was near.

The elves scrambled to their feet, slipping in my blood while they fanned out to face the new threat about to come through the door. Conveniently, this took their attention off me.

I gathered my magic. I unleashed my alchemy, pouring it over the cuffs binding my wrists, claiming them for my own.

Then, slamming a kick to the ankle of the elf nearest to me—only because I couldn't reach his knee while lying on the floor—I cracked through the cuffs, freed my hands, and made it up onto my knees. Calling my jade knife forth, I stabbed the elf I'd kicked as he tried to break his fall, pinning his hand to the floor. Then I slugged him with the hilt of Warner's knife.

He went all the way down, clearing the way for the neighboring elf to attack me.

Still holding the blade backward, I caught the overhand strike headed my way with the edge of Warner's knife, slicing the elf's crystal blood-blade in two. I stabbed him in the gut with my jade knife as he stumbled forward a step.

The magic of his blade crumbled into a fine powder as he fell to his knees.

I hadn't even made it to my feet yet.

I staggered upward, punching the elf still kneeling before me in the forehead. His gemstone cracked and he fell, unconscious but not dead.

See?

Even brain-damaged, I tried to not murder indiscriminately.

Still sealed inside his cell, Warner slammed his shoulder into the door again. Or maybe he was kicking it. But though the steel door buckled outward, the locks and the magic sealing it still held.

"Jade!"

I faced off against the two remaining elves, grinning through the blood streaming down my face as I shouted, "I'm here, Warner!" I didn't know if my fiancé could hear me through the warded walls and door, but he could clearly feel my magic.

Okay, it was actually the proximity of the instruments of assassination that he could feel.

Which reminded me ...

Thinking I was distracted, the two elves lunged. Holding my jade knife awkwardly, I ran three fingers across my necklace, teasing two of the silver centipedes from the gold chain—then flicking them in the faces of the elves as they charged me.

I raised both knives before me, ready to fight if necessary.

It wasn't.

Churning with deadly metallurgy, the centipedes latched onto the elves, hitting one on the cheek and one on the forehead. The warrior elves screamed in unison, attempting to claw one of the only three ways to kill a guardian dragon from their faces.

Apparently, the silver metallurgy that powered the centipedes wasn't picky about who it felled. Or maybe because I had claimed the weapon, imbuing it with my alchemy when I added it to my necklace, the centipedes simply did my bidding now—attacking whoever or whatever I wanted to destroy.

I knew it was best not to think about that tangle of possibilities. Not right at that moment, anyway.

I didn't bother to watch the elves fall. Didn't bother to watch the centipedes drilling into their brains.

I turned to the dented steel door that was all that separated me from Warner. Starting at the top right, I sliced through the magic that sealed it with my jade knife. Halfway down the edge of one side, the taste of chocolate and cherry—smoky and sweet—rolled across my tongue, filling my senses. Momentarily frozen in the grief of all that I'd almost lost, I pressed my ear to the door, sobbing in relief.

"Warner…Warner!"

"I'm here, Jade." His words were husky and soothing, filtering through the long slice I'd made in the magic sealing the door.

"I'm sorry, I'm sorry. I'm going to get—"

"Stop!" Magic reverberated up the hall, slamming into me and knocking me back a few steps from the door.

Reggie.

The power housed in the gemstone in my pocket flared. In response, even while slipping in my own blood and stumbling around the limbs of the fallen elves, I instinctively smothered it with my own. I found my footing, raised my weapons—my jade knife and Warner's blade—and looked down the hall.

Reggie, still dragging her stupid green cloak around with her, was standing at the far end of that hall, maybe twenty feet away. At least a dozen elves were arrayed beside and behind her. The warrior elves were all taller and broader than the sickly looking telepath, and sheathed in the white armor that was a manifestation of their blood. No pesky, tripping-hazard cloaks for the warriors.

It was a pretty picture.

Reggie and her artfully arrayed warriors, intending to be intimidating. Instagram worthy, really.

Too bad I didn't have a camera.

The only thing between us, other than unconscious or decomposing elves, was my katana. It was lying at the edge of the hall. I reached for its magic, calling it to me. It settled over my back. Then I tugged my satchel forward on my left hip, tucking Warner's knife back into its magical depths.

"I said stop!" Reggie snarled. "Drop your weapons."

This time, the magic she threw my way didn't even buffet me. I flicked the pitiful power away with my jade knife, holding up my left hand in the shape of an L at my forehead. Which probably would have been a more effective insult if I hadn't had a blood-soaked T-shirt tied around my head.

"Reggie. I was just coming to get you." The words came out more slurred than the sassy tone I was aiming for. "Give me a second would you? I have a feeling my fiance would like to say hello as well."

As if he agreed, Warner kicked his door again, snapping one of the locks at the edge I'd partially sliced open. A couple of more kicks and he'd be free.

I took two measured steps back, clearing the area so the door wouldn't hit me when Warner freed himself.

I was still unsteady on my feet, and oddly cold suddenly. Shivering but trying to hide it. That might have been a side effect of wandering around in a bra. It could also have been the blood loss. But I only needed to hold the elves off for a few more minutes ...

Then Traveler shouldered his way through the crowd of elves, pausing to loom over Reggie. He was at least a foot taller than the telepath.

I realized he was talking, but I understood only every few words. "... my liege ... ward builder ... sealed ..."

Had they been speaking Elvish this entire time? And I'd only understood it because of the gemstone? Yes. I'd known that already. That the gem also operated as a translator, and had apparently fixed at least a few words in my head. But then why had I been able to talk to Alivia? Ah—she'd been speaking English. That was why I'd picked up her accent.

Intense, golden magic blew open at my back. It raged forward, consuming the fallen elves, scouring every drop of my blood from the floor and walls. It engulfed me, searing the blood from my flesh and clothing, churning around me, lifting me forward and up onto my toes.

Dragon magic.

Guardian magic.

Someone stepped up behind me. Someone almost too large to fit into the narrow hall.

At the mouth of the corridor, Reggie's eyes widened in pure terror.

A strong hand grasped the back of my belt. I screamed, twisting, but I couldn't break free from his hold. "No! I have to get to Warner. Warner!"

Pulou the treasure keeper yanked me against him, practically shouting in my ear, "I can't hold the portal open any longer, dragon slayer."

I fought him, but I was wounded and weak … and the magic of the portal was so, so overwhelming.

"You!" Pulou shouted, pointing at Reggie. "I'll be back for you!"

Then he picked me up and tossed me through the raging portal standing open behind us. I flew through its golden magic, tumbling into the gilded interior of the dragon nexus. And as I did, I slammed into one of its nine pillars and fell senseless to the marble floor.

Chapter Three

The intense taste of black tea and heavy cream churned around Pulou as he stepped through into the nexus. His massive fur coat brushed the edges of the door that led to the North American territories. He was alone.

Alone.

He was leaving the others behind.

His tumultuous power settled, folding back on itself. The First Nations-carved door behind him began to close. The portal leading to the stadium was about to be shut down.

"No!" I screamed, struggling to gain my footing on the white marble floor. I managed to gather all four limbs beneath me, then launched myself across the central hub of the nexus. "Warner is there. He's almost out. Kandy ... Kett ..."

I slammed against Pulou's outstretched arm. He had raised it to block me from throwing myself through the portal as it closed. I hadn't even seen him move. His thick fur coat did nothing to mitigate the blow. My lower ribs snapped.

I fell to my knees, choking on the pain. The door was half closed ... only inches away from me ...

"I told you, no." The treasure keeper's English lilt was edged with a full-throated growl. He loomed over me. "Punching through the witches' city ward was de-stabilizing enough. Now the elves have sealed the breach in their own ..."

Not listening, not caring, I started to crawl. Pulou placed his booted foot in front of me. I edged around it.

The door clicked shut. And a completely different type of pain shot through my chest. Heart-wrenching, soul-sucking terror.

"They're dying ..." I whispered, reaching for and digging my fingernails into the edges of the elaborate carving etched into the heavy wooden door. I slowly pulled myself up, making it onto my knees. My ribs healed.

I reached for the door handle.

Pulou knocked my hand away. "That doesn't lead anywhere now, stupid child. I won't be the one to tell your father you've gotten lost in the portal network. Again." Derision laced every one of his words.

Anger flooded through me—a deep, simmering outrage that helped me make it all the way to my feet. I turned to face the treasure keeper.

His frown deepened, creasing the skin around his eyes and dour mouth. His dark gaze swept over me, head to toe.

I pulled the strap of my satchel over my head, dropping the bag to the ground. I'd lost hold of my katana when I tumbled through the portal. It was lying on the far side of the nexus, sheathed. The dragon slayer ... waiting for me to retrieve it.

Pulou's eyes narrowed, assessing me.

"You will reopen the portal," I said, my voice clogged with emotion. "If you are too much of a coward to come with me, I will go myself."

"Coward?" he snarled. "You dare—"

I jabbed my finger at his chest. "You have done this! Your arrogance and prejudice—"

"That is enough! You will not speak to me—"

"Open the portal!" I screamed. Pain raked through my brain, pounding, pulsing within my skull. I felt blood start to seep through the T-shirt on my forehead again, so I reached up and tore the sodden mass off. I'd ruined the shirt Kandy had made for me. *Never mind the cup-cakes. I can totally kick your ass.*

I'd...I'd ruined everything.

Something shifted in Pulou's expression. His anger was suddenly muted by concern, maybe. But I didn't care about what he thought or felt.

"I have to get back," I whispered.

"Be patient."

I sneered at his suggestion as I turned my back on him. I focused on the door, shutting him out.

I had absorbed Shailaja's magic. The daughter of the former treasure keeper had been able to manifest portals...tiny ones, and possibly only short range. But still portals. So therefore, it was possible that I could make use of her magic now to open the goddamn door back to the stadium myself.

I called forth the magic teeming in my blood. I filled that energy, that power, with every ounce of intent I could muster through my anger, and my fear, and the agony of my damaged brain.

I reached for the handle.

Pulou's hand fell on my shoulder.

Frustration carried by a fierce wrath flashed through me. I screamed, giving voice to my terror of losing those I loved, those I'd left to the terrible mercy of the elves.

I attacked the treasure keeper.

A guardian.

My one-time mentor.

I grabbed his wrist with my left hand, twisted within his grasp on my shoulder, and slammed the heel of my right hand up under his chin.

Pulou grunted.

Bones shattered in my hand and wrist.

He tossed me to the side, using the hand I was trying to hold him with. I flew across the hub of the nexus, and my back and head slammed against another gilded pillar. I fell to my hands and knees, disoriented and dazed.

But rage had me in its grip. Fury overrode my pain. I called my knife into my right hand, facing off against Pulou, who hadn't moved except to glance my way.

Wiping away the blood seeping from the wound in my forehead and threatening to obscure my vision, I reached up and untwined my necklace, bringing all the lethal magic I wielded into play.

Pulou pulled his shortsword, its power thick and potent. The emerald embedded in its cross guard was gleaming with magic.

But the treasure keeper's blade wasn't anywhere near as powerful as the weapons I carried.

With a flick, I coiled the entire length of my thick gold chain around my left hand, wrist, and lower forearm. I held the combined power of the three instruments of assassination in my fist.

Pulou curled his lip. "You dare to use the instruments against me."

"You dare to stand between me and those I love," I purred, deadly and focused. "Maybe it's time for you to understand the meaning of caring enough to die for something. For someone."

"You dare to suggest—"

"Yeah, yeah, asshole. The daring is done. It's time to do." I lunged for him.

The guardian's stance shifted as he made ready to backhand me, to knock me sideways, executing a move I'd seen him use when Desmond had attacked us in his living room in Portland years before. Unfortunately for the guardian, he was about to find out that some moves only worked once.

Pulou's reach was longer than mine.

He should have led with his sword.

I slid under his backhand. Completely sacrificing my footing and the strength of my legs in order to draw first blood, I stabbed through his fur coat and into the meat of his thigh.

He grunted, predictably grabbing me by my arm and hauling me to my feet. I let go of my knife, leaving it embedded in Pulou. But instead of giving him an opening to gut me, I used the momentum of him yanking me upright and coldcocked him with my fistful of necklace.

Potent, deadly magic exploded between us. Pulou flew backward, pulling me with him for a few feet before losing hold of me.

I tumbled but eventually landed on my knees, sliding halfway across the nexus.

The guardian crashed into a golden pillar, practically snapping it in half, then tumbled to the marble floor. The floor cracked, radiating out far enough that the spiderweb fissure brushed my knees.

The magic of the nexus shifted, rolling, writhing underneath me as I tried to gain my feet, to press my attack.

I scrambled forward, on all fours for a few feet, then stumbling fully upright. I called my jade knife into my right hand, wrenching it from Pulou's thigh with a mere thought.

The treasure keeper reared up on his undamaged knee, bringing his sword into play. He was bleeding.

Bleeding.

From a cut that ran across his jaw and chin.

I grinned nastily, meeting the tip of his shortsword with my left fist. Its golden blade crumbled underneath the assault of my alchemy and all three instruments of assassination.

Magic erupted between us again, but I pressed forward against the onslaught, leaning into it until I was holding the tip of my jade knife only inches from Pulou's throat.

The first hints of disconcertion flitted across the treasure keeper's face.

"Open the portal," I demanded.

"You open it," he snarled.

"I was trying to—"

Then he punched me in the gut.

Apparently, even a five-hundred-year-old dragon understood the power of distraction when dealing with an infuriated child.

I flew across the room, fairly certain that a few of my internal organs were imploding. I hit something…wood…stone…then fell to the floor, limp limbed and face first.

The white marble underneath me rumbled with the might of the treasure keeper as he stalked across the nexus toward me.

I lifted my head. I got my hands underneath me, but I couldn't seem to put any of my weight on them. I couldn't control my arms and legs at the same time.

Something was badly broken. It might have been my spine.

Pulou pulled another blade out of the depths of his fur coat. A steel knife with a gleaming golden edge—sharpened with magic. He was still bleeding from the slash across his jaw, and also from the knuckles of his knife hand.

I got one knee under me, but I couldn't get any leverage. There was blood everywhere. Under my hands, my head. It sizzled and spit each time it dripped onto the instruments of assassination still twined around my left hand and wrist.

Pulou raised his knife.

He was going to kill me.

And then…and then…who would survive in the time it would take for the guardians to realize they needed to go back to Vancouver? If Reggie managed to fix the gateway and bring her army through, who would be caught in the invasion?

Everyone.

My entire world was in Vancouver.

Every single person I loved would die.

"Please…please …" I tried to speak, but I wasn't certain I was doing so out loud. "Have to…go…back …"

Blood started gushing out of my nose, choking my words in my throat.

Dear God …

I was already dying.

Pulou hesitated. His knife was still raised, hovering somewhere over my shoulder blades.

The door closest to me slammed open, nearly taking the top of my skull off. Magic thundered through the activated portal. The warrior of the guardians, dressed in black, hard-shelled armor with his golden sword at the ready, entered the nexus in a blinding torrent of smoky, dark-chocolate power.

The mind-boggling magical power of the warrior's broadsword vowed the utter annihilation of anyone who stood before it.

My father stepped over me, avoiding the pool of blood forming around my head and shoulders.

Pulou took a step back.

My father bellowed.

Bellowed.

It was a vicious sound, saturated with anger, fear—and retribution.

His magic raged through the nexus, ricocheting off the walls and back again. Between that and the open portal, my mind turned to mush. Even my teeth ached as I let my head drop, cheek pressed into the blood cooling on the marble floor.

"What have you done?" My father's question was fiercely cold.

"Warrior." Pulou held up his hand, but he didn't drop his weapon. "Your daughter attacked me. With the instruments."

"Was that before or after you attempted to take them from her?"

Pulou looked affronted. "I did no such—"

"And the wound?" My father glanced down at me. I blinked up at him. His sword was glowing so brightly that it hurt my eyes. "On her forehead? Was that before or after?"

Pulou hesitated.

"I see, treasure keeper. You chose to assault my child while she was mortally wounded?" My father shifted his stance, sword at the ready.

That sword was the only other weapon that could kill a guardian dragon...or so I'd been told.

Well...I hadn't put that together before. The wielder of the instruments of assassination was also the warrior's daughter. It fit, didn't it?

I started giggling. Yes, apparently I could laugh while dying.

"What is so amusing, my daughter?"

I somehow found the strength to roll over to my side, then sort of slump onto my back, allowing the arm wrapped with the instruments to rest across my chest. I tried to flap my free hand at the question. I managed to wiggle my fingers. "It's not funny...it shouldn't be funny."

The door leading to my father's territories in Australia clicked shut. Yazi hunched down, gently tucking his fingers underneath my chin, examining the wound on my forehead. Fear replaced the fury etched into his face.

Pulou cleared his throat, sheathing his knife in his coat pocket. "Warrior, my judgement was—"

"The healer," Yazi snapped. "I presume you've called him already, guardian?"

"No, I ..." Pulou spun away, reaching for the nearest door. I could see only his feet and the edge of his fur coat as he stepped through into the portal magic he'd wordlessly called forth.

I tried to sit up. My father placed a gentle hand on my shoulder, holding me down.

"Dad. I have to go back."

"Yes."

"Now. I have to go back now."

"Listen to me, Jade. My darling girl. You are very badly wounded. I need you to lie still. And stay awake. You should be healing ..."

"Tell me something I don't know." I coughed up more blood, then had to hawk up the rest so I didn't choke on it. "Oh...that's...disgusting."

My father swore in Cantonese...or maybe Mandarin. Or maybe I'd damaged my brain so much that I was losing my grasp of English.

"No...Dad, the elf...Reggie, she made me do things."

My father touched my cheek lightly. "Never mind now."

"It's important now."

"It's not."

"It is. What if I'm dying?"

"You are impossibly stubborn."

"Kettle meet pot."

"I have no idea what that means."

"I opened a dimensional gateway. I managed to curtail its...aperture so that only one elf could pass through...every...hour...or ..." The gilded room around me went black at its edges. I kept trying to explain, kept trying to talk, but I didn't think I was forming words anymore.

Then suddenly, there was music and magic.

And pain. So, so much pain.

Searing, questing pain focused through my forehead, pushing deep into my skull, radiating down my back.

I cried out.

Somewhere nearby, my father was shouting.

"I'm sorry, dragon slayer," a gentle voice said.

The music increased. I couldn't quite hear the tune...or maybe it was that the tune was every note ever played, all at once ...

The pain faded.

Numbness tugged at my limbs. I relaxed into it.

"Jade…Jade …" The gentle voice with its delectable, irresistible Latin accent belonged to the healer. Qiuniu. But he didn't sound so gentle now. "Stay with me."

More magic radiated out across my chest, then my forehead. Qiuniu was trying to heal me.

And it hurt.

"Stop it," I said. I tried to brush the magic away, but I couldn't lift my arm.

"Jade, Jade. Stop." Qiuniu sounded stressed. His voice shifted away, indicating he was talking to someone else. "The instruments are fighting me. Who does she trust enough to hand them over to?"

"Not you," my father snapped.

"Of course not," Pulou said, affronted. "Blossom can do it. Yazi, warrior, I had no idea—"

The treasure keeper's voice cut off sharply. As if, just maybe, someone might have punched him.

I smiled. But only on the inside.

I let the numbness tug me under again. The pain was exhausting. Letting go of it would be …

Qiuniu touched my shoulder and the music swelled. "Jade. I need you to hand the necklace to Blossom."

"Mistress?" The taste of lemon verbena tickled my taste buds. The brownie's deep, gravelly voice was shaky. Fearful. "Mistress?"

"The instruments, Jade," the healer repeated. "They are hindering my healing. Hand the necklace to Blossom. Please. Time is of the essence."

"That's all good," I muttered. "But I can't move my hand."

"Just give her permission, then."

"Blossom?"

"Yes, mistress."

"Please look after my necklace."

Magic shifted around me, carrying a caress of lemon. Then it was gone, along with the weight of the chain I'd wrapped around my left hand and wrist. Qiuniu's power overtook the light touch of Blossom's magic, spreading through my stomach and chest, down my limbs.

The healing didn't hurt this time. But my head still ached. I really just wanted to sleep ...

If I could just sleep, I was certain I would heal.

They were arguing again. The three guardians. Or maybe they'd never stopped. The power rolling off them and radiating back from the walls and floor was annoyingly and intensely persistent, making it difficult to sleep.

I opened my eyes. My lashes were stuck together, most likely with dried blood. The room came into focus. I blinked at the decorated ceiling, realizing it showed a scene like an old-fashioned oil painting. A demon of some sort was peeking around the pillar just over my head. Right where it joined the ceiling.

A demon in the nexus seemed like a terrible idea. But no one else appeared to notice it.

"I've healed everything but the wound in her head." Qiuniu was hovering over me but looking away, talking to someone else. My father, by the taste of his magic. "She looks as though she's been in a war zone. And the damage to her organs ..." The healer shook his head.

Pulou grunted, somewhere nearby as well. "That was me."

The healer appeared to momentarily consider attacking the treasure keeper. That would have been a sight to behold.

I giggled.

The healer cranked his head to look at me, moving so quickly that I was surprised he didn't hurt his neck.

"Does your magic work on you?" I asked him, slurring the words. "I can't taste my magic...can you heal yourself?"

"No," the healer said grimly.

"That's too bad. There's a demon on the ceiling."

The healer flinched, looking up. Then he sighed. "It's a painting, Jade."

"Really? Who would paint a demon on the ceiling of the nexus?"

"Who did paint the ceiling?" my father asked. "Baxia?"

Qiuniu looked as though he might have been contemplating murdering us all.

I grinned at him.

"Who cut you, Jade?" the healer asked. He was awfully pretty, perched over me with his smooth, darkly tanned skin, his melted-milk-chocolate eyes, and looking all concerned.

"I'm about to be married," I said, feeling a need to remind myself and the healer of that fact. Qiuniu preferred to heal via a lip lock. At least when he healed me. "No kissing."

He sighed heavily, firming his tone to a no-nonsense level. "I'm having a difficult time healing the wound on your forehead. Who sliced into your head? What magic did they use?"

"I did."

"You cut into your own brain? Deliberately?"

"No," I mumbled. "That happened when I yanked this out." I dug into the pocket of my jeans, pulling out the gemstone that Reggie had embedded in my forehead, and displaying it in my open palm.

The healer swore.

My father started pacing and muttering to himself.

But Pulou surged into my field of vision, laughing huskily. Then he plucked the gemstone from my hand before I could protest. "You brilliant, brilliant girl. Daft and rash, to be sure. But brilliant." He held the stone up, peering through it. Tendrils of magic still clung to its edges. "I've never seen one intact. With this, we can stem the tide." Then he hustled off without another word.

Portal magic bloomed, then faded.

"He just stole my gemstone," I muttered. "He is such an asshole."

"Yes," the healer said agreeably. "But with the elves attacking at multiple points, stemming the tide is a good idea." He glanced up at my father. "So we'll forgive him the theft."

Yazi nodded curtly. "If you save my daughter, healer, I'll gladly follow your lead."

"And if not?"

A terrible smile bloomed across my father's normally jovial face. "Then the elves will have competition for the treasure keeper's attention."

Even with my mind in its present state, that sounded like a bad idea. The warrior couldn't be pitted against the treasure keeper ...

"Don't worry about it now, Jade," the healer murmured, as if maybe I'd been talking out loud. "I need you to concentrate just a little longer."

"I think I'll just lie here for a moment more," I whispered. Though I had managed to make my arm work earlier, I was actually having a hard time feeling all my limbs. Or my torso ...

"Jade, Jade." The healer touched my cheek, pulling my attention to him. "I need you to key me into your knife. Then you can sleep."

"I usually just stab people with it."

"That would work as well. But I'd prefer to not be bleeding as I heal you."

"Okay," I murmured. "But no kissing. I'm about to be married."

"To that, I make no promises." He laughed. "And the sentinel would want you healed above all else."

The sentinel. Warner. "I have to go back." I tried to move but didn't manage to even flinch. "I have to rescue the others."

"First healing. Then rescuing."

Qiuniu laid his hand over my knife, which had returned to its sheath at my hip. Then he placed my hand on top of his. "Just one more thing, then you can sleep. Allow me to wield the dowser's knife, Jade Godfrey."

"I allow it, Qiuniu, healer of the guardians. Thank you."

Magic shifted between the knife and me, between the knife and Qiuniu.

His eyes narrowed thoughtfully, then he smiled sweetly. "Ah, I see. Pulou is right. You are brilliant."

He leaned over and brushed a kiss to my lips. I closed my eyes and accepted his offer. Magic tasting of dark, bitter chocolate and darkly roasted coffee flooded through me. I breathed it in. I gathered every last drop I could hold.

I had to get back.

I had to rescue the others.

And I had to be able to at least walk to do both those things.

A comforting darkness swept over me, along with a whisper of sweet, soothing music.

"Why does that feel like it won't be the last time I'll kiss death from Jade Godfrey's lips?" the healer murmured.

Then I slept.

Chapter Four

I woke in the middle of an enormous bed, swaddled in silk, cotton, and goose down. For a moment, I envisioned myself drowning in the luxury fabrics. Then my conscious mind intruded and I remembered ... everything.

Where I was—the nexus.

Who I'd left behind—Warner, Kandy, Kett, and Haoxin.

And what was about to happen with the elves and the gateway—if it hadn't happened already.

I bolted upright. And was rewarded for that hasty movement with a slash of pain emanating from my forehead, then rebounding back and forth inside my skull to blur my sight. I held myself as still as possible through successive rounds of dizziness.

I wasn't wholly healed, then.

I worked one arm out of the silk sheets that someone had attempted to mummify me within, then carefully touched my forehead. It didn't hurt to do so, but a thick ridge of scar tissue marred the skin there. I traced the edges, discerning a circular shape. From the gemstone.

I was ... scarred ... disfigured. Maybe permanently.

That was ...

Warring emotions rolled through me. I squeezed my eyes shut, absorbing the shock and the sadness, denying the pitiful tears that welled up. I was being silly, stupid. I was alive. That was what counted.

I untwined my legs from the sheets, perching on the edge of the bed to get my bearings. The mattress and bed frame were so tall that my feet dangled about a foot and a half from the floor.

I didn't recognize the room. Well, with a sitting area and what appeared to be a huge marble-encased bathroom off to one side, it was really more of a suite. But despite the luxurious sheets and huge four-pillar bed, the remainder of the room's decor was austere. Dark-stained, heavy wooden furniture. Thickly layered rugs. And weapons.

I was in my father's quarters. The three sets of armor lined up against the wall, all of varying weights and materials, gave that away. Another space where a fourth set would have stood was empty.

A picture of my mother and me on the bedside table was another pretty obvious clue to my location. It sat next to a leather-bound book, with a title along the spine in lettering that I was pretty sure was Greek—which, of course, I couldn't read. The photo was set in a jewel-encrusted, magically imbued frame that my father must have fished out of the treasure keeper's stash. But I didn't immediately recognize the picture itself. The shot had been clearly taken on the beachfront at my grandmother's house. I appeared to be around nine or so.

Enticed by the magic I could feel emanating from it, I reached for the frame just as the picture faded and was replaced by another more recent photo of my mother. In that picture, my mother's blue eyes sparkled. Her strawberry-blond hair was wild in the wind, long tresses cascading over her bare shoulders. She gazed at the camera—at the photographer—in a way that was … loving and sultry and …

I glanced away, suddenly feeling as though I was invading my mother's personal life. And my father's, for that matter.

The idea that Yazi had pictures of us, of the people he loved, by his bedside was so ordinary that it was completely unexpected. Ordinary and utterly heartwarming.

I slipped off the bed, testing my ability to stand—and actually managed to stay upright. I was dressed in white cotton drawstring pants and a tank top. A combo that I'd once worn while imprisoned by Pulou.

But it was a safe guess that the treasure keeper wouldn't be locking me up this time.

My stomach growled. Loudly.

Accompanied by the taste of lemon verbena, a tray of food appeared on the bed beside me. Breakfast in bed, replete with scrambled eggs, multigrain toast, blackberry jam, and what appeared to be fresh-pressed apple juice. A note scrawled on a small piece of ragged-edged parchment sat propped on a banana. I recognized the handwriting as Pulou's, and I knew even before I read it that I wasn't going to be pleased with the instructions it was certain to contain.

You are to remain in the nexus until further notice.

Yep, I had that pegged.

He had added a second line. The color of the ink was slightly diluted, almost as if he'd jotted it down as an afterthought.

*Your family has been informed of your
survival and ongoing recovery.*

I snorted as I tossed the parchment onto the tray. Then I propped up the pillows against the headboard, climbed back onto the bed, and tugged the silk sheets around me. Settling back, I placed the tray over my lap and spread some jam on the toast.

I needed a plan.

I needed help.

But first, I needed food, clothes, and my weapons.

As if summoned by my thoughts, a familiar wooden table pockmarked by magic materialized at the foot of the bed. The same table had materialized to hold my weapons when I'd been summoned to stand trial before the guardians. My katana, my jade knife, my satchel, and my necklace—including the instruments of assassination—were arrayed across it.

"You read minds now, do you?" I asked the empty air around me, speaking to Blossom, who was obviously in the process of anticipating my needs.

I reached for the necklace with my magic. Because my hands were rather busy shoveling food into my mouth. It settled around my neck, its weight comforting even though the gold was momentarily cold against my skin.

I ate the eggs, sipped the juice, then explored the rest of the room while nibbling on the last piece of toast. A large dark-wood wardrobe was filled with my father's 'off-duty' clothing. Though I was only a couple of inches shorter than Yazi, anything that stretched over his shoulders was going to totally swamp mine. Which wouldn't have presented that much of a problem unless I was planning to race into battle.

I was.

"Blossom?" I had to hope that the brownie would be willing to fetch me some clothing, if she wasn't otherwise busy.

I waited, finishing the toast and the juice, but Blossom didn't appear. Though I would have sworn that I could feel her nearby, I couldn't taste her magic. But then, the brownie could hide from me if she so wished.

She was probably just busy. As I should have been.

So I made a decision. I would return by way of the portal into the basement of the bakery, then outfit myself at home. I had an older set of training leathers that would do just fine.

I availed myself of the facilities, then grabbed my weapons and satchel. Then I headed off in search of the hub of the nexus.

I expected to get lost on my way. The nexus shifted aspects, or so it seemed. As far as I'd been able to figure out, the other-dimensional space was anchored in Shanghai, China, but its interior architecture was prone to...mood swings. Yes, as if the site had some form of sentience. I'd previously suspected that the heart of the guardians' power base simply didn't like a half-dragon—namely me, since I was the only half-dragon in existence—wandering around unaccompanied. Because I had never gotten turned around when accompanied through the halls by Drake or Warner.

Still, I didn't get lost this time.

I was just locked in.

Yep. Every single door in the nexus was warded against me. Every single door along the long twisted corridor between my father's rooms and the hub of the nexus was sealed. I was certain of that because I'd tried all of them, one at a time, after I'd tried all the portal doors in turn. The only door that would open for me was the door that led to the treasure keeper's chambers.

So I could stay in my father's chambers. Or I could visit Antarctica. But I, being the wielder of the instruments of assassination and the dragon slayer, certainly wasn't in need of anything from the treasure keeper's chambers.

What I needed was to go home, grab some clothing, and carve out Reggie's heart.

All this power hanging around my neck, all the stolen magic thrumming through my veins, and I couldn't open a single freaking door. And I knew without even trying that these weren't just simple wards I could cut through with my knife. It was as though the passageways themselves no longer existed. For me, at least.

I was trapped in the nexus. And not for the first time, though my current prison featured a larger footprint and an actual bed. That was a massive step up from the white-cubed cell that had nullified my magic.

Freaking know-it-all guardian dragons.

My head was hurting again.

I stopped pacing, pausing in the center of the hub of the nexus. Surrounded by gilded pillars and nine decorated doorways, I simply breathed. Then I divested myself of my satchel and katana, sat in a lotus position on the white marble floor, and tried to meditate.

I noted that the damage the nexus had taken during my brawl with the treasure keeper had disappeared. Whether that was the doing of Blossom or one of her fellow brownies, or whether the nexus was fueled by self-repairing magic, I didn't know.

What I did know, and all that really mattered in the immediate moment, was that I needed to get home and rescue my fiance and BFFs. Eventually, a guardian would walk through one of the portals. Then I would persuade whoever appeared to transport me … somewhere … and from there, I could figure out how to get to Vancouver. The particulars didn't matter. I needed to be focused. I needed to heal.

I needed to be ready.

"Mistress?"

I opened my eyes. Blossom had appeared—without a hint of magic to announce her arrival. The brownie was standing between me and the carved door that led to the North American territories, twisting her large hands together fretfully.

A piece of folded paper was sticking out of the pocket of the Cake in a Cup apron she wore as a dress.

I recognized the thickness of the paper stock and the darkly smudged edges. My stomach squelched. Ignoring my cowardly reaction, I steadily met Blossom's gaze. Her large dark-brown eyes were rounded with what appeared to be agitation...and concern.

Oh, God. I so, so didn't want her to be delivering bad news.

"Blossom." I forced myself to smile. "Thank you for breakfast."

She bobbed her head, casting her gaze around the nexus. "The treasure keeper wishes you to remain here, mistress."

"Yes. I got his note. But you know I have things to do. People to care for. Like you."

"Yes. I understand." Blossom shuffled her bare feet, gripping the white marble of the floor with her toes.

"What's happened?" I asked, my voice catching in my throat. "Please just tell me."

She nodded, looking at her hands now. "I'm bound to the treasure keeper...and to you, mistress. And to the oracle."

Ah...suddenly her demeanor made perfect sense. She was conflicted in her sense of duty. "I'm sorry if we're all placing you in an uncomfortable position, Blossom. I would never ask you to betray the treasure keeper."

Then the brownie surprised me—by smiling slyly. "He has not given me a direct order."

I laughed.

"I have placed items you will need in your father's chambers."

I touched my sheathed katana. The weapon was sitting on the marble floor by my left knee. "Yes, thank you."

"No…those are yours, mistress. I bring you gifts…wedding gifts, from your father and the sentinel."

Painful emotion flashed through me, compressing my chest and clogging my throat. "Have you seen Warner?"

"Not with my own eyes."

That was a very specific wording that I wasn't certain I wanted to dissect. "But, to the best of your knowledge, he is alive."

"As I understand it."

"And the others? Kett and Kandy?"

"I do not know, mistress."

"But …" I hesitated, afraid to voice the question I'd been holding back even from myself. A question of time. I'd been badly wounded, both by the removal of Reggie's gemstone and by the brawl with the treasure keeper. Badly enough that I was still scarred, still weakened even after Qiuniu had healed me. So it was an easy guess that more than a day had passed—but how much more was a detail I'd been avoiding thinking about.

"I missed the wedding, didn't I?"

"The wedding was canceled, yes."

"How long...how long was I held by the elves? And how long have I been here?"

"Judging the passing of time from your territory, it is the morning of December 29."

I nodded, fighting back tears over the thought of missing my own wedding. I'd lost almost two weeks. To Reggie and to healing.

"They need you now, mistress." Blossom touched the edge of the folded paper in her pocket, but she didn't pull it out. "The witches. The oracle. They have done what they can, but they need you now."

I surged to my feet, then crouched to retrieve my katana and satchel. "Are you...can you take me to Vancouver?"

"No. That, I am not capable of doing. But the oracle has found you a path."

I nodded, spinning on my heel and racing back to my father's chambers. If saving the others meant following orders, then that I could do. Rochelle hadn't steered me wrong yet.

A fourth set of armor had joined the three sets already hanging in my father's chambers. The newest set wasn't as bulky, though, and appeared to have been constructed out of supple black leather. It glistened with grassy witch magic, likely layering it with defensive spells to repel magical assault. It would fit me like a glove—so much so that I was likely to have trouble lacing it up on my own.

"I'll do your hair, mistress." Blossom spoke up from behind me. She'd followed me into the bedroom.

I set my weapons on the table at the base of the bed, then settled on the floor, cross-legged before the armor.

Blossom stepped up, gently teasing her fingers—along with her magic—through my curls.

"The armor was to be a wedding gift from Warner?"

"No, mistress. The armor is from your father."

I laughed. Of course it was. Because what baker didn't need a full set of armor as a wedding gift?

Blossom dressed me. I couldn't actually remember the last time anyone had done so, and the process was awkward but ultimately necessary. The leather was lined with silk, so it slipped on easily enough, but there definitely wouldn't have been any way to get every piece cinched into place and laced up without help. The armor went on in overlapping sections, likely so that a single piece could be removed or replaced without having to remove the entire suit.

Skintight pants that ended at my lower calves were tucked into knee-high laced boots. A vest was layered over top of a long-sleeved shirt. An invisible sheath was built into my right thigh for my jade knife. Another invisible sheath was set across my back for my katana. Twined around my neck three times, my necklace sat within a collar that could be left unbuttoned, or closed over the artifact and laced up to protect my neck.

Since nasty creatures had a habit of trying to gouge out my throat, I could see the practical appeal. Still, I had Blossom leave it unlaced for the time being, because it was a trifle tight and rather choky.

I glanced into the full-length mirror on the inside of the door to my father's wardrobe, not recognizing the fierce visage that stared back at me. Blossom had twisted my hair into short rows held tightly against my head, then coiled each separate twist into a series of almost flat spirals at the back. Between the hair and the armor,

I looked...imposing. Deadly. Especially with a large circular crimson scar in the center of my forehead.

"I can't really walk the streets of Vancouver looking like this," I said.

"No, mistress. But the sentinel had this made for you. It might help."

She was holding a swath of fabric in her hands. It glistened with witch magic, shifting from a beige to a dark gold in color when it caught the light. I kneeled down, running my fingers across it. It felt like and appeared to be chain mail, but when Blossom settled it over my head, it turned out to be a sleeveless sweater. In form, at least.

The delicate chain mail hung off my shoulders all the way down to the middle of my thighs, covering enough of the black leather armor that I looked as though I might have just stepped off the pages of some slightly edgy fashion magazine. The mail's wide neckline didn't interfere with my katana or my necklace. And slits up to my lower waist on either side meant I could access my knife and move without being hindered.

I gazed at myself in the mirror, desperately wishing that Warner had been the one to give me this beautiful, intricate piece of magic. Wishing that Blossom hadn't felt it necessary to bring the armor to me. Wishing that whatever I was about to face hadn't demanded that action from the brownie in the first place.

Then I cleared my throat, shoving the wishes and the trepidation down as deeply as I could. I kneeled solemnly before Blossom. "I think you have delayed as long as you can," I said, knowing that whatever the brownie had to tell me, whatever path the oracle was about to open for me, placed Blossom in an uncomfortable position with the treasure keeper.

She nodded. Then she carefully pulled the folded piece of paper from the pocket of her apron dress.

For the first time since I'd met the oracle, I reached for the sketch eagerly. Rochelle had rescued me from the elves. She'd known what I needed to see. So I would follow wherever else she needed to lead me.

Before I opened the drawing, I met Blossom's eye. "Thank you. For bringing me the sketch in the stadium. And for this…the armor, taking care of me. You are a good friend. A blessing. For me and my family."

Blossom nodded. When she spoke, her voice was husky. "It is an honor to serve you, Jade Godfrey."

Then she disappeared without another word.

Or perhaps to avoid further interrogation.

I opened the sketch. Darkly smudged charcoal delivered the path the oracle had found for me in one simple image—the head and shoulders of a smiling Buddha statue wearing a necklace. An amulet, to be more specific. An amulet bearing a single large stone.

Rendered in black and white, at least, it looked identical to the magical artifact that Blackwell wore. An artifact that gave the dark sorcerer the power of teleportation.

"I know you," I whispered to the Buddha captured grinning on the paper. "Sneaky, sneaky oracle."

I grabbed my satchel, double-checking that I still had Kandy's cuffs and Warner's knife tucked within its magical depths.

Then I headed out to plunder the treasure keeper's stash.

Breaking into the treasure keeper's chamber was as easy as opening a door, walking through the portal magic, then appearing between mountains of haphazardly piled magical artifacts—furniture, jewels, gold coins, and actual treasure chests.

You know, loot. A pirate's hoard times infinity.

Seriously, Pulou needed to invest in some shelving units.

Granted, I had experienced a split second of doubt in the in-between—the moment during which I was suspended in the portal magic until my foot made contact with the marble floor on the other side. The last time I'd walked through a portal without permission, I hadn't made it all the way through. Warner had been the only person capable of retrieving me then. Though that might have been because the treasure keeper had just had his brain scrambled by one of the three silver centipedes currently clipped to the thick gold chain dangling around my neck.

Anyway.

Treasure. A trove. More than a trove. Dozens upon dozens of troves, hidden somewhere in Antarctica.

Right. Now was seriously not the time to wonder how many feet of ice Pulou's chamber was buried underneath. I had a Buddha statue to find and a teleportation amulet to steal—assuming I was reading the oracle's sketch correctly.

It wasn't the value of the precious metals or gems that dictated what artifacts were collected and housed by the treasure keeper. It was their magical significance. Specifically, Pulou collected magical items that could be used in nefarious ways—which, honestly, was anything of a certain power level. In many cases, it was the user, the owner, of a particular item that was the real issue. And as such, a lot of so-called owners didn't survive Pulou's retrieval of the object in question.

The point was, I was surrounded by so much magic that I had to shut down my dowsing ability as tightly as I could. As I did, I used the magic in my necklace and my knife to form an extra layer, an extra buffer between me and everything else.

But as a result, even if I hazarded a guess that the amulet had been created by the same alchemist who made the artifact Blackwell wore, and that this new amulet might also share the taste of baked potato, sour cream, and chives, I couldn't use that taste to narrow my focus. I wouldn't be able to sense it through the magical sensory assault that was the treasure keeper's chamber. I was going to have to search for the ivory Buddha by sight.

Unfortunately, the last time I'd been in the chamber, I had inadvertently collapsed a few piles of treasure—and sort of caused an avalanche throughout the entire place. As such, the jovial Buddha that had once worn my mangled and blood-crusted katana as a crown might well have been buried.

Nonetheless, I followed my instincts—because my sense of direction seriously sucked. I strolled forward as if I knew where I was going, clasping my hands behind my back so I didn't linger, caressing treasure after treasure—

Ooh, that burnished-gold high-backed chair was awfully pretty. And that low, square-edged chest would make a perfect coffee table—

Focus, Jade. Focus.

Buddha. Buddha. Buddha.

I wondered if praying would work. I mean, I wasn't a Buddhist, but it might be worth a try.

I was supremely hilarious.

In my head, anyway.

I skirted a large chest containing golden goblets, gem-crusted bowls, and piles of leather-bound books. And as I did, I spotted the smooth, ivory-carved head of the Buddha in the next pile over.

Yes!

Jade 1, treasure keeper 0.

Seriously, though. Organizational skills were not to be treated this lightly.

I rounded the treasure pile, seeing the three-foot-tall Buddha half buried in coins of various sizes and metals. A steel broadsword large enough to be wielded by a giant was angled across the ivory statue's lap, which seemed disrespectful. Granted, my understanding of Buddhism was a little thin.

A golden chain adorned with a large teardrop-shaped sapphire was hanging around the statue's neck. Blackwell's amulet held a ruby, similarly sized but differently shaped. But otherwise, the artifact adorning the Buddha's neck appeared to be a match to the sorcerer's amulet, including the runes etched onto the links of the chain and the setting that housed the gem.

"Bingo," I whispered. Reaching for the artifact with my dowser senses, I immediately got a hint of buttery, creamy potato lightly sprinkled with chives.

I was on my way to Vancouver.

You know, once I figured out how to teleport. The artifact didn't appear to come with a user manual.

But when I tried to remove the amulet from the Buddha's neck, I couldn't budge it.

I couldn't curl my fingers around it. I couldn't even wiggle it. It was stuck to the ivory statue.

That was odd.

I tried to lift the gigantic sword off the Buddha's lap. Again, I couldn't even wiggle it.

I'd never stopped to think about what place the Buddha held as a permanent fixture in the treasure keeper's collection. Maybe it attracted other magical items? Then held on to them? Which was maybe why my katana had adorned its head? But Shailaja had easily retrieved the mangled sword, right before she'd used it to slit my father's throat. So that didn't add up.

Dropping some of the defensive shielding I'd gathered around me, I reached out with a trickle of my dowser senses. I tasted the Buddha's magic, then the magic of the sword, then the coins scattered all around …

And overwhelming the taste of the magic of the artifacts themselves was the taste of the treasure keeper's magic. Black tea topped with a large slosh of thick cream.

I crouched down, reaching for a coin sitting on the marble floor. It was off by itself, separated from the nearest magical objects.

I couldn't pick it up.

I grabbed for a different coin. Then a goblet, then a small dagger.

I couldn't move a single thing.

I jogged over to the neighboring pile of treasure. Once there, I tried to pick up a gold-framed mirror, an emerald-crusted bowl, and another handful of coins in turn.

Everything was magically glued in place.

The freaking treasure keeper had warded everything in the chamber against pilfering. Or, I suspected, specifically against me.

Apparently, I only got to rip Pulou off once.

Jade 1, treasure keeper 1.

Panic welled up in my heart.

I was trapped, either in Pulou's chamber or in the nexus—assuming I could even make my way back. Elves were invading Vancouver. And I was helpless.

Losing the tight grip with which I'd been holding my shit at bay, I repeatedly kicked the pile of treasure nearest to me in silent but fierce frustration. Because it was either that or burst into tears. My only reward was a seriously bruised toe, but the pain provided some much-needed focus.

Pacing and limping, I tried to wrap my head around the puzzle I'd been presented. I pulled the oracle's sketch out of my satchel, stepping back to contemplate the Buddha and the amulet, then comparing Rochelle's charcoal rendering to the actual statue and artifact.

Rochelle wouldn't have sent the sketch to me if I hadn't been meant to retrieve the artifact. I obviously needed it for some reason. My supposition had been that it would help me break out of the nexus, but whatever the case ...

Wait. Not 'it.'

I didn't need the actual amulet.

I needed the magic it held. I needed the teleportation spell.

I wasn't just a thief. I was a freaking alchemist.

"Jesus, Jade," I muttered to myself. "You seriously are a moron sometimes."

Stepping forward, I untwined my necklace from my neck, then carefully looped it over the Buddha's head. Doubling it to shorten the chain, I aligned the golden chain with the sapphire artifact as closely as possible, making certain to never lose contact with it—just in case Pulou's warding spell tried to collect and keep my magical artifact as well.

Then I threaded my fingertips through the necklace's wedding rings, touching the amulet underneath but not the Buddha. I reached for the artifact's baked-potato-imbued magic with my alchemy. I teased the power housed within the gold and sapphire of the amulet forward, gathering it underneath my fingers.

As delicately as I could, I pulled the power from the amulet, feeding it into the golden links of my necklace as I did.

Carefully.

I didn't want to absorb the power that the amulet held. I just wanted to house it, as I housed the instruments of assassination. Draining the teleportation spell, then subsuming it with my own power, might have actually nullified it.

Pulou might have been able to lock down every last magical artifact in his chamber, but apparently he couldn't stop me from stealing the magic that powered those hoarded items.

Jade 2, treasure keeper 1.

I twined my necklace around my neck three times, making sure it rested tidily within the folded collar of my new armor. Then I stepped back, moving well away from the piles of treasure all around me in the hopes of avoiding any magical interference. Not that I knew what the hell I was doing, of course.

I called my jade knife into my right hand, weaving the fingers of my left hand through the wedding rings adhered to my necklace. Power churned eagerly underneath my touch—the siren call of the instruments paired with the almost-bubbly magic I'd just stolen from the sapphire amulet. Could something be effervescent and creamy at the same time? Apparently, yes.

If I could pop back into the hall in the elves' maze that Pulou had snatched me from, I could appear right beside Warner's cell. Then I could free him before the elves even knew I was in the stadium. Together, we would free the others, then kick some elf ass. If we were lucky, the element of surprise would help guarantee that the brawl didn't spill out onto the streets.

Vancouver—and everyone I loved—would be safe again.

I coaxed out the taste of the teleportation spell that had been embedded in the amulet, bringing it forward from the other power held in my necklace. The taste of buttery, fluffy, perfectly salted potato and its accoutrements rolled across my tongue as I visualized the white-walled hallway, as I remembered the feel of the elf magic coating the door that Warner had been moments away from breaking through.

My stomach grumbled.

Seriously? I'd just eaten.

Though time did run oddly in the nexus, so I had no real idea how many hours might have passed since then. Hours in which those I loved could have been consumed to fuel Reggie's gateway. A gateway that only existed because I'd managed to rebuild it.

Another wave of panic gripped me. I had to stop thinking about everything so much. Taking action was much easier than continually fretting about every last little thing.

Focus. Focus on the hallway. Focus on the door that had stood between Warner and me. The tenor of the magic that the elves had wielded to erect the walls of the maze.

I envisioned myself standing before the door, in the hall, my knife held ready …

Ready … ready.

Nothing happened.

Okay. Fine. Refocus.

I took a deep breath, stirring the teleportation spell simmering in the golden links of my necklace underneath my fingers. Maybe I couldn't travel directly into the stadium because of the exterior wards. Pulou had mentioned not being able to hold the portal open because the wards had been repaired after I'd torn a hole in them. So the same probably went for any type of transportation-based magic.

The bakery, then.

I sheathed my knife, envisioning my beautiful kitchen. My haven of stainless steel. The feel of the tile underneath my feet. The scents of icing sugar and vanilla, the taste of moist chocolate cake.

My stomach growled a second time.

I ignored it. I also shoved down another round of aching panic that was boiling in my belly, threatening to spread through my torso.

Nothing else happened.

I envisioned my bakery pantry. The tidily stocked shelves. The lingering scents of spices and cocoa. The door that led to the basement and the portal.

Nothing happened.

I focused on my bedroom. The double bed against the wall. The neatly folded knitted afghan from Gran on the chair in the corner of the room. The art tube that contained Rochelle's engagement present propped against the bureau.

Nothing happened.

My grandmother's house. The library. The living room. The beach I'd just seen in the picture on my father's bedside table.

It wasn't working.

It wasn't going to work.

All this magic, all this power hanging around my neck, and I was trapped.

Trapped.

I pressed my fingers to my forehead, to the scar. The reminder of what Reggie had done to me, of what she'd made me do, the people she'd made me hurt only days after we'd gathered together in the Whistler bakery and celebrated—

The baked-potato magic of the necklace perked up suddenly. Becoming... receptive.

Usually it wasn't a good sign when magical items demonstrated feelings. Or, even worse, when they offered opinions—as Warner's knife often did when I held it. But I would go down that rabbit hole if it got me closer to rescuing everyone I loved. Willingly. Eagerly.

"The Whistler bakery," I whispered. The tiled kitchen. The long countertop that bisected the room, white granite thinly veined with gray. Double ovens and a walk-in fridge on one side across from the—

The magic of the necklace exploded outward, wrapping backward over my shoulders and torso and literally crushing me. My bones crunched. My insides churned. My mind went fuzzy.

I couldn't breathe.

Everything went black.

Something I couldn't see through the haze of magic holding me clattered to the ground a few feet away. Calling my knife into my hand instinctively, I lunged forward, ready to deflect whatever assault was coming my way.

I blinked rapidly. The teleportation magic snapped back into my necklace. My surroundings came into view.

A dark-haired woman wearing a brown-ruffled apron emblazoned with a white Cake in a Cup logo was standing before me. She appeared to be frozen in place, her mouth hanging open in surprise and fear.

Bryn.

I had teleported into the Whistler bakery. Into the kitchen, to be specific. White and gray granite counters, stainless steel appliances, and all.

She was standing beside the swing doors that led to the storefront, one hand still raised to push the door open. An entire tray of beautifully frosted cupcakes had dropped at her feet. *Love*, *Lust*, and *Hug in a Cup*, as far as I could tell, all of them scattered across the tiled floor.

"Jade…I…I…you…look …"

"I can explain," I said. Except as soon as I said it, all the possible ramifications of that explanation flashed through my mind. I really didn't have the time. Bryn wasn't magically inclined. And the Adept world was crazy secretive. I didn't want to get my friend and business partner's mind scrambled. I wouldn't have wished that fate on my worst enemy—not now that I knew what it felt like myself.

"Actually…I can't explain. But…can I borrow your car?"

Maia stuck her head through the swing doors. The skinwalker had her braids twisted up on top of her head and was wearing a gorgeous beaded and feathered necklace over her brown Cake in a Cup T-shirt. She glanced around, taking in the destroyed cupcakes, then scowling at me. "Oh, it's just you. I heard a noise."

"She…she just appeared!" Bryn cried.

"Oh, yeah." Maia waved her hand offishly. "Magic is real. Jade has a lot of it. Though I didn't know she could teleport." Then she exited back into the storefront without another word.

I could hear a murmur of conversation, most likely Maia greeting a customer. Cake in a Cup Too was open, but Bryn was still baking. So it was probably midmorning. It felt to me as though only a couple of hours had passed in the nexus at most, but unfortunately, that didn't mean it was still December 29 on the Pacific West Coast.

Bryn was gazing at me as if utterly wounded. Even betrayed. "Magic? Is that how you get your icing so fluffy?"

I laughed. I couldn't help it. I held myself upright on the counter bisecting the kitchen, laughing until I was weeping.

"Well, you don't have to be an asshole about it," Bryn said crossly, crouching to retrieve the fallen cupcakes.

"I'm sorry. I'm so, so sorry." I wiped tears from my face, fairly certain they were tears of relief. "I don't mean to be rude. You know I just whip the buttercream more than you do."

"So you say," Bryn said stiffly, crossing into the office and retrieving a mop. "That's some outfit. And... knife."

I glanced down at myself. I did look completely different than usual. Then Bryn made a soft noise of concern, abandoning the mop and crossing to look at me more closely. She reached up, hovering her fingers over my forehead, but not touching the scar puckering my skin.

"You're hurt, Jade."

"I'm okay, Bryn. But... other people might not be."

"Right. Right. My keys." She threw her arms around me, hugging me fiercely, then releasing me just as quickly to hustle back to the office and dig through her purse. "I spoke to Gabby this morning. She called to clarify the amount of cocoa in the *Blitzen in a Cup*. She said you were on vacation." She crossed back out of the office, keys in hand. "And now, I just remembered the last time you went on an extended vacation without warning."

I nodded. Bryn was referring to the first time I'd crossed through into the nexus. When the far seer wouldn't let me return. When Sienna had kidnapped Mory, for the second time. And then I'd hunted her through Europe and back home again.

"Magic, eh?"

"Yeah, magic."

"And Maia?"

I smiled. It wasn't my place to out the skinwalker.

Bryn snorted. "This explains a lot." She reached for the mop, then looked back at me with a dawning look of dismay. "Please tell me that Kett isn't a vampire."

"Um …"

"Damn it. Why do all the really good-looking guys come with such heavy baggage?"

I laughed, pressed a kiss to Bryn's cheek, and took her keys. "I'll take care of the car."

"And text me on the hour."

"Deal."

I hustled over to the door, but then turned back. "Oh, Bryn? Get Maia to text me anything her grand-mother knows about elves, would you? I asked her to ask before … um … I went away. Again."

"Elves?"

I grimaced. "Yeah. Elves. And … maybe let her know that her people might want to stay away from Vancouver for a bit?"

Bryn glowered at me. "Her people?"

"I'm not being racist. I just … um …"

"You'll explain later."

"Yeah. I'll explain later." I grinned.

She smiled back begrudgingly.

I looked forward to a chat all about the Adept world over cupcakes with my business partner and friend. Right after I convinced Gran that it was ridiculous at this point to not have Bryn in the loop, and that there was no need for any mind wiping to occur. Even with her away from Vancouver so much while running the second bakery, I'd feel better about not having to hide the truth from her anymore.

Bryn sighed, flapping her hand at me. "Go, go."

Feeling my mood lighten more than it had in days, I exited through the back of the building and hightailed it to Bryn's car.

Chapter Five

I had driven halfway to Squamish before I realized that I'd forgotten to grab cupcakes while at the bakery. So apparently, I did rank something as more important than chocolate and treats—specifically, rescuing friends I'd personally put in mortal peril. Good to know.

The console of Bryn's car helpfully provided me with the date—December 30. So I'd lost another day messing around in the nexus. The time was 11:23 A.M., but when I tried to double-check that with my phone, I realized I should have grabbed Bryn's cell as well. Mine was still safely tucked into the side pocket of my satchel, along with some cash—but it was completely fried from having crossed through multiple portals without being in its lead-lined case. So much for texting Bryn on the hour like I'd promised. Or receiving any insider information from the skinwalkers.

I would have blamed the treasure keeper, except I was fairly certain I wouldn't have healed from carving the gemstone out of my forehead without his intervention. Though I might have managed to free Warner before collapsing myself.

Of course, if I'd been splayed on the floor at Warner's feet, dead or dying, even he might not have been able to fight his way through a dozen or more elves.

And either way, I could still be angry about Pulou's lousy timing.

In the end, being behind the wheel of Bryn's sporty sedan meant I didn't want to stop, not for a single moment. And certainly not for a cellphone or a chocolate bar. Thankfully, the car had a full tank of gas, and it wasn't snowing, so the roads were clear. And my disregard for speed limits didn't draw any attention.

My first glimpse of the city while speeding along the Upper Levels Highway produced confusion, then shock. The highway spiraled down from Whistler, through Squamish and into West Vancouver, and as it cut along the North Shore Mountains, it offered a gorgeous view of Vancouver on the other side of Burrard Inlet from multiple vantage points. But I wasn't beguiled by the pretty steel-and-glass skyscrapers, or the bridges spanning the deep gray-blue waterway, or the large evergreen-filled park along the edge of that water.

I was thrown by the massive dome of blue magic encasing the entire city.

Yep. As far as I could see in a glimpse—while speeding in a car that wasn't my own and looking for my exit—it appeared as though the witches' grid had been transformed into a magical boundary.

I had to check my speed down Taylor Way—the West Vancouver police were big on handing out speeding tickets. Then instead of making the turn and trying to head over Lions Gate Bridge, I pulled into the upper-level open lot at the north side of Park Royal Mall and parked Bryn's sedan.

Stepping out, I stared. Tracing my gaze along the span of the massive green-painted steel suspension bridge leading into Stanley Park, I stared some more. Then I peered at the city beyond. More specifically I gaped, utterly dumbfounded at the sight of the magic covering...everything. It sealed the exit from Lions Gate Bridge into the park, running along the entire shoreline on either side of the bridge.

I had no idea whether I'd be able to drive through that boundary. I mean, I was fairly certain Bryn's car would pass through the magic without issue. Vehicles were coming and going in and out of the city along the bridge, just like normal. But cars weren't magical. And though I'd been tied to the first incarnation of the witches' grid—back when it was just being used as a magical detection system—I wasn't going to blithely assume that I could pass through the barrier it had turned into now.

Adding two and two and getting completely brain fuzzled, I began to get the feeling that the glowing blue dome was the reason I hadn't been able to teleport into the bakery, or to Gran's, or to anywhere else in Vancouver. And if that was the case, it was an easy guess that this massive shield was why the elves had been so focused on the witches' grid right from the time they'd broken out of Pulou's prison. As soon as Reggie had sensed the grid in the park that night, she must have recognized its potential.

So it was going to be safer all around to approach on foot, rather than attempt to drive the car through. Because what was the possible alternative? Hitting the boundary and getting ripped out of the vehicle through the back window, even as it continued along on the causeway driverless?

That seemed a bad idea on multiple levels. There was no way it wouldn't cause a massive accident—and most likely expose the Adept world in the process. And even beyond that was the fact that I wasn't completely healed yet, and I wasn't certain I'd survive that kind of impact—let alone being hit by numerous cars in the aftermath.

After locking Bryn's sedan, I zigzagged in a light jog through the mall parking lots, upper and lower. Then I darted between the tall glass-fronted apartment buildings that stood between me and the bridge. I eventually found the stairs that I hadn't totally remembered the location of, down at the base of the northern bridge entrance. Lions Gate Bridge had always had sidewalks for pedestrians, but a number of years before, it had been widened to include a bike lane as well.

I jogged up the steel stairs. Even though it was only midday, the traffic was practically bumper-to-bumper as it merged from four lanes—two from North Vancouver and two from West Vancouver—onto the two lanes of the bridge. That included the reversible center lane that allowed flow in both directions, to or from the city. Its direction was switched at certain times of the day to help mitigate rush hour traffic, and it was currently open in favor of the North Shore.

I darted right. Walking, but quickly. I was slightly concerned that jogging alongside slow-moving traffic and zigzagging around cyclists and other pedestrians would draw too much attention—particularly while swathed in black leather and a chain mail sweater. It was chilly but thankfully not raining.

Lions Gate Bridge arced up over the first narrows of Burrard Inlet, which was speckled with freighters, float planes, and intrepid boaters not averse to being on the water in winter. The view was breathtaking, but I didn't spare it more than a glance. I had eyes only for the thick layer of blue witch magic tracing the edges of the park in either direction for as far as I could see. The dome even encased the skyscrapers that dominated the downtown core to my immediate left.

As I passed the midpoint of the bridge and started downhill toward the Stanley Park entrance at Prospect Point, I spotted two men of similar heights standing just in front of the magical boundary. On the bridge side, with me.

One was dark haired. The other was golden blond. The dark-haired, darker-skinned male was slighter than the suntanned male. But both were arrayed in leather armor similar to mine, though without the pretty chain mail sweater. I couldn't taste a single drop of magic from either. But both men turned to greet me with matching grins when I was about fifty feet away.

The healer. My father, the warrior.

Waiting for me.

"I'm not going back!" I yelled, picking up speed as I jogged downhill.

"Of course not." My father chuckled.

A cyclist zoomed by, nearly shoulder checking me off the sidewalk, then passing through the shimmering blue boundary line as if it didn't exist. Followed by vehicle after vehicle, the cyclist sped off down the causeway that cut through Stanley Park. Because for him and everyone else on the road, the boundary simply didn't exist. But as I watched them go, I wondered just how much magic a person needed to wield to be thwarted from coming and going from the city? And what if a person didn't know they were magical?

How many freaking traffic accidents had occurred since the boundary had been erected? What kind of massive pile-up would result by the concrete lions that guarded the entrance to the bridge if one did?

Something terrible must have happened for the witches to have raised the barrier. For my Gran and Scarlett specifically ...

My pace slowed as the sum total of what had actually occurred, what had precipitated the witches erecting the boundary, hit me.

Of course something terrible had happened.

Reggie had taken control of me. And I had taken out three of the most powerful magical beings in the city—plus a guardian dragon—without breaking a sweat.

I started firing questions at my father from about twenty feet out. "Are you waiting for me?"

"Yes."

"If you were coming to the city, then why the hell did I have to break out of the nexus?"

"I have no idea. You were already gone when we came to find you."

"Jesus Christ."

"How did you get out of the nexus?" Qiuniu asked.

"Never you mind."

My father laughed, reaching for me with both hands. I closed the space between us. He grabbed my shoulders, gripping me too tightly, but then brushed a soft kiss to my forehead. "You look magnificent."

"I'm supposed to look intimidating."

"That you do," the healer said. I could hear the humor in his tone, though. "You were supposed to wait for another healing, dragon slayer."

"I'm on my feet."

"So I see."

"What's with the boundary?" I gestured toward the magic shimmering only a few feet away from us. It soared overhead so high that I couldn't see the curve of the dome from my vantage point.

"Impressive," my father said, not remotely answering my question.

"I mean, is there a reason you're just hanging around on this side? Is the boundary why I couldn't teleport into the bakery?"

"Teleport?" Qiuniu asked. "I was unaware that teleportation was within the wielder's arsenal. That is disconcerting."

Again, I was fairly certain he was teasing me. I gave him a scathing look for his effort.

"The guardians have been concerned about entering the city and damaging the witches' casting." My father scanned the magic of the dome. "Pulou was willing to punch through, but only after you'd breached the elves' wards encasing the stadium. Even then it was ... risky."

"Risky?"

"Traditionally, this type of magic ... boundaries, wards ... is fueled by the caster."

"Right. Of course. When Shailaja tore through the wards on my bakery, before I'd fortified them myself, she hurt Gran. Badly."

"Exactly." My father sounded grim. "This level of magic is often ..."

"Soul fueled." The healer helpfully filled in what my father was hesitating to say.

"What do you mean? Soul fueled? Like, life force energy?"

"Exactly."

I stepped closer to the boundary, raising my palm to it. As expected, it tasted of grassy witch magic. But the undertone was all sweet, tangy strawberry.

My mother's magic.

Fear gripped my heart. I turned to my father. "You think that if we have to tear through the magic to get into the city we might ... hurt the witches?"

"Possibly kill them." My father touched something at his hip, most likely the hilt of his sword. He didn't wear it in an invisible sheath as I did, though. His weapon was a pure manifestation of his guardian magic.

"And asking Pulou a second time …" I murmured—but I was already certain I knew the answer.

Qiuniu shook his head. "It is one thing for the treasure keeper to step through, and risky enough to pull you through, even accompanied by him."

"And completely another thing for him to send two guardians. That would be too much magic slicing through the witches' magic."

The healer nodded, waiting on me to put everything together as if he had all the time in the world.

Except we didn't have that time. I was certain that Reggie had managed to open the gateway fully even before Pulou had snatched me, using the gemstone Alivia had brought. Which meant the telepath had had eight days to recruit while I healed. Eight days of bringing in new forces, unchecked. There could be an entire legion of elves crammed into BC Place stadium, ready to take the city and slaughter anyone who dared stand between them and utter dominion.

So, yeah. That was cheerful.

Thinking madly, I threaded my fingers through the wedding rings on my necklace. Specifically, Warner's parents' rings. They hung nearest to my heart.

Another cyclist sped past us. And I realized that I hadn't yet seen people cranking their necks to stare as they drove by. I wondered if the magic coating my chain mail sweater and the guardians' armor was layered with spells to hide us from casual glances. If so, it was definitely working.

"There's a lot of magic in the dome," I murmured. "But the bulk of it tastes like my mother's."

"I can feel that as well." Yazi clenched and un-clenched his fist. I could tell how badly he wanted to cut through the witches' boundary magic with his sword. And I could tell he was … worried. Afraid.

I recalled the pictures on my father's bedside table, of my mother and me. Guardians didn't usually have children, or spouses. As far as I'd been able to figure out, I was the only child among the current generation of guardians. Haoxin had replaced her mother over a hundred years before, and Chi Wen had been centuries before that. Warner and Shailaja were in between those two. But Warner's mother had passed on, replaced by the current Jiaotu. And the former treasure keeper had died centuries before I'd taken his daughter's head and absorbed her magic.

The impasse currently stymieing our forward mo-mentum was likely one of the reasons why guardians didn't often breed. I was watching the warrior weighing the lives of his loved ones over the safety of the city.

My stomach squelched. "I've made a terrible mess. I never should have taken up the instruments."

"I gathered you didn't have any choice, wielder." The healer smiled, thin lipped.

Yazi grunted, agreeing. "Destiny cannot be thwarted, Jade. But we must push forward from here. The healer and I have cleared our own territories of in-cursions. But based on what Pulou has gleaned from the tight-lipped brownie and the barrier we are currently fa-cing, Haoxin hasn't been able to do the same. The other Adepts of North America have been scrambling to deal with the incursions themselves, along with myself and the healer. But it cannot be allowed to continue."

"Haoxin ran into a bit of a road block," I muttered.

"The gem Pulou stole from you proved most helpful in sealing the breaches," Qiuniu said. "Possibly permanently. But choices need to be made here. Which is why we waited for you, wielder." He smiled grimly. Again.

I could read epic amounts into his expression. "Which is why you're here? Not to heal me further, but in case my mother ... in case she's tied herself too tightly to the grid. And ..." I looked over at my father. "Pulou should never have punched through to grab me!"

"He did what he was asked to do."

"Except for the beating," the healer murmured.

Yazi gave Qiuniu a withering look. "He will answer for the beating."

I ignored them both. My mind whirled with all that could have happened to my mother, to the witches, to the city, just because I needed to be rescued. "He could have ... what if ..."

"The boundary still stands, daughter. You say it tastes of your mother's magic."

"Yes, but—"

My father raised his hand to silence me—and for the first time in my life, I obeyed him. "The far seer's counsel is never overlooked. The treasure keeper and I would never ignore a surety for what might possibly happen."

I felt a little lightheaded. Overwhelmed at the idea that Pulou rescuing me could have killed my mother. That even entering the city to rescue the others now could kill my mother.

"We gave Haoxin time to resolve the incursion here herself." Yazi's tone was gruff—and rather judgemental, frankly, for someone who'd tangled with the instruments of assassination himself.

And then it hit me. They didn't know.

Somehow, they didn't know that it was me—or, rather, through me and the instruments—that the elves had gained a foothold in the city.

"But we cannot wait any longer," Qiuniu said kindly but firmly. "Not only have we not heard from Haoxin, but the far seer cannot clearly see what is occurring beyond the barrier. Not since he caught the glimpse of you and asked Pulou to retrieve you."

"He's not sharing what he sees, healer," my father said. "That is different."

Qiuniu nodded, acknowledging Yazi's statement but continuing with his own line of thought. "We are hoping you will be able to cross through without ramifications, then allow us entry."

I cleared my throat, trying to loosen what felt like epic amounts of guilt clogging my vocal cords. "Right. Um, I thought Drake would have told you ..."

"He sent word as you bade him, Jade," my father said. "That the elves had attacked, that you and Haoxin were bargaining with them on behalf of the treasure keeper. He was most frustrated that your grandmother sent him away without more information. But the elves have kept Suanmi and Drake busy throughout Europe and Asia, playing games."

"Keeping us distracted and divided," the healer added.

"Yes." My father nodded curtly. "And the boundary was in place before I could return to Vancouver."

"This is ... all of this is my fault."

"You've been clouding Chi Wen's sight?" Qiuniu asked. Once again, his tone held more amusement than was healthy for him—especially since I apparently wasn't opposed to unleashing the instruments of assassination with only minimal provocation. Well, maybe a little more than minimal.

"No...I...I assume it's the elves' wards on the stadium, BC Place, that have blinded the far seer. If he actually isn't seeing anything. That's where they're holding Haoxin, Warner, Kandy, and Kett. But what I meant was...it was me...who took out Haoxin."

"Took out?" the healer echoed.

"Yes. With the instruments." I rubbed my forehead, which was starting to ache. Again. "Haoxin and Warner. I thought maybe...I mean ..." I looked at my father. "I said I had things I needed to tell you. In the nexus. Actually, everything is a little hazy. Except my culpability. That I remember clearly."

"Rapid healing can muddle memories." The healer narrowed his eyes at me. Well, at the center of my forehead. I gathered the huge scar there was bothering him.

I pushed forward with my confession. "Reggie...the elf that the others refer to as their liege. She got that gemstone on me."

"Yes," the warrior said. "And you carved it out of your forehead." Daddy-O was starting to sound just a little impatient.

"Before that, she made me use the instruments. Haoxin was taken because of me. The witches have been alone in the city...with...with...a bunch of fledglings. Because of me."

My father's gaze rested on me heavily. I could see that he understood, finally. His eyes were narrowed, his jaw tense.

I waited for his judgement. For his condemnation. I deserved nothing less.

"Are you done confessing things that were completely beyond your control?" he asked pissily.

"I just...I thought you would have heard...from ..."

"Who?"

"I really thought, I hoped, that maybe Blossom might have mentioned something."

"Your brownie?" My father snorted. "She'd rather die than betray you."

Good to know. And a little overwhelming in its implications. "Right. Okay. Well, we'll just go retrieve Haoxin from the elves, along with the others, and everything will be ... fantastic." I sounded as though I didn't believe a single word coming out of my mouth. I was going to have to work on that.

"Jade," my father said gruffly. "It isn't for the healer or me to absolve you. Things happen. We all do our best, but despite how some of the other guardians act, we aren't gods. We aren't infallible."

The healer chuckled quietly in agreement.

"Okay."

Yazi touched my shoulder lightly. "My heart is full, seeing you striding over the bridge a moment ago, rather than teetering between life and death. I ... I wouldn't know what to do if I lost you so soon after having you tumble into my life."

I nodded, holding back tears.

My father lifted his gaze to the dome of magic shimmering behind me. "The elves will fall beneath our swords, my daughter."

"There are a lot of them here now," I said. "Even more than I let through myself, if Reggie managed to fix the damage I was doing to the gateway."

Yazi grinned at me. He rested his hand against the side of my head gently, brushing his thumb over the scar on my forehead. "Against all odds, from birth ever after. That's you, my Jade."

The healer cleared his throat. "Not to interject, but we really need to assess the boundary and move forward. With the other seven still dealing with the last incursions, I don't imagine I will be at leisure for long."

Nodding, I turned back to the boundary, raising my hand to it a second time. I could definitely feel a resistance, despite the fact that it was constructed at least partly from my mother's magic. I didn't think it was going to let me pass easily.

"You can walk through the wards on the bakery without any issues," I said, questioning my father without looking at him.

"Of course. They are of your construction. All the guardians will be able to pass. We all share the same magic."

Well, that was news. And a little staggering. And best left to be examined at a much later date. "And Gran's wards?"

"I have an open invitation."

"What's different about these?" I murmured, more to myself than my father. "They feel different...not just witch magic. Maybe ..." I caught a fleeting taste of tart apple. Then something...green, mossy. "Rochelle. And an elf."

"The oracle," Yazi murmured behind me, talking to the healer.

"Adepts working together? Intriguing."

I glanced around, trying to discern the specific anchor point—one of thirteen points arrayed around the city—from the boundary magic. I knew that one of those points had been situated at the base of the bridge, but I couldn't remember who among the witches had cast it.

On the other side of the boundary, a set of concrete stairs led upward from the sidewalk through evergreen trees to a lookout point. Vehicles streamed steadily past us, still crossing through the magic effortlessly.

Picking out the anchor point was beyond me. But honestly, the hope that knowing the witch who had cast it would help me figure out how to get through was just grasping at straws. The boundary shimmering before me was exceedingly different than the witches' original grid. It was almost as if it was composed of completely different magic—power that had maybe consumed the anchor points in order to utilize them.

I rubbed my forehead. Again. "We're going to have to cut—"

A brown-haired woman in her early twenties and a tall, darker-skinned man in his mid-twenties were walking up the sidewalk toward us. I could see fading blue streaks in her hair that matched her wool peacoat. Her watermelon-infused witch magic was riper and richer than it had been when I first met her. He was well over six foot—easily Warner's height—dressed in a hoodie over sweatpants. Though I knew he could stop traffic anytime he wore a suit, this outfit had been chosen in case of any sudden need to shift into his tiger form.

Burgundy and Beau.

I smiled. "Well. It seems the oracle isn't having any trouble seeing us."

"Welcoming committee?" the healer asked.

I nodded, lifting my hand to wave at the approaching witch and shapeshifter.

Burgundy smiled, picking up her pace. But her tentative glance at Beau let me know that trouble was brewing. Of course, the werecat's intense glower and fixated focus—on me—was also a dead giveaway. His obvious anger immediately irked me. Whether or not I deserved it.

I turned my attention back to Burgundy as she approached close enough that I didn't need to shout, gesturing toward the wall of magic between us. "What the hell is this?"

Burgundy opened her mouth to reply, but Beau interrupted her. "The witches' grid. Nothing magical can cross through. Not even the elves, though they can still hide from scent and sight." The green of his shapeshifter magic rolled across his eyes, brightly enough that I was able to easily distinguish it from the blue of the witches' boundary magic.

Burgundy dug into her purse. "We're here to let you in."

"Not yet," Beau said darkly. Then he pulled a folded piece of paper from his pocket. Opening it, he stepped up to the boundary so that only the blue barrier and about a foot of space stood between us. He held up a charcoal drawing that had obviously been torn from one of Rochelle's sketchbooks.

I glanced at the rough sketch—and felt instantly numbed by its contents. Then I resolutely returned my gaze to Beau. The drawing looked unfinished, at least compared to the sketches the oracle usually shared with me. It depicted a young girl standing on a perch of rubble with some sort of demon. The nature of the taloned, black-scaled creature was unmistakable, even though I'd never seen its like before. It was dwarfing the girl it appeared to be guarding.

"Who is that?"

"Our daughter," Beau said, threat underlying every one of his words. "After you destroy Vancouver."

I continued to meet his blazing green gaze steadily, refusing to look at the soul-crushing sketch a second time. When I spoke, my own tone was hard edged. "Did you steal that sketch from your wife, Beau?"

Tension ran through his clenched jaw. He spat out his demand. "You will listen, Jade. You will obey."

My father and the healer shifted forward, tightening the space behind me. Beau's gaze flicked to them, momentarily disconcerted. Then he looked back to me.

"Or what?" I asked, quietly dangerous. "Will you kill Burgundy? Snap her neck before she can open our way?"

Burgundy took a step away from the irate shifter.

"Will you kill your own mother tearing through the grid yourself?" Beau spat back.

"Threatening the mother of my child will not be tolerated," Yazi growled. His magic shifted around him, intensifying. Smoky, spicy dark chocolate flooded my mouth. And for the first time ever, the taste wasn't comforting.

All the hair on the back of my exposed neck lifted. I shook my head, raising my hand to the boundary magic that stood between me and the pissy shifter. Beau took an involuntary step back.

Burgundy was gripping the focal stone she'd pulled out of her bag so harshly that her knuckles were white. If looks could kill, Beau would have already been lying at the junior witch's feet.

"I don't have to tear through this magic, Beau. It would be easier, safer, to have Burgundy grant us passage. But I have no doubt I could slice through. It's my mother's magic, after all."

Beau swallowed. He glanced at me, then at my father and the healer in turn. His face had turned ashen. He'd miscalculated. Badly.

But what else was a shifter desperate to save his wife and unborn child to do?

I dropped my hand. "I was planning on taking the oracle's advice, shifter. She's gotten me this far. But I assume if she wanted me to see the sketch you're holding, she would have chosen to show it to me herself."

Beau closed his eyes, pained. "Right. Maybe don't mention this to Rochelle?"

"The sketch is a little difficult to unsee."

He swallowed. "Yes. But ... you're right. Rochelle will show it to you if she thinks you need to see it."

"And then I'll react accordingly."

Beau nodded, then looked over at Burgundy.

The witch jutted her chin out at him. "I'm never partnering with you again."

"I'm sorry—"

Burgundy raised her hand, effectively shutting Beau up with a single gesture.

Now why didn't that sort of thing ever work for me?

The young witch stepped off the sidewalk, slipping off her shoes and curling her toes in the sparse grass that edged the pavement. "The anchor point is right over here. Olive talked me through creating a doorway, then resealing it."

"Olive?" I stepped to the edge of the sidewalk, but the boundary magic prevented me from going any farther. "Not Gran? Not Scarlett?"

Burgundy glanced over at Beau, disconcerted. "I ... I thought you'd know."

My chest constricted as if my heart was being wrung out. "Know what?"

Burgundy dropped her gaze, hunkering down to place her stone at the edge of the boundary.

"Know what?" my father growled behind me.

Beau cleared his throat. "Easy. We have orders. We're going to follow them."

"Now?" I asked, snarling. "Now you decide to follow orders?"

Beau ignored me. "Burgundy?"

The young witch nodded, pulling a box of salt out of her bag. With her back to the magical barrier, she generously sprinkled a half circle about two feet across around her feet. "The salt is better for uneven ground," she said, chatting nervously. "Better than just drawing in the dirt. For me, at least."

I clenched my fists, feeling my father doing the same beside me. The healer remained silent. His magic was neatly contained—which honestly was probably prudent this close to a magical working of unknown construction. My father and I didn't share the healer's natural equanimity, though.

"Just tell me that everyone is still alive, Beau," I finally whispered.

"Everyone is still alive," he said. "Everyone we have eyes on, at least. Since the last time we've seen them."

I pressed my hand to my chest, trying to physically force away the pain that had lodged in my heart. "Who haven't you seen?"

"The elves changed up their wards," the shifter said. His gaze was on Burgundy, who had hunkered down again and appeared to be murmuring to the focal stone in the grass a few inches from her bare feet. She looked cold. "They closed down the final weak spot a couple of hours ago, though the Talbots are still conducting tests."

"Mory's turtle," I murmured.

"Yeah, Ed. We've been using him to map the stadium."

I glanced over at my father. "Mory is a necromancer—"

Burgundy abruptly stood, her eyes glowing bright blue. She clapped her hands together, then swept her arms forward, out to the sides, and up over her head.

The magic of the boundary shifted. Thinning, then slicing open. Just wide enough to step through sideways.

"I did it," the young witch gasped.

The magic wavered.

"Keep your focus, fledgling," my father growled, already brushing past me.

Burgundy bit her lip, stepping carefully out of her salted half circle while keeping her arms aloft.

My father ducked, slipping through the opening she'd created in the boundary. I followed, with the healer right behind me. We all carefully avoided touching Burgundy's focal stone or stepping on the salt line.

My father was suddenly chest to chest with Beau. And even though the shifter was easily five inches taller, he prudently kept his gaze downcast.

"It's okay, Dad," I said. "We all go momentarily insane for our loved ones."

My father nodded, but he didn't step away.

Burgundy stepped back into the salted half circle, retracing her hand and arm movements in the opposite direction, then clapping again. The boundary magic knitted back together. The young witch bounced on her bare feet, squealing quietly to herself.

Yeah, effectively using your own magic was a huge thrill.

Scooping up her focal stone, Burgundy shoved her feet into her shoes. Beau capitalized on the momentary distraction, stepping away from my father.

I cleared my throat, desperate to simply run off and single-handedly storm the stadium—but understanding that caution might have been a better choice. For a brief moment, at least.

Also, I realized introductions were in order.

"Yazi, the warrior of the guardians," I said, formally sweeping my hand toward my father. "Beau, werecat, husband of the oracle, Rochelle."

Beau nodded.

I continued as traffic sped by us. "Burgundy, witch, apprentice of the Godfrey coven, specializing in healing."

Burgundy bobbed her head, practically glowing.

I turned to the darker-haired guardian on my right. "Qiuniu, healer of the guardians."

"Oh!" Burgundy cried, digging into her bag. "I have something for you. From the oracle."

She didn't mean me. Or my father. She offered a folded piece of paper to the healer, who took it with a nod.

I exchanged a glance with my father. He grimaced. Yeah, that couldn't be good.

"We've been expecting you," Beau said. "I parked just on the other side of these trees." Then he took off without another word, cutting through the forest rather than traversing the sidewalk.

Not that I could blame him. It was an easy guess that he'd rather be doing anything else than welcoming me back into Vancouver.

I followed at Beau's heels, Burgundy beside me and Yazi behind. All of us pretended to ignore the healer as he lingered on the sidewalk, studying the charcoal sketch that Burgundy had given him.

I glanced back just before I lost my line of sight within the thick trees, catching Qiuniu nodding to himself as he refolded and tucked the sketch into a front pocket that had no business existing in tight leather pants.

But then, all our armor was layered with magic, including invisible pockets and sheaths. We were about to mount a rescue and quell an invasion, after all.

I hoped.

Though it was still early afternoon, it took just a few steps off the sidewalk and into the thick woods that made up the majority of Stanley Park to dim the light as though evening had fallen. The forest was old for such a young city, but no matter the thickness of the fir, cedar, and hemlock tree trunks, I didn't think it was considered old growth. Still, the park didn't allow any trimming or clearing of trees or underbrush, so our path to the parking lot required a lot of stepping over slowly decomposing deadfall and being careful to not trample large ferns.

I had just caught a glimpse of parked vehicles through the foliage when magic bloomed in the branches of a slimmer tree to my left.

My father's blade was out and swinging—almost too fast for me to react.

"No!" I screamed.

Yazi froze, his golden broadsword only inches from the dimly manifested shadow leech that had just made an appearance in the lowest elbow of a young fir tree.

The leech chittered madly, then disappeared.

"Dad! That's Freddie!"

My father frowned. "You've named it."

I ignored his pissy tone. "The leech doesn't usually appear during the day. It must be extremely hungry."

"You're feeding a demon."

I jutted my chin out belligerently. "It's a … it's my responsibility."

My father sighed heavily, releasing his hold on his sword. It winked out of existence.

The healer stepped past us, chuckling under his breath. My father gave him a look that would have curdled milk in an instant.

Beau and Burgundy had already disappeared into the parking lot.

I dug around in my purse, finding nothing that contained magic—residual or otherwise—except Warner's knife and Kandy's cuffs. And I couldn't feed either of those to the shadow leech. "Have you got any money on you?"

"It eats money?"

"It eats magic."

My father grumbled something I chose not to hear. But he dug into the pocket of his well-worn leather pants and pulled out three golden coins.

"Perfect!" I plucked them out of his open palm. "Now, go away. Freddie won't come back with you here."

My father's lips thinned grimly.

"I owe the shadow leech, Dad. And it's better that Freddie's coming to me to feed, rather than the alternative."

My father turned, stalking off through the trees and into the parking lot. I lifted up onto my tiptoes, carefully placing the coins into the elbow of the branch on which Freddie had appeared. Their gold glistened with guardian dragon magic.

"Freddie?" I whispered. Then I waited. Muted sounds filtered through the quiet forest. I heard a slight rustling overhead from the birds that overwintered in the Pacific Northwest. Voices came from the direction of the parking lot, and the steady drone of traffic continued from the causeway, completely incongruent to the setting.

"Come on, Freddie."

A sliver of magic bloomed on a fir branch higher above my head, as if the shadow leech was only begrudgingly manifesting. I'd never seen Freddie during the day before, though, so perhaps appearing at all was difficult. Either that or the leech had been hanging out with Mory too much and had picked up the necromancer's generally belligerent attitude.

A thin shadow flowed down the tree trunk, shifting over the three coins. The barest hint of burnt cinnamon toast tickled my senses.

Freddie was starving. I hadn't thought about that, hadn't planned to be gone so long. But it was terribly irresponsible to have left the leech without a more permanent food source.

"I'm sorry, Freddie," I murmured. "I'll make it right ... well, I'll fix it as best I can. I promise."

Freddie chittered quietly, but the leech's form was just a wisp of shadow. I could barely see it.

"Come see me later. After dark." I strode off toward the parking lot without giving in to the guilt that had been riding me since I'd woken in the nexus. Guilt never got anything done.

Revenge, however, was much more effective.

"What do you mean, no?" I asked, my hand resting on the top of the back passenger door I'd just opened. "I want to head straight to the stadium."

"The oracle has given us our orders," Beau said stiffly, staring at me over the top of the black SUV.

Kandy's vehicle. "We're to return with you to your grandmother's house."

Yazi had already climbed into the front passenger seat, with Qiuniu and Burgundy in the back, waiting on me. Beau was driving.

Well, he was supposed to be driving. But he had decided to argue about our ultimate destination with me first.

I opened my mouth, intending to insist. But instead, I strode purposefully around the car and made an attempt to snatch the keys from Beau. Actions spoke louder than words, right?

Beau didn't step back as I got up in his face. The green of his shapeshifter magic rolled over his eyes as he shoved the keys behind his back.

Damn it.

I was trying to be intimidating without actually having to follow through. And, you know, hurt more of the people I was pretty much sworn to protect.

Beau's gaze flicked to my forehead—and the mass of pink scar tissue I could still feel marring my skin. Concern flickered across his face. He clenched his teeth, squelching the emotion. "You said you'd listen, Jade."

"To the oracle," I retorted, knowing I was becoming more and more irrational as I spoke, as I insisted. Becoming more childish. Again. But this time, I had a purpose. A real need. "The people I love are trapped—"

"Rochelle knows that. And you have to trust her."

"That is ridicu—"

"Why?" Beau softened his tone. "Because you're older and wiser?"

"No, but—"

"Because you're stronger?"

"That's not what I—"

"Because you wield more weapons?"

I gnashed my teeth. "Just drop me off. My father and I can handle the elves."

Beau nodded agreeably. "Yeah. We know. Rochelle has seen as much."

The image of the charcoal sketch Beau had shoved in my face floated to the forefront of my mind, like a bad memory imprinted on my brain.

Beau nodded, apparently seeing some dawning understanding in my expression. "Yeah, that."

"You think … Rochelle thinks that … I'm going to make it worse?"

"Well, you ain't going to make it all better by going in guns blazing." The shifter touched my shoulder lightly. "We need to go. Rochelle was hoping the healer would come."

And just like that, my heart was thumping in my chest and blood was rushing in my ears. I turned away from the concern lurking in Beau's blue-green gaze. No, not concern. Compassion.

I crossed around the vehicle wordlessly, climbing in beside Burgundy, who was perched in the middle of the back seat. Beau was reversing the SUV out of the parking spot before I even got my seatbelt buckled.

"All right then, Jade?" my father asked from the front. His magic was buttoned down so tightly that I couldn't taste a drop of it, likely in deference to the mechanical and electrical systems of the vehicle. Some magic wore on technology.

"Yeah, Dad." I gazed out the window at the mostly empty parking lot, then at the heavily treed park as it blurred by. Not because Beau was speeding, but because I was struggling with unshed tears. "We're just going to Gran's first. The oracle needs to see us."

And someone needed the healer. But I didn't say that part out loud. Because it was obvious even to me that the only reason Beau and Burgundy were being so tightlipped was that they thought I would become unmanageable if I knew who it was who'd been so badly hurt that the healer of the guardians was needed.

And you couldn't have the wielder of the instruments of assassination lose her shit. Apparently, based on the sketch Beau had stolen from Rochelle, that was one of the ways to bring about the end of days.

"Prudent," my father said.

I couldn't remember what we'd been talking about. Something cool slipped into the palm of my hand. A stone. The image of a smiley face was painted on it. I closed my fingers over it, feeling soothing magic similar to my mother's, yet tasting of sweet watermelon.

I smiled at Burgundy. "Thank you."

She nodded happily.

And now the fledglings—Kandy's so-called misfits—were comforting me, when it was supposed to be the other way around.

I stared down at Burgundy's stone, desperately trying to sort through my hazy memories. "The Pack must know Kandy's missing. Are they here?"

"No," Beau said. "They've been busy tracking elf sightings themselves."

"How did you manage to keep Desmond from showing up with an army?" I asked, trying to keep my tone light.

"I told him five words. 'Rochelle says to stay away.' "

Because of me. All of it…the kidnapping, the magical grid…had happened because of my inability to fight Reggie off, my arrogance, and…untethered by all the raw emotion I was trying to deny, my magic welled up, threatening to smother Burgundy's delicate charm work with my guilt. My stupid, useless guilt over everything I'd wrought.

I didn't want to destroy Burgundy's thoughtful gift. I didn't want to subvert her gentle magic with my own destructive tendencies. I might have been the wielder of the instruments of assassination, but I preferred cupcakes over murder. I craved friendship over making enemies.

I was Jade.

Just Jade.

First and foremost.

I relaxed my fingers, allowing Burgundy's calming charm to soothe me, ground me. "Thank you," I murmured again.

"I'm glad you're back," the young witch said earnestly. "Everyone has been so worried. Plus Gabby's good and all, but you make the tastiest cupcakes."

I smiled, chuckling quietly. But my father threw his head back and guffawed, flooding the interior of the SUV with his spicy magic.

The engine thumped weirdly, stuttering, then catching again.

"What the hell?" Beau muttered.

I threw my head back and joined my father in his amusement, laughing until I'd used up Burgundy's charm. Until I'd burned off the misplaced guilt I'd been carrying.

The SUV sputtered again.

"So ..." the healer drawled. "We'll be walking the rest of the way, then?"

My father cranked around in his seat to smile at me, and I grinned back. The magic that had filled the interior of the vehicle dispersed, and the SUV's engine stopped sputtering and carried on.

Life happened. Enemies invaded. Then the warriors gathered, and the invaders were eventually beaten back. Just as it had been in Tofino.

So we were at the gathering part. I could deal with that.

For a little while, at least.

Chapter Six

My grandmother lay in the center of her bed, ashen and still. The dark-gray silk duvet and white sheeting underneath were neatly pulled up to her chest, her arms lying over top. A flickering, fading dome of witch magic that held only a hint of blue covered her from head to toe.

My heart stopped in my chest as I stepped through into the bedroom, tripping over my own feet. Then Qiuniu was brushing past me, making a beeline for the bed. He paused before Olive, who was sleeping propped up in an antique chair in the corner of the room. The witch appeared just as drained as her normally robust citrus magic tasted. The healer brushed his fingers against her pallid cheek, but she didn't wake.

The dome of witch magic over my grandmother—more of a fine mist, really—collapsed.

Gran sucked in a shuddering, pain-filled breath. But before she could exhale, the music that accompanied the guardian of South America's healing powers welled up. Qiuniu settled on the bed at Gran's side.

"Jade." A female voice called to me from the hall. "Jade."

I turned away, selfishly thankful for the excuse. I needed to be helpful. I needed to be doing anything but watching Qiuniu wrestle with death for my grandmother's life.

Burgundy brushed by me in the doorway as I glanced back into the corridor. The junior witch's gaze was glued to Gran and the healer. She unbuttoned her wool coat as she crossed over to the other side of the bed, placing a hand on a wooden box on the bedside table.

But it was Jasmine who was calling me from the hall, not the junior witch. The golden-haired vampire's bright-blue eyes were rimmed with the red of her magic. She reached for me, offering me both of her hands. In friendship.

The pain that felt as though it had stopped up my heart eased a tiny bit.

"I can help," Burgundy murmured behind me. "I can set my stones."

"Please do," Qiuniu said kindly.

I stepped into the hall, taking Jasmine's hands. She squeezed—a bit painfully. The bones of our fingers ground against each other, but I didn't flinch. I didn't drop her gaze.

The vampire tried to smile, but managed only a twist of her lips. "We'll get them back. With you returned to us, the oracle thinks we can, at least."

I nodded. I could feel the well of magic underneath my feet, undoubtedly coming from the map room in the basement. Its intensity was nothing like it had been before. I had assumed that was where the others had gathered as I'd rushed upstairs to see my grandmother. I had tasted the muted tenor of Gran's lilac magic instantly upon entering the house, but the other magic contained within was mixed together so thoroughly that I didn't actually know who else was in residence.

Jasmine looked almost as drawn as Olive. Her cheekbones were much more defined than before, and deep shadows were beneath her eyes.

"Are you hurt?" I asked.

"No. No, I'm fine." But she was still gripping my hands as if I might have been a lifeline. "I drank some elf blood, which has had an...effect, but otherwise I'm okay. The elves are still keeping to themselves."

"Your eyes. I'm sorry if it's rude, but I can see your magic. You look...hungry or hurt."

She nodded. "Again, I'm okay. Ben has been helping me, but...he sleeps during the day."

"Okay. Just...let me know. I can try to help."

Jasmine offered me a saucy grin that was more in keeping with her personality. "If only, my sweet, spicy dowser. If only."

I shook my head, managing to grin. Fleetingly.

Jasmine nodded, her own expression sobering. "You're needed downstairs."

"Yeah, I guessed something was up, based on the mass of magic underneath my feet and the huge freaking dome protecting the city."

The vampire didn't drop my hands, though. "I...I think I hated you for a bit."

"Understandable."

"It really wasn't. I saw what that elf did to you." She shuddered. "I know what it feels like to be controlled."

"I'm sorry."

She shrugged offishly. "But something about the elves' wards around the stadium cut me off from Kett, severed our connection. And I thought...I thought he was dead."

"I really am so sorry."

"Jade. Come on. I'm trying to say something important, and you're being all Canadian with the 'sorry'."

"Right. Sorry about that."

The golden-haired vampire laughed. "I was there when you tore that hole in the elves' defenses. Watching over Mory, trying to hold her back from charging inside to rescue you. Even Liam misplaced the stick up his butt for a moment, fully prepared to back the silly necromancer. Anyway. I...I could feel Kett again. Just for that moment. So...I knew. I knew he was still alive...well, that he still existed. And I didn't hate you anymore."

Jasmine squeezed my hands one final time. Then she let me go, heading off down the hall and the stairs without another word.

Okay, then.

My mother was floating in a column of brilliant white magic slashed through with pale blue. The column sliced through the very center of the map room in my grandmother's basement. More tendrils of power writhed across the ceiling, spiderwebbing down and across the map of Vancouver that had been painted in black on all four walls. The large space that had once been a rec room contained a number of other people, including my father. The taste of everyone's magic shimmered underneath the torrent of power that had absorbed and overwritten the witches' grid.

But I had eyes only for my mother. Her strawberry hair was a brilliant halo around her head. Her calves, ankles, and feet were bare, skin pale against the black silk sheath she wore.

"What the hell?" I whispered past the fear that was threatening to clog my throat. First Gran, and now

Scarlett. "Is she trapped in there?" I asked no one in particular, taking another step into the room.

"Yes," a woman said. It took me a moment to identify Angelica Talbot. The dark-haired sorcerer was unobtrusively standing in the corner to my left, but her dark-eyed gaze was on my father, not me. Magic glistened from each and every piece of jewelry she wore—dozens of bracelets, bangles, and rings, including a set of toe rings visible on her bare feet. "But she isn't in pain."

"Isn't in pain?" I snarled. I was striding forward before I'd even realized it, already reaching for the column of magic. Ready to tear it all down. That was something I could do. I could free my mother, at least.

"Jade!" my father barked, stepping between me and Scarlett. "Wait."

"Wait? Wait?! How long has she been like that? This is how the witches are fueling the boundary? It's insane!"

"Yes. But we can't just rip it down now. The backlash would kill your mother. And quite possibly Rochelle and Jasmine as well."

I took a fortifying breath, tamping down the instincts roaring in my ears so that I could actually listen to my father's concerns. "Rochelle and Jasmine?" I glanced around the map room. "Why?"

The oracle wasn't in the room, and neither was Beau, though I'd felt both of them nearby as I crossed through the house. Jasmine was leaning in the doorway. I must have brushed past her when I'd charged into the room.

"It's Rochelle's spell," the golden-haired vampire said grimly. "Some kind of sorcerer working channeled through the oracle magic with Rochelle's version of runes. Cast by Scarlett...and me. Activated by the blood of an elf, anchored by your mother." She nodded toward the column of magic containing Scarlett.

I sidestepped around that stream of magic until I could see my mother's face. Her eyes were closed. She looked thin. Too thin. "When? When was the last time she ate?"

Jasmine grimaced.

"The magic is sustaining her," Angelica said. Her tone carried a matter-of-fact, no-nonsense quality that it was easy to imagine her using with her unruly brood.

"How do we get her out?" I whispered. "Does … can I take her place?"

"No!" Jasmine practically shouted. "That would be …"

"Terrifying," Angelica muttered, likely thinking I couldn't hear her.

"But you think that an object of magic could take Scarlett's place?" my father asked, as if he was continuing a conversation he and the sorcerer had been having before I'd shown up.

"If it's powerful enough." Angelica stepped up beside me. "But even then, only in the short term. An artifact won't have the same reserves as a witch of Scarlett's power. We just didn't have enough people capable of casting in order to try." She glanced at me. "Or an alchemist to fuel it."

"Okay." I breathed deeply, steadying myself further. I could do this. I could focus past my panic. I could be rational. I could command the power that the witches and the sorcerer needed. "I have …" I looked at my father. "I have Kandy's cuffs. Warner's knife. I assume I shouldn't use my necklace, though. Or my katana?"

Yazi shook his head grimly, raising his hand to the column of magic holding my mother in its grip. He was assessing the spell siphoning her magic, slowly draining her, killing her ...

I clenched my fists.

"We already know the object," my father said, steady and sure, though his expression was deeply conflicted. "It has already been tied to Scarlett Godfrey by Chi Wen, the far seer of the guardians."

My heart beat painfully, once. As it always did when the far seer was brought into any conversation. Then a couple of puzzle pieces clicked into place. "The dragon-wrought sword."

"Yes. Constructed by the sword master himself."

Relief flooded through me. I wasn't big on walking in the steps of destiny, but if it meant that Chi Wen had seen a way to save my mother, then I was all for it. "She keeps it in her umbrella stand."

"No," Jasmine said. "It's here. In the house. She was ... she was kicking some elf ass with it the last time I saw it."

Yazi laughed, a low, hearty rumble. "Of course she was." He touched my cheek gently. "She's the mother of the wielder of the instruments of assassination." He glanced at Scarlett suspended before him. "I wouldn't have expected anything less of her."

Movement drew my attention to the doorway.

My grandmother.

She was alive.

Gran, supported on Qiuniu's arm, paused behind Jasmine, who stepped away to clear the elder witch's path into the room. She looked tired ... withered ... weak, swamped by a thick, dark-gray cotton robe. But her fierce, blue-eyed gaze was firmly glued to her trapped, dying daughter.

"Healer?" Yazi asked.

"My apologies, warrior," Qiuniu said ruefully. "I found myself unable to refuse the head of the Convocation's demands without...well, without being rude."

Gran pushed away from the healer, taking a tentative step into the room. Magic rippled all around her as the anchor point of the boundary spell reacted to her presence. It might have done the same when I'd entered, but I hadn't noticed. Energy rippled across the walls and over the ceiling, then filtered down into the column that held my mother.

Gran took another step, then another. She brushed away my attempt to reach for her, circling the stream of magic with her hands raised before her. Feeling the power.

"Mom?" my mother whispered suddenly. Her eyes blinked open, blazing the blue of her witch magic to obscure her expression. But I could hear the desperation in her voice.

My heart squelched.

"I'm here, my girl." Gran held her palm to the shimmering column of magic between her and the daughter she'd always underestimated. "My beauty." She cleared her throat of the emotion threatening to swallow her words. "You've done marvelously. But it's time to get you out." Then she brushed her hands together, looking at each of us in turn. Me, Yazi, Angelica, Qiuniu, then Jasmine. She nodded. "Is there a plan?"

"I need to find and fortify a sword," I said, utterly relieved that my grandmother was going to take charge. Beyond grateful that even despite the healer's obvious caution, she was well enough to do so. "Angelica?"

The dark-haired sorcerer nodded. "Jasmine, Olive, and I have been formulating a spell. But we needed at least two more experienced casters and an object of power."

"Myself and Jade, of course," Gran said.

"The oracle is sleeping," Jasmine said. "Involuntarily, I might add. It's been a rough couple of weeks. But she needs to see Jade as soon as she wakes up."

"Liam and Mory are on their way back," Angelica said. "Despite the extra protections provided by Jade, the elves have finally found a way to block the necromancer's incursions."

"Extra protections?" I echoed. "Incursions?"

Angelica ignored me, intent on filling my grandmother in. "Tony has been working nonstop with Liam and Jasmine since Jade requested his help, developing tech and—"

"The time to talk is over," my grandmother barked. "Jade, find the sword. Angelica and I will set up the spell to free Scarlett. We need the room cleared."

And with that pronouncement, my grandmother practically shoved everyone but Angelica out of the room and into the hall.

"Pearl," the healer said, gently protesting. "You really should be resting."

"Yes, yes. Thank you, guardian. Just as soon as my girl is on her own two feet."

Then Gran shut the door in the faces of those of us clumped together in the hallway. Cut off from the potent magic spilling out of the map room, it was suddenly dark.

I glanced over at Jasmine.

She snorted, shaking her head. "I'll get you the sword. I know where to look. Then I'll fill you in." She took off toward the stairs.

My father touched my shoulder. "I'd prefer to not leave the house, but I'd like to scout the area around the stadium. Beau will escort me, so you can remain here and help your mother."

"Okay."

He turned to the healer. "Will you stay?"

"For as long as possible. Though I might need to cross through the boundary quickly, so if the witches can provide passage, that would be ideal. I'm not sure if Pulou can even contact me while I'm within the city ward. Have you tried to speak to him since we entered?"

My father shook his head. "The treasure keeper and I aren't on speaking terms."

Because of me. Warmth bloomed in my chest, and I stifled a pleased, childish grin. "It's funny that the portal in the basement of the bakery doesn't work. I mean, the elves have the dimensional gateway running despite the witches' boundary …"

My father was staring at me, narrow-eyed.

"What? Am I missing something?"

"A portal in the basement? Of the bakery?"

I glanced between my father and the healer. Right. Was that still a secret? Even with Drake and Warner using it regularly? "Um … yes?"

Qiuniu started chuckling.

My father's glower deepened.

"The guardians do like their secrets," the healer said.

"I just assumed Pulou put it in when he stored the elves in Vancouver," I said. "And, you know, didn't mention the portal or the elves to anyone."

"I've been having to ask permission to travel here," my father spat. "Every single time. When there was an anchored portal in the basement of my daughter's bakery."

"All good, Pop-Pop," I said pertly, patting his bulging bicep in an attempt to derail the rage he was working himself into. "If the portal is working, it means the healer can come and go as needed, yes?"

Tension ran through my father's jaw. "Yes."

"All righty then." I nodded to them both as I took off down the hall after Jasmine. I didn't want to leave my mother trapped for a second longer than necessary. I heard my father and the healer talking behind me as I went, though.

"Haven't you been to the bakery multiple times?" Qiuniu asked.

"Yes."

"And you didn't notice a portal?"

"No."

"So the treasure keeper can mask his magic," the healer murmured. "From us."

My father grunted, then changed the subject. "Look after my girls while I'm gone?"

"For as long as I am able, warrior. Pearl needs another round of healing as well, after she sleeps."

Their voices finally faded as I cleared the stairs and hit the main foyer, then followed Jasmine's sweet peppermint magic up to the second floor.

The taste of Jasmine's magic led me past Gran's bedroom and into the guest room connected to the main bathroom. The glimpse I caught of it was all smoky blues. Gran had painted and spruced up all the linens in preparation for Warner's and my engagement party in September.

And at that stray thought, a sharp pain shot through my chest, forcing me to actually pause in the doorway to absorb it. I should have run off with Warner a year before. We should have gotten married on an obscure beach somewhere. But I'd allowed all of Gran's coven politicking and Warner's unpredictable schedule to push the date further and further.

And now I'd missed my own wedding.

Ruined my own wedding.

"Jade?" Jasmine whispered. She was in the guest room, and had backed away from me as I faltered. Retreated from me. Her fists were clenched at her sides, the red of her magic overwhelming the natural blue of her eyes.

She was scared of me.

Another deep ache sliced into my chest, settling heavily around my heart. The golden-haired vampire had witnessed my...my... Jesus, I couldn't even stand to recall what I'd done to those I loved most. I pressed the heel of my hand to my forehead, covering the scar that broadcast my shame.

"I'm fine," I said. But I really wasn't. More and more, it seemed as though each time I found my footing, it would get kicked out from underneath me by a mere thought.

Suddenly Jasmine was wrapping her arms around me, hugging me and cooing. "I know...I know...it's okay. You aren't responsible...you didn't ask for it, Jade. You didn't do anything to cause it."

I stifled the sob threatening to tear through my throat. I was the one who was supposed to be comforting, to be caring. Yet Jasmine, who'd had every reason to think I'd murdered her master, was the one voluntarily touching me. Holding me, even though her hunger must have been acute.

I wrapped my arms around the golden-haired vampire, clutching her like a child.

And I wept.

I sobbed.

I cried until I couldn't see through the torrent of tears, until I could no longer breathe through my nose.

I cried for everything I'd done. For the plans I had ruined. The people I'd hurt. Then I cried for the elves I'd slaughtered—even they were simply acting under orders from Reggie. The warrior elves were ultimately just as compelled as I had been, by their upbringing, by their training. By their responsibilities.

As Jasmine rocked me, I sobbed for everything that had been taken from me, stripped from me. Without my consent.

My mind invaded. My body abused. My magic subverted for another's gain.

My soul raped.

And I'd been powerless. Powerless to stop it.

"It's okay," Jasmine murmured over and over again. "It fades. It fades. Trust me. It's okay. No one blames you."

Jasmine loosened her hold on me, guiding me into the bathroom and sitting me down on the toilet. She shoved a handful of tissue into my hands, then wet and wrung out a navy-blue facecloth.

My sobs eased into an occasional shudder. I blew my nose, my hands shaking. Weakened by my grief, by my self-loathing.

Jasmine pressed the cool, wet cloth to my face, holding it over each of my eyes in turn. When it started to warm, she rewetted it at the sink.

"I'm sorry," I murmured, blowing my nose again. "I'm just so, so sorry."

"I know," Jasmine said. "I also know it'll take time for you to recognize that you weren't responsible."

"I just felt ... I felt ... I feel ..."

"Powerless. Complicit. Damaged." The vampire hung her head, momentarily hiding her face behind a cascade of dark-gold curls. "Ruined," she whispered.

I looked at her, distressed by the utter truth that backed her words. And at the confession implied by them.

She twisted her lips wryly, then closed the space between us to press the cool facecloth to my eyes again. "Yeah, I get it."

"You ..." A terrible thought occurred to me, one too painful to even bear. "Not ... not Kett?"

"Not Kett." She cleared her throat, returning to the sink with the cloth for a third time. Then she lingered there, not speaking for long enough that I assumed she wasn't going to elaborate.

I pulled the chrome tissue holder off the box of Kleenex on the back of the toilet, settling the cardboard box on my lap for easier access.

Jasmine handed me the cold cloth again, and I laid it across both my swollen eyes. My head was pounding—but thankfully just from sinus pressure, not from the scar.

"My uncle," Jasmine murmured.

I kept the cloth across my eyes, listening without looking at her. Not wanting to involuntarily inflict judgement, or pressure her to share details.

"He abused all of us. Wisteria, Declan, and me." The golden-haired vampire's tone was quietly contemplative but not distraught. "It was part of our training. A Fairchild tradition."

I dropped the cloth into my hand in response to that. Needing to look at her now.

She shrugged one shoulder. "The abused abuse. It's cyclical. Except ... he ... Jasper. He took it further with me. Beyond the magical applications, for lack of a better way to explain."

"Jasper Fairchild." I tasted the name eagerly, with vicious intent. A nasty grin spread across my face.

Jasmine laughed huskily. "He's already dead. But thank you."

"Kett?"

"Wisteria."

I didn't find that at all surprising. The reconstructionist was more than capable of taking care of those she loved. "And his death freed you?"

"No. No, I'd been working through it before that, of course. I'm sure I still am. But...I had Wisteria and Declan."

"And they knew. They knew it wasn't your fault."

"Exactly. Like I know that what that elf did to you, what she made you do, wasn't your fault either."

I nodded. But I only partially believed her.

She laughed quietly, then sobered quickly. "We need you, Jade."

"I'm here. I'll do whatever it takes."

"I know. But this can't be about you punishing yourself. Because if you do something stupid, like racing off to the stadium to save everyone singlehandedly, then getting yourself killed in order to prove something to yourself, it doesn't help anyone."

I narrowed my eyes at the golden-haired vampire.

She grinned at me snarkily.

"It's troubling that you've come to know me so well in such a short time, vampire."

"You aren't hard to read, dowser. Thank God. I've got enough obscurity in my life."

I snorted. Then I gave my nose a final blow. I was such an ugly crier. Everyone would know I'd been blubbering like a baby at a single glance. My eyes and nose would be red and puffy for hours.

I breathed in deeply. Then I got my wallowing ass up off the toilet. "The sword?"

"Tucked in the bedroom closet."

"Thank you." I crossed to the door, taking the box of tissues with me. Then I paused to look back at Jasmine.

The young vampire was leaning against the counter, her head bowed slightly and her hair a mass of riotous golden curls. She had her arms crossed, fingers digging into her biceps. It must have been difficult controlling her bloodlust in order to hold me, comfort me.

"Kett has survived worse," I said. "Worse than me."

She raised her red-hued eyes to meet my gaze. "Worse than the elves?"

"By my count, in the short time I've known him, he's died or been dying at least three times."

"Three ..." Jasmine furrowed her brow.

"In London, he took a blow that would have killed me."

Jasmine snorted doubtfully. "You aren't easy to kill, Jade."

"It dissolved the life debt I'd inadvertently formed between us when I rescued him from execution by the guardian dragons. So that magic was pretty certain he'd died for me."

Jasmine's lips parted slightly, shocked. "And the second?"

"Peru. He was badly injured by a swarm of shadow leeches, then he drank deeply from Shailaja, the dragon we were fighting."

"And ... the blood should have killed him?"

"Or poisoned him, at least. But the executioner of the Conclave is powerful. Still, the magic in her blood screwed with him, I think. He didn't talk about it much."

"Astonishing." Jasmine chuckled. "And the third time?"

"In the mountains...somewhere in China." I fell silent, remembering Kandy slung across Kett's arms and both of them so badly wounded that I'd actually been able to force them to retreat. Of course, they couldn't see our attackers. The shadow leeches, again. Fighting what you couldn't see was foolhardy—and the executioner wasn't given to folly. "He saved Kandy. Though she tells the story with a different twist."

"Of course she does." Jasmine pushed away from the counter. "I have to go...it's still a couple of hours until sunset, and...I should try to drink something to hold me over. I'll bring you a glass of water."

She joined me in the doorway. "You know both of them, Kandy and Kett, would follow you to hell, somehow manage to burn it down, then gleefully watch you bake cupcakes over the embers. Right?"

I smiled, a little stiffly. "It goes both ways. All three ways."

"Of course it does."

I brushed my fingers against the back of her hand, tentative about touching her but needing that last little bit of physical contact. "Thank you. For the cry. For the companionship."

Jasmine squeezed my hand, then slipped swiftly from the bedroom without another word.

And I went to work.

I sat cross-legged in the middle of the bed and the blue-gray duvet, with my mother's rapier lying across my knees. The thin weapon's cross guard was constructed out of an elaborate twist of gold and set with sapphires. I spaced my fingers as evenly as possible across the blade and hilt, closing my eyes. Then I just...settled. Just breathed. Feeling my weight, feeling the power of the weapon writhing under my touch.

I relaxed everything I held so tightly, all the magic at my disposal. I allowed it to unfurl and well up, then flow down my arms, through my hands and into the blade.

I didn't think about filling the weapon, because that would suggest it had a capacity. And I needed it to teem with magic—enough power for it to be able to take my mother's place in the magical grid. I simply channeled, giving it everything I had, everything I held, knowing that my own resources were vast.

I slipped deeper and deeper into a meditative state, filtering out all the other occupants of the house, all the other magic.

I might have slept, but it felt more like a shift into an inner awareness. Simply breathing. Simply living in the magic that constantly surrounded me, untapped. Doing more than just trying to endure what had happened to me, what I had been forced to do.

Doing more than just surviving.

I embraced that moment, making the most of each breath. Allowing it to heal me, to allow me to give more of myself to the rapier, to my mother.

The light had shifted in the room when I finally opened my eyes, heralding the setting of the sun behind the layer of clouds covering the city.

A turtle was watching me from the corner of the bed. A dead turtle, to be exact. He had hollowed out a nesting area, flattening the downy duvet in a circle.

"Hey, Ed," I whispered. "Fancy meeting you here."

A giggle drew my attention to the necromancer curled on a high-backed antique chair in the corner of the room.

Mory.

Knitting. Of course and always.

"He likes you," she said, tucking her knitting in her bag, unfolding her legs, and standing to cross over to the low bureau by the door. She was wearing her bright red poncho, with the multicolored beaded fringe. The sight brought a smile to my face, though I wasn't certain why.

I glanced back at Ed. Magic glistened across his upper shell. He stretched his neck, as if craning to get a good look back at me. "He looks different."

Mory laughed snarkily. "He sure does." She turned away from the bureau, taking three steps to the end of the bed and shoving a glass of water in my face. "Jasmine says drink this."

I took the heavy, etched-glass tumbler. A matching crystal pitcher filled with ice and water sat on a silver tray on the bureau. Someone had rummaged through the good china cabinets in the dining room. Gran would have a fit.

The necromancer critically eyed my chain mail sweater and the black leather armor beneath it as I downed the entire glass of water. "That's a new look."

"Yep."

"Is it going to be a thing?" She took the empty tumbler from me, crossing back to the pitcher of water and filling it again.

"I hope not."

"Yeah, okay. Good."

I snorted, reaching my fingers toward Ed and wiggling them. The turtle open its mouth, mimicking a smile. "Seriously … Ed feels different."

Mory shoved the second glass of water into my extended hand. "You don't remember?" She ran her forefinger and middle finger along Ed's back in a long caress. The turtle shimmied contentedly under her touch. "Jasmine calls it an obfuscation spell."

"Jasmine cast a … witch spell?"

"No, moron. You did."

Right. Nothing like three minutes with a belligerent necromancer to bring you right down to earth.

"He's, like, invisible now," Mory clarified.

"I can clearly see him."

"Yeah, well, it's your magic, ain't it?"

"Wait …" I racked my brain, pulling at the edges of a hazy memory. "This sounds vaguely familiar …"

"You picked Ed up, carried him upstairs …" Mory trailed off. Apparently, she was hoping to prompt me, but then she didn't actually pause long enough for me to fill in the blanks. "And you fiddled around with his charm. The one that let him pass through the wards."

"Right … it felt like my mother's magic. But it was wearing thin." In my defense, the healer did say I'd be a little fuzzy about exact details for a while.

Mory nodded. "But the next time Ed saw you, you were bleeding everywhere." She helpfully pointed toward the huge scar on my forehead with a grimace.

"How could I forget?" I said, heavy on the sarcasm.

"Yeah, well. I think you bled all over Ed and made him superpowered."

That didn't sound quite right. "Superpowered?"

"Yep!" Mory crowed, sweeping Ed up and cooing in his face. "Like the spider biting Peter Parker, or gamma radiation for Bruce Banner."

I narrowed my eyes, not too pleased with being compared to a radioactive spider. Or radiation in general. "So now Ed is invisible."

"When he wants to be."

"When he wants...I thought you controlled him? Thought for him?"

Mory just grinned at me. "And he's immune to the magic of that device you were fixing for the elves now. And you fortified my connection to him. So we were able to map the entire stadium and get a good look at everything without having to pull Ed out constantly."

"You think I gave your dead turtle invisibility and a magical immunity? Plus somehow tied your magic to him...tighter?"

"Yep." Mory scooped up her satchel, then made a beeline for the door. "The oracle is awake. I'll let her know you're ready." She exited into the hall.

I almost asked *'Ready for what?'* Except I knew the answer. Ready to be shown all the terrible that was about to occur. Everything I couldn't control, but had to somehow survive. That sort of ready.

Mory popped her head back into the room. "Oh, and Pearl and Angelica are almost ready for you. They need you to 'place the sword' when they cast whatever spell they're using to release Scarlett." She did air quotes with one hand, since the other was occupied holding Ed. "Or something like that." She took off again.

"That's two different things, Mory," I called after her snarkily. "Two things I need to be ready for."

I returned my attention to the thin rapier still slung across my lap. I'd pumped up the magic that it had been honed with so much that it now glowed—even to my own eyes, and I rarely saw my own magic. Good.

Good.

This I could do. This I could control. Inch by inch.

I unfolded my legs, crossing to pour myself a third glass of water. I could already feel the oracle climbing the stairs from the basement, could already taste her tart-apple magic preceding her. I was going to need more than another glass of water to get through my next conversation. Unfortunately, I was out of chocolate—and was fairly certain Rochelle wouldn't be pleased if I tried to make a run to Chocolate Arts or even my bakery pantry ...

Except, of course, I could now just teleport there and back with a mere thought.

I ran my fingers along my necklace, but ultimately rejected the idea as utterly frivolous. Even I couldn't justify the use of rare magic simply to collect chocolate. No matter how much I wanted to.

I settled back on the bed, cross-legged again. Then a petite, white-haired oracle, swathed in a graying black hoodie over slim-legged, faded black jeans, entered the room and closed the door behind her. The hoodie was three times too large for Rochelle's shoulders, but slightly tight across her rounded belly. She looked more than six months pregnant now. And I fervently hoped it wasn't stress and weight loss that made it appear so.

I let her cross toward the bed without harassing her with questions, allowing Rochelle to set the tone of the meeting—even though doing so went against every one of my protective instincts. Because I understood that this sort of terrible situation was exactly why my grandmother had nearly lost her cool when she discovered that Rochelle and Beau wanted to live in coven territory.

Oracles were rare. A valuable resource for a coven. It would be utterly foolish for me to ignore Rochelle. For me to not at least listen, not at least try to understand. Of course, I was all kinds of a fool for those I loved. So I didn't have any doubt that my resolve to face the oracle's visions rationally wasn't going to last particularly long.

Rochelle looked tired. But her magic simmered in her eyes intensely, as if it was maintaining some sort of epically alert status.

"Jade." The oracle's light-gray gaze flicked over me, taking in the rapier on the bed beside me, then assessing my leather-and-chain-mail getup with less emotion than Mory had. Until she homed in on the scar on my forehead. There, she paused.

"Rochelle." It was an easy guess that she'd been expecting my arrival, but not necessarily the scar. A silly flush of relief flooded through me at that thought. If the oracle had seen me, but not the wound, that might mean it wasn't going to stick around long. Yeah, that made me feel vain and completely self-centered. Which was why I kept such things to myself. Usually.

God, I missed Kandy. And Warner. And Kett. In that moment, I understood with perfect bitterness how liberating it was to be able to tell my fiance and my BFFs anything. I could admit to anything, any dark or silly thought, and they wouldn't look at me as lesser for having done so.

"We need to talk," the oracle said quietly. "And I have some...tasks I require of you."

"I'm looking forward to it immensely," I said, not even remotely attempting to hide the fact that I was lying.

Rochelle twisted her lips into a tight but amused smile. "But we need to get Scarlett out of the grid first. That's... well, she's a big puzzle piece, and I want to make certain that removing her from the grid doesn't affect what I've been seeing."

"An apocalypse. Triggered by me."

Rochelle narrowed her eyes at me. "Beau has been sharing. Ahead of schedule."

"He's concerned for you."

"It's not me he needs to be concerned about."

Rochelle's tone was grim. Even a little too grim for my liking, frankly. I was just hoping she'd seen something. Something that would get us out of the mess we'd made. Yes, we. Pulou, the elves, and me.

There. I could manage to at least share the responsibility. That was a step away from completely blaming myself. My golden-haired vampire psychologist would have been proud.

Rochelle tilted her head, taking in my involuntary and inappropriate smile.

"Sorry," I said. "Random amusing thought about my own fallibility, and being counseled by a vampire."

Rochelle laughed quietly. "Jasmine has been an asset."

"Yeah? An asset?"

The oracle sighed, heavy on the suffering. She rubbed her eyes.

"I didn't mean to mock you, oracle," I whispered.

"No, you're right. I meant that Jasmine's been a good ally, a good friend to me and the coven. I'm just... worn a little thin."

146

"I can imagine. And with the baby—"

Rochelle waved her hand, effectively cutting off the round of inappropriate mothering I was about to launch. "I just wanted to see you before Pearl hauls you into the basement."

She reached for me with her left hand, something completely formal in the gesture.

I unfolded my legs, sliding off the bed. I felt ungainly and awkward standing before the tiny oracle. So I kneeled instead.

Shock, replaced by a grim acceptance, flitted over Rochelle's face. Then she nodded.

I reached for my necklace, ready to pull it off. The last time Rochelle had tried to 'read' me, the necklace had been an issue for her. And that was even before it had absorbed the instruments of assassination.

"Leave it," Rochelle said, her voice thick with magic. "Please."

I dropped the chain, taking her offered hand. She placed her other hand over mine. Her oracle magic rose, shifting up my outstretched arm, questing around my head and shoulders. Tart apple filled my senses.

Silence stretched between us. The oracle's cold hands warmed in mine. I could feel the edge of her tattoos, the black butterfly fluttering underneath my fingers.

But I didn't flinch, didn't pull away.

I was all in.

I was a believer.

Rochelle sighed, but the sound was tinted with satisfaction. "You are a maker of chaos, Jade Godfrey. A disruption to ... what is possible."

"Not by choice."

She laughed quietly. "It's not necessarily a bad thing, is it? Though neither of us can control destiny.

Not even with set patterns or schedules. Not even with the careful application of cupcakes."

I looked up, checking to see if she was mocking me this time.

She wasn't.

Rochelle smiled, her gaze a wash of white-tinted power. She looked older than her twenty-three years, as though the magic that channeled through her was ancient, all-knowing. And maybe it was.

"What am I to do about it, then?" I asked. "About attracting chaos?"

Rochelle lifted her top hand from mine, brushing her forefinger and middle finger across the scar on my forehead. More magic writhed under her touch. "I don't quite know yet. But ... I have a plan. As I slotted in each piece, the future shifted. Sometimes slightly, sometimes significantly, though not always for the better. Let's free Scarlett from the boundary spell, just to make certain that doesn't alter anything. And then ... we can gear up."

"We?"

"Yes. You aren't storming the castle, as Jasmine says, alone."

"My father—"

"Jade." Rochelle squeezed my hand.

I shut my mouth.

"I need you," she whispered. "I need you, dowser, alchemist, wielder of the instruments of assassination. I don't think I can do it without you."

"Do what?" I whispered, though I already knew the answer.

"Save my daughter from the future waiting for her."

The confirmation was overwhelming. If I was a supposed 'chaos maker,' then I had no idea how to avoid my own destiny.

"We'll work through it together." Rochelle's tone was suddenly matter-of-fact as she dropped my hand. Then she abruptly turned toward the door.

"I am grateful, oracle," I said.

She paused, her hand on the doorknob, turning to look back at me.

"I would never bring harm to your family," I said. "Not if I could help it."

She nodded curtly. "I know, Jade. I think … it's not just something you do … I think … what I saw … starting two weeks ago is what happens if you die."

My stomach bottomed out, but Rochelle just pushed forward, determined—but trying to be rational, detached. "You have to let us help you," she said.

"I trust you, Rochelle. I wouldn't be here without you. Without you sending Blossom with the sketch. Twice. Without—"

"It's not just me you need to trust, Jade. Just … I know you want to protect everyone. Just please … let us, all of us, play our parts."

Then the oracle opened the door and exited into the hall before I could come up with an answer.

I stayed on my knees, feeling the magic shifting around in the house beneath me. I could pick out individual tastes. Lilac and shortbread. Toasted marshmallow. Spiced, dark chocolate …

Rochelle didn't know what she was asking, what the elves were capable of. She couldn't know. Otherwise, she'd never have asked me to allow anyone else to risk their lives …

Except when had that become my decision? Why was it my place to dictate what the other Adepts who called Vancouver home could or couldn't do?

Protecting those who were mine to protect wasn't the same as controlling them.

And with that uncomfortable thought, I stood and crossed to the bed to retrieve my mother's powered-up rapier.

So. The oracle thought she was seeing my death in her daughter's future. Well, it certainly wouldn't be stupid to give her a bit more time to figure out how to thwart that, would it?

Chapter Seven

My father was standing in the hall outside the map room, leaning against the wall across from the open door with his arms crossed and brow creased. He might simply have been frustrated. Or he might have been holding back a simmering fury that told of a mounting need to manifest his sword and start slashing through magic until there was nothing left.

I knew exactly how he felt.

Thankfully, though, neither of us was stupid enough to ignore the warnings and concerns of those who were much, much wiser regarding the casting of that magic.

"Hey, Dad," I said, a few steps away.

My father tore his gaze away from the empty doorway. It was an easy guess that he had a direct sight line to my mother from his position. "Jade."

His gaze fell to the rapier in my right hand. So much of my alchemy had been pumped into the delicate golden blade and the sapphires that decorated the intricate cross guard that it glowed.

"You've worked with your mother's weapon, then?"

"Yes."

"Then it will hold for as long as we need it to." My father pinned me with a fierce gaze. "I would like you to see the healer again before we confront the elves."

"You took a walk around the stadium?"

"It is well warded. More than expected. And I cannot sense the size of the force contained within."

"Alivia," I said. "They were joined by a ward builder. She brought Reggie a gem of power." I rubbed my scarred forehead. "As best I can remember. That's probably why Mory couldn't get Ed through their wards anymore."

My father grunted in acknowledgement, his gaze angling back through the doorway. "I can cut through it."

"Of course."

"But I cannot predict the consequences of doing so." He flexed the fingers of his right hand, most definitely recalling the feeling of wrapping them around the hilt of his sword. A frustrated growl edged his tone. "So we will do it your grandmother's way. For now."

"Actually, I think Rochelle is running everything behind the scenes."

My father's shoulders relaxed slightly. "Yes. Right. That makes much more sense. I am comfortable working with the oracle."

Yeah, Dad and Gran weren't the best of friends. I wasn't completely certain what Yazi held against my grandmother, though I certainly suspected it might have to do with her managing to hide me from him for twenty-three years. In Gran's defense, though, she hadn't known who exactly she was hiding me from at the time.

"They're almost ready for you," my father said.

I stepped into the open doorway. And then I stopped, because I needed just a moment to wrap my head around what I was seeing within the map room.

Gran and Angelica Talbot had painted a series of concentric circles radiating out from the column of magic that still contained my mother at the center of the room. They were approximately two feet apart, with a series of runes painted within them. Different symbols for each circle. Each with an opening on a diagonal with the door—creating a direct pathway to my mother from where I currently stood.

Angelica was crouched a few steps to my right with her back to me, adding more runes to the outermost circle nearest the wall. Her brown-sugar-shortbread magic tickled my senses as she dipped her brush into black paint, then carefully added a second leg to the end of what looked like a diamond set on the tip of a triangle without a base.

"Careful to not splash the baseboards, Angelica," my grandmother said, straightening from where she was carefully placing flat stones around the innermost circle, just feet away from the base of the column of magic that held my mother aloft.

"I know, Pearl," Angelica said testily. "I can feel the magic."

The room pulsed with power. Layer upon layer of magical energy roiled so strongly that I found it hard to believe the house was still anchored to its foundations. It should have been hovering two feet off the ground along with my mother, floating within the sea of magic.

Gran sniffed, brushing her hands together as she spotted me within the doorway. "Paint," she said with much disgust. Then she curled her lip into a sneer that was somehow also a smile. For me.

Angelica sat back on her heels, surveying her work. "Yes, you will have to replace the carpet, unfortunately. I wouldn't mind waiting until Stephan and Liam are back to check over the runes."

"The oracle has them tasked elsewhere—"

"I know that—"

"Jade is ready. We must proceed."

Angelica flinched, turning to spot me in the doorway. The dark-haired sorcerer straightened, her magic shifting around her. And for the briefest of moments, I felt as though she might attack me.

"Lots of magic here," I said carefully. "I couldn't even taste either of you from the hall. Or this...magnificent spell."

Angelica nodded, turning to survey her and Gran's work with some satisfaction. "It is a sight. Perhaps the most complex spell I've ever attempted. In this short a time, at least."

"Yes," Gran said. "Let's hope it—"

My mother sighed so softly that I barely heard her. The magic writhing across the ceiling and walls contracted into the center column that held her aloft. Then it all just dimmed. My mother dropped an inch closer to the floor, and as she did, the boundary spell tying Scarlett to the witches' grid slowly feathered back out across the map etched along the walls and twined over the ceiling.

The magic brightened as it resettled. I might have been imagining it, but the white tendrils of power appeared shorter and thinner than they had a moment before.

"About five minutes this time?" Angelica asked.

"Yes." My grandmother pursed her lips. "We need to cast. Now."

"It would be safer with Stephan and Liam."

"Perhaps. But we are spread thinly. And my daughter is dying."

A flush of weakness ran through my limbs. "What can I do?"

"Wait there, Jade." My grandmother stepped over to the opening to the innermost circle, gazing past me. "Yazi? We'll need Rochelle and Jasmine." She hesitated. "And Burgundy."

Angelica gave Gran a look. "Olive would be a better choice."

"Not if it goes badly."

"You need to fill me in, Gran," I said, trying to keep my voice calm and even.

"Yes, yes. I'm sorry. We've just been working on the fly. Angelica and I have devised a way for you to substitute the rapier for your mother. This should allow the boundary spell to naturally fade after it has consumed the magic within the weapon."

"Without also killing Mom."

"Exactly. I have every confidence we will make it work."

"It works in theory," the dark-haired sorcerer interjected. "But a casting this complicated usually takes months to perfect."

"Yes," my grandmother snapped. She almost snarled. "But we have Jade."

Angelica eyed me without comment.

Jasmine stepped into the doorway behind me. The magic in the room was so intense that I only sensed the golden-haired vampire a moment before she appeared.

"Ah, good, Jasmine," Gran said. "I believe the outer circle is yours to seal, yes?"

Jasmine studied the room for a long moment, then nodded.

"Shouldn't the junior witch seal the outer circle?" Angelica asked quietly. "She is the least…tested of us."

My grandmother threw her shoulders back imperiously. "My understanding is that when the original spell was cast, Jasmine triggered it from the four corners."

"Yes, but—"

Burgundy brushed past the golden-haired vampire, standing shoulder to shoulder with me. She was cupping her focal stone in both hands. Next to everyone and everything else in the room, her magic was dim, confined to an almost imperceptible blue hue around her fingers.

A tiny fissure of terror cracked open inside me. That magic, Burgundy's magic, could be snuffed out so easily...overwhelmed, swallowed, consumed by the spell waiting to be unleashed in the black paint etched across the floor.

"Gran?"

"You will leave this to me, Jade." My grandmother gave me a stern look. "Burgundy, I believe your spot is in the second inner circle. That is where your magic wants to rest. But you must look for yourself. You must choose. And once you have done so, when we begin to cast the spell, you will cross through the circle along the pathway, stepping nowhere else, and stand before the first opening."

Burgundy swallowed hard. Then she lifted her chin, cast her gaze around the room, and nodded.

My stomach churned uneasily.

The magic holding my mother aloft contracted again. Scarlett moaned softly, sounding pained. Then she slipped farther down toward the floor.

"We need to go now, Pearl," Angelica said tensely—and suddenly more than ready to throw her previous caution aside. She stepped toward the door, carrying the open can of paint while carefully avoiding the runes still drying underneath her feet.

Rochelle appeared behind me in the hall. She was holding three paintbrushes. She nodded as she met my gaze.

"Yes, yes," Gran said, also crossing to the closest opening between the circles. "We will proceed in a procession, entering the room one at a time. Jade first, crossing toward the innermost circle. Burgundy will follow, sealing Jade in. I will be third, sealing Burgundy."

"And I will seal you, Pearl," Angelica said. "Then the oracle behind me. With the vamp…Jasmine sealing the final circle."

"Each of us is powering a separate section?" Burgundy asked.

Gran nodded. "Bare feet for everyone but Jasmine, I believe."

The golden-haired vampire laughed quietly. "Yeah, magic doesn't work like that for me anymore."

"You will anchor us perfectly, Jasmine," my grandmother said. "Burgundy, you'll want to place your stone down first, before the opening. Then seal Jade within. I have already imbued the paint with some of my essence. But when you close the circle, you will add your own. Do you understand?"

Burgundy nodded. "Like I'm healing the circle."

A pleased smile flitted briefly over Gran's face, cracking her stern exterior. And through that crack, I saw that she was scared.

Underneath all her brusque orders, my grandmother was afraid. That realization was chilling.

The magic in the room shifted again. My mother cried out, a brief and utterly forlorn sound.

My father pushed off from the wall across the hall, where he'd been silently listening. "Now!" he barked.

"Jade," my grandmother said, shooing us all back out of the door to cluster together in the hall. Then she stepped to the side. "You first."

"But I... I don't know the spell."

Angelica plucked two of the new paintbrushes from Rochelle's hands, practically shoving them at Burgundy and Jasmine. "You don't need to. You're the lightning rod."

"I'll talk you through it, Jade." My grandmother touched me lightly on the shoulder. "After all the circles have been sealed, you will release your mother. And hopefully, the spell will accept the rapier as her replacement."

"Fingers crossed," Jasmine murmured, stripping the protective plastic off her paintbrush. "Otherwise it's going to be a hell of a backlash."

"Not helpful, Jasmine." My grandmother turned to my father. "I'm sorry to ask the mundane of you, guardian."

"Just ask, Pearl."

"Would you hold the paint can here by the door, so we may wet our brushes in turn?"

Angelica offered the open can of paint to my father. He grabbed the handle, stepping to one side of the door. I met his gaze.

He nodded. "Go get your mother."

"Okay."

Shoving all my worries aside, I stepped back into the map room. The magic twined across the walls and ceiling reacted to my entrance this time, tugging lightly at the rapier in my hand. I quickly crossed through the rune-scribed circles until I stood before my mother. Her toes were almost touching the floor now, making her shorter than me even though she was still suspended in the column of magic.

I glanced back as Burgundy stepped up behind me, carefully placing her focal stone between her bare feet. Her toenails were painted bright yellow. She was holding a paintbrush slick with black paint in her other hand. It glistened with magic.

The young witch crouched over her stone, hovering the paintbrush over one side of the narrow opening in the circle between us.

"Wait," I said, carefully setting the rapier down so that it didn't touch either circle or the painted runes. "Wait, wait."

"Jade," my grandmother snapped from the hall, "we don't have time for second-guessing."

Ignoring her, I hunkered down so I was eye to eye with Burgundy. She met my gaze. The whites of her eyes were wide and round. She was scared. But being brave about it.

"May I add some protections to your focal stone?" I asked.

Her eyes widened even further, but she nodded, palming her stone and holding it before her. She had carved a single rune into the stone's face, its edges smooth to suggest it was the result of repeated etchings.

"What does the rune stand for?" I asked quietly. I tried to block out all the other frantic energy in the room, and to simply focus on the witch crouched before me. "Strength?"

A faint blush bloomed across Burgundy's face. She had a dusting of freckles over her nose and cheeks that I'd never noticed before. "No. It's a ... passed down from my grandmother. A grounding. The symbol for earth combined with a healing rune."

"That's even better," I murmured, hovering my hand over the stone. "It suits your magic more than brute force or a simple amplification ... but let's just add a little something, shall we?"

Burgundy exhaled in a rush, as if she'd been holding her breath even while speaking. "All right."

Pressing my fingers to her inner wrist and the heel of my hand to the focal stone, I reached out for her magic. Feeling for what made her utterly unique, even among the powerful Adepts that waited impatiently in the hallway behind her. Her watermelon magic tickled my taste buds, sweet and thirst quenching.

"There you are," I murmured. I twined my own magic around Burgundy's, carefully coaxing the energy forward so as to not overwhelm the delicate watermelon power. "You're already a healer. That comes to you naturally."

"Yes," Burgundy said reverently. "I like ... helping."

I pulled more of the young witch's power forward, trying to not rush, trying to not just grab and shove. I channeled her sweet, delicate magic into the stone, cementing her inherent abilities with my own magic. Intensifying them. Then tying the stone back to her. A conduit. For her use only.

Burgundy gasped. "The stone is ... it's getting warm. And ... can you ... I can see it glowing. Just ... a glimmer, a halo ... is it ... is that my magic?"

I smiled at her. "Yes. That's you." I closed her fingers around the stone, outlining the rune carved through its center with my forefinger. "You'll be able to channel your healing through the stone now. It will ground your magic as it did before, but even more so. It will amplify that magic with focus and intention. But you must be careful not to drain yourself. And no one else will be able to take the stone from you, or use its power against you."

"But if I give it to someone?"

"The magic can pass from you to another by choice. That's always the way. Love is given freely. But it can't be taken by force."

"Yes. I understand."

I straightened, meeting my grandmother's disgruntled gaze over Burgundy's bowed head. The younger witch was staring at the stone in reverence. "Sheer power isn't always the way through a difficult situation."

My grandmother stiffened her shoulders. "Yet you casually hand an object of immense power to a young witch who has no idea what she now holds. What she now commands."

"I do understand," Burgundy said, gently but firmly.

I opened my mouth to back the young witch up, to explain why I'd felt an instinctual need to protect her from the spell we were all about to cast. But my grandmother raised her hand to silence me.

"Fine, Jade. I'd like to save my daughter if you're done making speeches."

My tone grew low. Dark edged. "It wasn't much of a speech, Gran. And we won't make it through any of this by treating anyone as expendable." I turned my back on my grandmother before she could respond. "Put the stone in your pocket, please, Burgundy."

"Under your foot or in your opposite hand while you seal the circle," my grandmother corrected. "Against skin is a better choice."

I didn't bother to counter that. My grandmother was the senior witch in the room, after all.

Magic shifted behind me as Burgundy applied her paintbrush to the carpet and closed the circle, sealing me in with my mother and the column of power.

A moment later, more energy bloomed, twisting through the next circle, then feeding back through mine, as Gran stepped forward and sealed the younger witch into the spell.

I kept my gaze on my mother's face. She looked serene, but I could see a single track of tears across each of her pale cheeks.

Another circle was sealed, adding the taste of brown-sugar shortbread to the intricate spell circling around me.

"Get ready, Jade," Gran whispered behind me. "It must be an equal exchange. Your mother for the rapier."

Tart apple tickled my senses as Rochelle sealed her circle. The carpeted floor began humming under my bare feet. At the edges of my peripheral vision, the runes were glowing a deep sea-blue. Then they began to vibrate.

Angelica was murmuring something, needing to vocalize the spell that the witches and the oracle could simply channel through themselves.

I raised the rapier before me in my right hand, holding the blade just under the cross guard, point down.

Jasmine sealed the final circle. Sweet peppermint topped all the other tastes filling my senses. A gentle breeze of energy twisted through each of the circles, swirling all the magic that had been called forth. Peppermint combined with apple, with shortbread, with lilac, and with watermelon into one gigantic bite. Then all those tastes mellowed into a single mouthful of power.

Power primed and waiting.

For me.

"Hey, Mom," I whispered, lifting my left hand so it was even with my right. I was ready to grab my mother and to shove the rapier into the column of magic at the same time. But...I hesitated. The spell was so intricate, so delicate. Just shoving my hand and the sword into the center of it seemed violent.

"I'm the lightning rod," I murmured. Angelica had called me that. But it wasn't quite right. That wasn't how my magic worked. It was more like I was—

Magic contracted around me. But it was the original boundary spell, not the one we were attempting to cast. My mother's eyes snapped open, her face etched with silent agony as the column of power dimmed again.

"Now, Jade!" my grandmother shouted. "Reach into the magic with the sword. Free your mother. You can do this, dowser."

Dowser. Alchemist.

I wasn't a lightning rod at all.

I was the storm.

I gathered all the magic circling around and thrumming under my feet. All the magic in the runes painted across the floor. All that combined power, carefully keeping it separated from the spell holding my mother hostage.

I channeled that energy up through my body, feeding it through into the rapier already imbued with dragon magic and fortified with my alchemy. Then I took all of that energy, the entire sum of the spell painstakingly painted across the floor by Gran and Angelica, and I channeled it into the sword.

Burgundy slumped to the floor behind me.

Angelica let out a sharp cry.

I slipped both my hands and the rapier into the column of magic, allowing the power of the boundary spell to flow around me and the weapon. I closed my empty hand around my mother's upper arm.

She opened her eyes.

And smiled.

"Hello, my Jade."

"Hi, Mom."

I gently tugged my mother from the column of magic. She slumped against me, unable to hold her own weight. But that was okay. I was strong enough to hold her for as long as she needed.

Then slowly, I loosened my grasp on the rapier. I let the energy of the column, of the boundary spell, lick along its edges. I let it sip at the blade's magic. Then I allowed it to consume it.

I started to withdraw my hand. The boundary magic resisted, attempting to hold onto me and all my power as well.

My mother wrapped her hand around my forearm, her grip weak as she tried to add her strength to mine.

I tugged my hand free, afraid to breathe as I waited to see if the grid would accept or reject the rapier. Holding my mother upright, I waited to see if the spell would try to take her back—or whether its energy would lash out against her.

I was ready to step forward myself, to take her place in the central column, even though I knew I shouldn't.

The magic held.

"Thank you, my darling girl," my mother murmured.

Then, preceded by a teeth-aching wash of his guardian magic, my father was striding through the room despite my grandmother's weak protests. He lifted my mother, cradling her in his arms and gazing at her with a desperate fierceness. "Don't you do that again."

My mother laughed weakly. "I would do much, much more if needed. You know that. Plus, I knew our daughter would come."

Yazi grumbled under his breath as he swiftly turned toward the door with my mother in his arms. "Healer!" he bellowed.

Qiuniu was already standing in the doorway. "I'm here, warrior."

"A boon, if you please."

The healer waved his hand as if brushing something away. "There are no favors between us, Yazi. I'm here by choice." He reached for my mother, meeting my gaze over my father's shoulder. "I'll be back for the others." Then he carried Scarlett from the room with my father on his heels.

I cast my gaze around the map room. The magic of the column held, writhing through the walls and criss-crossing the ceiling. But all the energy that I'd felt in the circles and the runes had faded. The black paint remained, but the spell was dormant, evaporated.

No … consumed. Channeled by me into the rapier.

Burgundy was curled up where she'd collapsed onto the carpet. She was cupping her focal stone in both hands and murmuring as if talking to it. And maybe she was. Who was I to judge?

The junior witch smiled at me softly when I caught her eye.

Gran was sitting cross-legged behind the younger witch. She looked exhausted, but she held my gaze steadily. "A magnificent casting, Jade."

Angelica was kneeling behind my grandmother, looking at me as if I were … well, some kind of dreadful monster. "You … you pulled all the magic from the spell …"

"What did you think she was going to do, sorcerer?" my grandmother snapped. "She's an alchemist. How else was the weapon to take Scarlett's place?"

Angelica shut her mouth, then smoothed her expression. "The barrier won't hold for long now. I'd estimate we have two days at the most."

"But it won't bounce back," Jasmine said. The golden-haired vampire was leaning against the wall next to the door. Her eyes were closed. "It won't consume Scarlett."

"No. It won't," Gran said smugly. "It should simply fade. Or we can turn it off. Jade can easily retrieve or replace the weapon now."

Ah, there it was. The other shoe dropping.

Somehow, my grandmother had gotten her way after all. The witches' grid had been weaponized, albeit accidentally—but still courtesy of me. Kandy would be pissed. Thankfully, I didn't feel tied to the grid in the same way I had been when it was first created, but Gran now thought that I could control it. Fuel it.

Rochelle, who'd been standing quietly and listening to us chatter, suddenly gasped. Her eyes glowed with a bright, searing light.

"Here we go," Jasmine murmured. "Time to see which way magic wills us. Again."

"I see...I see..." Rochelle murmured, reaching out with both hands. "Yes. I see." The oracle smiled, deeply satisfied. "Gather the misfits."

Jasmine snorted. "They're on their way."

"What?" I asked. "The misfits? Like who? Mory? Ben? The twins? That...that can't be right."

Beau strode into the room, carrying Rochelle's army-green satchel. Angelica's flinch let me know just how quickly the shifter was moving. He was also carrying a sketchbook. But before he could pick Rochelle up or hand over her drawing supplies, the white of the oracle's magic faded from her eyes.

She gazed at her husband, reaching up and touching his cheek adoringly. "It's going to be okay, Beau."

He grunted noncommittally, but Rochelle just smiled and laid her hand on his arm, allowing him to lead her from the room.

No one had answered my question. "What misfits?" I asked again, a bit more caustically.

Jasmine smiled tightly. "All of us, Jade. It's going to take all of us. You know there was no chance of it being any other way."

Gran sighed, reaching for me. I stepped by Burgundy and helped Pearl to her feet. She patted my shoulder as she stood. "It's not always about you, Jade." Then she turned away. "Come, Angelica. I believe we deserve some tea."

Angelica nodded, rising, then following my grandmother into the hall. I listened to the satisfied murmur of their conversation as they traversed the hallway and mounted the stairs.

Jasmine met my eye, smiling sneeringly. "Piece of work, your gran. But believe me, she doesn't even hold a candle to my mother in the nastiness department."

"It isn't ever all about me," I said belligerently.

Jasmine laughed. "Of course not. But it shut you up, didn't it?" She turned her head slightly, listening to something I couldn't hear. "Benjamin just arrived. Unfortunately, he brought his mother, speaking of pieces of work. I think Teresa Garrick might eat souls for breakfast."

Before I could figure out how to respond, Burgundy reached over and touched the back of my hand lightly. "I'll stay here, Jade. And keep an eye on the map."

"Are you sure?"

"Yes." She dropped her gaze to her focal stone, holding it reverently before her. "Thank you for this gift."

I touched the smooth stone lightly. It felt … pleased. Contented. "Thank you, Burgundy. For being here when I couldn't be. For doing what I can't."

"We all have different talents."

"Yes. Neither more important than the other."

The junior witch grinned at me.

I tried to smile back, but my face felt tight, so I didn't force it any further. Meeting Jasmine's gaze with a nod, I strode past the golden-haired vampire, exiting into the hall.

"I'll stay," Jasmine said to Burgundy behind me. "Go with Jade. You might never get another chance to learn from the most powerful healer in the world."

"But … you said Benjamin was here … don't you need … um …"

"Just go, witch," Jasmine said. "Let the rest of us sort ourselves out."

Coming from another vampire, addressing Burgundy as 'witch' instead of using her name might have sounded derogatory, but I could hear the smile in Jasmine's tone. And I could imagine the answering grin on the so-called witch's face.

Eager to check on my mother, I jogged up the stairs, leaving the rest of the overheard conversation behind me.

Chapter Eight

Following the taste of the healer's and my father's magic, I slipped into the guest bedroom where I had found and fueled the rapier. My mother, looking more petite than she had ever appeared to me before, was lying in the center of the queen-sized bed with a guardian standing to either side. Qiuniu hovered his hand over Scarlett's forehead, but her indigo-blue gaze was glued to my father on her right. Yazi reached down to touch her hand, but Qiuniu warned him off with a quiet murmur. They were speaking Mandarin, or maybe Cantonese, in hushed tones. I really had to figure out the difference. And, like, learn the language. Because it was becoming apparent that the guardians liked to use it to exclude the rest of us from their discussions.

Warner spoke fluent Cantonese. He'd be able to translate, to teach me. Then I …

A wave of grief gripped me, freezing me in place as I tried to fight it and appear unaffected at the same time.

"Jade," Gran said, calling my attention to my left. Her magic was so muted that I hadn't tasted her lilac under the chocolate and coffee permeating the bedroom. She was holding the neatly folded blue-gray silk duvet in her arms. It had likely been torn from the bed by my father when he'd carried my mother in. "You will not be going running off now that Scarlett has been removed from the grid."

I opened my mouth to protest, but Gran decided I needed a spanking on top of orders.

"You running amok in the city is what got us to this point. This impasse."

All of my anger, all my fear, rose. I wanted to let loose, to defend my choices and decisions. But Burgundy stepped into the room before I could speak, so I curbed my ire, knowing I was on edge for all the wrong reasons. Knowing that the same was true for Gran.

"Healer. May I assist you?" Burgundy asked formally.

My grandmother looked aghast. She stepped forward as if to admonish the young witch, likely over some perceived breach of protocol. But Qiuniu simply nodded and waved Burgundy forward.

My grandmother snapped her mouth closed.

The junior witch stepped to the opposite side of the bed from the healer, bobbing her head to my father shyly. The warrior of the guardians stepped aside for her, begrudgingly joining me at the foot of the bed.

"Hold your hand over Scarlett's chest," Qiuniu prompted softly. Burgundy did so. "Can you feel her magic?"

The witch tilted her head to one side, then shook it.

"Try with your focal stone."

Burgundy gently placed her stone on my mother's upper chest, resting her fingers on it. "I see," she murmured. "So … drained."

"Yes," the healer said. "And your instinct is to try to fill that reservoir, yes?"

Burgundy nodded eagerly. "Yes. Shall I?"

"No. When someone is this depleted, their magic might not be receptive. And you might drain your own resources attempting to ..." He paused, searching for the correct term. "Attempting to fill a leaky bucket. Do you understand?"

"I should test the connection first."

"Yes."

"And then?"

Qiuniu gazed at Burgundy intently. "You must never give more than you have to give. It is far better to heal slowly and efficiently than to harm or even kill yourself in order to heal swiftly."

My mother shivered.

Gran bustled forward, shoving herself into the lesson. "Might I cover my daughter now, healer? So she doesn't freeze to death while you chat?"

"Of course, Pearl." The healer stepped to the side, meeting my father's gaze with a wry twist of his lips.

Gran clucked her tongue at Burgundy, and the younger witch helped her spread the silk duvet over my mother. Apparently, somewhere between seeing him heal me on the beach in Tofino, then waking to find that Vancouver had gone to hell and almost killed her daughter in the process, Gran had lost her shine for the healer.

Then Qiuniu reached his hands toward me, and I had to refrain from snapping at him myself. I'd just heard him tell Burgundy that they couldn't simply pump magic into my mother, but I didn't want to divide his attention. And I didn't even feel like I needed healing.

Or maybe it was that I didn't think I deserved healing.

I removed my necklace so it wouldn't impede the healer's abilities, laying it on the bureau and ignoring the instruments' protest over being set aside. Then I stepped forward, accepting the healer's hands and the magic he offered. A whisper of music swelled around us, but the healer didn't lean any closer or kiss me. Possibly because all three of my parental figures were currently in the room.

Qiuniu shifted my left hand so that he was holding both my hands in his right palm. With his left hand, he reached up to brush his thumb across the scar on my forehead. I felt it smooth under his touch—even as his utterly affronted frown informed me that it hadn't completely faded. Then he gave me a look informing me in no uncertain terms that I was the one to blame for that.

And since it was my knife that had done the damage, it kind of was.

"Thank you," I murmured. Then I offered the healer a shallow bow that transformed his frown into a curl of a smile.

"I will see to your mother, dowser. And then your grandmother ... if Pearl will allow ..."

My grandmother harrumphed from behind him, letting us know that she was cataloging everything being said even though her attention was glued to my mother.

I retrieved my necklace, twining the chain three times around my neck so that it lay within the collar of my armor. Once again, I ignored the mutter of indignation that came from the instruments.

"I haven't heard from the other guardians, and would like to check in on them myself," the healer said. "Will you escort me to the portal?"

"Not Jade," Gran said. "Jasmine or Benjamin can see you to the bakery."

I twisted my lips wryly. "I'm not allowed out of the house."

My father chuckled under his breath.

"Well," the healer murmured. "If you were mine to protect, I wouldn't let you out of my sight either." He winked at me.

Gran cleared her throat. And then, I put two and two together and figured out what Gran held against Qiuniu.

Warner.

I smiled at the thought. Even though, if examined too closely, Gran's affection for Warner and her dislike of the healer's propensity to flirt could also be read as her distrust of my ability to remain focused and faithful. Of course, I knew that dragons weren't a prolific species, and the healer's flirting had more to do with me being female and half-dragon. I was already fairly certain he and Haoxin, the two guardians closest in age, had an ongoing thing.

"Yazi …" my mother whispered, struggling to keep her eyes open. "Jade …"

My father stepped around to my mother's side. "We're both here. You can sleep now." He glanced up at the healer, who nodded.

My grandmother reached for me, and I accepted the arm she offered and the comfort meant to accompany it.

"We won't go anywhere before you wake." My father glanced my way pointedly.

I gave him a look, somewhat pissy over being blackmailed while standing at my mother's sickbed.

He flashed an unrepentant grin at me in response.

Yeah, yeah. I wasn't going anywhere.

Yet.

"Get your stones please, Burgundy," the healer murmured. "I'll help you align them."

Burgundy nodded, already hustling toward the door before the healer had completed his request. I suspected the stones in question meant the box of healing charms I'd seen her use on Gran.

"Your tea must be getting cold, Gran," I said. "Do you want me to bring a cup up for you?"

My grandmother sighed wearily, patting my arm. "No. There are many things to discuss, and your mother is in capable hands." But as she spoke, she sounded as though she might have been trying to convince herself.

I had no doubt as to the healer's abilities—and not just because I was fairly certain I'd been mortally wounded when he'd healed me in the nexus. But then, I hadn't spent the last two weeks having my magic drained from me, fueling a massive magical working that encased an entire city.

The thought of other loved ones fueling another magical working—namely, the dimensional gateway—surfaced in the forefront of my mind again. And as it did, it made me keenly regret all my promises to wait. To listen to reason.

"Jade," the healer said with a sigh. "It would be better if you stepped out."

"What?" I cried.

"You're throwing magic around, my girl," Yazi said, his gaze on my mother. "As you do when you get upset. Disruptive magic."

"Yeah, well... so do you!"

My father gave me a look.

The healer laughed quietly. "It's the instruments, I believe."

Well, that quelled my pissiness instantly. The instruments had impeded Qiuniu from healing me. "Oh. Okay."

I stepped into the hall, brushing past Burgundy returning with her wooden box. Gran followed me out.

With nothing else to do, I eventually found myself pacing the main-floor living room and waiting on the oracle. Mory had informed me that Rochelle needed to refine her sketches before meeting with me. And, of course, the fact that the oracle needed to do so wasn't intimidating and annoying at the same time. Not at all.

Everything apparently hinged on the delicate point of what Rochelle was seeing. So I was all armored up but not allowed to leave the house. And worse, Mory was my assigned babysitter.

The necromancer was currently curled up in one of the two antique love seats that bookended the gray-and-white marble surround of the living room's retrofitted gas fireplace. She was napping. With Ed on her stomach.

As he'd talked of earlier, Qiuniu had headed to the bakery. He was going to attempt to contact the treasure keeper through the portal in the basement and see if he was needed elsewhere. As Gran had ordained, Jasmine and Benjamin Garrick were accompanying him, because apparently even one of the nine guardians of the world wasn't allowed to wander Vancouver alone.

I had returned to a totalitarian regime, evidently. Except I still wasn't certain who I was supposed to be bowing down to.

"You know that Jasmine and Benjamin are watching out for each other," Mory murmured, her eyes still closed. "The healer just didn't know where the bakery was."

"Was I talking out loud again?"

"Yeah."

"Damn it."

"You're freaking out. That's cool. We're all just in survivor mode already." Mory's eyes opened and she pinned me with her dark gaze, effectively chastising me without even lifting her head. "Since we lost you. Since we almost lost Pearl and Scarlett."

I threw myself down on the second loveseat, facing the curtained front windows. I had laid my katana across the coffee table, even though the spindly legs and antique oak top—matching the arms of the couches—looked too delicate to hold the weight of a folded steel blade that teemed with magic. All the power drained from Sienna, from all the Adepts she'd murdered, and from Shailaja…the rabid koala. That was way too heavy a burden to be resting…waiting…endlessly waiting in my grandmother's living room.

"Wow, you've got a lot of shit rolling around in your head, Jade."

I snorted, leaning forward to run my fingers along the twenty-four-inch blade, stirring the magic contained within it. The dragon slayer. Though the built-in sheath on the back of my new leather armor was invisible, it had felt weird wearing the weapon while sitting.

"I know," I finally said. "I mean, about Jasmine and Benjamin, and you all being in survivor mode. I'm just worried about who else you might lose the longer I hang around doing nothing."

"You've been pretty active for a person doing nothing."

"Don't try to make me feel better, Mory."

"Why?" she asked mockingly. "Because you're a bad person now? Evil Jade?"

I narrowed my eyes at her.

She looked utterly nonplused. "Visions take time. You don't want to be going in blind, Jade." She softened her tone. "That's the fastest way to get the rest of us hurt, yes?"

I clenched my teeth but didn't answer. I was so all over the place emotionally. And yeah, rationally, I knew I'd been severely mentally traumatized, then badly physically injured. But I just ...

I just wanted it done. All of it. No matter how childish it was, I just wanted to be moving, moving through it, past it.

Magic shifted, announcing the oracle's approach along the upper hall and down the stairs. I looked up at the doorway a moment before Rochelle appeared. Beau loomed behind her.

The petite, white-haired oracle smiled at me wearily. She was holding three sketchbooks. The edges of each were smudged to a solid black.

"When was the last time you slept? Properly?" The question was out of my mouth before I could hear my own hypocrisy. I wanted desperately to charge forward—but apparently, everyone else should be getting a solid eight hours of sleep every night.

"Certainly you aren't suggesting I can't look after my own mate, dowser?" Beau growled from the doorway.

I lounged against the arm of the loveseat, resting one foot on the coffee table and slinging my left arm across the back of the couch. As if I didn't have a care in the world.

The green of his shapeshifter magic edged Beau's eyes.

I grinned, completely egging the werecat on.

Rochelle sighed.

Mory snorted.

"A battle is coming," Rochelle said, stepping forward and angling her body so she could speak to Beau and me. "A battle like I've never seen before, not even with the demons on the beach." She paused, resting her light-gray gaze on me. She wasn't wearing her sunglasses, which was a rarity. Even inside.

I straightened, nodding to indicate I understood. I hadn't even known her then, but Rochelle had seen a vision of the final battle with Sienna. The mass demon summoning in Tofino.

"We need to focus on that battle." The oracle glanced back at Beau. "Not on needling each other."

"You're not going into any battle," he growled. But the sound was more desperate than angry.

Rochelle reached up, caressing his face.

Mory looked away at the same time I did. We met each other's gaze, exchanging awkward looks.

"Okay," Rochelle whispered.

"Okay?" Beau sounded incredulous, as if they'd been having the same argument for days and he'd expected to never win.

"Yes, okay. But you need to give me time to explain everything—"

Beau swept his pregnant wife into what looked like a soul-searing kiss, crushing the sketchbooks between them.

Yeah, both Mory and I peeked.

The shifter broke the embrace, smoothing Rochelle's hair behind her ears. He placed a delicate kiss on her forehead, then strode off toward the dining room and kitchen with his cellphone in hand.

Rochelle turned toward us, crossing to the antique chair upholstered with delicate pink flowers nearest the doorway. As she sat, she set the three sketchbooks at the end of the coffee table, then looked over at Mory. "We're going to need to gather everyone."

"Everyone?" Mory echoed, reaching for the satchel she'd propped against the leg of the love seat. "Including the twins?"

Rochelle paused, contemplating the question and looking beyond Mory for a moment. The white of her magic rolled across her eyes. "No...but we need Liam first, because he needs to rejoin his parents and the necromancers at the stadium. Jade's already given Burgundy what she needed—"

"What's this all about?" I asked, not actually expecting an answer. I was fairly certain the general of the army of misfits had just walked into the room.

Still, I didn't have a problem being a soldier.

Well, not much of a problem.

Rochelle awkwardly grabbed the arms of the antique chair and shifted it closer to the coffee table so that she could more easily reach her sketchbooks. I resisted the urge to lunge forward and help her get settled. But it was a near thing.

Perched on the edge of the chair, Rochelle leaned over her rounded belly and tapped her sketchbooks, as if indicating that all my answers lay within those pages.

And seriously—no matter how foolhardy my grandmother might accuse me of being, playing a game of show-and-tell with the oracle was one thing I would never look forward to.

"After Liam, Benjamin Garrick," Rochelle said to Mory. "Then Jasmine. You last."

"Me?"

"Yeah." Rochelle cleared her throat. "We're going to need you, Mory. Getting Scarlett out of the grid didn't change that part."

Mory exhaled sharply. "Okay. Okay." She looked over at me, clutching Ed to her chest. "I can do it, Jade."

I raised my hands in surrender. "I'm not going to fight over something I don't know anything about."

The necromancer jutted out her chin, back in belligerent pixie mode. "But you are going to try to stop me."

I glanced over at Rochelle, recalling our conversation in the bedroom. Her left hand was resting on top of the sketchbooks. On top of the destiny she'd seen. The destiny she needed my help to thwart. "I will do my best to follow the oracle's directives."

"Fine," Mory said, tucking Ed into her bag. "Good."

"But …" I hardened my tone, keeping my gaze on Rochelle. "I'm not sacrificing anyone."

Rochelle smiled tightly. "No matter what Angelica was implying, Pearl placed Burgundy in the strongest position she could. Directly between you and her. Having the junior witch seal your circle was barely necessary. Because your magic doesn't work like that, right?"

She meant that I naturally contained my dowsing and alchemy abilities. I didn't pull energy from the earth like a witch did. And as such, I didn't need the same boundary precautions. "Right."

"And if Burgundy had gotten into trouble on her own, while you were doing your thing and getting Scarlett free, she had Pearl right next to her. Pearl's magic sealing her circle."

Sometimes I was such an idiot. A blind fool.

"I would never ask you to do anything you weren't capable of doing, Jade," Rochelle said softly. "Because I see … you. I see your actions, your choices."

"Okay."

"But …"

Ah, crap. With the oracle, there was always a freaking 'but.' "But?"

Rochelle eyed me for a moment. "We'll talk about that part later."

Lovely.

Delightful.

This was going to be an ongoing conversation, because apparently it was something I could handle only in bite-sized pieces.

"Give us ten minutes. Then bring Liam in," Rochelle said, speaking to Mory again. "Please."

Mory nodded, slung her bag across her chest, and hustled out of the living room.

"So," I said. "Alone at last." Trying to be playful and failing miserably.

Rochelle chuckled quietly. Which was kind of her.

"Three sketchbooks," I said. "Three total, or just three for me?"

"Three for you."

"Jesus."

"Yeah, I'm going to need a vacation."

"We'll hawk some of Pulou's gold. It's the least he can do."

The smile slid from Rochelle's face. "I have enough gold, Jade."

I shifted uncomfortably. And for another truly painful moment, I desperately missed Kandy and Kett and Warner. My true companions. My soul mates. They understood me. Understood my need to keep the darkness at bay with sarcasm and humor.

Rochelle took the topmost sketchbook off the pile, set it on the coffee table, and slid it toward me as far as she could without getting up. I pulled it the rest of the way, setting it before me. But I didn't open it.

"I debated showing you this one," Rochelle said. "Because I'm not certain it's wholly relevant to the immediate situation."

"Okay."

"But I understand that Beau gave you a preview already, and I didn't want you to think I was hiding anything. I'd ... I'd like you to just flip through it quickly. To get an impression, but not dwell on anything."

"Because I can't change it?"

Rochelle shook her head. "I'm not certain. It's set about nine years from now."

"That's a long way to see."

"Yes. With many, many things in between now and then."

"But you believe that what occurs in these pages, in this vision, is tied back to the elves?"

"I believe so. But not because I see the elves, not nine years from now. Because of how the vision came to me. And the timing."

I waited for the oracle to elaborate.

She twisted her lips wryly. "A tale for another day? I haven't had time to sort it all out myself."

"Okay." I took a deep breath, reaching to flip open the first page of the sketchbook.

Mory jogged back into the room, sliding through the doorway and past Rochelle on the hardwood floor in her hand-knit striped socks. "I almost forgot," she cried, thrusting her hand toward me.

She was holding a chocolate bar. A dark-chocolate bar with pistachios and dried cranberries, to be exact. From the ever-delectable, soul-fueling Chocolate Arts, to be even more exact.

"Oh my God," I whispered reverently, gently prying it from Mory's grasp. "Where have you been, my beauty?" I was practically cooing.

"In my bag," Mory said. "I picked it up for you this morning. I have another one." She looked at Rochelle. "In case things get really bad."

The oracle stifled a chuckle.

The misfits were totally laughing at me. But, as I carefully slipped the paper wrapper off the bar and lifted the clear sticker sealing the flap, I didn't care one bit.

Then the full implication of Mory's words actually sank in. "Wait!" I cried. "You were holding out on me?"

Mory laughed—apparently unaware that I was not freaking joking. Then she spun away, dashing back out of the room.

I let her go without protest, allowing myself to nibble on a single row of the bar—which smelled insanely good—while opening Rochelle's sketchbook.

A dreadful future etched in charcoal on paper flashed before my eyes. It unfolded picture by picture as I flipped the pages and savored the treat Mory had thoughtfully bought for me.

A young girl with a whip.

A demon.

A city destroyed.

"This is what we'll be unmaking?" I asked, glancing over at Rochelle because I couldn't bear to continue to look at the future contained in the sketchbook. All the sketches showed the girl—a younger, female version of Beau—abandoned in a derelict cityscape with only a demon at her side.

The oracle toyed with her wedding ring, looking resolutely away from me. And the sketchbook. But she nodded. "Yes."

"All right." I closed the sketchbook, hiding that future from my sight—but not from the forefront of my mind. I had no doubt that the images would haunt me ever after. Assuming I survived the following nine years. "Show me your plan."

Rochelle shifted to the love seat, perching beside me to flip through the second sketchbook—and revealing pages upon pages of elves and swords and bloody mayhem. I saw scenes with my father and me, swords flashing. I saw the gateway practically vomiting forth dozens of elves at a time.

Then more sketches of me, looking...well, half-dead, and tearing through the magic I'd helped erect. Destroying the gateway. And apparently, as it was all laid out for me in black and white and accompanied by a helpful narration from the oracle, that gateway was going to collapse and swallow us all.

Yeah, not just me or my father.

The entire city.

Destroyed.

Consumed by a magical backlash. Because of me. My choice. My decision.

My future.

My destiny?

Despite my resolve, I practically inhaled the rest of the bar, smothering my terror in smooth chocolate, candied nuts, and sweet-and-sour fruit.

"Okay, Jade?" Rochelle asked, laying her hand gently on my forearm.

I carefully folded the now-empty plastic wrapper, ignoring my almost desperate desire to rip it open and lick off any tiny slivers of chocolate still stuck to it. "I assume you've figured out a way to …" I waved my hand over the sketchbook.

"I've figured out a beginning. We're still taking steps, so…I can't tell you if it works. I can't tell you if we've thwarted what's going to happen until we have thwarted it. Until I see a different future."

"Or until I kill you. Along with the rest of the city."

Rochelle sighed softly. "Not me." She lifted her hand from my arm, pressing her palm lightly against her rounded belly.

Right. The girl and the demon. Rochelle would survive the destruction. For long enough to give birth, at least.

The oracle shook her head. "So…the only thing I can tell you for certain is that you can't be the one to close the gate. But it must be closed. It has to be closed. And…logically, that has to happen after the elves have retreated back through it. So they can't just go into hiding until they get an opportunity to reopen the gate."

I stared at her in horror. "You want me to talk the elves into retreating?"

"They don't seem like big talkers."

"They aren't." Unbidden, a fissure of pain for the lovely elf who'd washed away in the rain opened up in my chest. Mira. Mira didn't mind trying to communicate. "Mira wanted to go home," I murmured. "After I killed her brother."

"The illusionist?"

"Yes."

"So…what about the others? What if they had the option?"

A ping of hope bloomed within the pain that I seemed to be constantly recalling, constantly holding, constantly fighting through.

Rochelle was watching me closely. This was part of it, part of her magic, part of constructing the plan. She needed me to move in some specific way, but neither of us knew what direction that was yet.

Then I remembered the gemstone that had been embedded in my forehead.

"Even if they did want to go home, Reggie controls them," I said.

"All of them, all the time?"

"Yeah. She's annoyingly powerful."

"She'd have to be. To take you down, dowser." Rochelle touched my arm again, lightly. "But she never really had you, not completely. Did she?"

"I don't know. She had a damn good hold."

"I couldn't see you. It terrified me. But then Mory and Liam got Ed through the elves' wards, and that started giving me glimpses." She tapped the sketchbook I'd just been paging through. The one in which I destroyed everything and everyone. "And I knew ... I saw your knife and Blossom. I knew there was going to be a moment where ..." Rochelle's steady resolve cracked infinitesimally, but she shored it back up. "I knew there was going to be a moment when you would need me. Need us."

"When I tore through the wards."

"Yes. You did that, Jade. And then the floodgates opened, and I saw." She laid her hand over the third notebook. "Possibilities."

"But this ..." I touched the second notebook. "It's not destiny?"

"It might be," Rochelle murmured. "But ... I've been seeing other things, other people, not contained in that set of visions. Things and people around the edges of that future." She looked over at me. "And you're good with an edge, aren't you, Jade?"

"I can do a lot with an edge," I said. And for the first time in a while, I heard my own resolve. "Point me in the right direction, oracle. If I'm going to die either way, if it's a fight I can't win, I might as well go up against destiny."

"Yeah. I thought you'd say that. But I need you to do a few things first."

"Are you going to set me trials? Am I to prove my worthiness?"

Rochelle offered me a tiny hint of a smile. "I need you to wield your alchemy. To arm your misfits, as you call them."

"Kandy calls them that," I murmured. "And I can't just wave my hand over any object—"

"I've sorted that part out."

Liam Talbot stepped into the open doorway, unbuttoning his dark-navy wool coat. I'd been so focused on the conversation that I hadn't heard the dark-haired sorcerer arrive, or even tasted his magic.

"Jade," he said, slinging his coat over the back of the antique chair Rochelle had abandoned. His gun was holstered at his hip, teeming with his creamy peanut-butter magic. "Good to see you so ..." He grinned, sweeping me head to toe with a warm, brown-eyed gaze. "So primed."

I'd never seen him look so relaxed. Apparently, the end of the world appealed to him. "Liam."

Nodding toward Rochelle, the dark-haired sorcerer's gaze fell to the sketchbooks on the coffee table as he pushed up the sleeves of his sweater, revealing muscled, naturally tanned skin. "Oracle."

"Sorcerer. Did you bring your badge?"

"Yes. Mory said you'd asked." He pulled his Vancouver Police Department badge out of the back pocket of his dark-wash jeans. "Do you need me officially on duty? I, uh, took a leave of absence, but I can reverse it fairly easily."

I narrowed my eyes at him. Liam's hesitation and the casual suggestion that he could reverse his so-called leave easily sounded a lot like he'd tossed some spells around at the police department.

"I'm not sure it needs to be official." Rochelle reached for and opened the third sketchbook, flipping through the charcoal sketches so quickly that they were a blur of dark gray. "I haven't had the time to refine many of these, but I picked what I thought were the most important." She paused near the back third of the book, angling it toward me.

The sketch she'd selected showed Liam's badge, but held in a decidedly female-looking hand.

"Is this the first of my tasks, oracle?" I asked, just a little caustically. I wasn't certain how I felt about creating magical objects on demand.

Instead of answering, Rochelle flipped back to a set of earlier pages in the sketchbook. Those sketches depicted less-refined details of the badge, then showed Liam standing by a concrete wall, or maybe the corner of a building—and wearing that badge.

I glanced over at the sorcerer. He had sat and was now leaning forward in the chair, his eyes glued to the sketches. As far as I could tell in black and white, he was wearing the same clothing now as he was in Rochelle's vision.

"What do you want me to add to the badge?"

"Is there enough magic in it? For you to work with?"

There was. I could taste the residual—a hint of Liam's peanut-butter power. "Enough."

"Persuasion."

"Excuse me?"

"Persuasion," Rochelle repeated calmly.

Liam looked up at me, his dark eyes rounded with wonder.

"You want me to add a layer of persuasion to a sorcerer's badge?"

"Yes."

"A sorcerer who already wields a dangerous weapon?"

"Hey," Liam interjected.

"Yes."

"You want me to make it possible for him to … persuade people to do whatever he wants?" I jutted my finger at the image of Liam on the table before me. "This is somewhere in the city, right?"

"Yes. By the stadium."

"So who will the sorcerer be persuading? Non-magicals, right?"

"Possibly. Or possibly elves. I'm not asking that you give Liam the ability to brainwash people. Simply to … imbue them with a feeling of well-being. Of easy-going, good-natured compliance."

Liam leaned back in the chair. His steady, rapt gaze darted between me and Rochelle.

"And when he uses it to compel someone to do something … illegal?"

"It's all going to be illegal," Liam said. "Today, to-night, tomorrow. With the elves, according to human laws at least. Isn't it?"

I looked at him, utterly aghast.

He shrugged. "Breaking and entering. Destruction of property. Assault, murder. Hell, the elves started it with a mass kidnapping."

I glanced back at Rochelle in disbelief.

She sighed softly. "You know you can just destroy it. If he uses it in a way you don't like."

"They don't just hand out badges like candy," Liam said crossly.

We ignored him. I flipped back through the pages of the sketchbook, finding the first one of me holding the badge.

"Just a little compulsion, maybe," I murmured. "A little extra to back the sorcerer's natural ability to charm. However deeply he usually hides it."

"Yes." Rochelle fiddled with the cushions, settling back on the couch with her hands splayed across her belly.

I eyed Liam. He let me look at him, assess him, without comment. "Is this the worst thing you're going to ask of me?" I directed the question to Rochelle.

"Not even close."

I sighed. But then, I had already known that was going to be her answer. I gestured toward Liam.

He leaned across the coffee table, offering the badge to me.

"No. You need to hold it."

"In the sketch—"

"Sure. I'm certain I'll hold it at some point, but magic doesn't come from nowhere. I use the power within you, anchoring it to the artifact with my own."

"The power within me," Liam said, sounding horrified.

I laughed. "Yeah, sorcerer. You've got to have it to wield it. Just like witches. Or necromancers. Or oracles."

"But I use spells, objects, runes to cast."

"And the spark that ignites those objects is within you. The trigger."

Liam muttered disconcertedly under his breath. Then he stood up, crossing around the coffee table. He hesitated before attempting to cram himself onto the love seat beside me—there wasn't much space. Pushing the coffee table aside to make room, he kneeled next to me instead, holding his badge in the palm of his hand.

I almost teased him about the kneeling, but decided he didn't know me well enough for me to pull it off. This was a difficult enough situation already without any miscommunications. Well, any further miscommunications.

I cupped Liam's hand in mine. He flinched. Adepts weren't big on being touched by other Adepts. Yeah, that must have totally been the issue. It had nothing to do with him having seen me in full-on 'Evil Jade' mode.

Ignoring his reaction, I concentrated on the glimmer of magic already coating the badge. Residual from being worn, being touched by him constantly. I'd worked with less. I cupped my other hand over top, sandwiching Liam's hand and badge in between my own hands.

Then I closed my eyes, reaching for Liam's peanut-butter magic—his spark, as I'd called it. I stirred that energy toward his hand, coaxing it to pool within his palm. Then I siphoned it into the residual contained in the badge, anchoring it there with my own magic.

The taste and scent of creamy peanut butter filled my senses. I thought about Liam's easy smile when he'd stood in the doorway, and the good nature that simmered beneath that expression. I thought about how that good nature was often dampened by his fierce need to protect those he cared about. I recalled his systematic thoroughness when investigating the elves. And his willingness to adapt when his methods hadn't worked.

I thought about him standing sentry at the stadium when I'd asked him to wait there for Kandy. Of how he'd retreated only when necessary.

He could have run that night. He should have run, but he'd stayed. And ultimately, it was his bravery that had led to the others knowing I'd been captured, and to me being rescued.

"The badge is you, Liam Talbot," I murmured. "An extrapolation of everything you already are. Kind, caring, forceful when needed. Tempered by your rational nature. Persuasive."

Magic settled between our hands, embedding into the badge.

I opened my eyes, pinning the sorcerer with my gaze. "No one can take this from you, Liam. No one can use it but you."

He nodded, epically serious.

"Except me. So don't make me take it from you."

"I won't." He swallowed, then firmed his tone. "It is a great privilege to wield an artifact of your creation, Jade. I will use it carefully."

I nodded, plucking the badge out of his hand before he'd even seen me move.

He flinched. Again.

But it was never a bad thing to instill just a little fear into someone I wasn't quite certain I could completely trust yet. Even though I knew my reservations about the sorcerer, and about the other Talbot sorcerers in general, had more to do with my own prejudices than it did with them.

I held the badge in my palm, glancing down at the open sketchbook to make certain I mirrored the vision that Rochelle had captured on the page. Then I smiled at Liam. "Just to fulfill the oracle's prediction."

He nodded solemnly. I offered him the badge and he took it, gazing at it with wonder.

I turned to Rochelle. She had her eyes closed and her head resting on the back of the couch. "What next, oracle of mine?"

She smiled tightly, leaning forward to flip the page of her sketchbook, revealing a drawing of a pen. Benjamin Garrick's fountain pen, at a guess.

"Great," I groused, trying to infuse the proceedings with some humor but failing miserably. I touched the scar on my forehead and reminded myself that I could be a good soldier.

Both Liam and Rochelle were watching me. Too closely. As if waiting for Evil Jade to make an appearance. Or maybe I was just reading too much into everything, like usual.

I dropped my hand. The tense moment passed.

Liam clipped the badge to his belt and picked up his wool coat. "We'll be ready for you. But give us some notice before you head our way?"

Rochelle nodded, but her attention was already back on her sketchbooks.

Mory returned with Benjamin Garrick and Jasmine in tow. A junior necromancer hanging out with two vampires would have been great fodder for an Adept comedian, though it wasn't presently giving me the giggles. Even though I trusted both the vampires in question.

Well, I trusted that the bone bracelet seething with necromancy on Benjamin's left wrist would keep his bloodlust under control. And I trusted the blood of the executioner that ran in Jasmine's veins and made her far stronger and less easily distracted than a newly made vampire usually was. But in general, vampires and necromancers didn't mix. Like, on a fundamental level. Predators didn't like being controlled by their prey.

Benjamin, wearing a thin brown sweater, faded black jeans, and heavy work boots, paused in the open doorway to the living room, spotting me by the front windows where I'd been pacing. Yes, again.

A slow smile spread across the dark-haired vampire's face as he swept his dark gaze over me, head to toe and back again.

I'd forgotten about my warrior get-up. Again.

In what I thought might have been an unconscious gesture, Benjamin pushed the sleeves of his sweater up his forearms, exposing the aforementioned bone bracelet on his left wrist. He'd been reluctant to reveal the necromancy working previously. But as his innate magic—his ability to beguile—brushed against me, it was obvious he was distracted. By me, it seemed.

I allowed myself an answering smile.

"Benjamin," Rochelle said from her vantage point on the couch. "Thank you for coming."

"Of course, oracle." Though the young vampire's response was pleasantly polite, his gaze didn't leave me. "It is my pleasure as always."

"Hey, Benjamin," I said.

"I like the new look, Jade. Very formidable. Very ..." Benjamin rubbed his fingers together. And as if finishing his unspoken thought, the dark-haired vampire's magic attempted to tease me toward him, inciting me.

I laughed quietly.

"Please," Jasmine snorted. "What are you going to do with her if you catch her, Ben?"

Benjamin frowned, glancing over at the golden-haired vampire. His inadvertent attempt to captivate me faded. "What do you mean?"

Mory threw herself onto the love seat beside Rochelle. "You were trying to beguile Jade."

Benjamin looked aghast. "I wasn't."

I shook my head at Mory.

She frowned, but quieted.

"I apologize, dowser," Benjamin said. "If I was…doing anything untoward. You look magnificent." He glanced at Mory, then over at Jasmine. "I wasn't aware that saying so broke any sort of rules."

Jasmine shrugged in exaggerated fashion. "You can lust after whoever you want. That's none of my business." She looked pointedly at Mory. "Or the necromancer's."

Benjamin had gone still, watching Jasmine intently. The junior vampire was a sponge. Give him another year, and he'd have us all catalogued, assessed, and completely figured out. I had wondered more than once whether that predilection—his need to gather as much information about the Adept world that he had found himself adopted into—was something that had been inherent in his human self. But even if it was, it had clearly been amplified by his transformation.

"Shall we move on?" I asked, trying to be polite, but coming up belligerent. There was a lot of movement happening in and around Gran's house. Magic being tested, plans being laid out. And so far, none of it included me tearing through the elves' wards and rescuing my best friends.

Granted, I understood that Rochelle was moving forward with a master plan, testing it step by step to see if a task she set for me, or the plans the others were implementing, triggered a new vision. She was trying to figure out if she was moving us all in a direction that countered the destiny laid out in the first and second sketchbook she'd shown me, rather than bringing that destiny to fruition.

The oracle nodded, gesturing Benjamin toward the sketchbook that lay open on the coffee table. Jasmine folded herself into the antique chair nearest the doorway as Benjamin crouched down to peer at the charcoal sketch. It was a drawing depicting me—or, rather, my hand—holding the fountain pen.

Benjamin studied the sketch intently. When he nodded, Rochelle flipped the page. He then studied the new reveal, which showed him standing in a long hall before a steel door. Rochelle flipped to a third page, and Benjamin leaned forward, face practically pressed to the paper, intently examining the final sketch—the pen pressed against a lock.

"Benjamin, what I'm asking you to do...what I'm going to ask you to do is dangerous," Rochelle said. "I haven't seen the outcome yet. At least, I'm hoping I haven't seen the actual outcome yet."

"Have you given Mory and Liam and Jasmine the same warnings, oracle?" Benjamin's tone was pointed but not confrontational. He lifted the edge of the page with long, delicate fingers, carefully flipping back to the first sketch Rochelle had shown him. The pen sitting in the palm of my hand.

Me holding random items had apparently become a bit of a theme for the oracle. First the gemstone, then Liam's badge, and now Benjamin's fountain pen.

Rochelle glanced up, ceding the conversation to me.

I laughed inwardly. Apparently, I was better suited to outlining exactly how perilous hanging out with me was. "While I'm not a fan of Rochelle's plan, or at least what little I understand of it so far, Mory has...been involved in life-threatening situations before."

"Three times," the junior necromancer interjected. She had curled her legs underneath her and pulled out her knitting while I'd been focused on Benjamin's reactions. Of course.

I skewered her with a look. "Once by choice. Twice by being an idiot."

Mory snickered. "Plus, Jade totally plans on trying to talk me out of coming along. Just as soon as the oracle's back is turned."

"I don't even know what your task is yet," I grumbled.

No one offered any further illumination. Yes, it was all about baby steps for me today. Which obviously meant that whatever I was being eased into was going to be an utterly horrible idea.

"And Jasmine? And the others?" Benjamin asked.

"Jasmine," the golden-haired vampire drawled, "is bound by magic to try to rescue her maker." By her tone, she evidently didn't enjoy being talked about while she was in the room.

Benjamin sat back on his haunches, looking at all of us in turn. "But that's not my point. You'd all face this, you'd all stand up, answer the oracle's call without a second thought. Yes?"

"Yes," I said. "But it would still be a choice."

"And why should I be any different?" Benjamin asked softly. "It can't be because I'm a vampire. Kett and Jasmine are vampires, and they're by your side unquestioningly. And it can't be because I'm weak, because logically, Mory is more physically vulnerable than I am."

"That's debatable," Jasmine interjected before I could answer. "The necromancer's necklace alone is powerful enough that even I can feel it across the room. Not to mention the zombie turtle in her bag."

"Ed!" Mory exclaimed proudly, setting her knitting aside to pull the aforementioned dead turtle out of her satchel. Ed did indeed teem with magic now.

"But it's a question of morality, not mortality, isn't it?" Benjamin pressed. "You're not certain I would risk my life…my existence. You're not certain I would choose to save others over myself."

I crossed my arms. My jaw was starting to ache with frustration. I didn't want to be crafting artifacts and waiting around, making small talk with fledglings about freaking morality.

Benjamin took my silence, my attempt to maintain some control of myself, as a reason to flip through the three sketches again.

Jasmine eyed me warily.

"What am I doing with the pen?" Benjamin finally asked Rochelle, pointing to the third sketch. The close-up of the locking mechanism. "What do you see me doing?"

"It's a lockpick," Rochelle said. Then she looked at me and pointedly added, "For magical locks."

"Well, he doesn't need it for nonmagical locks, Rochelle," I said pissily. "He can snap those with his bare hands."

Benjamin looked intrigued. Though whether it was from the idea of a magical pen or being strong enough to break into wherever he wanted, I didn't know.

"Though that wouldn't be terribly polite," I added.

Benjamin offered me a slight smile. "And why do I need a magical lockpick?"

Rochelle tugged her sketchbook toward her, flipping it open to the drawing that showed Benjamin in the hallway. "The elves have built a maze within the stadium. Yazi, Jade's dad, confirmed that this is a fortification technique to narrow and direct any possible…ingresses."

Benjamin nodded. "Limiting, funneling access. So that any invaders can be picked off easily at specific choke points. Like narrow stairwells in castles and fortresses."

"Uh, yeah …" Rochelle blinked at Benjamin a couple of times, seemingly surprised at his level of insight into combat tactics. "And…they've also built rooms on the ground floor where they've imprisoned the warriors. Mory verified this with Ed." The oracle tapped the charcoal sketch lightly. "I see you in this hall, Benjamin. By this door."

"You think I need to open this door?"

"Three doors," I said. "The fourth will already be open. Because one of the…warriors will be powering the gateway."

A bright smile slowly bloomed across Benjamin's face. "You want me in the rescue party."

I shook my head. "Not me. I would never choose to put you in harm's way. But apparently, I don't have any say. Not this time, anyway."

"You always have a say, Jade," Rochelle said, mildly reprimanding me.

Except on this particular occasion, when my actions, my choices, could get everyone killed and the city destroyed. I kept that dark thought to myself, though.

"I had to cut through the magic sealing the doors, oracle," I said instead, pointing toward the drawing. "With my knife. A pen in the locks isn't going to do it."

Rochelle nodded. "I can only speak to what I've seen, Jade. I'm sorry I can't offer you more assurances."

I sighed, frustrated with myself more than anything else.

"You need more chocolate, eh?" Mory asked.

"Yes!" I snapped. "I need more freaking chocolate."

"Right," the tiny necromancer tucked her knitting away, keeping Ed in hand. "You make Benjamin's pen and then whatever Jasmine needs, and I'll see if Pearl has milk, sugar, and cocoa."

"What about the chocolate bar in your bag?"

"It's for later."

"Fine."

"Fine."

Jasmine bowed her head, trying to hide her amusement. Mory sauntered across the room.

"Check for *fleur de sel*, as well," I called after her. "Please."

"I would, but I have no idea what that is." The snarky necromancer waved dismissively over her shoulder, crossing out of the room in the direction of the kitchen.

I turned to the dark-haired vampire still peering at the sketch of himself in the hallway. "You haven't said yes, Benjamin."

He slowly stood, smoothing his sweater.

"You came to Vancouver as a ... safe haven." I tried to keep my tone neutral, but was struggling to do so. "Not to fight in some elf war."

"It's a privilege." Benjamin smiled softly. "For a vampire to be taken in by a coven. This coven, specifically. To be given access to the city and the Adepts who reside here. To have conversations, build relationships. I understand that. I also understand that the oracle hasn't seen everything that is to come, and that she can't guarantee my safety. That you, Jade, can't always watch over me."

He looked down at Rochelle, then to me. We both nodded.

Benjamin grabbed the black leather satchel he'd set by the leg of the coffee table, fishing his fountain pen out of its depths. Then he gently laid it down next to Rochelle's open sketchbook, flipping back to the image of me holding the pen in my palm. It was an exact match—the shape of the barrel, the top of the cap, the design of the clip, the overall length.

Benjamin looked up at me. "I'd say fate has already decided for me."

I shook my head. "That's our point. Choice is still a factor."

"I choose to stand by you, Jade. You, and Rochelle, and Mory, and Jasmine. All of you. Even if I'm just a cog in the wheel. You wouldn't do any less for me."

"Bring me the pen," I said gruffly, trying to hide the welling emotion threatening to clog my throat.

Benjamin plucked up the pen and was standing before me in practically the same motion, moving quicker than he usually did. Most likely unconsciously.

I took the pen from him, feeling the residual magic that already resided in it.

"This fountain pen is an antique," I said as I first stirred, then tried to taste the energy embedded within it. "Actual gold. A little too heavy, I suspect, for a mere mortal to comfortably wield. Given to you by Kett, yes?"

"Yes."

"But it belonged to a vampire powerful enough to leave behind residual magic. Perhaps even the executioner himself. Though there isn't enough magic in it to hold a taste, so I don't know for certain."

"The pen is magical?"

I laughed quietly at the wonder in Benjamin's tone. "No. But if an Adept uses or wears an object receptive to magic for long enough, it accrues a…lick of their power. Like the wedding rings on my necklace."

"Or the coins on Mory's?"

"Yes. Metal, especially gold and platinum, collects the most. Or certain gems, raw better than polished."

Benjamin eyed the pen in my hand. "You think that's a solid gold pen?"

"The housing, at least." I pulled off the cap, peering at the tip. "And the nib is white gold, I think. Hold out your hand."

He complied.

I recapped the pen, placing it in his palm. I folded his fingers over it loosely, so that I could still weave my fingertips through his and touch the pen. "I take some of your magic and weave it into the residual contained within the pen. Then I cement it with my own, and I…direct the alchemy. I inform it of its function."

"Wait, my…magic? I mean, I know you said I tasted like …"—he lowered his voice—"… sour-grape jellybeans. But I don't…I can't wield magic."

"Grape jellybeans. Well, that makes sense," Jasmine muttered from the other side of the room. I had no idea what she was talking about. As far as I knew, I was the only one in the room—possibly the only dowser in the northern hemisphere—who tasted magic.

"You don't wield like a witch," I said to Benjamin. "But you still have magic within you. Within your every cell. And I steal a bit of that power and feed it into the pen to create a magical artifact."

Benjamin twitched, as if he had just stopped himself from shoving his hand into his satchel and pulling out his notebook to write all that down.

I smiled at him. "I can explain it again later. If you don't remember it word for word."

He nodded, prompting. "So you tie the pen to me …"

"Yes." I coaxed strands of his magic forward as I spoke, weaving them through the residual already in the pen and cementing the combination with my own alchemy. "Which means that no one but you can use the pen, not unless you've given them explicit permission."

"Like how? With a spell?"

"No. Magic is about intention. Witches use words and candles and compass points. And sorcerers use pentagrams and runes and magical objects. But those items are just focuses for their intention."

"Focal points."

"Yes. And triggers, I suppose. If I'm simplifying it. So I tell the pen and all the magic contained within it that its job is to open locks for its wielder." And then I did just that. Closing my eyes, I smoothed the layers and layers of magic I'd coaxed forth into the pen.

Shifting through my hazy recent memory, I recalled the magic I'd sliced through to free myself from my room. Then the door that had stood between Warner and me, remembering the feel and tenor of the power that had locked him within and me without.

I had used my knife, which could cut through any magic. Well, any magic I'd had the chance to try it on so far. But the pen would have to somehow fit the locks of the doors—three locks in each steel-reinforced door, if I was remembering correctly. And in turning those locks, the pen would need to neutralize the magic that sealed the entire door.

I stole a lick of magic from my knife, feeding it into the pen sandwiched between Benjamin's fingers and mine. Then, with all of my gathered remembrances and all the intention I could muster, I allowed the energy to settle within the pen.

It had to work. An oracle had said it would be so.

I opened my eyes and dropped my hand.

"Just like that?" Benjamin whispered, enraptured.

"Pretty much."

Jasmine chuckled. "If you're an alchemist. No one else can perform such magic."

I took the pen from Benjamin, holding it in my hand for a moment to reflect the oracle's vision. Then I offered it back to the dark-haired vampire.

Benjamin looked at me solemnly. We were exactly the same height. Then he took the pen with reverence. "It is a blessing to wield an artifact of Jade Godfrey's creation. I shall cherish it. And I will never use it for evil purposes."

"Okay," I said, matching his serious tone. "All objects of my crafting are tied to me, Benjamin. Don't make me take it back."

"I won't." He ran his fingers along the pen.

I wondered if he could feel the magic embedded in it now—it tasted of vampire and sugary-sweet jellybeans to me—but I didn't want to be rude and ask.

I glanced beyond Benjamin's shoulder to where Rochelle was perched on the couch. She was hovering over a blank page in her sketchbook with a piece of charcoal in hand. Waiting. The dark-haired vampire tugged his notebook out of his satchel, sat in the window seat, and began writing madly. Every couple of sentences, he would pause to admire the pen in his hand.

Rochelle looked up at me, shaking her head. She had apparently hoped that something would shift when I gave Benjamin the pen.

I took a breath before speaking. "I still don't know that it's going to open the rooms the elves have warded," I said. "Sending Benjamin in with just a pen seems … risky."

Rochelle nodded, then she glanced at Jasmine. "He won't be alone."

"Batter up," Jasmine said chuckling. "What piece of magic am I to be gifted with?"

Rochelle shook her head, then she flipped back in her sketchbook to a charcoal rendering of Jasmine. It was a head-and-shoulders detail of the golden-haired vampire in profile, wearing her necklace decorated with a cluster of tiny cubes. Reconstructions from her cousin Wisteria.

I reached for it, I'd be able to taste the hint of nutmeg that always accompanied Jasmine. The nutmeg that defined the taste of Wisteria's witch magic. Though I had no idea what reconstruction each cube held, I did know that Wisteria had collected one of them in the bakery over a year before. Before Jasmine had shed her mortal coil and become Kett's child.

"Just hit me with it, oracle," Jasmine said. "I don't need to be eased in."

"Okay."

"Wait!" I cried, just a little mockingly. "I get treated like a freaking baby, but you're just going to lay it all out for Jasmine?"

"Yeah, well, I'm not going to run off and try to take it all on myself, am I?" The golden-haired vampire offered me a toothy smile. "I'm a good foot soldier."

I gave her a scathing look that I hoped expressed my utter displeasure.

She laughed.

"Invisibility," Rochelle said. Her tone was becoming slightly edgy. Yeah, I wouldn't want to put up with myself for very long either.

"Excuse me?" I asked. "Invisibility?"

"Yes."

"You want me to spell Jasmine's necklace invisible?"

Rochelle gave me a look.

I laughed, a little harshly. "Invisibility isn't a thing... for people." I glanced over at Jasmine, who was gazing down at the sketch of herself thoughtfully. "That's not possible."

"Not if you don't think it is," Rochelle said. "If your magic is controlled by intention. So Jasmine will have to go without your protection."

She reached over to close her sketchbook.

Jasmine, moving so quickly that the oracle flinched, touched the edge of the book, keeping it open on the coffee table. Bent down to hover over the sketch, she looked up at me, her golden curls falling forward all around her head and shoulders. "The oracle can only try to articulate what she sees. So ..." Jasmine glanced over at Rochelle. "You believe you see me abruptly appear? Or disappear?"

The oracle nodded. "Appear."

"That could simply be Jasmine's speed," I said.

"Not in a vision." Rochelle settled back on the love seat, arranging the cushions behind her lower back again. "I'm meant to see, to understand what magic wants me to see in my visions. If I study it closely enough. Plus, the necklace glows briefly."

"It can't be invisibility," I said, speaking to Jasmine—who was way, way better versed in magic than I was. "Even Warner... or Kett for that matter... can't turn themselves invisible. They simply use light and shadows to their advantage."

"You're right. So whatever the oracle is picking up isn't true invisibility ..." Jasmine's gaze was on the sketch again.

I stepped forward for a better view myself. But all I saw was Jasmine's lovely face. She was clearly wearing her necklace, which was drawn in great detail, while looking at something beyond the edge of the page. No fangs, no fear, no joy.

"Can you…move like Kett does?" I asked. I tried to phrase it vaguely because questioning someone about their personal magic was considered rude in Adept society. And there were many ears in the room, and in the house beyond.

Jasmine straightened, stepping closer to me, but shook her head. "I can move quickly and slip partly into shadows, but nowhere near as well as my master does."

I nodded. Kett could blend so well into the night that even I couldn't see him, though I could always taste his magic.

Just then, Mory slipped back into the room, crossing toward the love seat.

Without my hot chocolate.

I narrowed my eyes at her.

She shrugged as she pulled out her knitting. "Not enough milk. There's tea."

"Tea?" I echoed pissily.

Jasmine snorted, drawing my attention back to her before I could demand the chocolate bar that the necromancer had flaunted before me earlier.

The golden-haired vampire lowered her voice. "Not all abilities are passed through the primary blood exchange at rebirth. But…I'm not certain without having Kett here to ask, but I might have gained his ability to absorb the magic of those I drink from. The, um…after inadvertently drinking from the elf, I could see magic for a while. In color."

"That wouldn't cause the necklace to glow in the vision, though." I was thinking madly. "If it was an ability you were supposed to absorb. If we even knew anyone who could become actually invisible, who you could then drink from." A sinking feeling hit me. "What about Blossom?"

I definitely wasn't a fan of the idea of the brownie offering up her blood, but she was the only Adept I knew who could sneak up on me. Maybe true invisibility was the magic behind that little trick.

Thankfully, though, Jasmine shook her head. "No. Brownies have an exceptional ability to mask their magic, especially if they're bonded with and moving within their chosen abodes. But they don't actually become invisible." Then the golden-haired vampire hesitated, glancing toward Benjamin.

I followed her gaze. He was still perched in the window seat with his notebook in hand, presumably transcribing every word we were saying.

"Estelle can teleport," Jasmine whispered.

"Kett's maker? Jesus. That's an unsettling thought."

"Exactly."

"But Kett can't."

"Ve can. Kett's granddaddy. You call him the Big Bad of London. But maybe the blood thins? You know, from generation to generation?"

"Or like with other Adepts, abilities can skip generations."

Jasmine sighed. "If I can teleport, I'm fairly certain I'd know it. Like all magic, it would be triggered instinctively the first couple of times."

I nodded. Extreme situations or extreme emotions often triggered latent powers in Adepts. Jasmine had just experienced a rough couple of weeks. So if she had the ability to teleport, then—

Wait …

I had the ability to teleport stored in my own necklace. Could I transfer that to Jasmine?

"What are you thinking, Jade?"

"It's one thing, I think, for me to add certain protections to Mory's necklace, or to give a single intention to Benjamin's pen. But they don't have to be able to wield magic to trigger that ..." I glanced over toward Rochelle. "What are the chances that the sketch you sent to me in the nexus wasn't about me breaking out?"

"You're thinking about Blackwell's amulet," Rochelle said, indicating that she knew what I was talking about.

Mory stiffened at the mention of the dark sorcerer's name, but she kept her gaze on her knitting.

Seriously, speaking frankly would have been way, way easier on everyone. "I couldn't collect the twin amulet, couldn't pick it up. The treasure keeper had warded the entire place against pilfering."

"By you specifically?" Jasmine asked, way too skilled at interpreting clues—and far too amused at coming up correct.

I side-eyed her. "Apparently."

"I'm certain that sketch was for you, Jade," Rochelle said.

"Yeah, but when I finally made it to the other side of Lions Gate bridge, my father and the healer were already waiting. They'd wanted to bring me with them, but I was already gone. So ... technically I didn't actually need the amulet."

Jasmine was glancing back and forth between the oracle and me. "You just said you couldn't collect it anyway, Jade."

"I stole its magic."

Jasmine laughed breathlessly. "Teleportation?"

Yeah, the golden-haired vampire was far quicker than me at putting two and two together—and coming up with rare magical abilities. Of course, she was originally a Fairchild witch, trained in magic from infancy. Then she'd attended the Academy and worked for the Convocation as an investigator.

Still, I had two successful bakeries and the ability to make pretty magical artifacts. So maybe we were even on the blessings scale?

"What do you think, oracle? Could it be teleportation you're seeing, not invisibility?"

The white of Rochelle's magic ringed her eyes. "I see the hallways, then Jasmine appears," she murmured. Then she paused, as if reviewing the vision in her own mind. "It's not teleportation. I've seen Blackwell teleport many times. Jasmine … slides into focus. Like … like she's part of the walls, but then steps forward into the hall."

"Obfuscation!" Mory blurted, proving that she could listen closely and knit at the same time. "Like what you did for Ed when you bled all over him."

Jasmine gave me a look. "Not sure bleeding all over me would be a good idea, dowser."

I laughed, involuntarily shoving all my pissy fretfulness to the side as I did so. "I agree, vampire."

Jasmine bared her teeth at me, sans fang. "Maybe next time." She looked over at Rochelle. "I wouldn't mind a bit of that teleportation power, though."

Rochelle shook her head sternly.

"Spoilsport."

That comment got an extra round of giggles from me. And, honestly, it felt good to laugh. I missed my BFFs so desperately.

"Okay, okay." I calmed myself. I seemed to be flipping from one extreme emotional state to another—and trying to drag everyone with me. No wonder they were being cautious and close-mouthed. "So my concern with that sort of thing...if I can do it consciously and without bleeding all over Jasmine...is that she...you, Jasmine, need to have the ability to turn it on and off, to trigger it. I assume you don't want to take the necklace on and off, right?"

"You assume correctly, dowser. But since we're faced with an oracle's vision, I have a feeling it'll sort itself out." Jasmine became completely serious. "I believe. I have to believe."

I nodded. "All right. Let's give it a try. I'm going to have to touch you."

"I'm all atingle in anticipation."

Mory and Benjamin laughed quietly. Apparently, Jasmine could only maintain a serious note for micro periods of time. But then, who was I to judge?

I shook my head ruefully, reaching for the gold chain half hidden under Jasmine's bronze silk blouse. I pulled it out, revealing the twelve...no, thirteen tiny reconstruction cubes attached to it. Each of the miniature cubes glowed softly blue with witch magic. Wisteria's nutmeg magic, to be specific.

Jasmine touched the back of my hand tentatively. "This...this won't effect the reconstructions, will it?"

"No. There's enough residual magic in the chain to work with. That's your magic. I won't need to use the power stored in the cubes." I laid my thumb and forefinger on the chain, splaying my other fingers across Jasmine's upper chest and collarbone. Her skin was cool to the touch, still creamy in color, but paler than my own.

"This is a little personal...but can you still trigger and view the reconstructions?"

Jasmine looked surprised. "Yes. I…I hadn't thought about it when I do, but yes. I can." She smiled. "That's a witch ability."

"Actually, I'm pretty certain it's only a specific witch ability. Can Gran even view reconstructions without having a reconstructionist around?"

"I would think so, but we'd have to ask to be certain." Jasmine's smile had widened, and there was nothing snarky or sarcastic about her expression now. "I can still do some magic. I mean, I knew about the tech. I'm not as good as I was before, but …" She trailed off happily.

"Yeah. Let's see if I can jump through the oracle's hoops. But if I can, I'm going to guess you won't have any issue triggering the new magic."

Jasmine nodded, still softly smiling.

"First things first," I murmured, stirring the residual within the gold chain and coaxing Jasmine's sweet peppermint power to pool under my fingers. "No one will be able to take the necklace from you. Though you can gift it voluntarily."

"Thank you."

I smoothed Jasmine's magic into the chain, cementing it there with my own alchemy. I focused on the feel of the combined power filtering up and down the chain, the tenor and taste of it. I thought about Rochelle's sketch, and of her description of Jasmine appearing, fading in from the white halls. As if she'd camouflaged herself with those walls, using them as a visual cloak. Similarly to how her master Kett moved through the shadows. An ability that Jasmine already had to some extent. So…I just had to pull that ability forth from her own magic, then inform it that it could cloak the vampire from any of her immediate surroundings, not just within shadows.

I fed more magic into the gold chain—my own magic and Jasmine's. I could hear the quiet scratch of Benjamin's pen across paper, and a ticking clock from the entranceway. But all I could see was the magic glowing beneath my fingers, glistening from the edges of the chain, filling it full. Full of power, full of intention.

"You can't be moving for it to completely mask you, I don't think," I murmured, speaking without really thinking about what I was saying. "Not very quickly, at least. But ... you might be able to also shield whoever you're touching from direct sight? Maybe?"

"That makes sense," Jasmine said. "I'll test it."

A bit of feedback reflected off the necklace, as if it was telling me it was full, though magic couldn't really be measured as mass or volume. I lifted my fingers from contact with the chain and Jasmine, watching as all the energy I'd called forth settled into the necklace.

"Holy hell, dowser," Jasmine whispered, her chin practically pressed to her chest so she could look at her necklace. "It's glowing. Like, brightly."

"Yeah. Thankfully, not everyone can see magic. But ... you might want to tuck it under your shirt. Or a jacket. It'll probably fade. Eventually."

"I will endeavor to be worthy of your gift, dowser. Thank you." Jasmine carefully tucked the necklace into her cleavage again, then she winked at me saucily. "Kett is going to be jealous."

"More jealous about you being seen by the oracle than jealous of the necklace. I'm not sure he could pull that pretty piece of magic off quite as well as you do."

Jasmine chuckled. "Come on, Ben. Let's find a witch to spell some locks and run some tests with us. Olive is awake. I can ... hear her upstairs, moving around."

I raised an eyebrow at the hitch in Jasmine's wording.

"I'm not hunting the witches," she said crossly.

Yeah, in the long run, giving the vampire an obfuscation spell might have been a bad idea.

Benjamin dutifully shut his notebook, tucking it into his satchel as he fluidly rose from the window seat and practically appeared at Jasmine's side in the same motion.

The golden-haired vampire glanced over at Rochelle. "I imagine we don't have much time."

"As soon as the sorcerers are ready, we'll move forward. Unless magic tells me differently."

Jasmine met Benjamin's steady gaze. She was about an inch shorter than him in her brown suede boots. "We'll be ready to rescue the warriors. Won't we, Ben?"

He grinned at her easily. "We will."

Then they slipped swiftly from the room, heading upstairs instead of down. I could taste just a hint of Burgundy's watermelon magic within the well of power in the map room, but all the other witches, including Scarlett and Gran, were still upstairs.

I settled my gaze on Rochelle, then looked pointedly at Mory. The necromancer kept her attention riveted to her knitting. Ed was attempting to make a nest out of an afghan that was draped over the arm of the love seat.

The oracle grimaced.

"Just tell me, Rochelle. I feel like I'm going crazy waiting around. Just tell me."

Rochelle nodded, but then didn't immediately offer up any insight.

"I'm the one who's going to close the gateway," Mory said mildly.

"Close the gateway," I echoed incredulously. My mind momentarily blanked, as if I were incapable of even processing the idea. "I'm the one who fixed it! The one who opened it!"

"Jade," Rochelle chided.

"No!" I started pacing again, but stopped myself. "Just no. It's alchemy! It's magic."

"I'm magic," Mory interjected.

I ignored her, pointing at the sketchbook still lying open on the coffee table. "Show me."

"Some of this ... I've been shown a bunch of pieces, Jade. I've had to put them together. I see Mory at the gateway, Gabby at her side. I see you and your father shielding them both. I see an army of elves. More and more flooding forward."

I sat down in the chair Jasmine had vacated, feeling shaky and faint. "This can't be, Rochelle. Mory ... Mory can't do alchemy, not even amplified by Gabby. This is just insanity. This is what you've been pushing me toward?"

I realized I was yelling. I leaned forward, elbows on my knees, head in my hands, trying to simply breathe.

"It isn't alchemy," Mory said, setting her knitting aside and sliding off the couch onto her knees by the coffee table. "May I?" she asked Rochelle.

I felt more than saw the white-haired oracle nod.

Mory tugged the sketchbook toward her, flipping closer to the back. "You fixed the gateway, yes?"

I didn't answer. She already knew I had.

"But how are the elves fueling it?" She found the sketch she was looking for, letting me know that she'd already studied the oracle's sketchbook. They had already had this conversation, most likely multiple times. All while waiting for me to return.

She pushed the sketchbook across the coffee table so that it edged my peripheral vision. I caught a glimpse of a figure in the well of magic above the gateway. I squeezed my eyes shut so I couldn't see who hung there, slowly dying. Because of me. Warner ... Kandy ... Kett ... Haoxin ...

I clenched my hands. I'd been making pretty little trinkets for everyone while ... while—

"It's the magic of one of the others," Rochelle said gently. "The gateway is fueled by their magic. Yes?"

Before I could confirm, Mory spoke up smugly. "But not just magic. Their life force."

I looked up at her.

"That's what I do, Jade. I can see that much, feel that much, even through Ed's eyes. I couldn't get near enough, not until after you amped up Ed's charm and made him seriously sneaky. And then I got kicked out when the elves strengthened the exterior warding. But I figured it out. The gateway is being fueled by life force. Soul magic."

I rubbed my forehead, feeling the puckered skin of my still-healing scar. "The oracle said that collapsing the gateway causes a backlash that destroys the city."

"Yeah, but I'm not going to collapse it to close it. I'm going to ... unweave the life force. Release it, so it no longer fuels the operation of the gate."

"That's delicate work ... precise, time consuming ..."

"Yes."

"Which is why we need you," Rochelle said. "You and your father. And all of the others, in fact. To give Mory time."

"And the sorcerers and witches?"

"Backup. To hold a boundary if the elves try to bolt. Or ... if the worst happens, to try to protect the city. They've been setting it up for two days."

"The necromancers are ready with secondary defenses as well," Mory added.

"Jesus Christ."

"Yes."

"Jesus freaking Christ."

"Yes."

"You want me to escort Mory, and Gabby, to the gateway. Then with my father, hold off an army of elves while a necromancer unravels...life force—"

"Soul magic," Mory interjected helpfully.

I waved my hand in her direction helplessly. "The treasure keeper said that the gateway is too powerful, even for me. That the former warrior was damaged by it when he ..." I heard what I was saying even as I was saying it. But I finished the thought anyway. "When he destroyed the artifact."

"Yes," Rochelle said smugly.

"Don't even try to pretend you knew that part, oracle."

She grinned at me unrepentantly.

"Jesus. This is insane."

"Yes."

I pinned Mory with a look. "Your mother ..."

The necromancer shook her head, tossing her purple and red hair across her forehead and cheeks. "Nope. Her magic doesn't work like mine. And before you ask, neither does Teresa's. They deal solely in death magic. But I...I can work soul magic. That's how I tied Rusty to me. You know, he wasn't just a ghost. And recently, I ..." She slid her gaze to Rochelle, hesitating over whatever she was about to divulge. Then, obviously changing her mind, she looked resolutely back at me. "I know I can do it."

I opened my mouth to protest.

But before I could express more reservations, Mory emphatically declared, "I am the wielder's necromancer!"

"Plus, it's Mory I see in the visions," Rochelle said gently.

I slumped back in my seat. "What do I have to do?"

"Not stop me." Mory jutted her chin at me. "Even if you think I'm in trouble. You have to let me work."

"I meant, what magic am I adding to your necklace?"

"Oh." Mory looked sheepish.

"Not the necklace," Rochelle said, tugging the sketchbook back toward her awkwardly. Her reach was compromised by her belly. "Knitting needles."

"Knitting needles? This day is getting better and better."

Mory ignored my sarcasm. "Rochelle and I have discussed it—"

"Obviously."

"And we think you just need to tie my magic to the needles. Not, like, add a specific function or anything."

Rochelle found the sketch she was looking for and turned it toward me. It depicted Mory standing before the gate, which completely dwarfed her tiny figure. She was holding a needle-like object aloft in either hand, as if she might have been conducting music. Or magic, in this case.

A lone figure was floating within the magic, fueling the gateway. I forced myself to look closely this time, but the image was indistinct, not looking like anyone in particular. And Mory was so tiny that I couldn't guess based on scale. "Okay. All right. Who's going to be trapped in the gateway?" I gestured toward the figure.

Rochelle shook her head. "It changes."

"The vision changes?"

"This part. All the parts that take place in the stadium. They change, subtly or extremely, sometimes hour by hour."

"Because choices will be made in the moment."

"Yes."

"So you can't tell me who, if anyone, survives. Or even whether what we're going to try to do saves the city."

"No. I can't." The oracle carefully stacked her three sketchbooks, then shifted off the couch awkwardly. "I'm going to gather the others while you work with Mory. It's time to lay out the plan... and to begin."

She wandered out of the living room. I looked over at Mory.

The fledgling necromancer smiled at me tightly. "I'm sorry, Jade."

"Me too, Mory. Me too."

She pulled a pair of knitting needles out of her bag. "I brought every set I have. I didn't know which ones you'd want."

I nodded. But instead of taking the needles from her, I straightened and pulled her up off her knees and into a hug.

"I'm going to be okay," she said, muffled against my chest.

"I'm going to add more protections to your necklace," I said fiercely. "I just gave the shadow leech some coins. Freddie will bring them back and I'll add them to your necklace."

"Okay."

"And I won't leave you, Mory. I promise. No matter what."

"Okay."

"I might not be able to stop you from getting hurt, but I won't—"

"I'm not giving you the chocolate bar, Jade."

I laughed. I couldn't help it. I released the pissy necromancer and took the knitting needles from her.

I could be a good foot soldier too.

Chapter Nine

I wasn't entirely sure how much longer we all waited for the rest of the Talbot clan to arrive in full force, but it was longer than I liked. Then and only then, everyone finally gathered in Gran's front living room. Everyone, including Freddie—though I had to ask freaking permission in order to let the shadow leech through Gran's wards. Not everyone could actually sense Freddie's presence, obviously. But of those who could, everyone except Mory and me seemed to find the shadow leech currently perched on the mantel disconcerting.

Hazy memories or not, I still remembered Freddie trying to get between Reggie and me. At a point when letting me be taken, or even killed, would have been in the leech's best interests. Without me to rein it in, Freddie would have had the freedom to consume any magic it wanted. So yeah, I had fought my way past my grandmother and father, went outside the property wards, and brought Freddie back in with me. And the holier-than-freaking-thou Adepts gathered in the living room could give me as many disgruntled looks about it as they pleased.

They should have realized how freaking lucky they were that I hadn't sprinted off in the direction of the stadium once I set foot on the sidewalk, frankly. But I remembered the sketches in the first notebook. The young girl abandoned in a post-apocalyptic city with only a demon to protect her. So yeah, I just snagged the shadow leech and went back inside. As ordered.

Rochelle was perched on one of the love seats, with her right hand resting on the three full sketchbooks piled on the coffee table. A sketchbook and a set of charcoals sat to her left, both brand new. Beau stood silently behind his wife. The shifter's arms were crossed, but his expression was deceptively placid.

Apparently, I wasn't the only one getting frustrated about not moving forward.

The petite, pregnant oracle looked at each of us in turn, beginning with my father standing in the open doorway. The white of her magic was simmering in her eyes. Yazi nodded, acknowledging Rochelle's regard. Then he grinned at me as if he found the situation amusing.

And maybe it was. All of us, bristling with magic and weapons, waiting for the tiny oracle to release us to our tasks.

Problem was, I still wasn't completely certain what I was supposed to be doing, except trying to not trigger anything that would annihilate the city. Life was way, way easier when I just blundered around making mistakes that were patchable.

But the visions contained in Rochelle's sketchbooks weren't mere stumbles.

Rochelle let her gaze rest on my mother next. Having come directly from her bed against Qiuniu's express orders to rest, Scarlett was curled up in the love seat across from the oracle. Her strawberry magic was so muted that I had to seek it out specifically in order to distinguish it from all the other flavors stuffed into the living room. She still looked far too pale, but I wasn't hypocritical enough to demand that she stay out of the coming battle.

Gran, seated beside her daughter, looked stern and focused, but thankfully healthy.

The Talbots—all seven of them—were arrayed around the front windows, quietly clustered together. Except for Gabby, who wore white jeans and a white hoodie, each of them was dressed in various shades of black, dark navy, and charcoal. Peggy had practically flung herself at me when she'd arrived, and Gabby had actually smiled upon seeing me. The sorcerers—Angelica, Stephan, Liam, and Tony—felt swollen with power, making it an easy guess that they were currently carrying every magical artifact they possessed. And that was even after Tony had installed a bunch of magical gear in the map room the moment he'd stepped into the house. Bitsy stood with her brothers, just as tall and even fiercer looking.

The vampires and the necromancers stood on the opposite side of the room, making a highly unlikely grouping. Jasmine was closest to the fireplace with Benjamin. Mory was in the middle, next to her mother, Danica, and Teresa Garrick. Even distracted, I could sense the disdain and animosity that practically seethed between the golden-haired vampire and Benjamin's mother. Perhaps it was just the typical, seemingly inherent, dislike that those types of Adept bore for each other. But I couldn't shake the feeling that there was something extra going on between the two of them. Maybe with Benjamin, and even Mory, caught in the middle.

Burgundy and Olive were hovering behind the loveseat where Scarlett and Gran sat, nodding as the oracle looked to them. And then Rochelle looked at me last, standing on the opposite side of the fireplace.

Oddly, she reached out for me. I stepped forward. Kneeling, I took her hand, magic shifting between us.

And nothing happened.

The oracle sighed heavily. "All right." She nodded, releasing my hand. "What will be will be, now," she murmured. She glanced at me again, then over at my father. "We've been working on a plan for over a week, since we knew Jade was in the nexus. Since the visions ... shifted, became more specific. There were pieces we didn't have until she returned to us."

"Artifacts for the fledglings," my father said, indicating he'd been following along closely.

A slightly discontented murmur ran through the gathered so-called fledglings, and I almost laughed. To my father, a three-hundred-and-fifty-year-old guardian, everyone in the room was a fledgling. Well, not Gran, of course. She might have been almost three centuries younger, but no one in the room doubted she could kick all of our asses without lifting a finger.

Angelica cleared her throat, nervous but doing a fantastic job of hiding it. Her bangles and bracelets clinked quietly together as she stepped around the witches and the love seat, smoothing a detailed map open on the coffee table beside Rochelle's sketchbooks. "After Liam, Mory, and Tony started mapping the stadium, we were able to assess where the elves' defenses were thinnest, and where a small group might be able to infiltrate without being detected right away."

"As the map was pieced together, I started to get the visions of the items I've asked Jade to create," Rochelle said.

"Wait a second." I was still taking in what Angelica had said. "What do you mean by 'small group' and 'infiltrate'?"

"The oracle keeps talking around that point because you're not going to like it, dowser," Jasmine said.

"Yeah, that's been clear for a while now," I said snippily.

Angelica completely ignored me, continuing to lay out the plan for my father's benefit. And for Gran, presumably, since as far as I was aware, she'd been unconscious through all the formulating. "The sorcerers and witches will erect and hold a perimeter around the stadium."

"You've placed the fifth anchor?" my father asked.

Stephan nodded. "About thirty minutes ago. The elves haven't discovered our preliminary working yet, but they will need to be distracted so we can cast without worrying about being discovered in the act."

Every eye in the room settled on me.

"That's what I'm good for? Distracting the elves?"

A murmur of laughter ran through the misfits gathered around me.

Gran sniffed. "Well, you're certainly dressed for it."

The second round of laughter was far less suppressed than the first. And yeah, you'd have thought I was wearing a G-string and pasties by my grandmother's tone.

"Please continue," Scarlett said, frostily eyeing her mother.

"After the distraction is … implemented, Angelica, Stephan, Liam, and Tony, with Burgundy, will cast the perimeter," Rochelle said. "We don't have a fifth sorcerer, but Burgundy's magic is receptive."

"I'm a good conduit," the young witch added proudly. Then she glanced over at me. "We've done lots of tests."

When exactly had I been shoved into the position where everyone felt they had to justify every little thing they did? When had I become the substitute teacher for the class of misfits?

"Tony will return here," Angelica continued before I could get even pissier. "He will manage the map room in case the elves break ranks, or get by us and attack the city. We'll be communicating via text message, or through Peggy if the tech is compromised."

"We've been practicing," Peggy said, completely cheery as her mother laid out plans to thwart an invasion from another dimension. "Gabby will be with Mory, amplifying her. But also, as long as I can hear through the elves' wards, she should be able to communicate with me. Though we haven't been able to test that yet. For obvious reasons."

"From inside the stadium," I said bitingly. "Surrounded by an army of elves."

"Maybe we should pick up the pace," Jasmine said blithely. "Not all of us have that great an attention span."

I gave her a dark look—but then realized she was probably talking about herself. At her side, Benjamin was recording every word spoken in his notebook, and most likely cataloging every weapon and outfit in the room as well.

"I agree," my father said. "As much protection as the sorcerers, witches, and necromancers can hold around the stadium is paramount. And above all else, the witches' city boundary needs to hold whatever version of the future is about to unfold."

I looked at him, aghast. "To stop any backlash? If the gateway...explodes?" I didn't need to add the bit about that backlash killing us all. About it leveling the city.

He nodded grimly. "Based on the rate the magic is being consumed from the sword in the map room, I estimate we have a maximum of twelve hours."

"Eight," my grandmother interjected. "If the gateway isn't neutralized in the next eight hours, the youngest among us will be evacuated."

I opened my mouth to protest—to insist on evacuating right away.

But my grandmother continued before I could speak, pinning Rochelle with an intense gaze. "And the oracle will be evacuated as soon as Jade and Yazi enter the stadium."

"But not having me in the city might trigger the future we're trying to prevent," Rochelle said shakily.

"I will not discuss it further, Rochelle. At some point, you will need to trust us to do everything we can."

"Plus, there are always cellphones," Jasmine said.

Silence fell in the room. I would never have believed that so many people gathered in such a small space could be so quiet.

Beau laid a gentle hand on Rochelle's shoulder. The oracle's face crumpled, and she sobbed. Just once, but the sound twisted through me.

"I just kept hoping...that as we planned, as we implemented the plan, I would see more," the oracle whispered.

"You will, oracle," Gran said softly. "You will simply see it from a safe distance. And if the worst happens, you will retreat and regroup. With plenty of time to alter the fate you see for your unborn child."

Tears streamed down Rochelle's cheeks. She swallowed harshly, then nodded.

All the tension that had been ratcheting up since we'd gathered eased. Though it didn't completely disperse. It was obvious that I hadn't been the only one who'd been on edge about hauling a pregnant oracle into battle.

Mory shoved a package of tissue into Rochelle's hands.

Angelica cleared her throat. "To be brief, then." The dark-haired sorcerer cast a look at us all that suggested she wouldn't stand for any more interruptions. "Once we have the perimeter in place, Liam will hold it. I, along with Stephan, will help the witches break through the elves' wards. We doubt that we'll be able to disable them completely, but can hope to at least provide an egress, if needed."

Angelica and Gran exchanged nods.

"The necromancers will provide cover," Danica said. Then, with a sad but proud glance at her daughter, she added, "Teresa and I will."

"Benjamin, Bitsy, and I will rescue the warriors," Jasmine said. "Guided by Mory's maps." The vampire pinned her gaze on me, anticipating my rebuttal.

And naturally, I was going to give her one. "Benjamin, Bitsy, and you?" I echoed. "Why not me?"

"We've had this discussion," Rochelle said.

"We really haven't. Not to a level that's convinced me of anything." I pointed a vicious finger at Bitsy. "Can you even achieve half-form?"

"Nope," she sneered at me. "But I can run real fast."

"So can elves. This is insane. I can cut through magic—"

"There are three closed doors," Rochelle said, reaching for her sketchbooks.

"I don't want to see the damn sketches! I've been in there! By now, if they have the full gateway open, there'll be hundreds of elves in that freaking stadium!"

"And who can stand against them, my Jade?" my mother asked softly.

"Me!" I cried. "And...Dad! We'll go in. We'll free Warner, and Kandy, and Kett, and Haoxin. Then we'll regroup. Against all of us, the elves will be...will be ..."

Everyone was staring at me. But not like I was ranting. More as if...as if they pitied me.

"And then what?" Gran asked. "Then you'll tear down the gate? Or your father will?"

I brushed hot, angry tears from my cheeks, managing to contain a triumphant scream of *Yes!* Yes, I would tear the freaking gate down. It was mine, after all. I'd built it. It was my responsibility. To rescue the others. To close the gateway.

"Wait," Burgundy said hesitantly. "Isn't that exactly what Jade isn't supposed to do?"

Nervous laughter ran through the room.

I clenched my fists, then forced myself to relax my fingers. I wrapped my right hand around the hilt of my knife as I threaded the fingers of my left hand through my necklace, calming myself. "Just tell me the rest. Quickly, please."

Rochelle sighed softly. "You and Yazi will get Mory and Gabby to the gateway. Doing so will draw the elves' attention."

"You'd better believe it will."

"You will be the first line of offense and defense, providing cover for Mory. Then she, amplified by Gabby, will shut down the gate."

Angelica took over. "No elves will get past the perimeter, past us. But Jasmine, Ben, and Bitsy will be able to get the prisoners out of the stadium. They've been held for weeks, Jade. I doubt they'll be able to join you in the battle."

I didn't bother addressing her flawed assessment. I knew that nothing except death would keep Warner, Kandy, or Kett from waging war—because the same was true for me.

Except when I was repeatedly told that my doing so would trigger an apocalypse.

"And we're the distraction," I said quietly. "Yazi and me."

"Yes."

It was a carefully considered plan. One that would protect the city as best as possible. But it was insanely risky. In my mind, a two-person infiltration—my father and me—had a way higher chance of success.

"They won't go," I said. "Warner, Kandy, or Kett. Once they're free. You won't be able to drag them from the stadium, not if they have any strength left."

"The same will be true for Haoxin," my father added.

Yeah, there was no way the guardian was going anywhere once freed.

"That will be their choice," my grandmother said stiffly.

"I'm just saying that the egress won't be needed—"

"It's just smart, Jade. You don't want Bitsy or Benjamin trapped inside. Or anyone else, if they're wounded."

"And if the elves get by Yazi or me? We can't guarantee that our ability to distract them will work. They could go after the rescue team. They could even try to flee into the city. And en masse, they could overwhelm your protections."

"They aren't the type to break ranks and flee," my father said.

"We're prepared for some resistance," Jasmine said stiffly. "It's not like we haven't had to fend for ourselves, Jade."

"And if they do attempt to leave the stadium, they'll face the sorcerers, the necromancers, your mother, and me," Gran said. "We are more than up to the task. Formidable, in fact."

Yeah, I was stepping on delicate toes all over the place. And too freaking bad.

"Fine. You're all so, so much smarter and better prepared than me. There's just one tiny hiccup in your perfect plan." Yep, I was acting like an indignant toddler now, but I couldn't seem to rein my mouth in. "Cutting through the wards? Which, according to Mory, have been reinforced since I tore through them the first time? That's going to draw attention. Big attention. Like it did the first time. And, as I'm sure it's obvious to everyone ..."—I pointed to the map laid out on the coffee table—"... the maze has one purpose, and one purpose only. To bottleneck any incoming assault."

"Which is why you're sneaking in," Rochelle said, completely unruffled. "Then splitting into two groups and going your separate ways."

"Sneaking in? Shall I attempt to construct an artifact for that as well?"

"No, Jade," Rochelle said, far too patiently. Seriously, I would have been tearing my own head off at this point if I were her. "You've already taken care of the entry."

She tugged the top sketchbook toward her, flipping to the final sketch contained within. The most recent sketch, which I hadn't seen before. It depicted a fierce-looking elf, sword drawn, hand on a door latch. Her clothing was dripping with gemstones.

Mira's aunt.

"Alivia," I whispered, as all the wind was taken out of my high-and-mighty sails. "This is how she gets her revenge." I laughed harshly.

"Yes," Rochelle said. "Be ready to go in twenty minutes, please. I'll lead the infiltration group to the entry point, just in case a mass movement on our part triggers another vision."

Tony stepped forward, dropping an open backpack on top of the map on the coffee table. "Cellphones. Magically linked. If you don't have one already, take one. They're warded by Jasmine and me. We don't know if they'll work inside the stadium, but they should pass through the exterior wards." The fledgling sorcerer gave me a look, a proud smile curling at the edges of his lips. "We tested them thoroughly."

Everyone sprang into action, flooding from the room to gather supplies and coats and whatever else was needed. Gran took a cellphone from Tony's pile, as did Teresa.

My mother got to her feet carefully, but steadily. She crossed to me, placing her hands on either side of my face and just gazing at me lovingly for a moment. Then she tugged me forward so she could kiss the scar on my forehead. "You need a quick nap, Jade. You've expended a lot of magic today already."

"Mom—"

"Fifteen minutes. Now." She turned away from me without waiting for an answer, reaching out to my father. He immediately stepped forward, taking her hand and tucking her arm through his elbow. She leaned against him, in a gesture more about affection than weakness, I thought. Together, they wandered out of the room.

Without anything else to prepare, I snagged a cellphone. Then I coaxed the shadow leech off the mantel and onto the arm of the loveseat, laid down on that love seat, and closed my eyes.

Freddie shifted, curling into my shoulder and chittering so quietly that the leech might have actually been purring. I didn't mind one bit. I simply allowed all the tasty energy running through and around the house to lull me into a meditative state.

I could afford to recharge for fifteen minutes. I knew the others weren't going anywhere without me.

The touch of my mother's magic woke me as she brushed her fingers across my scarred forehead, murmuring a healing spell under her breath. Sharing magic with me that she didn't have the resources to expend.

I opened my eyes to meet her sad gaze, which warmed when she smiled.

"Time to go?" I asked.

"Yes." She pressed a kiss to my forehead. "I knew the elves would never be able to hold you, my darling Jade."

"Actually, I'm surprised they put up with me for so long."

The joke came out awkward and flat, but my mother laughed quietly anyway.

"I'm to stay here until Tony returns," she said. Then, as if anticipating my questions, she added, "Burgundy has left me some of her excellent healing charms, cast using her new focal stone. And I will not, under any circumstances, be stepping back into the witches' grid. If it falls, it falls. I'm not certain I could stop it now even if I tried."

"How many times have you made that promise?" I asked, trying for a teasing tone. Though I had to push through layers of my own grimness to do so.

"Three times." My mother laughed quietly again, and the sound carried more magic with it. It unfurled smoothly across my chest, easing the pent-up frustration and pain I was still carrying, and leaving a lingering, sweet strawberry aftertaste in my mouth.

I glanced toward the open doorway where I could feel my father's magic. Yazi was watching us—his family—intently. His golden hair was practically glowing in the dim light, his black leather armor all laced up and glistening with magic.

I sat up, threading my fingers through my mother's. She settled on the love seat beside me. Freddie had disappeared. I took in the dark room and the empty feel of the house around me, allowing myself the physical contact. Allowing myself the moment to acknowledge the love carried with my mother's magic.

"There's one thing we haven't discussed," I finally said, loosening my hold on my mother and standing up to face my father. "Another objection to using the misfits."

"And what is that?" my father asked.

"Reggie. The telepathic elf. Mory, Gabby, Jasmine, Benjamin, and Bitsy aren't going to have the immunity you and I have to her. Never mind what'll happen if she steps outside the stadium."

My father nodded. "We will keep her focused on us."

"Yeah? And how do we guarantee that?"

He grinned. "By continually pressing her warriors, forcing them to constantly defend her. The maze can be used against them, once we penetrate its center."

"By blocking the exits."

"Exactly. And your grandmother has provided us with some handy spells to that effect. Once the gate has been neutralized by the necromancer, you will kill this Reggie. Though if I understand anything about the elves, sending her back defeated would also be a death sentence."

"Okay."

"Okay."

I squeezed my mother's hand one last time, then retrieved my katana and satchel, joining my father in the doorway. The house felt utterly bereft of magic. I could still sense the map room, but most of the others had filtered out while I'd been napping.

My father reached his hand toward my mother. She stepped across the room to take it. "Take care of yourself," he said.

"And you," my mother whispered, brushing a kiss across his lips.

I probably shouldn't have been staring at them. But I found I couldn't look away. I had never seen my parents together. I'd never even wished for it, but there was something...something about that moment I wanted to mark.

Perhaps marching to your possible demise made your connection to those you loved more intense.

"I'll bring our girl back," Yazi whispered.

"I have no doubt." My mother smiled at me. "We have a wedding to celebrate, after all."

I grinned back at her. It was silly, but yeah, it was always good to have something to look forward to. Fuel for the fight, aka hope. To get me to the other side of the vision of death and despair that was my immediate future.

Two cars were waiting in the driveway, swathed in the deep gloom of the late December evening. Gran and Olive were to join Burgundy and the sorcerers, who I assumed were already on their way. And Beau, Rochelle, and Mory were apparently waiting on me and my father.

Yazi climbed into the oracle's vehicle, but my grandmother reached for me, so I crossed to her first.

She spoke before I could. "I cannot imagine how difficult this afternoon has been for you, Jade. Waiting while we moved about and set things in order as the oracle saw them. But together, we will prevail."

"I know, Gran."

She tilted her head, thoughtful but stern. "I'm not certain you do. But ..." She paused. Then she smiled as if something had just occurred to her. "Try to have fun, my granddaughter. There will not be many days that you will be able to wield unfettered what it is your destiny to wield. Enjoy it."

"Enjoy the elf slaughter?" I laughed edgily. "That's different coming from you, Gran. I always thought you saw cupcakes and trinkets as my destiny."

She smiled, oddly smug. "I was wrong, Jade." She squeezed my hands. "It's been known to happen on occasion." She turned to climb into her car. "We'll hold the line. Trust us."

"I do."

She nodded, shut the door, and started the car. I stepped away and watched her back out of the drive and onto the road. Then I glanced back at the vehicle waiting for me. Rochelle was leaning against the rear of the SUV, head bowed. The satchel slung across her chest emphasized the full round of her belly.

Even if everything went to hell, Rochelle would survive. Because her child had a future. Admittedly, it wasn't a fantastic future. But it meant that Rochelle, at least, wouldn't die today. That was another tiny ray of hope to take with me. A bit more fuel to get me through the next few hours.

I closed the distance between us. Rochelle raised her head, meeting my gaze. She hadn't bothered covering her light-gray eyes with her sunglasses.

"So …" I cleared my throat and tried for a playful tone, mostly failing miserably. "Despite all the planning and fussing about, if we're barreling toward destiny, I imagine this might be goodbye, oracle. I'm sorry if I fail you."

Rochelle reached up, placing her cold hands against my cheeks. Magic shifted between us, bristling up the oracle's arms and brushing against me. The taste of tart green apple filled my mouth.

But Rochelle's eyes remained their light-gray color. No vision rose within them.

As far as I'd ever been able to figure out, that meant we were currently doing what we were supposed to be doing. According to magic, at least.

Of course, that didn't necessarily mean that magic was on our side.

"Nah," Rochelle said. "If we weren't unmaking destiny, there wouldn't have been so much fiddling." She turned toward the open door of the front passenger seat, but looked back at me before climbing in. "And, Jade?"

"Yeah?"

"I don't think you are capable of failing. Because … you believe. You believe in all of it. In love, and family, and friendship. In protecting those who need to be protected. In accepting … everyone. So whatever is about to happen, it doesn't occur because you failed."

"Okay."

Rochelle laughed, seemingly without meaning to. "Okay."

Then we climbed into the SUV and headed off to thwart destiny. Because Rochelle was right.

I did ultimately believe.

I believed, in the simplest of terms, that good always triumphed. That good people could come together and vanquish any evil.

Even though there were always blurred lines. And over and over again, a price to be paid.

Rochelle pored over her sketches during the quick drive along the water, over the bridge, and across to the stadium. All around us, the city and its people just carried on as if everything wasn't about to possibly be wiped from the face of the earth. A steady stream of headlights reflected on the wet pavement. It had been raining earlier, but that had abated to just a mist across the windshield now. Pedestrians were walking their dogs on the seawall. Groups of friends chatted over lattes in the Starbucks on the corner of Yew Street. People heading home from work were grabbing sushi or falafel takeout for dinner.

Beau parked far enough away from BC Place that I could only see the white steel pylons that soared above the stadium. But the moment I stepped out of the vehicle into the well-lit but empty parking lot that bordered the Plaza of Nations, I could feel the magic of the exterior wards the elves had erected after I'd escaped.

And by 'escaped,' I meant after I was carted off by Pulou only moments away from rescuing Warner, and then was almost beaten to death.

Yeah, I was going to hold onto that grudge for a long, long while.

Assuming I got the chance.

A dark shadow manifested at the top of a tall white metal lamppost. Apparently, the shadow leech was ready to join in on the all-you-can-eat magical buffet. Well, a buffet for Freddie, at least. What the rest of us were about to experience wasn't likely to be quite as palatable.

I beckoned the leech toward me, then settled it on Mory's shoulder under the disapproving gaze of my father. The necromancer wagged her fingers at Freddie playfully, but her expression was tense with fear and determination.

After exchanging silent glances, Beau and Rochelle led us through the parking lot, underneath an underpass, and up a wide set of concrete stairs. I got the feeling everyone but me had spent a lot of time walking that exact route, including my father. Mory stuck close by me, not knitting for once.

We paused as a group at the top landing. The wide concrete walkway encircling the stadium branched out to the right and left, and another set of wide stairs led down to a lower entrance marked with a large royal-blue letter G. Though the building itself was almost pretty—soaring white steel and a mix of blue and clear glass—everything about the exterior architecture was big and broad, built for crowds of thousands filtering in before a football or soccer game, then thundering out all at once.

You could walk around the entire building via the concrete stairs and walkways without once needing to cross out to the surrounding streets or sidewalks. I'd never seen it devoid of people before, pedestrians or otherwise.

I'd also never entered the stadium from that particular section. But it took only a quick glance around to figure out that it was a smart choice, offering lots of overhead cover and multiple exits. And I wasn't surprised that it was a weak spot in the elves' defenses. If I was remembering correctly, the gateway was situated farther away from this entrance than any other.

Magic tasting of peanut butter shifted to our left, revealing Gabby, Bitsy, and Liam standing near one of the wide circular concrete columns underneath the overhead walkway. Jasmine and Ben slipped out of the shadows to the far left at the same time.

The windows on this side of the stadium were dark. And despite the thick layer of magic coating it, the entire building felt oddly abandoned. Lifeless, on the edge of a city that teemed with energy and light.

Rochelle opened a sketchbook, lifting it before her with both hands high enough that I could see it over her head. She held it open to a sketch that spanned both pages, depicting the scene before us. The concrete stairs, the ticket booths to the left of the entrance doors, the large G, and even the glass-and-steel-cable awning.

Gabby joined Mory. Bitsy stepped over to join Jasmine and Benjamin, who were both doing solid impressions of statues—if statues had a habit of glistening with magic. Benjamin's power was limited and shaped by the bone bracelet on his left wrist, which I could sense but not see underneath the sleeve of his thin ivory-colored sweater.

Actually, now that I was paying attention, Jasmine, Bitsy, and Benjamin had all changed into light-colored clothing. As had Mory and Gabby. All I could think about was that none of it was going to survive the coming fight particularly well.

Rochelle flipped a page in the book, revealing the sketch of Alivia at the door. We all shifted as one, just enough to peer down the stairs. The glass doors to the right of the ticket booth windows at the bottom landing remained closed.

All righty then. That vision wasn't happening yet.

Liam hunkered down beside the wide concrete pillar, murmuring as he ran his finger along a pentagram that had been etched into the concrete at his feet. This entrance was clearly one of the five anchor points the sorcerers had set up previously. Magic glistened around Liam, most likely a ward of some kind that I hoped was blocking him from view. He straightened, looking at me as he tucked his sweater into the front of his jeans and double-checked the placement of the badge clipped to his belt. Then he pulled his gun from his holster, holding it ready by his side.

From his vantage point, he had a perfect view of the entrance the oracle had led us to. And for some reason, that soothed me. Liam would be there to help if someone who needed it exited the stadium. And if an elf happened to be chasing that someone, I had no doubt the sorcerer would put them down.

I nodded to Liam and he returned the gesture, then tilted his head slightly as if listening to something I couldn't hear. He nodded again. "We're all ready."

Peggy, talking to him telepathically, at best guess.

"Okay," I said. "Let's keep moving." I stepped around Rochelle and Beau, striding across the walkway—and noting a large RV parked far down the street to my right as I did. It was dark enough that I couldn't make out the driver or passenger, but it was an easy guess that it was Rochelle's adoptive parents and her ride out of all this craziness.

Good.

Thank God, actually.

I was two steps away from the bottom landing when I felt the edge of the elves' wards. So, pretty much standing out in the open in full view of all the windows. My father had followed me partway down the stairs, but was standing off to one side. Mory and Gabby were tight behind me—right where I was pretty sure the oracle had told them to stay at all times.

I raised my hand, ghosting my palm against the magic that prevented me from getting any closer to the building. It felt different, tasting of evergreen and fern, damp moss, and a hint of what might have been fuzzy apricot. Though I'd been a little out of my head the last time I'd tasted the power encasing the stadium, that taste was now thicker, richer than before.

Soft murmurs rose behind me. At the top of the stairs, Jasmine, Benjamin, and Bitsy were glancing back and forth between Rochelle's sketchbook and pieces of paper that they each held. Most likely, they were comparing Mory's maps to the sketches of the halls and doors between this entrance and the place where the prisoners were held.

I clenched and unclenched my fists, fighting through an urge to tear through the wards, race into the building, and rescue everyone myself.

"That way lies the apocalypse, Jade," I muttered, reminding myself.

My father laughed quietly, then grinned at me when I shot him a look.

I lifted my hand a second time. "Ready or not—"

"Oh, shit. Shit!" Bitsy cried out behind me.

I whirled around, calling my knife into my hand—and almost skewering the junior werewolf as she barreled down the stairs toward me, holding a tiny black box.

"Tony gave this to me to give to you," she said. "He's been working on a locator device…with Jasmine." She glanced back up to the golden-haired vampire. "They siphoned off bits of the elves' wards. So, like the cellphones, it should hold against that magic. Um, hopefully."

She passed me the tiny device, not even glancing at the deadly knife in my hand, then jogged back up the stairs. A sourness churned through my belly. They were all so untrained. So not ready.

And I really, really didn't want to know why I was being gifted with a locator device, when as far as I knew, no one else had one. I met Rochelle's steady gaze, then tucked the tiny black metal box inside a pocket in my leather vest. The oracle nodded, satisfied.

Mory touched my forearm, her gaze on my jade knife. I released the hilt, and the blade settled back into its built-in invisible sheath.

"Cool," Gabby murmured.

"Tony worked on my phone as well," Mory said quietly. "Not just the ones he passed out. He added the tracking thingy to each of our devices, including Benjamin, Bitsy, and Burgundy. So the oracle will be able to get through to us if anything changes. And ... if we go missing ..." She let the thought trail off, offering no indication of why I'd been gifted with a secondary tracking device.

"Sure," I said as amicably as possible. "Until we're within steps of the gateway."

Mory nodded, undaunted.

"That's why we have Peggy," Gabby said. "She'll be tied to the sorcerer perimeter, so she'll be able to communicate with me, even when we're at the gateway. Once they open the egress, for certain."

"You know what they say about plans," I said, turning back to the towering wall of elf magic hindering my forward progress.

"Best way to stay organized?" Mory said pertly. "And to adapt to sudden changes?"

I shook my head, shoving my left hand into my satchel to brush my fingers against Kandy's cuffs, and then the hilt of Warner's knife. Soon, soon, my pretties. Soon the artifacts would be back with their proper owners.

Then, unable to wait one moment longer to make that happen, I raised my right hand to the energy simmering before me. But instead of ripping through the ward magic, I knocked.

Yes, three polite taps.

Time to trigger another of the oracle's visions.

My magic rippled across the elves' wards, quickly fading within their viscous energy.

I waited, loosening my grip on my own magic and allowing it to accumulate around me. Just in case we were about to switch to plan B.

Nothing happened.

I raised my hand to knock again when one of the lower doors opened and Alivia half-stepped out. She had a sword in one hand as she swept a glittering, green-eyed gaze across the Adepts arrayed on the steps before her. Then she glanced up at the dark sky. "Took you long enough, wielder," she said in her lyrically accented English. Her gaze settled on my father. "And you brought company."

"I did."

"Will you be attempting to close the path today?"

"We will."

"I am forewarned, then."

"And who else is forewarned, elf?" my father asked, magic threading through his words.

"No one, warrior," Alivia said, proving that she knew who was standing before her. Then she smiled, displaying wickedly sharp teeth. "No one yet." She settled her smug gaze on me. "She has yet to figure it out."

"Reggie? That we're coming? Or that you're helping us?"

She laughed mirthlessly. "No. She has yet to learn how much, much more powerful true loyalty is on the battlefield."

My father glanced toward me. "Are we being used to teach an elf a lesson?"

"It seems so."

"True loyalty?" Yazi stepped up beside me. "Is there any other kind?"

"Everything can be falsely created, warrior." Alivia swept her hand forward.

The magic shifted before me, creating a slight opening in the wards. "You call it magic. We call it science and technology. Both can be used to create, to connect, and to destroy and kill."

My father stepped through the opening in the wards, pausing on the other side and scanning the area before him. "They are one and the same, elf."

"Ah, but build your fortress on sand and what happens?"

"You are susceptible to the elements."

Alivia laughed, sounding actually delighted. "And so I invite the storm. To sweep this mess away."

I followed my father through the ward line, keeping Mory and Gabby close behind me. Jasmine, Benjamin, and Bitsy were tucked up behind my father.

Alivia eyed us for a moment, then glanced up to Rochelle and Beau on the stairs behind us. I didn't think she could see Liam from her low point of view. "This is all of you?"

"For now," I said.

She nodded. The magic sealed behind us. "I cannot clear your path any further than I have already. Not without drawing attention sooner than is prudent. And I will not aid you a third time, Jade. Magic moves differently in this realm, and I would not have you placed in my debt." She hesitated, then added, "Not all who stand before you wish to be here."

"I can't distinguish the difference if they're all trying to kill me."

"I know." The elf glanced at all of us, all the power arrayed on the concrete steps before her. "Try to be worthy of my betrayal."

"Try being the leader your people need," my father said.

Alivia twisted her mouth into a snarl, but quickly tempered her response. "I shall endeavor to do so." Then she slipped back into the stadium without another word.

My father darted forward, grabbing the door before it clicked shut, then stepping inside the stadium. The others filtered in after him. Mory lingered behind with me.

I glanced back up at Rochelle and Beau. The oracle was standing at the top of the concrete stairs with her sketchbook clutched tightly to her chest.

I waited, taking a moment to breathe in the cool night air. Waiting to see if she had any last-minute revelations.

But Rochelle only shook her head, then raised her hand in farewell.

I smiled but didn't wave back, because I really didn't want to say goodbye to an oracle a second time. Why tempt fate?

Beau took Rochelle's hand, and together they stepped away.

Still smiling, I turned back to meet Mory's earnest gaze. "Ready, my necromancer?"

"Yes, wielder," she said, nodding her head in a formal bow.

"I trust you, Mory," I said. Willing myself to accept my own statement, to believe it.

Mory lifted her chin. "I'll do my best."

The shadow leech on her shoulder ruffled its wings and chittered quietly.

"You too, Freddie," I said. Then I turned to lead us into the future, fervently hoping it wasn't the destiny pictured in the first two sketchbooks Rochelle had shown me.

There was nothing to do about the visions now. I could only follow the plan as best I could, save those I could save—and try like hell to not be the one to bring the gateway down.

As I remembered from escaping the stadium while brain-damaged, every inch of its newly raised white hallways glistened with elf magic. In the section through which we entered, ceilings had been added, effectively completely boxing us into the maze.

And of course that was the moment when I figured out why everyone but my father and me were wearing light-colored clothing. The other five practically blended into the walls—and would help guarantee that all the elves' attention would be on Yazi and me.

Following Mory's map of the interior, we regrouped at a three-way fork in the corridor. The way we'd come from the side entrance lay behind us. A long hall with no exits stretched out to the left and right.

Jasmine and Bitsy bowed their heads over the map in Benjamin's hand. "Left, then two right turns," the dark-haired vampire murmured.

Far, far away, I could feel the steady pulse of the gateway. It felt practically on the opposite side of the stadium, though I knew it was closer to the center than that. The feel of its power indicated it was open. Wide open. With God knows how many elves funneling through it.

Yazi pressed his palm against the wall closest to him. He was reading its magic by touch, as I did just by intention.

Jasmine, Bitsy, and Benjamin slipped away to the left without any fanfare, quietly following their portion of the oracle's carefully laid out plan. Mory and Gabby watched them go. But I tracked their magic much farther than I could see, until I lost the taste of it among the elves' walls and halls and ceilings, all pungent evergreen and moss. Layers and layers of enemy magic between me and those under my protection.

They were on their own, and I felt their absence as a chill down my spine. A dreadful, foreboding chill.

My father stepped away from the wall. "I suspect I could go through." He pointed in the direction in which I could feel the gateway.

I nodded. "I don't doubt it. But that would put us on the opposite side of the gateway than what was pictured in the oracle's sketch...if I'm remembering the layout of all this correctly. Assuming the elves haven't shifted or changed anything since I last laid eyes on it. But in any case, if we bust through, we might find a legion of elves between us and where Mory and Gabby need to be to close the gate."

My father nodded, already stepping forward, turning right. "Better to be sneaky then, and follow the oracle's direction for a little while longer. Getting the necromancer and amplifier closer to the gate before announcing our presence would be ideal, even if a little boring."

I followed, wanting to laugh at his 'boring' comment, but finding I needed to focus in order to force myself to put more distance between me and the rescue team. My every step felt weighted with guilt and terror.

"Usually there are guards patrolling the halls," Mory said from behind me. "Concentrated closer to the center. It actually feels weird that we haven't seen any yet. Sometimes Ed would have to wait ten or fifteen minutes for a hall to clear. Though that wasn't as much of an issue after Jade gave him the power of invisibility."

My father glanced back at me, oddly disconcerted.

"Not true invisibility," I scoffed, brushing off the necromancer's claim.

"The elf, maybe," Gabby murmured. "Alivia? She said she wasn't going to help again, but she also said something about clearing our path as much as she could. If I were her, I would have cleared the halls to cover letting us in."

My father grunted, unconcerned. But then, facing elves and other beings that wished the world ill was his life's work, so little about this situation would concern him. Being a demigod had to come with some perks.

"Left, right, or straight?" my father asked.

We'd arrived at another fork without me even seeing it. Everything in white all the time—walls, floors, ceilings—was playing hell with my vision.

The elves were smart, smart cookies.

Unfortunately.

Paper crinkled behind me. "Left," Gabby said, checking the map.

My father gestured to the left, ceding the lead to me. As I stepped past him, he fell in behind to sandwich the necromancer and the amplifier between us.

I whispered a prayer for the others, already feeling cut off from all the plans upon plans we were implementing. But I was just one small part of those plans. As it should be, really.

I called my knife into my hand, a not-so-nice smile stretching across my face. My facial muscles protested. "Coming for you, Reggie," I murmured, hoping that somehow, magic might carry my threat to its intended recipient.

The time for questions was long past.

And honestly, I always felt easier not thinking quite so much anyway.

At best guess, we were halfway to the center of the stadium and had just taken another left when three elves decked out in their white blood armor stepped directly into our path. Aside from their magic and their green eyes, they blended into the corridor perfectly.

I honestly hadn't thought about that function of the all-white decor. I always was a little slow to put two and two together. But I usually eventually came up with someone or something to knife, so it was all good.

I laughed. Yep. Utterly and manically delighted.

I blamed the head wound.

But even recognizing my own inappropriate anticipation didn't stop me from raising my jade knife and widening my stance.

Then Mory had to ruin it all, tearing through the mounting tension by piping up behind me as she attempted to peer around my shoulder. "With heads, please."

The elf in the center of the trio stepped forward, the two others directly behind. The hallway was too tight to fight three abreast. Each elf manifested short, deadly sharp, milky-crystal blades on the fly.

"What?" I asked Mory.

"It's just a theory …"

"Mory!"

"You said you trusted me."

My father started laughing, his magic rumbling through the floor and quaking along the walls.

The elves hesitated, disconcerted.

"Jesus Christ in a muffin basket!" I snarled, running my hand down my necklace and collecting all three silver centipedes in one swift pass. The metallurgy capable of killing a guardian trilled excitedly—though hopefully only I picked up on that.

My father continued laughing, though he managed to tone it down to a snicker.

Okay, it wasn't like I hadn't known where I got the whole humor-in-the-midst-of-adversity thing.

The elves recovered their bravado, raised their weapons, and rushed me.

I unleashed the centipedes with a flick of my wrist. The deadly artifacts arced forward, streaking silver-tinted magic through the blindingly white corridor.

The first centipede hit the chest of the nearest elf. He dropped so suddenly and heavily that the floor lifted underneath my feet.

The elf on the right got his sword between the centipede and his face, slashing horizontally to block the artifact with such vicious strength that he embedded his blade in the wall. Unfortunately for him, the instrument of assassination simply latched onto the crystalline weapon, then skittered up the blade, twining around the elf's arm—and apparently freezing him in place, still clinging to his sword.

The third elf, who'd been a step behind the other two, threw herself to her knees, attempting to slide underneath the centipede aimed for her head. She actually managed to clear its arcing path, twisting forward while pinning me with a smug look as she continued her attack.

The centipede reversed course in midair, slamming into and latching onto the back of her head. She fell flat, sliding to within a few inches of my forward foot and lying there, shocked still.

"Huh," I said. "They really lock onto their prey. Good to know."

Mory and Gabby shoved up next to me, peering down at the elf just as the centipede started burrowing its way into her ear.

"Holy fu…I mean …" Gabby gushed, talking over herself. "I knew you were…everyone said you put the 'bad' in 'bad ass'…but the cupcakes and the bakery…and the T-shirts…and the hair …"

"What's wrong with my hair?" I asked, genuinely dismayed.

"Nothing!" Gabby snapped up straight, staring at me with wide, rounded eyes. "Absolutely nothing! I…just…I mean…it's all curly and bouncy…and …"

"Blond," my father helpfully supplied.

Gabby pointed at him emphatically. "Yes. Yes, blond." Apparently, the amplifier had forgotten that she was also a blond, though without the bouncy curls.

I shot my father a look. Mirth danced in his eyes. And also…pride?

"Jade," Mory said crossly. "I said with heads. What is that silver thing doing?"

"Best guess? Scrambling their brains."

Gabby looked at Mory. "Do they need brains?"

"I'm not sure. Nah, probably not."

I glanced over at my father, who was watching the fledgling necromancer with interest. "So it's just me who can't believe we're standing around having this conversation?"

My father smiled, but perfunctorily. "Retrieve the instruments, wielder. Let's see what the necromancer can do."

I called the centipedes to return to the necklace. The three artifacts streaked back toward me, clicking into place and avoiding Warner's parents' wedding rings, as they always did. Gooey elf blood—and quite possibly brain matter—crumbled into fine flakes, dusting my black-leather-swathed chest. Well, now it appeared like I had breast dandruff, or a real thing for icing sugar. That seriously ruined the look.

"Ready?" Gabby asked Mory. Apparently, the two of them had discussed whatever they were about to do ahead of time.

I just utterly adored being kept out of the loop.

"Yes."

Gabby stepped up behind Mory, who tugged her knitting project out of her bag—a colorful hat, at best guess—and faced the fallen elves. She began to knit. Inexplicably.

The amplifier cupped the back of Mory's neck, threading her fingers through the necromancer's red-and-purple-streaked hair, cradling the back of Mory's skull.

Toasted marshmallow magic smeared in raspberry jam filled my senses, a flood of smell and taste.

Freddie abandoned the necromancer's shoulder, latching onto mine instead.

"Rise and shine," Mory said in a singsong whisper. Her necromancy power flooded out of her and sank into the elf nearest her.

The elf's feet twitched.

Then Mory's power flowed to the elf still hanging limply from the blade embedded into the wall. He shuddered.

My father laughed huskily under his breath.

"Up and at 'em," Mory said, claiming the third elf with her necromancy as she did.

All three elves stood, moving like puppets on Mory's string. Except in the necromancer's case, the string was yarn. She'd somehow knitted her power into the residual… what? Magic? Life force? The souls of the elves? Whatever it was, she'd used it to create herself some zombies.

Zombie elves.

Well. That was new.

The zombies stood ramrod straight, shoulder to shoulder, and staring blankly forward with deadened eyes. They weren't decomposing or crumbling into crystal, which made sense. Just like Mory's necromancy held Ed in an undead sort of stasis, it would do the same for them.

"Jesus Christ on a freaking cupcake," I muttered.

"Turn," Mory said. "Await instructions."

The elves turned in one smooth motion, then paused. They filled the corridor side to side, each standing at least a head taller than me.

Mory had created an elf shield.

I thought my head might explode. I turned to share my disbelief with my father, but he was grinning madly.

"Graduation day," he said, laughing quietly.

"We are supposed to be the distraction, right?" Mory asked, looking back at me. An uncertain tone warred with her defiant expression.

"Right." I shook my head. "Right."

Gabby dropped her hands, rubbing them together with satisfaction.

"Lead the way, necromancer," my father said. "Elves front. But you and the amplifier behind Jade."

Mory and Gabby slipped back behind me, dutifully standing between my father and me.

"You didn't use the new needles," Gabby said quietly to Mory.

Mory shrugged, keeping the bulk of her attention on the magic connecting her to the elves arrayed before me. I could actually feel the thin tendrils of toasted-marshmallow power stretching out past me.

"It didn't feel like I needed them yet."

Gabby laughed. "You totally didn't."

A thought occurred to me. "Hey, Mory. Can you, like, read their last thoughts or anything? I really wouldn't mind knowing how many elves have made it through the gateway already. Or what Reggie knows about us, if anything." Though I didn't say it, I was also worried about whether severing the telepathic elf's connection to the three elves-turned-zombies was already a dead giveaway that we were wandering the halls. I had no idea how often Reggie bothered to check in on her warriors between issuing orders.

Mory gave me an utterly disgusted look, though. "No. They're dead. That's a seriously creepy idea, Jade."

My father snorted back a laugh.

"Well," I drawled, "it's always good to know where the line is, necromancer." I gestured dramatically toward the elves. "By all means, lead the way with your undead minions. No one is going to think that's creepy as all hell."

Mory lifted her chin, sniffing her displeasure at me.

The elves started walking. In sync.

I glanced back at my father. "By the way, that's Jade 3." I gestured toward the undead elves with three fingers, then tapped my chest. "Yazi 0."

A grin spread across my father's face. "I've been hunting elves for over three hundred years. I'd say you've got some catching up to do, little one."

Ignoring the way my heart warmed at the term of endearment, I snarked back. "The count reset when we crossed through the exterior wards. Because if I can't remember how many I took down before, you can't count them either."

My father nodded his head formally. "By all means, wielder. Your invasion, your rules."

I laughed—and understood as I did how joking about murdering sentient beings made it really obvious just how close I was to the edge.

But what else was I going to do? Fall apart?

"Right," Mory muttered behind me. "Because necromancy is just so disturbing ..."

We continued forward, the zombie elves leading the way. After allowing us the time to get a few steps ahead of him, my father tossed a small stone over his shoulder. Magic tasting of freshly cut grass and lilacs exploded behind us—and the walls, floor, and ceiling all warped, as if the corridor had folded in on itself. We'd be safe from attack from behind.

But there was no exit anymore.

No way back.

Seven turns, six white-walled corridors glimmering with magic, and another half-dozen elves incapacitated later, and we paused for a respite—hunkering down behind what was rapidly becoming Mory's zombie-elf army.

And yeah, 'incapacitated' was a nice way of saying 'murdered then roped into service to a necromancer.' Three of the elves had fallen by way of the centipedes, one met my knife, and two had their necks snapped by my father.

I was pretty sure we'd all be suffering nightmares for years if we got through the next couple of hours alive. Except for my father. This was everyday life for a guardian. But I couldn't imagine myself living in this state of fearful anticipation, of continually meting out justice and violence. I'd never been more pleased to be only a half-dragon in my life. There was no guardian mantle in my future.

Brushing those thoughts aside, I pressed my hand to the wall, feeling the intense magic of the gateway just on the other side. I was achingly aware of how far away I was from where I really wanted to be—namely, releasing Warner, Kandy, and Kett.

"Mory," I whispered. "The gate is closer to one side of the stadium, yes? This side?"

The necromancer nodded distractedly. The bulk of her attention remained trained on her zombie elves, which were currently forming a blockade at the opening to the next fork in the maze, about a dozen feet in front of us.

Gabby pulled the folded maps out of her pocket, shuffling through them to find the detail of the center of the stadium. Tony had taken notes from Mory via Ed, using that and any camera footage that survived the intense magic emanating from the gate to generate various maps with different directions for each objective. Each group—the infiltrators, the rescuers, and the backup—held copies of everyone else's objectives, just in case everything went sideways. Because everything always went sideways, didn't it? Best-laid plans and all that, yadda yadda.

Gabby pressed the detail of the center of the stadium up against the wall, smoothing it out.

I tapped the map, indicating the hall I was fairly certain we were currently standing in. A notation on the map informed me that the gateway was approximately twenty-five feet away. Through that wall.

"Given the tenor of the magic," I said, tapping the map again, "It feels like we're here."

My father glanced over my shoulder, then down the hall behind us, watching our backs. He had closed two more halls behind us as we'd drilled farther into the maze, spiraling ever closer to our objective, but none of us were taking any chances. "I concur."

"I'm surprised we haven't encountered more resistance."

"They know we're here." My father nodded toward the zombie elves. "The telepath, if she's any good, would have been able to sense when she loses connection to one of those under her command."

"If she cares to check. I'm fairly certain she only keeps tabs on those she's utilizing in some way."

Yazi twisted his lips grimly. "Yes. If she cares. But either way, the telepath has chosen to hold the open ground instead of utilizing the maze as soon as she became aware of our presence." He gestured to the large space around the gateway. "The elves will attack en masse when we try to exit this hall, keeping us bottlenecked."

"Tony said their plan would be to drive us back if we got this far," Gabby offered helpfully. "Keeping us trapped and confused in the maze. Easy to pick off. Especially if we get separated from each other."

"Exactly." My father offered the amplifier a quick smile.

She grinned, pleased.

I nodded thoughtfully. "So what if we do something a little more … unexpected? We are supposed to be the distraction, right?"

"Whatever we're going to do," Mory said, "we need to do it quickly. The others are waiting on us before they implement their part of the plan. We don't need them getting snatched before they've even attempted the rescue."

My father flashed me a grin, glancing up at the open girders way, way above our heads. The elves hadn't added ceilings to this section of the maze yet. "Go over the wall?"

I answered his gleeful anticipation with a grin of my own. "Or through? Like we discussed before, except now we're on the right side of the gateway. So going through won't contradict the oracle's visions. Plus, it'll be easier for Mory and Gabby to follow."

My father laughed huskily. He gestured Mory and Gabby back against the far wall. "Zombies for cover, necromancer."

Mory shifted four of her nine dead elves in front of her and Gabby. The zombies' movements weren't as smooth as before, as if Mory was jerking on them with her own power. Nine might have been pushing the limits of what she could command, but despite her drawn face, the necromancer didn't complain. And I didn't question her. As promised.

My father stepped back to eye the wall before us.

Gabby pulled out her phone, applying her thumbs to her screen. "Texting Jasmine," she murmured.

"The walls haven't appeared to be unusually thick," my father said.

"Coated in magic, though."

Yazi pulled his golden sword out of thin air. Its magic rushed through the corridor, reflecting back at us from the walls. "And what is such magic to the likes of you or me, my Jade?"

Mory snorted from behind us, talking to Gabby. "Good call. Looks like the sneaky part of the plan is about to be tossed out the window."

"Nah." I stepped back from my father, giving him room to move as I covered the exit. "We've got to make the window first. Or, rather, a doorway of our very own."

Mory and Gabby peered around the shoulders of the zombies.

"Behind the elves," I said, momentarily forgetting I was trying to be cool about their involvement.

Mory stuck her tongue out at me. Then she and Gabby hunkered down behind the zombies. I was fairly certain there was some snickering involved.

Seriously, even I was quaking in my freaking boots. Mory had seen what we were about to face through Ed's eyes. I would have thought she'd have been a little more—

Ah. The difference was ... the necromancer had me standing between her and dismemberment. Me and the warrior of the guardians. But I knew that neither of us were automatically capable of quelling an army of elves and getting our companions through unscathed.

My father carved an arc up and through the wall in front of him. His brilliant sword sliced through the elves' magic like a spoon through creamy chocolate mousse—with the deep, smoky cacao aftertaste and all.

My father took a step back, barking over his shoulder, "You step through after Jade, necromancer. With your zombies tight at your and the amplifier's backs. You will stay between us and the zombies at all times."

"Yes, sir," Mory said, without a hint of sarcasm in her tone. Gabby threaded her fingers through Mory's. She was wearing gold bangles on her other arm that I hadn't noticed with all the other magic surrounding us. Angelica's bangles, most likely powered up with all the magic the sorcerer could layer into the jewelry to protect her amplifier daughter. Generations of magic, if I was correct about the origins of Angelica's jewelry.

My chest squeezed, pained with the insanity of involving Gabby and Mory and all the others in any of this. Not all of us were going to make it out whole.

"Ready, my Jade?" my father asked.

"I've been ready for half a freaking day."

Yazi laughed. His guardian magic vibrated across the walls and floor, electric against my skin.

I stepped up behind him, calling my knife into my hand. "Go to Mory, Freddie," I whispered to the shadow leech perched on my shoulder. "No one touches her, no elf brings her harm. Drain anyone who tries. Drain them down."

The leech chittered quietly in my ear. Then its magic contracted and disappeared with a snap.

"Hey, Freddie," Mory whispered.

I didn't glance back. We were past that, past the point of no return. All of us were barreling forward into a future with only a single thread of hope. A hope that by following the oracle, we were carving a new path into the unknown.

I swiped my fingers across my necklace, releasing the centipedes into my left hand. The metallurgy bit into my skin—gleeful pinpricks of contentment and anticipation that echoed my own.

I inhaled.

Without another word, my father slammed a thrust kick to the section of the wall he'd cut. Magic reverberated, literally rippling around us as an archway cracked open. We charged through the opening even as the chunk of wall flew forward, revealing the center of the stadium. I was right on my father's heels.

Dozens of elves hit us from either side.

Apparently, they'd been waiting.

My father's sword moved, streaking golden magic through the air. I unleashed the centipedes, even as I jumped up to skewer the warrior closest to me through the gemstone embedded in his head. Landing on my feet, I called the centipedes back to my left hand.

Four elves down.

I exhaled.

The section of the wall my father had freed with a kick got sucked into the gateway, which rose up about twenty feet in front of us. It was wide open. Its narrow aperture was rooted in the tech that I'd been deliberately sabotaging, but it appeared completely functional now. The gateway spiraled upward in a conic shape for about twelve feet, easily spanning twenty feet across at the top.

Haoxin was suspended in the churning well of magic above the gateway, fueling it with her life force. Her limbs hung limply. Her hair was a blond maelstrom around her head, her eyes closed. If not for the epic amount of power radiating from her—being siphoned downward into the tech, then converted to fuel the gateway—I would have thought she was dead.

She was still wearing the T-shirt that Kandy had designed. *Fueled by coffee. And epic mystical powers.*

A fierce, desperate anger seized me. It infused my torso and limbs, grounding my heart, quieting my fears.

I caught a glimpse of Reggie standing on the far side of the gateway, her arms akimbo and head thrown back. But I lost sight of her and whatever magic she was engaged in as the thirty or so elves arrayed between us and the gate shuffled back to form a blockade. Bristling with weapons, they stood shoulder to shoulder between us and our objective.

Mory and Gabby pressed up behind me, practically climbing into my back pockets. Not that I had any in my leather armor. It wasn't because they were scared, though. They were simply following Yazi's orders.

I could practically feel courage radiating off them. Courage that tasted like sticky-sweet, toasted marshmallows dipped in tart raspberry jam. And I decided in that moment that if I ever made it back to the bakery, back to the haven of my kitchen, I would design that exact cupcake.

Mory's nine zombie elves stepped up, covering us to the sides and rear. All of them held weapons at the ready, plucked up from the warriors my father and I had felled as we came through from the hall. I didn't know if Mory had enough control to actually use the zombies to fight. But that wall of undead drew more than a few disconcerted glances from their former fellow warriors.

My father gestured before himself with a sweep of his sword, chuckling. "Five. Which makes nine for me."

I glanced over. There were five headless warriors arrayed on the ground around him.

"Four," I said. "Which makes nine for me. See if you can continue to keep up, Daddy-o." I took a step forward, raising my left hand and allowing the centipedes to twist and twine around my palm and wrist. I wrapped my bravado around me as if it were another level of protection against the death and destruction I was about to unleash.

And maybe it was. A thing protecting my heart and soul.

I thrust my jade knife toward the three dozen white-armored elves standing between me and my objective—the gateway.

"The wielder of the instruments of assassination has returned," I yelled. "Give way, or I and my father, the warrior of the guardian dragons, will carve a path through you."

The elves glared and snarled back at me. Then each one in the front line defiantly thumped their milky, iridescent sword against their chest once, advancing toward us in perfect step with each other.

My father laughed. "I thought you were very clear, my daughter. But some people just don't want to listen."

The first wave of elves attacked before I could respond with a smart-ass remark.

Three more fell to my centipedes. One to my knife.

Four fell to my father's sword. Another to a left-hand uppercut backed by a blast of guardian power.

The elves kept coming.

And falling.

Magic continued to boil from the gateway—magic pulled from Haoxin, draining her, slowly killing her. Reggie was still trying to get more elves through, and it was an easy guess that doing so was what had kept her occupied while we'd been sneaking through the maze.

Weapons and magic flying, we marched over the fallen. Side by side, my father and I pressed forward, swiftly and decisively. Moving as if we'd fought together, as if we'd waged war together, for centuries. Gabby and Mory stayed tucked up safely behind us.

If an elf managed to slip by me or Yazi, one of Mory's zombies latched on to the attacker, holding them at bay for the moment it took for one of us to turn and dispatch them.

Freddie helpfully burrowed into one elf's eyeball, slithering out of the other only after I'd skewered the elf through his gemstone.

Amplified by Gabby, Mory picked up three more of the fallen, boosting her elf shield to twelve. I knew that her being able to do so was something to marvel at, even with the amplifier's help. But I didn't have time for pride or praise.

I thought of nothing but the next step, unleashing the centipedes over and over again. Slitting throats, cracking gemstones.

Not a single blow made it through my defenses. What my own magic didn't deflect, the magic embedded in my new armor mitigated.

We were still about five feet from the gateway when the energy radiating from it ebbed to a trickle. Then a wave of magic tasting of salt water and decomposing wood crashed over us like a tsunami. It prickled across my forehead, trying to find purchase on my scar and slip into my brain.

Gabby grunted in pain.

Reggie had decided to join the fight.

Finally.

I slashed through her telepathic onslaught with a casual flick of my knife. My father did the same at my left.

The final wave of elves fell back, but they stayed facing us as they circled back around the gateway—momentarily stepping out of our sight.

I called the centipedes back, clipping them into place on my necklace. Then, without bothering to discuss our next steps, I reached back for Mory, hitching her up on my back like a toddler.

The necromancer wrapped her arms around my neck without hesitation.

"To the right," my father barked, reaching for Gabby.

Picking up the necromancer and the amplifier, we moved together, quickly circling the gateway. The stadium was a blur of magic as we moved. Then just as suddenly we stopped, depositing our companions next to the churning magic feeding off Haoxin.

Mory gasped, falling to her knees.

"What the hell?" Gabby murmured, wobbling and clutching her stomach.

I didn't have time to make sure they were okay, though. I was already turning to face Reggie.

Not only did I have a personal score to settle, I also had to keep every single elf in the stadium focused on me. I had to keep the fight centered on Yazi and me.

Because even though it was so faint and brief that it might have been only a long-lost memory, I could have sworn I'd tasted sweet stewed cherries, thick whipped cream, bittersweet chocolate, and the barest hint of cool peppermint.

It was there one moment, then gone, overwhelmed by the blistering, mind-warping power of the gateway at my back.

Warner. Kandy. Kett.

They'd been freed from their cells.

Maybe we were going to pull this off after all.

Chapter Ten

I met Reggie's vicious, green-eyed gaze across the wide expanse of the very center of the massive fifty-thousand-seat stadium. Then I slid my eyes toward my father. "I lost count."

"Not counting the wounded who retreated, it's twenty-five for me, nineteen for you, and three for the necromancer and amplifier. With help from the leech," my father said loudly and clearly amused.

Mory and Gabby shifted around behind us. The pixie necromancer settled down cross-legged on the edge of the platform, directly in front of the gateway. Gabby kneeled, tucking up behind Mory with her hands on her shoulders. Six zombie elves—Mory had apparently lost hold of the others, or the elves had taken them out—lurched around the pulsing magic of the gate, three to either side, shielding Mory and Gabby.

Alivia and Traveler backed Reggie, who was still wearing her stupid cloak. And as I made a very fast count, I estimated that close to three hundred elves were arrayed around their liege, all of them sheathed in their white, flexible armor and bristling with crystal blood-swords and magic.

Hundreds of elves. Between me and my target.

Except I was supposed to support and defend Mory in this stage of Rochelle's master plan. Sneak in, trigger a distraction, then watch over Mory while she closed the gateway. So revenge was going to have to wait until the necromancer managed to free Haoxin.

Three smaller subgroups of elves suddenly broke off in different directions. I counted six elves in each group, heading down three different passageways into the maze—including the one we'd avoided using.

So Reggie had finally seen through our distraction attempt. Or maybe she'd known there was a separate rescue attempt going on at the same time, but had been focused on shoring up her forces with as many new re- cruits as she could get through the gateway before we made it through the maze.

Fear slipped down my spine, spreading a numb- ness through my limbs. All I could think about was how we should have cut through the walls earlier. We should have brought some heavier-duty spells with us, not just sealing off the maze behind us but letting us blast our way through.

I took a deep breath, trying to quell the terror rising in response to all the unknowns. But there was nothing I could do, other than what had already been done. Nothing I could do for anyone other than Mory and Gabby.

I had to stick to the plan. I had to hope.

So. Might as well keep the diversion tactics going and buy the necromancer some time.

I took a single step forward, pulling my katana from the built-in sheath on my back. The front line of elves raised their crystal weapons in unison. They were puppets, like Mory's zombies. Except that Reggie's strings could theoretically be severed, freeing the elves. Just like I'd severed her connection to me. Of course, I'd almost killed myself doing so, so that wasn't a terribly practical solution.

My father chuckled.

Good to know a freaking legion of elves all controlled by a megalomaniac telepath amused the warrior of the guardians.

Behind me, I felt more than saw Mory pull her newly powered-up knitting needles out of her satchel, then hold them up in the air, pointed toward Haoxin.

"Ready?" Gabby whispered.

"Not yet."

I leveled my sword, pointing it directly at Reggie. She pressed her hands forward, then swept her arms open. The elves directly between us took three steps to the side, opening a pathway and exposing a circle that had been scribed on the floor in what I assumed was Elvish script.

"I am Jade Godfrey, wielder of the instruments of assassination," I cried, projecting my voice as much as I could. "I stand before you with my father, the warrior of the guardian dragons."

Traveler flashed Reggie a disconcerted look, but she waved him off without taking her gaze from me.

I twirled my katana, using the magic embedded in it to flip it around my hand, then tossing it back and forth in a glittering display. "This is the dragon slayer," I proclaimed. Then I captured the katana in my right hand, absorbing all the magic I'd generated into its twenty-four-inch blade and pointing it at Reggie again. "After today, it will have a new name."

I gestured to all the elves on my right, then back to my left. "Elf slayer."

I paused, hoping to let the threat sink in. "But ... I'm also here to close the gateway. I can do that with all of you on this side, likely dead at my feet. Or after you've chosen to return to your own dimension. But I will slaughter anyone who stands between me and Reggie." I thrust my sword toward the telepath. "Hand her over to me, and we can shortcut the maiming and decapitation."

The hundreds of elves arrayed before me didn't even blink.

I hadn't expected them to.

"Do you always declare your intentions so thoroughly?" my father asked. "I usually just start lopping heads off."

"I know, Dad. But the elves are just pawns in Reggie's game. I wanted to give them a chance to make up their own minds."

Yazi looked at me doubtfully.

"Plus," I said huffily, "I was being intimidating."

A wide grin bloomed across my father's face. "That you were, daughter of mine. That you were."

A flush of warmth triggered by his pride filled the empty space in my heart, if only for that moment.

"Got it," Mory murmured. "I can see the threads …"

"Okay … okay …" Gabby whispered.

I glanced back to see the amplifier wrap her hands around the back of Mory's head, pressing her fingertips to the necromancer's temples. Magic welled between them.

Freddie disappeared from Mory's shoulder, reappearing perched on the head of the zombie elf next to the necromancer. The shadow leech spread its wings, beady red eyes pinned to the elf army, needle-like teeth flashing. Then it chittered madly.

So I wasn't the only mouthy one in the group. Good to know.

Now the leech and I just had to prove we could back up the boasting.

Reggie took a step forward into the circle with Alivia at her side. Magic shimmered through the Elvish script, then a ward slammed into place around them, streaking upward in a thick column all the way to the domed ceiling.

I could feel the intensity of the magic from where I stood, easily over fifty feet away.

Traveler strode forward through the pathway Reggie had created, and the elf army stepped back into place as he passed. Once again blocking me from my target.

The taste of Alivia's magic—the primary forest-after-a-rainstorm scent that all elves seemed to carry, plus her apricot undertone—channeled downward. A platform rose underneath the telepath and the ward builder's feet, raising them about three feet from the concrete floor. So they could see the battle about to be waged.

I'd been too distracted to notice it before, but the floor around us was plain concrete. The elves must have torn up all the synthetic turf at some point. I snorted. "Fancy."

My father grunted, rolled his shoulders, and manifested his golden broadsword out of thin air. A few of the elves arrayed in the front line actually flinched in response to the intense power rolling off the weapon.

Traveler barked a series of orders in a language I could no longer understand. And a flush of relief actually ran through me at the confirmation—minor or not—that the gemstone hadn't left any unwanted residual in me. Nothing that Reggie might harness and use against me.

With Traveler at their center, the first wave of elves raised their swords and began methodically stalking toward us, making a wall about twenty warriors across.

Another uniform line began marching a half-dozen steps behind the first.

"The big guy in the middle is a teleporter," I said. "Traveler, they call him. He survived Haoxin."

My father grunted. "Reckless and adventurous likes to play," he said, referring to Haoxin's secondary title. "She likes to test her powers." He shrugged. "I am not so ... young."

His hesitation before the word 'young' made me wonder what he'd stopped himself from saying. But the elves were quickly closing in, so I didn't ask.

The first wave was about twenty feet away when my father randomly leaped fifteen feet into the air, coming down deliberately hard on his right foot in front of us.

Guardian magic exploded as he hit. The concrete floor cracked as if it had been struck by a massive meteor. A meteor that then caused a shockwave that radiated in only one direction, leaving the floor beneath my feet untouched, but crumpling concrete and rebar in a wide arc forward.

Caught in the wave of guardian magic and roiling concrete, the first two lines of elves flew backward, including Traveler. They slammed into the hundreds of elves behind them, knocking them asunder. Elves smashed into the column of magic Alivia had erected around Reggie, falling senseless to the floor before being accidentally trampled. Other white-armored warriors crashed into and through the outer walls of the maze. Some were even tossed up into the stadium seating. Easily two dozen didn't get back up.

I lost track of Traveler. He might have teleported out of the way.

That assault was really going to tip the body count in my father's favor. Which was okay, actually, because it was a stupid game to have been playing anyway.

The cracked floor abruptly settled, creating a wide ridge of jagged concrete and twisted rebar in a rough half circle in front of us. The barrier ranged from eight to ten feet high in places, and looked treacherously unstable. The elves would now be forced to climb over the barrier to get to us. The area directly before us was relatively clear. The concrete was slightly cracked, but smooth enough that we wouldn't need to worry about tripping.

But now we'd be able to pick the elves off in small groups as they scrambled over the ridge. Also, Reggie's viewing platform likely wasn't high enough to see completely over the barrier. So the telepath would have to rely on filtered information if she planned to command the battle.

"Freaking brilliant," I whispered.

Yazi threw back his head and laughed. The ground shook with his power, shifting the unstable barrier so that a number of the elves already attempting to scale it slipped and got their legs caught in various crevices.

"You're going to have to teach me that one, Dad," I said.

Still laughing, Yazi stepped forward and lazily decapitated three elves who'd managed to make it over. Then he turned back, still grinning, to wink at me.

Then, one by one—well, sometimes two by two, or three by three for my father—we slaughtered any of the elves that made it over the concrete and rebar, keeping Mory and Gabby safely tucked at our backs.

Every time my father dropped an elf, he kicked that warrior back over the barrier. When the pile around my own feet grew too cumbersome, he would switch places with me and clear it. Slowly and steadily, the concrete barrier was blanketed with the bodies of Reggie's army, growing higher and higher. Forcing the warrior elves to scramble over their own dead and dying to reach us.

We were butchering and maiming the elves faster than they could decompose and crumble into fine crystal. That was utterly disconcerting, even as we used it to our advantage.

There was no sign of Traveler, though he could have easily teleported in. No sign of Reggie or Alivia peeking over the ridge. The absence of Traveler, who loathed me enough to want to confront me directly, worried me. Either he'd been badly wounded when my father erected the barrier...or Reggie had sent him elsewhere.

Yet another thing I could do nothing about.

So I kept my focus narrow, trying to ignore the destruction that I...that we unleashed. Whenever my katana grew heavy with elven blood, I simply absorbed its magic into the steel blade, watching that blood crumble into flakes of crystal. Over and over again.

At some point, the centipedes started singing. They made a thrilled trill as I released the instrument of assassination from my grasp and they sped toward their targets. Then a contented hum when they returned to me. It was as if they were feeding, adapting, growing with power.

And all I could do was acknowledge it, understanding that this was the purpose of the instruments, and of the katana soon to be known as the elf slayer. Understanding that this was the destiny of the wielder.

My destiny.

All I could do was keep myself between Mory and Gabby and the onslaught. All I could do was keep moving.

The nightmares, for all of us, would come later. If we survived.

The steady assault eased to a trickle, barely enough to keep both my father and me engaged. Freddie settled on my shoulder as I turned back to check on Mory. The leech was heavy with magic, its form as substantial as I'd ever seen it. It was more winged demon, red eyes, and hooked claws than shadow now.

I realized that my movements during the fight had opened up too much space between me and the gateway. I couldn't let any elves slip around and past me. Returning my gaze to the top of the corpse-littered barrier, I took a few quick steps back.

My father glanced over at me, frowning and stepping back as well. "They're regrouping."

I nodded.

Then I felt a pulse of magic from the gateway. A churning spiral of power.

I spun back. Mory was standing now, her arms stretched out over her head. Gabby was still behind her, still amplifying her. Thick cords of magic twined around both of them—as Mory began to slowly unravel the energy holding Haoxin aloft.

"Dad!" I cried out. "The gateway is opening!"

A massive cloven hoof stepped through that opening gateway, landing only a couple of feet away from Mory. It was followed a moment later by a broad, tusked face.

A creature was crossing through the gateway, apparently made out of some sort of metal. It was massive. Far larger, in fact, than the aperture it was attempting to squeeze through. The magic that was calling it forth didn't have to obey the laws of physics, though. Or any laws of nature or science, for that matter.

The metal beast glowered at Mory and Gabby, blinking eyes that were too small in comparison to its massive head.

Gabby screamed. Then she screamed again.

But she didn't run.

Foolishly brave. Ridiculously brave.

My heart rate spiked, but my limbs felt sluggish. Slow to respond—even though I knew that was just the feeling of the creature moving faster than me.

Mory was windmilling her arms, rapidly coiling up the magic—the life force—that she'd been untangling, then wrapping it around her.

"Run!" I screamed, even as I attempted to close the space between us. "Mory!"

She didn't run.

The beast thrust its shoulders through the gateway. It tilted its head, angling its tusks to the side as if intending to knock Mory and Gabby out of its path.

There was nothing that would save them from that. Nothing in any magical protection that either of them wore that would be strong enough to protect against such a blow. Not even the bodies of Mory's zombie elves.

I screamed, weapons forgotten, reaching for the necromancer and amplifier as I ran toward them. Terror had seized my heart.

A mass of elves swarmed the barrier behind me, engaging my father as one coordinated force.

Called forth by my desperate need, magic welled in my necklace, burrowing into my skin. And suddenly I was standing beside Mory and Gabby.

I had inadvertently teleported. I'd forgotten I could do any such thing.

With no time to do anything else, I wrapped my arms around the fledglings, taking the creature's vicious blow across my back. My ribs shattered. Pain ricocheted through my torso and filtered through my limbs. But I held on to the girls.

The three of us were lifted off our feet and flung across the stadium. Zombie elves flew through the air all around us.

I tried to twist, get myself between Mory and Gabby and the barrier speeding toward us, to absorb our landing. But inexplicably, we slowed. Then we slowed some more.

The zombie elves splattered against the barrier. But we didn't. We were somehow decelerating, suspended …

I glanced back toward the beast and the gateway.

Thick tendrils of magic—the life force that fueled the gateway—were still attached to Mory. Specifically, attached to her arms. Arms that I had clamped to her sides in my crushing hug. The ropes of magic were thinning—but were somehow still elastic.

"Let go, Mory!" We paused for the instant it took for me to put everything together, suspended about twelve feet off the floor. "Let go!"

"No," Mory grunted. "I can't."

"Jesus Christ!"

The life force magic jerked, yanking us back the way we'd come. The metal-plated beast, now about halfway through the gateway, lowered its tusked head, watching us return.

I swear to God it was freaking smiling. Toothily.

Either that or the beast couldn't properly close its mouth. You know, because of the massive tusks and the full complement of jagged, sharp-edged teeth.

"Gabby!" I cried. "Grab my arm!"

Unbelievably, the amplifier did exactly as I asked, grabbing hold of me with both hands. I dropped my arm, holding onto Mory one-handed while lowering the amplifier. We sped back toward the beast.

I had time to notice that it had two-foot-long metal spines jutting out all over its back. Delightful.

I dropped Gabby three feet from the ground. She hit hard, then rolled.

Mory shrieked defiantly, bringing her knitting needles up over her head, both in her one free hand, as if she was ready to stab the beast through the eye.

It opened its massive maw, already anticipating chomping us down.

I got my feet up and forward seconds before we hit that maw, jamming each foot against a tusk on either side of the creature's mouth. Then somehow, I managed to hold myself in place just long enough to lower Mory a bit closer to the ground before I dropped her.

The beast roared, flipping its head upward—and me along with it—before I could see if Mory was safe.

I slammed into the well of magic fueling the gateway, hitting hard like it might have been a solid wall—and came face-to-face with Haoxin.

The guardian of North America's eyes were open.

I saw the moment she recognized me, as anger contorted her pretty features. The gold of her guardian magic was literally bleeding from her sky-blue eyes.

Her mouth moved, forming the word, "You!"

Then I was falling, tumbling down from the gateway and landing on the back of the beast. With those metal spines. Which sank into my own back like I was a pincushion. I wasn't certain my ribs had healed yet from the first hit I'd taken.

As agony seized me, holding me in place, I got the strong feeling that Haoxin wasn't going to forgive me.

And that a guardian's retribution might be way more dangerous than hundreds of elves, or dozens of elven metal-spined beasts, or Reggie.

The beast snarled and spat, twisting to get me off its back. Unfortunately for me, I appeared to be skewered to it. The creature completely cleared the gateway as I managed to peel myself off its spines. My armor had apparently saved any vital organs from being punctured. But I was leaving way, way too much blood behind.

Then, because I was an absolute moron, I called my knife into my hand and tried crawling toward the creature's head. Mory had the right idea. Stabbing it through the eye would certainly—

The beast bucked.

I slipped, slamming down—hard—with one leg on either side of its metal-plated back. I stifled a scream. Black dots swam before my eyes, and I just had to hang on for a moment, blinking, absorbing the pain.

Yeah, that was going to bruise.

"Get down from there, Jade!" my father shouted, peeved. "Now is not the time for a piggyback ride!"

A snarky retort rose up, but I didn't have the breath to voice it.

"Yeah, it's you I'm calling a piggy!" my father crowed.

Yep. My father was smack-talking a metal beast from another dimension. A creature that was the size of a freaking bus. A double-decker bus. From my vantage point, at least.

The beast swung its tusked head around, completely forgetting about the annoyance currently, though involuntarily, straddling its back. Namely, me.

My father's sword flashed, its magic singing a gleeful, hungry chorus.

Lovely.

Singing weapons of mass destruction. That ran in the family, apparently.

Thankfully, the beast was easily distracted.

I slid down its back, landing hard on my ass as it charged my father. I crawled, then scrambled in the opposite direction.

A cluster of elves had surrounded Mory and Gabby, who were pressed together to one side of the gateway. Freddie was perched on the necromancer's shoulder.

Screaming fiercely, I pulled my sword and launched myself forward. And only then realized that these elves were under Mory's control. Her zombies. Or maybe replacement zombies.

I had to abort my attack in midair, landing seriously awkwardly.

My father bellowed. Then he laughed. Not at me, though. Apparently, he found the metal beast entertaining.

I pushed through the zombie elves, glancing over at Yazi. He was dancing around and slashing at the beast, goading it. It was already missing an upper tusk. So much for my father not playing with his prey.

"Jade!" Mory was hunched over, holding her ankle. But she still held onto the life force she'd untangled. "I can do this. I can still do this."

I glanced over at Gabby. She was holding her arm, looking too pale. Badly injured.

The amplifier nodded.

"That's ridiculous—" I started to say.

Mory jabbed her finger, pointing past my shoulder. "You take care of the elves, Jade. I've almost got Haoxin out."

I snarled.

"You promised," Mory hissed.

"Yeah," Gabby echoed. "You promised."

Clenching my jaw down on my need to argue, I spun away. Heedless of my own injuries, which were thankfully already healing, I pulled my sword again. I shoved my way free of Mory's zombies.

A half-dozen elves had made it over the barrier while my father was distracted with the beast.

I charged toward the warriors, unleashing the centipedes on three moments before I attacked the other three, decapitating one with my first strike.

The other two drove me back a step before I incapacitated them. The next half-dozen drove me farther back.

I fought.

The elves kept coming.

From the corner of my eye, I saw my father take the beast down, then hack off its head for good measure. But the elves simply swarmed over and around it as it began to decay and crumble. The refreshed onslaught beat both of us back, pushing us closer and closer to the gateway.

"Mory!" I shouted. "Now, Mory!"

"Don't rush me, Jade!" she screeched.

There were too many of them. Reggie had managed to get too many warriors through the gate while I was injured and healing. Then she'd buoyed her numbers even more while we snuck through the maze.

And she was willing to sacrifice every last one of them.

We were going to lose.

The elves would take Vancouver.

I tripped on a fallen elf, taking a blow to the head and stumbling. I blocked the next hit … but just barely. Desperate, I called the centipedes back into my left hand.

Then I tasted salvation.

I risked a glance to my right.

Warner and Kandy were charging over the top of the barrier. The elves nearest to them were already spinning to protect their rear flank.

"Jade!" Kandy screamed. Then she flung out her arms and simply leaped up into the air.

I shoved my left hand into my satchel, ripping the golden cuffs out of its depths and flinging them toward Kandy in the same motion.

The elves pressing me stumbled back, unsure of what I'd released.

The cuffs flew upward.

A seven-foot-tall monster with three-inch claws tore through Kandy's human visage, stretching her stained and torn clothing. The cuffs clicked into place on her wrists. She tucked her knees to her chest, deliberately stalling herself mid leap. Then she dropped to the floor, riding three elves down as she landed. She tore off two of their heads with her massive clawed hands, then ripped out the throat of the third with her teeth. And all the while, she chortled madly through her misaligned, toothy jaw.

Meeting Warner's fierce gaze and not wanting to look anywhere else ever again, I cleared my closest opponents with the centipedes. Then I tossed him his weapon.

Having some understanding of what was happening this time, the elves in the path of the wicked-looking knife tried to knock it out of the air. I watched the weapon actually swerve around them, homing in on, then setting neatly into Warner's raised hand.

He took two more heads with it before the elves even saw him move.

Hope bloomed through my chest, energizing my limbs. I began to cut down any elves that stood between me and the two people I loved beyond anything else, beyond destiny, beyond death.

The elves shifted before me, trying to reorganize on the fly in order to fight opponents on two fronts. But Warner and Kandy steadily carved a path toward my father and me, fighting side by side, her with tooth and claw and him with fist and blade. Moving together as if they'd been fighting in tandem for years.

I didn't have any time to admire their battle prowess, though. I had my own war to wage.

A taste of peppermint tickled my senses. I quickly scanned the barrier but didn't spot Kett or Jasmine.

"Jade!" Kandy shouted. Her words were mangled by her misaligned jaw, though she was only a few feet away from me now. "Benjamin needs you. You need to get his bracelet off!"

"What?" I called the centipedes back to me, then stabbed an elf standing between me and Kandy through the eye.

Kandy flung her arms around my neck. "Jasmine and Bitsy took out the guards while Benjamin got the cells unlocked with that brilliant pen you made him. But ..."

Warner put his back to us, covering our embrace and taking over for Kandy as she struggled to speak. "Kandy and I were attacked in the corridor while the fledglings went to free Kett. Unfortunately, the executioner wasn't in possession of his usual control, and he injured them before we could intercede. Bitsy said the witches were supposed to open an exit, but we couldn't find it." He growled with frustration. "Without my knife, I couldn't get them through the exterior wards."

Kandy mumbled into my hair, "Benjamin is seriously hurt. Dying. I tried to feed him, but he can't ... you have to get the bracelet off him."

"Go, Jade," my father shouted. "Warner, the wolf, and I will keep the elves from the gate and protect the necromancer and amplifier."

The elves pressed against us. My father and Warner hacked them back, brutally efficient.

"Warner or I have to lead the dowser to Benjamin," Kandy said. "And have her back while getting to him."

My father laughed. "Jade has upgraded."

I snorted. Then I realized he meant the teleporting.

"I have to be able to see ... or to visualize where I'm going, don't I?"

My father shook his head. "You know the taste of the vampire ... of Benjamin's magic?"

I did. "Sounds risky."

My father grinned.

Yeah. I hated being right.

Warner swept me forward into a fierce embrace, practically savaging my mouth. And I welcomed the strength beneath his touch, the taste of his magic. As if I might have been dying of dehydration, and only he could—

Kandy pressed her face against ours. She slobbered across my left cheek—then practically chewed it.

Warner threw his head back and laughed. Kandy joined him. Then she grabbed the arm of an elf intent on stabbing Warner in the back and tore it off.

"Come right back," Warner growled. Then he spun away, back to the battle.

Breathless, with a grin firmly etched across my face, I sheathed my weapons and tried to recall the taste of Benjamin's sweet-but-sour grape-jelly-bean magic.

I'd thought I'd have to beg for forgiveness from my BFF and fiance. For what I'd done. For leaving them behind.

Apparently not.

The effervescent teleportation magic embedded in my necklace snapped out and bit me, squeezing me from the inside out. Then the battle was gone.

I was standing in a white-walled, white-ceilinged hall, dizzy and disoriented.

Clawed fingers gripped my shoulders, yanking me backward. Sharp teeth scored my neck as I slammed my elbow back. Bone and cartilage crunched. My attacker grunted, losing her hold on me. I spun, knife already in hand. Then I tasted sweet peppermint.

I had thrown Jasmine all the way down the hall, tumbling over the bodies of the warrior elves that littered the floor all around me. Most of them were missing their heads, but a few had their throats gouged ... ripped out.

Kett was kneeling a few feet away with Benjamin in his arms. The fledgling vampire's naturally pale skin had grayed. Bitsy, propped up against the wall beside the executioner, didn't look much better.

Kett glanced down the hall toward the golden-haired vampire struggling to gain her feet. "I told you to stop biting everyone."

Jasmine managed to crouch, holding one of her arms across her chest. She pinned her gaze to me, snarling viciously. Her eyes were fully blood red—and not just from her magic.

Ignoring her, I stepped over to Kett, kneeling before Benjamin. The immediate area was littered with empty IV blood bags. Benjamin's satchel was tossed to the side, his notebooks spilling out. The dark-haired vampire's magic was dim, almost tasteless. I was surprised I'd been able to use it as an anchor to teleport.

I met Kett's gaze. He looked haggard, worn. His magic was blazing red through his eyes, his fangs on full display.

"He's dying," I whispered.

"Yes."

"No!" Jasmine howled. She abruptly appeared beside me, slamming her shoulder into mine and attempting to tear Benjamin from Kett's arms.

"I said stop!" Kett snarled. Magic lashed out with his words, freezing Jasmine in place.

Bitsy moaned, sliding sideways against the wall. Two bite marks on her neck weeped with blood. A bruise was slowly darkening the area around the punctured skin.

"Please, please," Jasmine whispered, pulling my attention to her. "Please, dowser." The golden-haired vampire had also been bitten, though the marks on her neck were mostly healed.

I met Kett's steady gaze again.

"I took too much." Regret cracked through his dispassion. "I...I tried to tell them not to open the door when I realized they were coming for me. Warner and Kandy eventually got me...quelled, but not before ..." He looked down at Benjamin in his arms, sorrow chiseled across his face.

I squeezed my eyes shut. "It's not your fault," I said, and I knew it was true. Because the fault was mine. "What can I do?"

"We need you to get the bracelet off," Jasmine said. "We can't get it off Ben. Kandy tried to feed him, but the bracelet is backfiring. Or maybe it's doing exactly what it's supposed to do in this situation, stopping Ben from becoming a slaughtering fiend when he's...when he needs ..." She sobbed harshly. "Please, dowser. Take the bracelet off. And...then...I'll feed him. I'll feed Ben."

"Absolutely not," Kett snapped. "I just watched you drink from two elves. Benjamin is already dying."

I turned my attention to the bone bracelet on Benjamin's left wrist. Half-healed scratch marks bloodied his arm and hand on either side. The bracelet seethed with blood, its magic deeply embedded into Benjamin, digging through flesh and bone. I could almost feel it burrowing deeper and deeper into the dying vampire, like a fast-growing malignancy.

"His mother should have known she needed to remove it," Kett said.

Jasmine started pacing behind me. "She offered. But with Bitsy with us...Benjamin felt he needed the control it brings him."

"Jade." Kett prompted me softly.

I nodded, reaching for the necromancy embedded in the bone bracelet, slowly coaxing it into my left hand. I called my jade knife into my right hand. Then gently, carefully, I cut away the magic I'd gathered. One tiny bird bone loosened, then another. The separated pieces fell from the bracelet, leaving a gaping wound on Benjamin's wrist.

Two warrior elves barreled around the corner. Jasmine launched herself at the nearest one, taking him down with a vicious snarl.

Bitsy was up and moving before I even knew she was actually awake. The young werewolf jumped into the air, slamming a vicious but gorgeously executed kick to the second elf's head that knocked him sideways. It looked remarkably like the way she would have air kicked a soccer ball. Except hard enough to destroy the hypothetical ball.

Still kneeling, I pulled my katana, inadvertently ripping the necromancy I'd been gathering from Benjamin's bracelet as I spun and took the stumbling elf out at the knee.

He fell.

Jasmine, having finished off the first elf already, grabbed the second one from behind and tore out his throat. With her teeth.

"Jesus Christ," I muttered, giving Kett a look.

He sighed. Heavily. "Stop biting the elves, Jasmine."

She looked up, face, neck, and hair slick with elven blood. "How else am I supposed to kill them?!"

"We've had this conversation," Kett snapped. "Twice."

Jasmine thrust her hand forward. "My claws aren't as long as yours!"

Bitsy stumbled, swaying on her feet. Jasmine's gaze snapped to her. Like a predator homing in on prey. I slowly stood, stepping over to the young werewolf. Holding my katana before the golden-haired vampire, I tugged the werewolf behind me.

"Excellent kick," I murmured.

Jasmine's gaze snapped to me, fading from hungry predator to simply peeved.

"Thank you," Bitsy said, making it to the wall and sliding down to sit beside Kett again.

I skewered Jasmine with a look.

"I'm not going to hurt anyone," she said huffily. "It was actually Ben who bit Bitsy. After Kett drained him and grabbed me …" She glanced at her maker, trailing off.

All righty then. I turned back to Benjamin, gently coaxing the final pieces of the bone bracelet from his wrist with my alchemy. The flesh underneath tore away, raw and bloody. I must have nicked a vein, because it started dribbling blood. Blood that I was fairly certain was supposed to spurt.

I cut Benjamin's sweater away at the shoulder seam, wrapping the wound.

"And now?" I asked Kett.

Jasmine pushed up beside me. "We feed him Bitsy."

"No. We don't." Kett's tone was steady and cool. But if his magic, fangs, and claws were any indication, he was only inches away from seriously losing it.

"You … you want me to—" I raised my wrist.

"Yes," Jasmine blurted.

"No," Kett said. "We are trying to save him, aren't we?"

Jasmine jumped to her feet, prowling back and forth.

Kett shifted Benjamin in his arms so that he was holding the back of his head in one hand. "Benjamin," he said softly. His cool peppermint magic shifted, swelling. "Benjamin."

Kett was also calling the younger vampire telepathically, I knew. He'd done the same to me when he'd almost broken Reggie's hold on me.

The dark-haired vampire's eyelids fluttered open. His eyes were blood red. "Kett."

"You're dying, Benjamin."

"I know. I know the feeling."

Jasmine let out a moan that she quickly stifled.

I pressed my hand against my aching chest. Not for the first time, I desperately wished I had some sort of healing ability.

"I woke you to give you a choice, Benjamin," Kett said. "A sip of my blood."

Benjamin's hands twitched, then clenched and unclenched. But I wasn't certain he was actually controlling the movement.

"A sip," Benjamin repeated. But his tone was remote, as if he might not have actually been hearing and understanding the offer.

"If I let you be," Kett said, his voice steady and cool, "you may simply slip into an … undead state. You may rise again."

"No," Benjamin said. "I'm dying."

Kett nodded. "I concur. If you sip from me … you might not have enough magic left within you to absorb mine. Or, if you do, my blood could drive you insane. And then I would have to kill you myself."

"I understand." Benjamin cleared his throat, trying to form the words he needed to say, to agree to the offer so it was magically binding. "I would be … honored …"

"Kett," Jasmine cried. "Please. Please! Now!"

"Let Benjamin answer, Jasmine."

A smile ghosted over Benjamin's face as he spotted Jasmine hovering over my shoulder.

"Benjamin." Kett called the younger vampire's red-eyed gaze back to him. "You understand that you will be tied to me, and possibly those of my bloodline."

"Jasmine …" Benjamin murmured.

"Not just Jasmine …" Kett hesitated, flicking his gaze to me.

"Do you want me to leave?" I asked.

He shook his head curtly. "I have another favor to ask. Two favors."

"The things we do for each other aren't favors, my friend." I smiled at him. "Anything I can give is yours."

Kett nodded, already refocusing on Benjamin. "It wouldn't just be me who you might have to obey, Benjamin."

"I understand."

"I'm not sure you do. Having someone else be able to control you—"

"He understands, Kett!" Jasmine cried. "Please, please. He understands. He wants to be with us. He wants to survive. You already know. You didn't even have to ask!"

Benjamin closed his eyes, laughing quietly to himself. And the soft sound brought a genuine smile to my face. Even while dying, Benjamin was…happy. Maybe even pleased. To be here in this moment. To be given a second…no, a third chance to survive.

Kett bit his own wrist, then pressed it to Benjamin's mouth. Blood smeared across the dark-haired vampire's lips and chin, but nothing else happened.

Jasmine collapsed between Bitsy and me, calling my attention to the werewolf. Bitsy smiled at me, but then immediately dropped her concerned gaze to Benjamin.

Kett bit his wrist again, once more pressing the wound against Benjamin's mouth. Again, nothing happened.

Then I realized I couldn't taste sour-grape jellybeans anymore. At all.

"You're going to have to force him." Jasmine reached for Kett's hand, scoring it over and over again with her sharp fingernails. Blood dripped down onto Benjamin's lips and chin.

I reached over, tilting Benjamin's face up and gently opening his mouth. I held him that way until five or six drops had made it past his teeth.

Jasmine raised her hand to claw Kett again.

"No," her master said. "That's enough. Perhaps too much." Kett looked to me. "We need to get him to ground before sunrise. And … I'll need to stay with him just in case …"

He didn't finish the statement, but I understood. In case some creature other than the thoughtful, kind, and steady Benjamin Garrick rose tomorrow evening.

"I understand. Do you have a place to go? What about the bakery basement?"

"We've got to get out of the damn stadium first," Jasmine said. "The witches haven't broken through the exterior wards yet."

"Okay. I can cut you out …" I said. Even though I really, really needed to return to the battle.

"No," Kett said softly. "I'll get the fledglings to safety."

"Then what do you need from me?"

Kett closed his eyes, pained. "Your blood. And … if possible, your knife. To cut through the warding."

Before I had a chance to respond, Jasmine reached over and took Benjamin from Kett, cradling him in her arms. Bitsy grabbed Benjamin's satchel and shakily stuffed his notebooks back into it.

"You want … won't my blood poison you?"

Kett opened his eyes. They'd reverted to their icy blue. He'd managed to retract his claws and fangs as well. "It very likely will. But …" He glanced over at Bitsy, who was using the wall for support as she made it to her feet. She followed Jasmine, who was carrying Benjamin, both of them moving around the decomposing elf corpses, giving us space. "As I understand it, the oracle needs you back at the gateway …"

"And you need the strength to get your … the fledglings out of the stadium."

Kett lowered his voice to a whisper. "And to control Benjamin, if needed."

"Risky," I teased.

He chuckled. "Indeed."

I closed the space between us, straddling his legs. He hesitated, then brushed his fingers gently over my face and wrapped his arms around me.

"I wouldn't have had it this way, Jade," he whispered against my neck.

I shivered at the cool touch of his breath, his magic. "What other way should it be between us, Kettil? You've done much, much more for me than what a few sips of blood will cost me."

He smoothed his hand down my back and up again. "You underestimate the power of your blood."

"You underestimate how loved and valued you are."

He laughed again, but in disbelief. "I like the new look. Dangerous. Intimidating. But I prefer the cupcake T-shirts."

"So do I."

Kett's fangs sliced into my neck with a whisper of pain. Then for the briefest of moments, he crushed me against his chest, as if gathering strength from the physical contact as well as from my blood. He suckled at me, feeling as though he was pulling the blood straight from my heart.

I gasped.

The instruments of assassination writhed, then bristled.

Kett immediately released me, shoving me off his lap and back a few feet. His now-red eyes were glued to the weapons hanging around my neck.

"Sorry," I said, lifting my hand to my neck. My fingers came away bloody.

"I apologize," Kett said. "Normally, I would heal you ..." But he trailed off as he saw the wound already closing over. He shook his head, smoothing his features. He looked better already. Not quite so gaunt. He stood in one fluid motion, then reached his hand toward me.

I accepted that hand, allowing him to pull me to my feet—though I actually felt better than I had just a few moments before. The time away from the battle had given my body the chance to properly heal. And whatever blood Kett had managed to sip in the short time the instruments had given him hadn't appeared to weaken me.

The vampire brushed a cool kiss across my brow, across the scar in the center of my forehead. "Thank you, Jade."

"You are very welcome. But I need to get back to the gateway."

He nodded, taking a step toward the trio waiting for him. Benjamin was still immobile and gray-skinned in Jasmine's arms. Bitsy was upright but leaning on the wall. "Jasmine informs me that the witches had planned to cut through the exterior wards themselves," Kett added. "Apparently, they've been unsuccessful."

"The wards have been refortified," I said. I was instinctively defending my grandmother, even though I'd thought the plan of an egress had been unnecessarily dangerous earlier. I palmed my knife, offering the jade weapon to Kett, hilt first. "This will help."

A smile flitted across his face. "Yes, my second request. I will return it to you."

I shook my head, already taking another step back and recalling the taste of Warner's magic—since the teleportation spell contained within my necklace could apparently pinpoint location guided only by that remembered taste now. The only way that made any sense to me was in thinking about how I'd claimed the teleportation spell. Then understanding how my inherent, instinctual power—my dowsing ability—worked with the taste of magic as its foundation.

It seemed like Alivia was right. There was a science to the energy we Adepts called magic.

Still, randomly teleporting into the middle of a battlefield was definitely going to come with its own complications.

"Just drop the knife when you're done with it. It'll return to me."

"I will not just be dropping a magical artifact of this caliber," Kett said, utterly affronted.

I squeezed out a laugh as the death grip of the teleportation magic cinched around me. "Just set it down then, old man. Take care of my BFF, Jasmine. Pretty please."

Bubbly, buoyant, creamy magic blotted out Jasmine's response, though I caught a note or two of her snarky laughter. Then my insides were turned outside once more.

I slammed into two elves, knocking them asunder, then tripping and tumbling into a pile of limbs and decapitated heads, all slick with elven blood. Warner's blade—trilling gleefully—whooshed over my head, nearly taking the top of my skull with it.

"Jade!" my fiance shouted, slamming a kick to an elf just past my shoulder.

Kandy yanked me to my feet before I could respond, throwing me behind her. I tumbled again, then found myself lying on a bed of decomposing corpses and staring up at the gateway.

Haoxin was hovering a couple of feet from the platform, facing Mory. Gabby was curled around the knitting-needle-wielding necromancer's feet. As far as I could tell, the amplifier was unconscious but breathing.

Mory wasn't holding or commanding her zombie elves anymore. Likely that had expended too much energy, draining her when she needed to focus.

As I watched, Mory gently teased forward another strand of the magic roped through and around Haoxin. Then somehow, the necromancer released it from her needles. The energy retracted, coiling into the guardian's chest, right around her heart. Her eyes flared gold, and she slipped another six inches closer to the platform.

Mory almost had the guardian out of the dimensional gate, which meant—

I sat up.

Reggie was mine.

My movement pulled Haoxin's gaze to me. Slowly, as if fighting the hold of the gateway magic to do so, she lifted her arm and pointed her finger at me.

Yeah, that couldn't be good.

My father was slaughtering elves off to Mory's right, letting them charge him, then cutting them down with almost-lazy flicks of his golden broadsword.

"Hey, Dad," I called, rolling to my feet. "Haoxin seems a bit pissed, eh?"

"She was displeased when I refused to simply cut her away from the gateway," my father said. "On the oracle's orders." He laughed, a little too gleeful for my taste. Especially since the guardian of North America's pissiness appeared to be focused on me.

I turned to survey the battlefield. To get my eyes on Reggie. Every inch of the floor, every foot of the ragged-concrete-and-rebar barrier my father had created was covered in white-armored bodies. Most of the elves were dead and dismembered, in various states of decomposition. But a few were still breathing, fallen but attempting to retreat.

The onslaught had slowed to a trickle.

Reggie was getting her subjects, those most loyal to her, slaughtered. For no reason. At this point, with Kandy and Warner joining the field and Haoxin almost freed, she had to know she was going to lose.

So why not surrender?

I strode forward. My father flashed me a grin, stepping back while clearing the immediate area until he stood only a foot or so away from Mory and Gabby.

Warner and Kandy stepped up behind me. The few elves still on their feet and facing us hesitated. I made a show of pulling my katana.

They suddenly convulsed, dropping their swords. The blades crumbled into fine crystal as they hit the concrete. Then the elves clutched their foreheads, driven to their knees in pain.

"They keep doing that," Kandy muttered.

"It's Reggie," I said, speaking through clenched teeth. "She's not allowing them to retreat, or even regroup."

I skirted the elves, leaving them for my father to deal with if they managed to shake off Reggie's psychic torture. I jogged up the barrier, easily finding and springing off footholds until I reached the apex. Warner and Kandy followed.

Maybe twenty-five feet beyond the ridge of broken concrete littered with the dead and dying, Reggie and Alivia were still standing on the raised platform. The ward builder's magic shimmered all around them, streaming straight up to the domed roof.

A few dozen elves were still on their feet. More than that number were wounded. And only a few of those were being tended to.

"Fuck this," Kandy muttered to my left. "This is completely insane."

Warner brushed his shoulder against mine, grunting in agreement.

"You're a coward, Reggie!" I shouted, climbing down the other side of the barrier. "A manipulative coward. Your people deserve your protection and you waste their lives. You were never going to win. Not even if you managed to hold me." I laughed harshly. "You couldn't even get past the witches!"

The remaining elves—maybe fifty or so, and most of them wounded—scrambled together, lining themselves up in neat short rows between Reggie and me. Momentarily halting our advance.

Traveler placed himself at the center front, directly between me and my target. His face and neck were scored with half-healed claw marks, his armor dented and chipped. Since I hadn't seen him on the battlefield—and because Kandy would have taken his head—I had the feeling he'd gone up against Kett, or even Jasmine, outside the cells. And he'd fled before he lost that fight.

The warrior manifested two knives now, his green eyes flicking to take in my companions on either side. Then his gaze glued itself to me.

I pointed my sword at him. "You don't even want to be under her control."

"I made a deal," he spat. His English was so heavily accented I had to work to understand him. "Some of us have honor."

I nodded. "Yeah. Just not all of you."

I looked across the mass of elves between me and the telepath, meeting Alivia's steady and inscrutable gaze. "Let's end this now, Reggie. One on one."

Reggie sneered. "You can't best me, alchemist."

Magic whispered across my right thigh, and my jade knife settled into its built-in sheath. I laughed, quietly delighted. "Kett and the others made it through the exterior wards," I said for Warner and Kandy's benefit.

The rows of elves before us began slowly advancing. One step. Two steps.

"What's the play here, Jade?" Kandy asked.

"Wait for it." I took a deep breath, then exhaled.

A shout of victory came from behind the barrier.

Mory.

Reggie flicked her gaze over our heads, frowning deeply.

Alivia dropped the ward surrounding the three-foot-high platform.

Sheathing my katana, I raised my foot to step forward, imagining myself stepping up beside the telepath. Magic squeezed me, twisting through my internal organs.

And then...I was standing behind Reggie.

She spun to face me.

Calling my jade knife into my hand, I stabbed her in the chest. Surprise smoothed out the anger etched across the telepath's face.

Kandy threw her head back, howling in victory. All the hair on the back of my neck rose in response to her undulating cry. Swords and claws clashed as the final wave of elves fell upon her and Warner.

Reggie stumbled, falling against me. Her magic rose up, wailing against me, scrambling for a hold—a raging hurricane thundering against every inch of my body.

Alivia watched, completely dispassionate.

I withdrew my knife, then stabbed Reggie a second time. I clawed the fingers of my left hand around the gemstone on her forehead, realizing for the first time that it wasn't actually attached to her, wasn't embedded in her skin. It was just a coronet. A crown she wore. A trinket she could have tossed aside at any moment, just as she'd tossed aside the lives of those under her control.

I tore the coronet off her head, letting her body slide off my knife and drop to the platform at my feet.

I thrust my hand above my head, holding the gemstone section of the crown against the palm of my hand and bellowing, "Stop!"

Elven magic snapped at me, swirling around my hand.

The warriors arrayed between me and the barrier froze, including those who were already fighting Kandy and Warner. The entire field of warriors pivoted, looking at me.

"The necromancer is closing the gateway. Those of you who wish to return to your own dimension may do so. Those who wish to remain and fight will fall to our blades."

The elves didn't move, didn't react.

"Allow me," Alivia said, suddenly manifesting a long crystal blade—even as she swung it toward me.

I stumbled back, raising my own knife to block the blow. But the ward builder wasn't aiming for me.

She sliced downward instead, taking Reggie's head. Then she held out her hand for the coronet.

Speechless, and way too uncertain to question the wisdom of the action, I dropped the elven artifact into her hand. She smeared the gemstone in the thick white blood sluggishly draining from Reggie's neck. Then she held the coronet before her mouth and whispered an Elvish word.

The gemstone in the center of the magical artifact shattered, crumbling into fine crystal.

Alivia met my startled gaze with a grim smile. "A simple break incantation. But I could never have torn the gem from her head on my own."

"Ah, okay. Cool." A breaking spell. I'd have to try that myself someday. Though I seriously hoped it wouldn't prove necessary to add any other magical implements to my arsenal for a long, long time.

Alivia turned to the assembled elves, all of them seemingly frozen in place. She said something in Elvish, then translated for me.

"I've told them to go home."

The warrior elves looked around, completely confused.

Traveler shouted something. He was standing near Warner, cradling one arm. He shouted a second time.

All the elves spun to look at him.

And for a brief moment, I thought he was egging them on. Encouraging them to continue fighting.

I was going to have to murder them all.

I clenched my fists, angry tears edging my eyes. But I firmed my resolve, not allowing them to fall.

Everyone made choices. Though sometimes the circumstances were thrust upon us.

Traveler shouted a third time. But then he turned and raised one hand, the other hanging useless at his side. And he crossed toward the barrier, toward the gateway.

"To me," Alivia murmured, translating. "Follow me home."

The warriors dropped their weapons, forming a long, tidy line behind Traveler. Alivia threw the coronet onto Reggie's body and stepped off the platform, immediately reaching down to help one of the fallen to their feet.

I met Warner's gaze over top of the elves' heads. He smiled at me, then returned his attention to the warriors shuffling past him and climbing over the barrier toward the gateway.

The defeated elves murmured quietly among themselves. The able-bodied were helping the wounded or carrying the nearly dead. But there were too many already-crumbling corpses for the elves to take their fallen with them.

I glanced over at Alivia. But I was remembering the unknown elf who had moaned, pained, when Mira had fallen. When Reggie had killed the pretty elf in order to enslave me. How many of the warriors had actually wanted to be there? How many had been compelled through the gateway?

"Alivia," I called, stepping down off the platform.

She half-turned to me, almost absentmindedly. Her attention was on a wounded elf at her feet, trying to fix his dislocated shoulder.

"Can you speak for your people?" I asked.

She smiled stiffly. "I can communicate to those who can."

"Okay. I think it might be time for a conversation."

"With you, Jade Godfrey? Do you speak for the Adept?"

I laughed. "Not me. But I might be able to set up a conversation with the guardians."

"As you promised my niece, Mira. Your friend. A promise she confided in someone she shouldn't have, though he regretted his unintentional betrayal and sought me out after I crossed through the gateway. And here we are." The ward builder's tone was darkly tinted, but she offered me a tight smile.

"Yes. As I promised."

"I'll hold you to your word."

"I would expect nothing less."

Alivia snorted as she dismissed me in order to help the wounded elf to his feet. Then she moved on to helping the next fallen warrior, and I turned away.

Chapter Eleven

*H*aoxin was standing on her own two feet now—and appeared to be interrogating Mory. The necromancer was still working to untangle the final strands of magic connecting the guardian to the gateway. By my count, about half of the remaining elves had already crossed back through the dimensional portal.

I just watched, in a bit of a daze.

Apparently, my job was done.

Warner was talking to me, but I only half-heard him. He had carried an unconscious Gabby out to the witches and the sorcerers, bringing back the news that Kett and Jasmine had helped tip the balance in a secondary battle I hadn't even known about. The elves had been fighting the witches, the sorcerers, and the necromancers, which was why the witches hadn't managed to open the promised egress. Even though everyone was banged up, they'd survived the secondary assault.

As far as anyone knew, Benjamin was still hanging on. But Kett and Jasmine had already disappeared with him. It was only a couple of hours away from dawn. Much more time had passed than I thought.

And it was all going to be okay.

I moved through the wounded with Alivia and Kandy, helping those we could to get to their feet. Those who couldn't walk, we ferried over the barrier so they could have a chance to cross through the gateway home. Once the immediate area was clear, all three of us started working our way up the barrier. I'd paused at the crest, crouching to check the elves sprawled there for signs of life. All of them were already decomposing, though.

Still riding the adrenaline high that was insulating me from the destruction I'd wrought—that we had wrought—I closed my eyes. Then I hoped to God that it wasn't ever on me to thwart an interdimensional invasion again.

The crash from this fight was going to be a bitch.

I was already certain I wasn't the same person as the Jade who'd danced at her own bachelorette party, just two weeks ago. Hell, I wasn't even the same Jade who'd torn the gemstone from her forehead, the same Jade who'd chosen to stand between Mory and hundreds of elves. The Jade who'd trusted an oracle.

I opened my eyes, seeking and finding Warner standing with Mory by the gateway. He held himself slightly between the necromancer and the almost freed guardian, but his gaze was on me.

I smiled.

An answering grin softened all the hard edges of his face.

We'd won.

Assuming that everything around us was what winning looked like.

My father stepped up beside me, brushing his fingers against my shoulder. "I should sweep the rest of the building for stragglers. Should I ask the elf to come with me? To mitigate any reactions should I find any of her people?" He nodded toward Alivia, who was still moving among the fallen elves on the far side of the barrier. They were decomposing steadily now, but I really couldn't blame her for checking again. Too few were crossing back through the gateway.

"Alivia. And yeah, that might be a good idea," I murmured.

He touched my head lightly, then stepped away to speak with the ward builder.

Kandy slumped down next to me, still in her half-beast form. The taste of bittersweet chocolate with a rich red-berry finish flooded my mouth as her magic whirled around her and she transformed into her human visage. Her torn and stretched T-shirt was hanging off her, and she had to cinch her belt tightly to keep what remained of her shredded jeans in place. She was rail thin, having lost way too much muscle mass while in the elves' not-so-tender care.

Perhaps that was why Mory was being so careful, so particular. Why she hadn't wanted me to slice through the gateway magic she'd held, even when our lives might have depended on it after the metal beast came through the gate. Was she hoping that carefully releasing the life force that fueled the gateway might somehow return it to those it had been forcefully siphoned from? I was fairly certain that the gateway would have burned through all that stolen life. That was why Reggie had systematically switched out the prisoners, aka her dimensional fuel cells.

"I wanted to come for you myself," I said quietly.

Kandy snorted. "Of course you did. Because you think you're responsible."

I huffed out a laugh. "Rochelle pretty much told me I was going to cause an apocalyptic event if I didn't follow her plan."

Kandy glanced to her wrist as if checking a nonexistent watch. "There's still time."

"Hilarious."

My werewolf BFF rested her head on my shoulder. "Your ass looks fucking fantastic in those pants."

"Priorities. Right."

"Right." She cleared her throat. "I knew…I knew you'd make it through, Jade."

"I missed you desperately. There is no one else I would want with me, no one else I would want to face anything like this with. You, Warner, and Kett."

Kandy laughed quietly. "Lucky for you I ain't the marrying kind. So I plan to stick around. But …" Kandy knocked me with her shoulder playfully, holding her arms out, then lifting her bare legs one at a time. She was covered in a thick layer of crusty elven blood. "I think I might be over the green thing."

I chuckled. "Some things do change. How about purple hair? Ooh, no. Pink."

"Screw you, dowser."

"Aw, just think how cute you'd look when you were in the bakery. Pink hair, cupcakes—"

"Speaking of which, have you got any chocolate?"

That perked me up. "No. But Mory does."

Kandy sprang to her feet, dashing down the broken concrete and somehow managing to not skewer herself on jutting rebar. "Finders keepers, loser!"

I laughed. I couldn't help it. Crouched among dozens upon dozens of the dead—a goodly portion felled by my own hand—I threw my head back and laughed at my werewolf BFF.

Over by the gateway, Haoxin keyed in on me. "You!" the guardian of North America bellowed. Her magic somehow rode her rage, crumpling the jagged concrete between her and me.

Kandy darted to the side, narrowly avoiding being taken off her feet.

Haoxin's ire rumbled the makeshift barrier under my feet. "Jade Godfrey! Wielder of the instruments of assassination!"

The guardian lurched forward.

"Wait, wait!" Mory cried, seated at Haoxin's feet, still holding her knitting needles before her. "I'm almost finished!"

"Haoxin waits for no one." The petite guardian's magic lashed around her as she stepped over the necromancer. And suddenly, she wasn't so petite anymore.

Haoxin was…growing…stretching…expanding…

I stood stock still, completely unsure of what to say, of how to calm the irate guardian. I'd be pissed too if I'd been taken down by the centipedes—especially when wielded by a supposed friend. An ally. Me.

"Haoxin," Warner said, stepping in front of her, "the wielder was—"

The guardian—now standing about six inches taller than the sentinel and still growing—backhanded him.

Warner flew across the stadium, slamming into and through at least three sections of the elves' white-walled maze.

Instantly incensed, I reached for my necklace, brushing my fingers across the chain. Magic welled under my touch. Then I hesitated.

Haoxin and the instruments shared a destiny. Namely, her death by strangulation. And I wasn't going to be…I couldn't be the wielder who brought that destiny to fruition. I dropped my hand from the necklace, allowing the anticipatory trill of the instruments to fade.

"Stand forth for your reckoning, dragon slayer!" The guardian was easily eight feet tall now, but her arms and legs were longer and thicker than the rest of her body. She was still expanding, stretching.

My father abruptly appeared, dancing in front of the irate guardian, hands held up and forward. "Settle, my friend. All will be well. Let the necromancer finish—"

Haoxin slammed her fist down, attempting to smush my father with a hand that was now the size of a tiny car.

Yazi rolled away.

The blow created a massive crater in the floor, throwing anyone still on their feet to the ground. Including me.

I tumbled down the other side of the barrier. The rebar wasn't kind to me. I smashed my head at least once. Then I just lay where I'd fallen, twisted around jutting concrete.

I'd been fighting for hours. I was drained. I wasn't certain I had the strength for another fight.

Mory screamed. "Stop! Stop!"

I made it to my feet. Jesus Christ. I could see Haoxin even over the freaking barrier. She was reaching for the roof, and tall enough to almost touch it now.

Mory screamed a second time.

Her terror flooded through me, leaving an aching fear in its wake. I closed my eyes and tried to focus. "Toasted marshmallow. Toasted marshmallow. Toasted—"

Magic flowed out from my necklace, wrapping around me, pinching, squeezing, wrenching my guts.

I teleported to right beside Mory. She'd been dragged a few feet away from the gateway. Thick tendrils of magic still connected her and her knitting needles to the raging guardian and the elves' gate.

About twelve feet away, Haoxin raised a foot the size of a freaking minivan and tried to stomp my father.

The gateway slipped.

Tilted.

Haoxin was pulling on it by way of the magic still connected to her. Following my father, she took another step, yanking Mory with her.

The necromancer was sobbing, but she was trying to hang on, trying to loosen the last of the magical ties connected to Haoxin.

A large hunk of concrete shifted a few feet away from us as Kandy freed herself from the debris Haoxin had stirred up. She rolled to her feet, shaking her head. She was bleeding from a head wound. Badly.

I reached for Mory.

She strained away from me. "No, Jade. No, Jade. No!"

Warner appeared beside us.

"Kandy," I cried. "Get Kandy clear, please."

He cast a grim gaze around us. The last dozen or so elves were frantically dragging their wounded toward the unstable gateway, desperate to pass through before it collapsed. Literally.

Jesus.

No.

The gateway couldn't collapse.

That would mean it had all been for nothing. Everything Rochelle had seen would come to pass.

Haoxin took another step, distracted by my father attempting to talk her down. He was shouting in Mandarin now.

Mory was yanked forward with the guardian's movement. She screamed in frustration and pain.

I palmed my knife, darting forward between the necromancer and the rampaging giant guardian.

Haoxin spotted me, whirling my way far too quickly for any creature her size.

Warner lunged, grabbing Kandy before she got crushed under the guardian's foot. Then he was gone, carrying my wolf to safety.

I sliced downward, intending to sever the final strand connecting Haoxin to the gateway. I remembered Pulou saying that the former warrior had never been the same after he'd walked through the gateway's magic. Haoxin was still fueling it. So getting her free might help contain her.

But before I could cut it myself, the thick tendril of magic loosened, snapping back toward the guardian.

"Got it," Mory grunted with satisfaction.

I dropped my knife, scooping Mory up in my arms.

Then Haoxin brought the roof down.

I clearly saw her reach overhead.

I saw her wrench two of the white metal pylons free, breaking off large chunks of concrete and shattering an epic amount of glass.

I wasn't going to be able to clear the area in time.

I hunkered down, covering as much of Mory as I could with my body. Then I prepared myself to take the hit, to hold whatever fell for as long as I could.

I felt the roof come down, dampening the light all around us.

Then...nothing.

I cranked my head, looking up over my shoulder. A barrage of twisted metal, glass, and hunks of concrete was suspended above me. Magic rippled across it all, tasting of apricots.

Alivia's magic.

I straightened, frantically looking for the ward builder and finding her off to one side of the gateway. Her hands were flung forward, her face etched with determination and pain.

"Oh, my God," Mory whispered.

"The gateway!" Alivia screamed.

One of the metal pylons was just above the gateway. Inches away from hitting it. The gate was tilted at a sharp angle, with the last of the elves still trying to cross through it, dragging the wounded. One at a time. Seven left, including Alivia. Six …

Something heavy slammed over my head.

Alivia moaned. Everything she was trying to hold aloft—an entire section of a freaking stadium roof—slipped down a couple of inches.

Another hit from above. More slippage.

Haoxin was trying to get through to us. To me. She was trying to crush me like a bug. And everyone along with me.

Five elves left.

"Stay here, Mory," I said. Then I sprinted toward the gateway.

"No, Jade," the necromancer shrieked behind me. "You can't! You can't close it!"

"I'm not closing it. I'm holding it." I knelt as I slid to a stop, shoving my hands into the magic. Turning my face away as best I could, I placed my hands on either side of the elf tech. Then I tried to hold it in place.

The next elf in line grunted, shifted the warrior he was dragging up over his shoulder, and stepped over me. He fell into, then through, the magic boiling over my head.

Four elves left.

Alivia's ward took another hit.

The gateway shuddered, pressing against me. A biting, twisting pain shot through my arms, but I held on. I looked up, catching sight of Haoxin—her body huge and distended—beating against the ward. A flash of gold informed me that my father had resorted to unleashing his sword.

"What a fucking mess," I murmured.

Three elves left.

Two.

I looked over at Alivia. "Can you move? And hold?"

She nodded. "I believe so. If I tighten the aperture." Then her gaze dropped to Mory. The necromancer was watching us with massively wide eyes, holding her ankle. "But … you need to clear the area first."

Haoxin hit the ward over us again. Hard. Like she might have resorted to kicking it. The magic cracked. Pieces of concrete and glass began to fall.

"We'll time it," I said, trying to focus despite the fact that I was starting to feel off. Stretched thin. As if the gateway might have been draining me now, fueling itself from my life force. "I'll get Mory out."

Alivia nodded, carefully stepping toward me while still concentrating on the shield she was holding overhead.

Haoxin swiped the area above me clear, shoving the debris of the roof aside so she could peer down at me.

I couldn't see my father anywhere.

The guardian grinned, cartoonish and maniacal. Then she reared back, raised her foot, and slammed it through Alivia's magic.

"Jump!" I screamed to Alivia, even as I rolled away from the gateway.

Something hit me on the back, then across my head.

Everything went black.

Someone was crying.

It wasn't me.

Mory.

Mory was crying.

I opened my eyes.

I was on the ground...on the metal...the concrete...the glass all around me. Blood was dripping into my eyes. Panicked, I wiped my forehead, but I could still feel the ridge of scar tissue there. I was bleeding from my skull, not a gemstone embedded into my brain.

I had killed Reggie. I'd freed myself from her, then killed her. I was bleeding for an entirely different reason now.

Something shifted on the edge of my blurred vision.

I blinked.

Hands.

Toasted marshmallow magic.

Mory.

The necromancer was crawling toward me.

I tried to twist toward her, but...aside from my arm, I couldn't actually move. I was...pinned? And something was tugging at my legs?

Right.

The roof had fallen.

Mory pulled herself over a hunk of concrete, making eye contact. Then she let out a terrible sob that sounded as if it tore through her heart and soul.

"Hey, Mory," I croaked. "Shh, shh ..."

Something rumbled nearby, the debris around us shifting. Magic exploded all around us, tasting of spices and chocolate ... and tomato. A combination of Yazi and Haoxin. Maybe Warner.

Mory squeaked then pulled herself closer, finally able to brush her fingers against mine.

"You're hurt," I managed to say, realizing with the words that something was terribly wrong with me...with my legs, my back and lower rib cage. Something was squeezing me, making it difficult to talk.

But there was no pain. Shouldn't I have been in pain?

"... Jade?" Mory asked, her tone suggesting she'd been talking to me and I'd missed it. "Jade? You look hurt. Bad."

"I'm okay. How about you? It's your leg?"

"Yeah, I think I broke my ankle ..." She glanced at me worriedly, mumbling the rest. "When you dropped me. But, um, now the other leg...won't ..." She sobbed, then got herself under control. "They'll come for us, yes?"

"Yes. Sure."

Except I had just figured out what was tugging at me, what was pinning me, above and beyond the hunk of roof.

The dimensional gateway.

It must have collapsed over me. And now...and now...I thought it might have been tearing me in two.

I cleared my throat, tamping down my panic. "Mory. Can you see the magic holding me?"

Mory's eyes widened in fear, then flicked over my head and shoulders. "No," she cried. "Is it the gate?"

"It's okay."

The rubble all around us suddenly rose up, then slammed back down as if an earthquake had just hit the city. Or a large body had just been thrown to the ground.

Pain exploded in my upper chest, my left arm, my head and neck.

Mory cried out. Then, even as wounded as she was, she started to try to dig me out.

Metal creaked and crackled overhead. I could see a sliver of lightening sky above us. It was nearing dawn. But I couldn't turn my head to see what was making the noise. The rest of the roof coming down, most likely.

Mory was grunting and sobbing, struggling to lift something off my back even though she couldn't stand herself.

"It's okay. It's okay, babe." I grabbed for her with my left hand. "Listen, listen. I'm going to try to teleport us out of here."

Mory panted through her tears, calming down enough to listen to me. "Yes. Yes." She gripped my arm.

And I tried…I tried to call the magic forth from my necklace, tried to wrap it around me and Mory. But I couldn't make it move lower than my upper back. It was as if it couldn't grab onto my lower half. The half the gateway was holding.

"Nothing is happening," Mory whispered. "Jade?"

A large chunk of the roof broke off and crashed to the ground about ten feet behind me.

We were going to die. Mory and me. And even if some miracle occurred and I survived the rest of the stadium collapsing on me, and if whoever found me could get me out of the gateway in the end …

Mory wouldn't make it.

Mory would die for certain.

"Help me," I whispered, reaching for my necklace.

"I'm trying. I'm trying," Mory cried, on the edge of hysterical now.

"No. Help me get my necklace off."

"What? Why? Why?"

"Mory!"

The necromancer slipped her fingers underneath the heavy gold chain. I helped as much as I could with my left hand, but the instruments protested, bristling and pulsing with displeasure.

"Shh … shh …" I whispered.

"I'm okay. I'm okay," Mory murmured. She eased the chain off over my head, then left it pooled underneath my palm.

I panted for a moment. It was becoming difficult to breathe. And the instruments were already fighting my unvoiced intention.

"Now put it on," I said.

"What?"

"I need you to put on the necklace, Mory. Leave it loose, please. So I can touch it."

"I'm not putting on your necklace!"

"Put on the necklace," I snarled.

Mory snatched up the chain, then remembered that I needed to keep in contact with it. She leaned over me, close enough that her hair tickled my cheek, and looped the chain over her neck.

The instruments screamed, shrieking their discontent.

Mory sucked in a breath.

"It's okay." I petted the chain as best I could with my torso, shoulder, and one arm pinned.

Another huge chunk of the roof fell. This one even closer.

"Stay with Mory," I said, speaking to all the magic contained in the necklace. "Protect Mory."

"What are you doing, Jade?"

I didn't answer the necromancer. I had to keep all my attention on the magical artifact. I had to calm it, direct it. "The treasure keeper will come. Everything is going to be okay."

"What do you mean?"

The magic of the necklace and the instruments settled. Keeping my fingertips on the lower two wedding rings, I called the teleportation spell forward. Then I looked up at Mory.

"Tell them I love them," I whispered.

"Who? Tell who?"

"All of them."

I brushed my fingers along the chain, feeling the comforting magic dancing underneath them. "Promise me, Mory. Promise me you'll make them understand."

"Understand what?" Mory cried, grabbing at my hand, grabbing my arm.

"To Warner," I said, speaking to the power of the necklace while I recalled the taste of Warner's magic—dark chocolate...sweet cherry..."Take the necromancer safely to Warner."

The magic balked at my command. It was an easy guess that the disgruntled instruments were impeding it.

"What?" Mory was sobbing now, tugging at my arm, trying to pull me free but getting nowhere.

I could feel myself truly fading now, numbness spreading over my shoulders and up my neck.

"Don't leave me, Jade. Don't leave me."

"It's not me leaving, darling. It's time for you to leave me."

I took the last bit of magic I could summon. I shoved it all at the necklace. "To Warner. Safely to Warner."

The magic of the necklace expanded. Somewhat pissily, I thought.

Mory shouted something.

The magic contracted.

And the necromancer was gone.

I sighed, finally able to rest my head in the rubble. I could hear voices shouting somewhere in the distance. I felt guardian magic. And the gateway, tug-tug-tugging at me.

And I understood. This was the future Rochelle had seen in her sketch of the Buddha. I hadn't needed the power of the sorcerer's amulet to escape the dragon nexus. I had needed it for this. For Mory.

Another hunk of roof collapsed. Debris pelted me around the head and shoulders.

Freddie appeared. As the shadow leech moved over me, its magic tried to grab hold. I tried to brush it away, but I couldn't move my arm anymore.

"Freddie," I murmured thickly. I realized that I was leaking blood from my nose and mouth. "Leave it. Go to Mory. Mory will take care of you. The ... the bakery wards. I give you permission to take magic from the bakery ..."

Freddie chittered indignantly, still trying to grab me. To transport me, maybe. As the leeches had once been able to transport Shailaja. But the rubble and the gateway held me fast.

I closed my eyes.

Then someone was screaming. Shouting. The sound coming closer.

Mory.

Oh, God.

Had something happened? Had something gone wrong with the teleportation?

I struggled to lift my head. And there suddenly was Warner, just on the edge of my sight line, climbing over the rubble. Mory was slung across his back, jabbing her finger in my direction.

I met his gaze.

I smiled. So, so glad that I'd had the chance to see him one last time.

I love you. My mouth wouldn't form the words, so I thought them over and over and over again.

I love you.

I love you.

Warner shouted.

Freddie shifted, latching onto my head and neck, spreading out across my shoulders.

The taste of burnt cinnamon toast filled my mouth.

I love you.

The roof collapsed.

Taking what remained of me with it.

Chapter Twelve

*P*ain.

Pain. Pain.

Pain. Pain. Pain.
Then blissful nothingness.

Coffee.
And chocolate.
But bitter…too bitter.
Choking.
Suffocating.
Someone was trying to force me to…drink…coffee…
I tried to shove it away…tried to turn my head…
The pain returned, or maybe it had never gone.

Too much.
Too late.

The damn coffee pusher was back.

Seriously, I didn't freaking like freaking coffee!

I mean, drink it if you want to, but …

Wait.

Music.

Wait.

Coffee … and chocolate?

Wait.

The healer.

I was … alive? Still alive?

Agony shot through my head, down my neck, and through my left arm. Then it was soothed away, carried off by a tune I could never remember.

But … I didn't want to be soothed. I didn't want to be shoved into oblivion.

I tried to grab hold of the healer's magic. I tried to hoard it … but I didn't have my knife or my necklace.

Where was my necklace?

I had to open my eyes.

I had to move.

I couldn't do either.

I was trapped on the edge of oblivion.

I was trapped.

I was trapped.

No.

No one held me.

I didn't need to be able to see or move.

I had magic.

I was magic.

"Oh, thank goodness," a voice murmured. "I've got her. I've got her back."

The healer. Qiuniu.

I tried to speak, but I couldn't move my mouth.

So I reached for the healer's magic instead.

I could suffer through a few sips of coffee, especially if accompanied by dark chocolate.

There wasn't much I couldn't do when motivated by chocolate, after all.

"We have to get the necklace off the necromancer."

"She can't even move yet, warrior."

"The girl will die. The instruments are not meant to be held, not together, not by anyone other than the wielder. And Jade will be angry if she wakes to find we did nothing."

"Jade's permission will hold a little while longer. The necromancer will survive."

Mory.

Mory was in trouble.

Dying?

Because of…me.

"Blossom."

A sudden spike of magic—my father's power—drilled into my head, deeply into my brain. I gasped, shying away from the intense energy.

"Jade! What did she say?"

I tried to speak again. I couldn't.

My father's magic brushed me…my cheek, my shoulder, my left hand.

No.

He was touching me. That was what physical contact felt like.

"Blossom tried, Jade," my father said urgently. "The necklace refuses to budge from the necromancer's neck. And for all his arrogant, ignorant declarations, the treasure keeper can't collect it either."

The pain rose, but I fought it back. I tried reaching out, seeking the tenor of the necklace. But I couldn't feel it.

"Bring the girl here," the healer said. "The proximity might help."

Mory. Not 'the girl.'

She was Mory.

The healer's music rose and I slipped away into the soothing tune before I could voice my complaint.

The intense taste of chocolate and cherries and whipped cream came and went.

Warner.

His magic was full of fury.

Later.

Bittersweet chocolate with a red-berry finish.

Kandy.

Later.

Cool peppermint.

I breathed.

The bed shifted. Cool fingers brushed against my left wrist, checking my pulse.

Kett.

I tried to talk but couldn't.

Then I realized I was touching something. The fingers of my left hand were threaded through … metal. Magic writhed, noting my attention on it. Needy, spiteful magic, full of declarations of vengeance.

"Shh, shh …" I whispered, soothing the power. It settled under my touch.

Kett pressed a kiss to my forehead. His cool magic smoothed away the dull ache that seemed to permanently reside in my head.

"We didn't get to save each other this time," he murmured, teasing.

He was gone before I could reply. Before I could thank him for reminding me who I was when I'd so desperately needed to know it.

Or … maybe it was me who'd slipped away.

Again.

I opened my eyes.

Blinking.

I was in my bedroom. Lying faceup on the bed. The light was muted. Shadows across the ceiling.

Someone was lying curled beside me.

I turned my head. Pain streaked up my neck, resolving into black dots across my vision. I blinked some more.

It was Mory next to me. And … and … there was something terribly wrong with her magic.

I couldn't taste it.

The fingers of my left hand were twined through the wedding rings on the necklace she wore.

That was odd … there was something odd about Mory wearing—

"Jade? Jade!"

I met Mory's gaze. Her dark eyes were sunken, her skin sallow. But a grin spread across her face.

"You look like hell," she teased.

"Right back at you," I croaked.

She shifted up, sitting propped up on one hand, but bent over me so I didn't lose contact with the necklace. Both her legs were in hard casts.

Her movement jostled me, and the resulting agony nearly pushed me back under the darkness waiting to consume me. To subsume me.

"I held it for you, Jade," Mory whispered. "The necklace."

The necromancer's face came back into focus. She looked...sick. Really sick. Like something was eating her from the inside out...consuming her magic. That's why I couldn't taste it.

"The necklace," I murmured.

"Yes."

"My necklace."

"Yes."

Magic shifted around us, around Mory's neck. Then I was holding the necklace, my fingers still threaded through the wedding rings.

Intense magic flooded up my left arm, streaking through my shoulder, neck, and head. Pain rampaged through every one of my nerve endings.

If I hadn't known any better, I would have thought the instruments were punishing me for abandoning them.

Pain snuffed out my sight.

Darkness swallowed me again.

Voices.

Raised.

Arguing.

My grandmother, my father, and…the treasure keeper?

But muffled, as if coming through the door.

I opened my eyes.

Warner was pacing back and forth by my bedroom door. Dressed head to toe in leather armor and with his knife visible in its sheath, everything about him promised death and destruction to anyone who dared enter the room.

My heart squeezed, then expanded until I thought it might burst. "I…I thought …" Tears flooded my eyes, choking my already reedy whisper.

Warner spun to face me, instantly dropping to his knees by the bed. Pure joy was etched across his face.

"I thought I would never get to see you again," I said.

"I'm not going anywhere."

I lifted my hand, intending to press it against his face. Desperately wanting to feel his warmth, the scrape of his stubble. But the necklace and the instruments of assassination came with me, twined around my fingers.

Warner laughed, quietly joyful. "Ah, my Jade. My Jade." He gently cupped my hand, necklace and all, and pressed a kiss to my palm. "You're moving. You're healing."

"What's going on in the hall?"

"Pulou," Warner spat. "Now that you've reclaimed the necklace, he thinks he can force Blossom to take it from you. You made some deal with the brownie before? The treasure keeper thinks it's still in effect." He paused, looking at me questioningly.

I nodded. "When the healer needed to heal me in the nexus. From the gemstone... and the brawl with Pulou. He couldn't do it with me wearing the instruments."

Warner nodded grimly. "He's driven poor Blossom into hiding. Don't worry, your mother is on the way. He won't be able to justify his behavior when she gets here."

"I wasn't aware she had that kind of power over guardians." I laughed quietly. It hurt, but it hurt worse not to laugh.

"Scarlett has them all wrapped around her little finger." He pressed a gentle kiss to my hand again. "It runs in the family."

I smiled at him, but I could feel the weariness threatening to take me under. "Open the door."

"You're going to let Pulou take the necklace?"

"No. Just open the door. I'll speak to him."

Intense emotion flitted across Warner's face, and I watched as he visibly struggled to not argue with me. Then he shook his head, stood up, and stiffly crossed to the door. He pulled it open so hard that the knob embedded into my standing bureau. He glanced back at me.

I gave him a look.

He grinned, deadly around the edges. But not deadly for me.

I chuckled quietly.

Everyone who had crammed into the narrow hall of my apartment had gone silent. Warner stepped to the side.

I angled my head so I could see partly into the hall. "Pulou."

The treasure keeper pushed past my grandmother and father, pausing just outside the door. He was massive in his floor-length fur coat, though his magic was dampened. Or maybe it was actually me who was drained. "Wielder," he murmured.

I lifted my left hand—the only limb I could actually move—to display the necklace. "The instruments will put up with no other mistress."

"Jade," Pulou said kindly. "They are dangerous even when you are...whole." He waved his hand. "And now, they nearly killed the necromancer."

"Mory. Her name is Mory."

"I am aware. I'm simply asking you to let me put them away, safely, until you are capable of retrieving them."

"And I'm simply telling you that when I die, you can rip them from my cold corpse. Until then, you must remain in a perpetual state of displeasure."

"Your death would not please me, Jade."

"There you go, then," I murmured, epically weary from holding my hand aloft. "The instruments stay with me. When I die, I shall give Blossom permission to hide them away in the treasure keeper's chamber."

"Fine?" Warner asked pissily. "Can Jade get back to healing now?"

"Of course, sentinel," Pulou said stiffly. "I meant no disrespect."

My eyes were shut before Warner got the door closed.

"There's something wrong with my legs."

"You're still healing." Kandy was curled up on the bed beside me. I could feel her magic, more than see her in the dark room. Not even a hint of moonlight filtered through the closed curtains.

"I've been healing forever."

"It's just … complicated. Qiuniu brought you back, right? But you … you weren't breathing when Warner pulled you out from under the fucking stadium."

"Not breathing …" I murmured. I was still so, so tired.

"They … the witches, Scarlett and Pearl … they pumped so much magic into you that they actually collapsed. All their reserves, just to hold you in stasis. Force your heart to beat. Mory says the damn leech helped saved you, so now we all have to be nice to the creep." Kandy sighed. She shifted again, scrubbing a hand over her face. "And the healer and Burgundy have been working overtime between all the rest of us."

"So … I'm … paralyzed? By the gateway?"

"Jesus, Jade. We thought you were dead." Her voice cracked, haggard. She pressed her face against my neck. I felt tears streaming down her cheeks. "I thought … I thought you'd left me. And that's not the deal. That's not the deal. I get to go first. Promise. Promise me, Jade."

I closed my eyes, terribly weary. "How about together?"

Kandy laughed huskily. "Okay. Together. In a blaze of glory. You, me, Kett. And Warner, if he wants. I thought old toothy was going to end his immortal existence when he set eyes on you, lying here … Pearl thought that she and the sorcerers were going to have to figure out how to contain him. With everyone so drained, they didn't know if they could hold him. And Warner wasn't being at all helpful."

She curled into me more tightly, gently threading her fingers through mine. "We thought you were dead. We thought you were dead."

I pressed my other hand to her head, finding I could move both upper limbs now. Slowly, I twisted around so I could actually see my BFF.

Her hair was pink. Like, neon pink.

"What the hell is wrong with your hair?"

Kandy laughed. "What? You said you thought I'd look adorable in the bakery."

Haoxin was standing by the side of the bed, peering down at me.

I moved, slamming myself up against the headboard, pain ricocheting through my entire body in response. But I had only enough focus for the guardian, who had danced away in response to my movement. Standing just beyond my reach.

Mory gasped. She'd been asleep in a high-backed antique chair of burnished gold standing in the center of the bedroom. I didn't recognize it. Dripping with magic, it looked like something Warner might have dragged out of the treasure keeper's chamber.

I turned my attention back to Haoxin. Her blue-eyed gaze flicked down to my hand, then up to meet my eyes.

My necklace was wrapped around my left wrist and forearm, though I didn't remember moving it. My jade knife had appeared in my right hand, called forth by a sharp spike of self-preservation. My fingers felt thick, almost numb, but I could close them around the hilt.

And I didn't need fingers to unleash the centipedes.

Haoxin snorted, watching me thoughtfully. "There you are. Your father said you were paralyzed."

"Apparently not."

"What are you doing here?" Mory demanded. She jutted her chin out belligerently even as she quaked in fear.

"Really, necromancer. You should curb that tongue when addressing your guardian dragon."

Mory clamped her mouth shut, shooting me a look that urged me to take the petite blond down a peg or two.

I was happy to oblige. "So. You look good for … you know … having been a beastly giant on a rampage only days ago. Fit, trim."

Haoxin smoothed her hands down her waist and hips, sneering cockily. She was wearing a sky-blue cashmere sweater over a charcoal-gray plaid wool pencil skirt. "Weeks, dowser. Not days."

My stomach bottomed out. Weeks. I'd been down for weeks? Keeping my gaze steadily locked to Haoxin, I gripped my knife tighter, ignoring the way my bent legs were starting to shake as I crouched against the headboard.

I flicked my wrist, loosening the twist of my necklace. Magic expanded, then contracted. The necklace settled around my neck.

Haoxin took another step back.

And yeah, I smiled. Not nicely.

Mory looked damn smug as well.

"No need to be feisty, Jade." Haoxin draped her arm across the back of the chair Mory was sitting in.

I wasn't certain if the guardian meant to be intimidating, but Mory shot out of the chair and hobbled around the other side of the bed, standing near the headboard. As close as she could get to me without climbing onto the bed itself, clutching Ed and her knitting to her chest.

A look of regret flickered across Haoxin's face.

Yeah, it was difficult to stay friends with people you'd just tried to kill.

"I come bearing a wedding gift," Haoxin said. She smoothed her fingers along the back of the chair, then dropped her arm. "The chair has healing properties."

"Blossom brought it," Mory said. Not contradicting the guardian, but just clarifying.

"It took me some time to find it," Haoxin said. "It was a gift from the former healer to my mother, when she was badly hurt." She cleared her throat, covering something painful in the pause. Then she added crossly, "I was unaware that the treasure keeper had collected it."

"He likes to do that."

"Yes, he does."

"A shelving system would help."

"Yes!" Haoxin cried. "We must force a trip to Ikea on him." She chuckled, then swept her gaze across Mory and me again as her smile faded. "I'm sorry I hurt you, necromancer. I understand you freed me from the portal, but I was…momentarily altered by its magic."

Mory nodded. "The oracle asked me and I accepted."

"Of course you did. I owe you a boon."

"A boon?"

"If something is in my power to give you, you have only to ask."

Mory stared at Haoxin, thoughtfully caressing Ed's shell. Then she nodded.

The blond guardian's lips curled in a hint of a smile. Then she pinned me with her intense blue gaze. "You and I are even."

"Neither of us were ourselves."

"Exactly." And with that pronouncement, Haoxin crossed to open the door, pausing to look back at the chair. "The chair is yours for life, Jade Godfrey. Have it returned to the estate of Haoxin on your death."

"I will."

Magic shifted through the room, flowing between Haoxin, me, and the chair. Reminding me that using mere words to make binding deals with demigods who controlled magic was far too easy.

"And Jade? That night, with the elves...thank you for using the centipede to take me down." Haoxin touched her neck. "Rather than the silk ribbons." Her gaze was remote, and I was pretty sure she was remembering the vision Chi Wen had shown her. Of her own death by strangulation.

She was gone before I could answer.

I lost hold of my knife. My legs collapsed under me, and I slumped sideways.

Mory grabbed for me, but one of her arms was in a cast. I hadn't noticed it underneath her bulky sweater. I touched the hard wrapping even as she struggled to get me under the covers.

"What...your arm is broken too?"

"Yep. Along with both legs. Though the ankle has healed."

"But...but...the healer?"

"The witches pretty much expended everything they had, first on Gabby. Her magic was so drained it wouldn't accept the healing. Then they worked on you and had nothing left. Then the healer couldn't heal me."

"Because of the necklace."

"Yep. So Mom took me to the hospital and claimed we'd been in a car accident. Later, the witches were able to help some. But...keeping you going was a little exhausting for them all. And the healer has gotten called away a bunch of times, leaving for days. A whole week one time."

She shoved a pillow under my head, awkwardly. It hurt. I closed my eyes. "Sit in the chair, Mory."

"I have been."

"Now."

She laughed, but I could hear her hobbling over to the chair and settling into it. A moment later, the steady click of her needles started up.

I smiled. "You were so brave, Mory."

"I was scared out of my mind."

"So was I. But never more than when I thought … when I thought you might not make it."

"Yeah. You died, Jade. Died saving me. Don't do it again."

I laughed, sleep tugging me down, down, down in a spiral of peacefulness. "I would have gotten both of us free if I could have. But … I'd do it again."

"I know," Mory whispered.

I slept.

"How did I get free?" I asked. I didn't realize that I'd spoken out loud—didn't realize I was even awake—until my mother curled her hand into mine.

"Warner," she whispered. "And your father. And Kandy with those magnificent cuffs, though she was badly hurt and magically drained. But Mory tells me it was the shadow leech she calls Freddie who really made the difference."

"Freddie … wrapped around my head and shoulders …"

"Yes, protecting your head. Warner was a terror. Your magic was…he couldn't find you without the instruments. And Mory was wearing those."

I sighed. "But Mory could feel Freddie."

"Yes. And Tony had that tracking device on you, steadily telling everyone they were looking in the right place."

"Did it…did Freddie survive?"

"She shows up every evening, even through the wards, and perches on your bedpost."

"She? Mory says Freddie is a she?"

My mother laughed quietly. "The necromancer insisted. Your father is most disgruntled that a demon saved you when he was otherwise occupied. The leech makes herself scarce when he visits."

"Freddie isn't just a demon," I said, smiling.

"No, my darling, she isn't." My mother smoothed her hand across my forehead. "You have that effect on otherworldly creatures."

I laughed quietly, then remembered the answer I'd been seeking, the concern haunting the back of my mind. "But what I meant was…how did I get free of the gateway?"

"You must have freed yourself, darling."

That didn't sound right. But there was obviously a lot I didn't know, that I couldn't recall. Maybe I had managed to pull myself free.

Except…I was fairly certain that wasn't the case.

Magic tasting intensely of lilac prickled across my shoulders as Gran tucked the duvet up under my chin. I opened my eyes just in time to see her close the curtains over the darkened windows, then pause to check the sill for dust. It was spotless, of course, thanks to Blossom.

"Hey, Gran." I cleared my throat, freeing my arms from the confines of the bedding to reach for the glass of water on the bedside table.

"Jade." Gran smiled, stepping back to turn on the bedside lamp.

A golden glow softened all the hard edges in the room. I drained the glass of water. The apartment felt empty of magic, other than Gran's and the wards. "Where is everybody?"

"What?" my Gran said, huffily playful. She plucked the empty glass out of my hand and hustled toward the door. "Am I not good enough?"

I shook my head at her retreating back, listening as she traversed the hall toward the kitchen.

Crispy cinnamon toast tickled my senses. Without looking, I reached up to the shadow leech, who had just appeared on my headboard, tickling her in return under the chin.

"Hey, Freddie," I whispered. "You hungry?"

The leech leaned down, nuzzling my ear and purring.

Gran hustled back into the bedroom, holding a tray. She paused, eyeing the leech with displeasure.

Freddie folded in her wings, wrapping her magic tightly to herself.

"You know where your food is," Gran said crossly. "You don't need to bother Jade while she's healing. I left you three charms. And one is from Burgundy. I know you prefer her magic."

Freddie took flight, zooming through the door and buzzing Gran in the process. The head of the Convocation shook her head, feigning disgruntlement—and completely ignoring my stunned expression.

"You...you're feeding Freddie? Wait—you can see Freddie?"

Gran hustled over to the bed, placing the tray over my lap. The smell of homemade turkey soup wafted up, momentarily distracting me from interrogating her. My stomach grumbled.

My grandmother huffed, pleased. Then she ruined our bonding moment by tucking a napkin into my tank-top neckline and trying to feed me.

I took the spoon from her. Ignoring the way my hand trembled, I took a sip of the hot soup. "I missed Christmas. And turkey."

"But not the soup," Gran said, straightening the already perfectly straight duvet and sheets.

"Tell me everything I don't know," I asked, taking another sip. Then another. The soup was doing a surprisingly good job of slowly soothing away my regrets over missing the holidays.

"Such as?"

I reached for the dinner roll on the tray. It was warm, braided into a rosette. My grandmother's baking. I tore it apart and buttered it. "What happened after, with the stadium? Your wards held?"

"Of course they did. No one outside them heard, saw, or felt a thing." Gran finally settled down beside me, folding her hands in her lap. Witch magic glinted from her rings. I'd never seen her wear so much jewelry or so much magic at once. "The guardians cleaned up their mess. As they should have. The treasure keeper. Haoxin, once she was up and about again. And the one to whom Warner owes fealty."

Fealty? "Jiaotu."

"Yes." Gran's lips twisted. Apparently, the guardian of Northern Europe had made a bad impression. "Couldn't spare a word for any of those who covered for his brethren's rampage. He sauntered around the stadium, what was left of it, three times. Counterclockwise." Gran sneered.

I offered her one of the sugar cookies that accompanied my lunch, shaped and decorated like a Christmas tree. It was cool to the touch. Gran must have frozen some of her holiday baking so I wouldn't miss out.

I tucked my chin to my chest, covering a well of emotion.

Gran touched my hand gently, then took the cookie from me. "You're still healing, Jade."

I nodded, pressing the napkin to the corners of my eyes. Then I took another comforting sip of soup.

Gran nibbled on the cookie, taking up her narrative with more gusto. "I must admit, though, the guardian's magic was impressive. His illusions were spectacular enough that the sorcerers and I could allow our shielding to fade. Then the city remained blissfully ignorant of the destruction of the stadium while Blossom oversaw the repairs."

"Blossom repaired the entire stadium?"

Gran chuckled. "No. She had a legion of brownies at her command. And it was done within a week."

"And...the elves?"

"Gone. Without a trace. Through the gateway, according to Mory, or crumbled into nothing."

I nodded, feeling saddened for all those I'd killed. Everyone who would have chosen to die in their own lands, if they'd had the choice.

"Tony is still monitoring the situation," Gran said, watching me intently.

"Monitoring?"

She waved the hand she held the half-eaten cookie in. "Social media sites and such. For chatter. Just in case anyone reports having seen something they shouldn't have. But I doubt anyone could have seen through the magic we held that day."

"How long, Gran?" I asked, knowing it was the only question I really wanted answered.

"For the cleanup? Under a week, like I said."

"No." I set my spoon down, suddenly feeling full. "How long have I been in bed? Haoxin said it had been weeks."

"It takes as long as it takes, Jade. For you to be … back to normal."

I met her blue-eyed gaze, feeling the tears welling in my own eyes again. "What if I never am? Normal?"

Gran stood, taking the tray and setting it on top of the bureau. "You're tired. I shouldn't have pushed you with a full meal."

"What's the date, Gran?"

My grandmother stepped back, holding the covers up so I could settle back down into the bed. I did, but only because I was tired.

"The date?" I asked again.

Gran smoothed her fingers across my cheek. "I'm so, so glad you are here, my granddaughter. When Warner pulled you out of the …" Her words hitched with emotion. "You mean … everything to me. Everything." She leaned over and kissed me on the forehead. "January 30. Sleep some more, darling. When you're ready, you'll get up. That's how life works. We keep moving."

She stepped back to retrieve the tray while my mind boggled over how much time I'd lost … to Reggie and to healing.

Gran paused at the door, looking back at me. "I'm so proud of you, Jade. So proud of the life you have built, and the strength with which you defend it. But I pray every day that I never lay eyes on your lifeless body again. I'm not certain I could survive it. I'm not certain I would want to."

"Gran."

"Sleep. I'll watch over you until you can take care of yourself again. And I have no doubt you will be able to do so. Soon."

She left without another word. I closed my eyes, tracking the taste of her magic and allowing the sounds of her bustling around in the kitchen to lull me to sleep. As I'd done as a child.

The room was empty and brightly lit when I next woke. I swung my legs off the bed, compelled to leave it behind me. I stood, unsteadily. And after struggling to change into a clean tank top and my cupcake pajama bottoms, I made my way down to the bakery.

To my kitchen.

My haven.

I should have showered. Brushed my teeth. I should have stretched, done yoga, made certain that everyone was okay.

But I wanted, I needed, to bake.

The storefront was empty. It was well past opening hour, so it must have been a Monday. The entire bakery felt almost…lifeless. As if it were slumbering.

But there was butter and cream cheese in the fridge. And eggs from Rochelle. A precious half-dozen, though her deathlayer hens hadn't been laying through the winter.

I found myself wondering if the oracle had sent the eggs because she'd seen me baking in a vision. Then I threw my head back and laughed at the idea.

The magic of the wards responded, caressing me. I ran my hand across the pristinely clean stainless steel counter as I crossed toward the pantry, collecting cocoa, vanilla, sugar, and flour.

I owed Gabby and Mory a cupcake. Something with raspberry and a marshmallow topping.

But not today.

Today, I was baking just for me.

I had the first dozen dark-chocolate-cake cupcakes in the oven when Kandy came barreling down the stairs from the upper apartment. She laughed breathlessly when she saw me.

"I step away for one minute ..." She shook her head. Her towel-dried hair—still pink—flapped around her face. She got herself a stool from the office and perched on the other side of my workstation. The bright pink hair was crazy cute on her, but I didn't say so. Because paired with faded-black skinny jeans, a black T-shirt, and the three-inch-thick gold cuffs, I was fairly certain the werewolf was trying to be edgy. I didn't want to ruin that for her.

I mixed up another round of cake batter.

Warner arrived next. Dressed in jeans and a printed T-shirt, he swung me into his arms and danced me around the kitchen while Kandy screamed at him to be gentle. The T-shirt was emblazoned with the text 'Looking good since 1507.' Kandy's handiwork.

"Let her finish icing the cupcakes, at least!"

Warner laughed huskily, then whispered in my ear, "I'm planning a surprise."

"For me?"

He grinned, stole a plain cupcake, then wandered into the office to make phone calls. Though first, he dragged my desk across the floor to the right, so he could maintain a direct line of sight to me through the open door. I caught snippets of his hushed conversations as he spoke to my mother, then to Gran. I couldn't get enough to figure out the surprise, though.

I flicked my gaze to Kandy. "I scared you. All of you."

She shrugged, beckoning for me to give her the beater currently covered in dark-chocolate cream-cheese icing. "You know what it's like. You've been on our side of that. Watching us dying."

The wards shifted, announcing Kett with a tingle of peppermint across my palate just before he slipped into the bakery kitchen through the exterior alley door. He stood just inside, watching me.

I frosted a half-dozen cupcakes. Then I smiled at him.

An answering smile ghosted across his face. Then he wandered into the office, had a muted conversation with Warner, and retrieved another stool.

He cast a cool gaze across my no-longer-quite-so-pristine workstation. "How many cupcakes were you planning to make, dowser?"

"Shut your wicked trap, vampire," Kandy snarled.

I laughed quietly, feeling tired but...contented. "Are Jasmine and Benjamin doing okay?"

"She's watching him," Kett said. "We're being careful around risings."

"Teresa still wants to put that bracelet back on him?" Kandy narrowed her eyes at Kett.

He ignored her, speaking to me. "It's a transition period."

My BFFs had obviously been bickering about the feeding and care of Benjamin Garrick.

I smiled at them.

"What?" Kandy asked snarkily.

I slid a frosted cupcake across the stainless steel workstation toward her. She fell on it like it was a lifeline to heaven and she was drowning in a sea of death and destruction. "It's going to take more than one, dowser."

An image seared across my brain ...

Slowly decomposing elf corpses littered throughout the stadium ...

Their lives thrown away, sacrificed to my sword by their leader ...

Hundreds dead ...

I blinked, forcing the image away. I was holding my jade knife, not the metal spatula I'd been using to frost cupcakes just a moment before.

Kandy and Kett were gazing at me steadily. My werewolf BFF smiled kindly. Kett stood, reaching across the cupcakes spread between us, then ghosting his cool fingers across the back of my hand.

I took a shuddering breath. Then another.

I loosened my grip on my knife. It disappeared. I wasn't wearing my sheath.

Kett settled back onto the stool. Kandy grunted happily, eating the last couple of bites of her cupcake.

I took another breath. Then I started frosting cupcakes again.

Warner wandered back into the kitchen from the office, looking pleased with himself. I fed him a cupcake and he looked even more pleased, leaning back against the counter while he ate it, brushing his shoulder against mine.

Someone knocked on the door to the alley. Someone the wards hadn't announced. I couldn't get a read on who it was, except to know they weren't human.

There weren't many people who could hide their magic from me in such a fashion. But oddly, I wasn't worried.

Warner, Kandy, and Kett stilled. Their every sense was now trained on the door, like predators homed in on prey.

"Come in," I said. The magic of the wards shifted.

An elf stepped through into the kitchen, sweeping her glittering green-eyed gaze across Warner, Kett, and Kandy—then immediately dismissing them. She settled on me. A smile tugged at the edges of her lips.

Alivia.

It was probably my pajama pants that amused her.

"You didn't make it through the gateway?"

"I didn't."

I gazed at her for a moment. The elf had ditched her gem-crusted clothing for perfectly pressed navy wool pants, a plaid wool coat, and an azure silk scarf. It was an outfit worthy of—and possibly purchased directly from—the Holt Renfrew display window.

No one spoke. The others were obviously waiting on me to set the tone of the conversation. But, to me, Alivia had already proven herself an ally. And now, stranded on this side of the gateway, she was standing in my bakery, presenting herself. The least I could do, after everything she'd done for us, was to treat her as I would any other Adept. Plus, despite the rampant bloodletting in the stadium, I always preferred to default to being kind. And to cupcakes, of course.

"Would you like a cupcake?"

Alivia looked startled, then pleased. "Yes. Thank you."

I picked up a cupcake, offering it to her. "Dark-chocolate cake with dark-chocolate cream-cheese icing."

She took the treat, hesitating. "I...might have to stay for a while. I might like to...or have the option to, choose to stay forever."

I laughed. "Try the cupcake first. Then we'll talk."

She looked concerned. "My...asylum depends on a cupcake?"

"You peel the paper off first. Before eating it."

She blinked. Then she peeled the cupcake wrapper away from the cake, carefully collecting crumbs in her palm. She bit into the cupcake. Her eyes widened.

"Oh, my," she breathed. "What is this?"

"*Lust in a Cup*, sweet cheeks," Kandy crowed. Then she snatched herself a second cupcake.

Warner reached past me, offering his hand to the ward builder, though his mood was restrained. "Thank you. Mory said you held a shield over her and Jade when the first section of roof collapsed."

Alivia stiffened, not accepting Warner's hand. "I was seeing to my people."

I laughed. "A smaller casting might have been easier to hold, then. One that didn't cover Mory and me as well."

"Perhaps." The elf smiled tightly. Then, after another tentative glance at all of us, she reached into the pocket of her coat and pulled out a large milky-white gemstone. The stone she'd brought to Reggie. The stone that had fixed the gateway, made it fully operational.

I met her gaze. "You closed the gateway."

"No. It was already compromised."

"You freed me from the gateway."

Alivia cleared her throat. "I...simply contained the situation."

"I didn't see you there, elf," Warner said darkly.

"You were rather occupied." Alivia turned the stone in her hand, gazing down at it. "And then, I wasn't sure what my status would be if Jade...didn't survive." She looked up to meet my gaze. Then she offered the gemstone to me as if she might have been offering up a piece of her heart. A piece of her home. Like Mira's black-sand beach.

I shook my head. "That belongs to you. With you."

"The gateway has been disassembled and destroyed by the treasure keeper," Warner said bluntly.

Alivia nodded. "I would expect nothing less."

"Thank you," I said, reaching out to shake the ward builder's hand. "You saved my life."

Alivia took my hand, squeezing. "I believe that was your kin, Jade."

I laughed quietly. Apparently, the elf wasn't interested in gratitude. Even I could take a hint, if it was repeated enough times. So I stepped back, angling my body toward my fiance. "Warner Jiaotuson, sentinel of the instruments of assassination," I said. "This is Alivia, ward builder...ambassador for the elves."

Warner reached toward the elf again. This time, she took his offered hand.

Kett and Kandy crossed around the stainless steel workstation, already holding their hands out to the ward builder.

"And Pulou thought cupcakes and peace treaty talks were a waste of time," I groused.

By the time I'd finished baking, Warner had to carry me to bed, leaving the cleanup to Blossom. But this time, he crawled in with me. Treating me to his own brand of gentle, healing magic.

Chapter Thirteen

I woke alone. Before I made any movement, before I stretched to document what parts of my body were working and what had yet to be fully healed, I reached out with my dowser senses. Seeking, tasting, every drop of magic in the building. As if summoned by that casual sensing, the hilt of my jade knife slipped into my right hand. My katana—the elf slayer—appeared in my left hand. The weapons, along with the weight of my necklace resting across my breastbone, murmured under my touch. Extensions of me, of my physical body and of my magic.

I reached farther, finding Mory's toasted marshmallow magic in the living room. The necromancer was most likely curled up on the healing chair that Haoxin had given me. While knitting, of course. My mother had deemed the chair too large for my bedroom, but said it was perfectly gaudy when paired with the worn leather couch in the living room. I had no idea that 'perfectly gaudy' was a thing.

Kandy's bittersweet chocolate and my mother's strawberry magic were in my second bedroom. I had the distinct feeling that Warner had roped them into whatever he was planning. Though my birthday was still two weeks away, so I was fairly certain sixteenth century wasn't planning a surprise party.

Gabby and Peggy were downstairs in the bakery kitchen. The taste of the twins' blackberry and raspberry jam intertwined, feeding and complementing each other. That was interesting. Something to investigate at another time, perhaps.

I could sense the bakery storefront so full of Adepts that I had no idea whether they'd left any room for non-magical customers. I caught Gran's lilac, Jasmine and Kett's peppermint, as well as Burgundy's sweet watermelon and Drake's salted almond and honey.

I smiled. Then I inhaled deeply, merging all the different tastes, all the effortlessly gathered power with the breath. The exterior blood wards rippled. If I hadn't known better, I would have sworn they sighed contentedly.

I exhaled, reeling in my dowser senses and tasting one lingering bit of magic. Magic I'd been ignoring for months now. Magic sitting right at the foot of my bed.

Tart green apple.

I opened my eyes, already rolling to the end of the bed and reaching for the art tube containing Rochelle's engagement gift. I popped the plastic cap, carefully shaking the tube so that the rolled sketch would slip out into my hand.

A whisper of oracle magic shivered across my palm and up my wrist. Carefully touching only the edges so that I didn't smudge the vision rendered in charcoal any more than it was already, I unrolled the thick art paper.

The drawing was large, easily eighteen inches across. It depicted two sets of entwined hands. One set was smaller, more delicate, and holding what appeared to be a small bouquet of chocolate cosmos. Each of the two left hands wore a wedding ring. Ribbons of magic—at least that was how I thought Rochelle depicted magic in her visions—twined around the hands where they clasped.

Warner's hands and mine. Wearing what appeared to be two of the wedding rings that adorned my necklace. Rune-carved rings that were currently hanging directly between my breasts, resting against my heart.

Warner's parents' rings.

We hadn't intended to use them. We'd had stacking rings designed.

I sobbed. Just once.

Then I laughed.

I was such a freaking idiot for not opening the sketch right away. The oracle didn't sketch the mundane. She'd seen Warner and I married. Months ago. Had I opened her gift right away, I would have had some extra bit of hope—something to carry with me through all the world-ending craziness with the elves.

Carrying the drawing with me, I stood up on my bed. Turning back toward the headboard, I smoothed the sketch against the wall, coaxing the magic of the exterior wards through siding, concrete, and drywall to hold the vision in place.

A hint of lemon verbena drew my gaze to the right. A wedding dress had abruptly appeared in the center of the bedroom, hovering about a foot from the hardwood floor. My wedding dress. An ivory French tulle soft A-line gown, strapless with a woven crisscross bodice and gathered skirt. An ivory cross-grain satin sash was set at the waist, loosely looped into a double bow. It was pristinely pressed.

Preceded by the taste of their magic, Kandy and my mother bustled into the room.

"Wakey, wakey, sleepyhead," Kandy crowed. "It's time to get married."

I laughed, stepping down from the bed. "Is this what Warner's been planning?"

My mother stepped over to me, brushing a kiss to my forehead. "Yes, my Jade. Proper permits and all." She turned to my bureau, setting down the small box she'd been carrying.

"Permits?"

Kandy grabbed my arm, gently dragging me to the bathroom. "For the alley."

"The alley?"

"Yeah, dummy. You wanted to be married where you met, right?"

A sharp, almost painful feeling bloomed in my chest. But it was joy, not fear. Not grief.

Warner had just barreled right over my grandmother's wishes, putting my happiness first.

"Oh, God," Kandy groused. "If you're going to get all mushy, I'm going to make you shower on your own."

I barked out a laugh.

Kandy snickered, then hustled out of the bathroom. "Get moving. We still have to do your makeup and hair. And Blossom needs to fit the dress. You've lost too much weight." Kandy turned back and sneered. "Ain't nobody around here that likes you looking like skin and bones, dowser. Thankfully, Gabby's been baking for hours!"

I waited. My hair and makeup were done, including antique hairpins tasting of grassy witch magic that had been worn by my great-grandmother and my grandmother when they'd gotten married. I was alone for a moment in my living room while Kandy and Scarlett hustled downstairs to make certain the groom and the guests were ready for me.

Ready for my wedding.

I laughed quietly, feeling a little ... out of body.

Lemon verbena called my attention behind me, toward the front door of the apartment. I turned to thank Blossom for everything she'd done for me and for my family. But instead of seeing the brownie, I found myself blinking at an ivory-carved, three-foot-high smiling Buddha.

An envelope was propped in the crook of the statue's arm. Delighting in the feel of the tulle skirt brushing against my legs, I crossed around the couch to retrieve the note.

My name and title, including a new attribute that I could have done without, were scrawled across the envelope in black ink:

Jade Godfrey
Wielder of the Instruments of Assassination,
Dowser, Alchemist, Elf Slayer

I cracked the seal, tasting a hint of Pulou's magic—strong tea and heavy cream. Opening the thick parchment envelope, I pulled out the plain card tucked within it. It read:

On the day of your wedding, I gift you with this Buddha. It appears to already have an affinity for collecting that which belongs to you. Should it ever be necessary, it will keep what you bid it to hold.

—Pulou, the treasure keeper of the guardian dragons

"Huh." I patted the rounded, smooth head of the Buddha. "Welcome to the collection of misfits. We love cupcakes and tend to draw a bit of magical mayhem our way ... like, constantly."

The magic of the statue shifted, tasting of Asian coconut-jelly dessert. And I would have sworn the Buddha licked my palm, teasing and tasting my magic in turn.

Delightful.

That was what I got for talking to inanimate magical artifacts.

Footsteps pounded up the stairs from the bakery, then Mory burst into the room. The necromancer was finally and thankfully free of her casts, and dressed in the sweetest dark-red baby-doll dress. Over army boots and paired with a multicolored, speckled shawl, of course. "Oh! Good. I thought I was going to be late."

She was holding what appeared to be miles of delicate, cobweb-thin golden lace. She strode toward me, unfolding an absolutely gorgeous shawl as she neared. The triangle was so large that it dipped in the middle even when Mory held it stretched out before her.

"It was still drying," the necromancer muttered as she circled around me to drape the shawl over my shoulders.

I had to bend my knees so she could reach over my head. She then secured the wings at my back with a lightweight gold pin, from which I could feel a hint of residual magic. Dragon magic, judging by its spicing.

I touched the beaded lace edging, feeling overwhelmed by the gift—and therefore oddly speechless.

"Warner collected the beads for me." Mory crossed around me to fuss with the way the shawl was decorating my shoulders and chest. "I think they might actually be diamonds. Which freaked me out, so I had to practice a lot on a swatch before I got to the edge."

"This…Mory…this must have taken you months."

She bobbed her head, not meeting my gaze. "I've been working on it since I got your engagement party invitation. The broach at the back is from your dad. Well, your grandmother."

"My father's mom?"

"Yeah. He says there's a story to go with it, but he wanted to tell you himself."

I smiled. I didn't know much about my father's family, other than the fact that he didn't have many blood relatives. I looked forward to the tale.

Mory flicked her dark-brown eyes up to meet my gaze, whispering, "Do you like it?"

"It's perfect."

She grinned, then she danced away to the stairs. "We're late!"

I trailed after her. Slowly, carefully, and deliberately taking the first steps into the next chapter of my life.

The alley was decorated with magic. Swooping, delicate ivory-and-gold banners shielded the small party of friends and family gathered just beyond the back door of the bakery from sight and from the rain. Everyone I truly loved—Kett, Kandy, Gran, my mother and father, and Drake—was in attendance. Mory pressed a small bouquet of chocolate cosmos into my hands. Then she stepped over to join Rochelle and Beau. Blossom was hiding behind the exceedingly pregnant oracle.

But from the moment I stepped through from the bakery kitchen, I only had eyes for Warner. My sentinel stood a few feet away, situated on the exact spot where I had called him forth. Twice, in fact. He looked absolutely delectable in a dark-gray suit, but it was the smile etched across his face and the way his golden dragon magic flecked his eyes that captured every ounce of my attention.

The tiny group gathered around us. A steady rain supplied the music as I stepped forward, reaching for my love, my soul mate.

The man, the dragon, who had pulled me from death. Who helped hold me in the world. Who helped me create and keep the life I'd carved out for myself.

Marrying him was just the icing on the cupcake.

I leaned in, brushing my cheek across Warner's smooth jaw. "Is the suit real?"

"Oh, yes," he murmured. "You can prove it to yourself a little later."

"By undoing every single button with my teeth?"

Warner laughed huskily.

Kett cleared his throat, surprising me when he spoke. "Jade and Warner, you are gathered here, surrounded by those you love, to cement your commitment to each other with vows. And, I have no doubt, with magic."

I laughed. "So you're an ordained minister now, executioner?"

My vampire BFF raised an eyebrow at my interruption. "We all have dark moments in our past that, on occasion, can be useful to resurrect."

Kandy cackled. "Especially when you've got a thousand years to collect them, eh?"

"Do you have the rings?" Kett asked Warner.

The sentinel reached into his breast pocket. "I do."

"Wait." I passed the bouquet of chocolate cosmos to Kandy. I slipped my hand under the shawl Mory made and tickled my fingertips, along with a dollop of alchemy, across the lowest two wedding rings on my necklace. I turned as I did so, seeking out Rochelle in the tiny crowd standing behind us. "The oracle has spoken."

Warner's parents' dark gold, rune-marked rings dropped into my palm. I held them out toward my husband-to-be.

He grinned. "You opened the vision in the art tube."

"I did."

He offered me his left hand. I rolled the larger of the two rings in my fingers, filling it with my magic, binding it with my alchemy. Then I slipped it partway up Warner's ring finger, pausing as it resized to fit him.

"For better, for worse?" He teased, grinning at me. "Till death us do part?"

I laughed softly. "Nah. You aren't getting rid of me that easily, sixteenth century."

"Promise," he growled.

"I do."

Warner swept me forward into a blistering, soul-searing, life-affirming kiss.

"Apparently, we're doing everything out of order," Kett said coolly.

Kandy practically busted a gut laughing. "Did you expect anything less, old man?"

Kett eyed her, then pointedly cleared his throat to take command of the ceremony again.

Only half listening, I reached up and stroked Warner's smooth jaw, tasting his magic. Tasting all the magic of all my loved ones surrounding us. And knowing I was exactly where I was meant to be in this moment, in this life.

When the ceremony was done, Gran happily presided over a storefront reception with all of the Adepts that now firmly called Vancouver home—including Burgundy, all seven Talbots, and the necromancer elders. Though, of course, my grandmother was already planning a second reception for out-of-town guests. Benjamin slipped in just after sunset.

After mountains of cupcakes, courtesy of Peggy and Gabby, gallons of dark-chocolate shots, and many, many congratulations, Warner carried me through the portal in the basement, which had been apparently realigned to open into his bedroom in Stockholm.

I didn't have much time to notice the rest of the furniture, but the bed was covered in more chocolate cosmos, the mattress was firm but bouncy, and the suit was definitely real.

Then together, with limbs and lives entwined, we moved into our own version of happily ever after ... with a cupcake on top.

Acknowledgements

With thanks to:

My story & line editor
Scott Fitzgerald Gray

My proofreader
Pauline Nolet

My beta readers
Terry Daigle, Angela Flannery,
Gael Fleming, and Heather Lewis.

**For their continual encouragement,
feedback, & general advice**
SFWA
The Office
The Retreat

About the Author

Meghan Ciana Doidge is an award-winning writer based out of Salt Spring Island, British Columbia, Canada. She has a penchant for bloody love stories, superheroes, and the supernatural. She also has a thing for chocolate, potatoes, and cashmere yarn.

For recipes, giveaways, news, and glimpses of upcoming stories, please connect with Meghan on her:

New release mailing list, http://eepurl.com/AfFzz
Personal blog, www.madebymeghan.ca
Twitter, @mcdoidge
Facebook, Meghan Ciana Doidge
Email, info@madebymeghan.ca

Also by Meghan Ciana Doidge

Novels
After The Virus
Spirit Binder
Time Walker
Cupcakes, Trinkets, and Other Deadly Magic (Dowser 1)
Trinkets, Treasures, and Other Bloody Magic (Dowser 2)
Treasures, Demons, and Other Black Magic (Dowser 3)
I See Me (Oracle 1)
Shadows, Maps, and Other Ancient Magic (Dowser 4)
Maps, Artifacts, and Other Arcane Magic (Dowser 5)
I See You (Oracle 2)
Artifacts, Dragons, and Other Lethal Magic (Dowser 6)
I See Us (Oracle 3)
Catching Echoes (Reconstructionist 1)
Tangled Echoes (Reconstructionist 2)
Unleashing Echoes (Reconstructionist 3)
Champagne, Misfits, and Other Shady Magic (Dowser 7)
Misfits, Gemstones, and Other Shattered Magic (Dowser 8)
Gemstones, Elves, and Other Insidious Magic (Dowser 9)

Novellas/Shorts
Love Lies Bleeding
The Graveyard Kiss (Reconstructionist 0.5)
Dawn Bytes (Reconstructionist 1.5)
An Uncut Key (Reconstructionist 2.5)
Graveyards, Visions, and Other Things that Byte (Dowser 8.5)

Please also consider leaving an honest
review at your point of sale outlet.

CPSIA information can be obtained
at www.ICGtesting.com
Printed in the USA
LVHW021818250819
628867LV00014B/843